LIM COUCH

— ARIZONA COWBOY —

JERRY HARRIS

Lim Couch

~ Arizona Cowboy ~

ISBN-13: 978-1507587355
ISBN-10: 150758735X

To Audrey, Paige, and Alexis

Contents

Chapter One

Mom Left on a Sunday

Lim Couch

Mom left on a Sunday. We were living in Benson, Arizona and I was five years old. It was a windy, March day in 1990. The night before, I had heard them arguing. I was supposed to be asleep in my room, but in our trailer, you could hear everything if you cracked the door and listened. My bedroom was just off the den where they were sitting. Mom was sitting on the old green vinyl couch and Dad was in the brown leather recliner.

When they had told me to go to bed, Dad was drinking a beer out of a cold mug he had taken out of the refrigerator. Mom was not drinking anything but she was smoking a cigarette.

I lay in the bed and I heard snatches of their conversation. I remember Mom saying, "Dewey, I am not leaving you and Lim. You just won't come with me. I am simply going to live with my sister, Doris. She has me a job making twice as much money as I am making working at that insurance agency answering the phone and typing and being a receptionist. A nowhere job in a nowhere town."

And dad saying in his low voice, "And being a cocktail waitress in Las Vegas is your idea of moving up in the world?"

She cried a little and then said, "Dewey, Doris can get you on at Circus, Circus where she works in a minute. You would be dealing black jack or poker. You would be a natural. People trust you. Money there. She makes five hundred or more just on Friday night."

"I just cannot see it. Me in one of them silly little outfits dealing cards," Dad said.

There was a lot of silence then. Only thing you could here was a big rig up on Interstate 10 in the West bound lane laboring up the long hill going out of Benson. Our trailer was on a smaller hill a few hundred yards just north of Interstate 10. I had part of my blue sheet and red and green blanket wadded up tight in my right hand.

A long time later, when I was just about to nod off, Dad said, "Rose, I love you. I have done a sorry ass job of providing for you and Lim, I know that."

"You don't want to move to Tucson or Phoenix or even El Paso where the jobs are? Benson sucks." Mom said.

The last thing I remember about that night was hearing Mom crying softly. A few minutes later Dad came to my door and looked in at me and said, "Go to sleep, son," and he shut the door.

The next morning, Mom woke me up and said, "Get up Lim, I guess you can stay with Mrs. White for a while. Your Dad is carrying me to Tucson so I can catch a plane to Las Vegas. You will have to do for yourself until I can send for you."

I got up and cleaned up and dressed and went in the kitchen. Dad was sitting at the kitchen table. He was sipping coffee out of a thick black mug that had a white chip in it. The table was right there in the kitchen across from the stove and refrigerator. I could sit by a window and eat and look outside and see the trucks and cars climbing that long hill out of Benson going west to Tucson.

"Lim's going with us." Dad said.

Mom looked like she wanted to say something but she didn't. I saw a big brown trunk and a large pink suitcase by the door. Mom pulled a skillet out of the cabinet and reached in the refrigerator and took out some eggs and a package of bacon. A loaf of wheat bread was on top of the refrigerator and she took some slices out and laid them by the toaster.

Dad said, "I can do that."

Mom said, "I am tired of arguing."

She walked slowly down the dark and narrow hall to their bedroom and shut the door. Dad fried up some eggs in hot bacon grease after he had taken the bacon slices out and put them on a platter. He told me to set the table while he cooked and I took forks and knives and spoons out of the tray in the top drawer and pulled three strips of paper towels off the roll and laid them under the silverware.

When the toast was done, Dad told me to get the strawberry jelly out of the refrigerator and pour us some orange juice. He sat the food on the table and walked down the hall. I heard him say, "Rose, come on and eat. You got a long day ahead of you."

Wasn't much said at breakfast. When Mom was through eating, she said, "Come here boy," and I got up from my chair and she pulled me to her and held me for a while and I could hear her sniffling a little and then she said, "Go on and finish your breakfast."

When we were through eating, Dad and I cleaned the plates and loaded the dishwasher. After he shut the dishwasher door, Dad went out to his old blue truck and cleaned the bed out a little. I took the trash out to the big, green plastic barrel and sat out on the little wooden porch in one of those white plastic chairs.

After a while, Mom came outside and said, "Well, son, we might as well get going and I will call and write when I can."

She was wearing a nice blue skirt and a white blouse and a little red and yellow scarf around her neck. Her pretty blond hair went on past her shoulders and she had gathered it up in a ponytail. Dad came out in a minute and locked up the front door. He was wearing his black

Stetson and clean jeans and a white long sleeved western shirt with a big yoke in the back.

We went to the truck and Mom told me she loved me and that one day I would understand and Dad did not say anything all the way to the Airport in Tucson. We pulled up in the lanes for departing United Airlines passengers and Dad set the pink suitcase out and motioned for a fellow in a blue uniform to come over and take the suitcase. Mom kissed me and held me for a minute and went on into the airport.

Dad stood at the front of the truck and watched her as she went in the door along with some more folks. They were all in a hurry. Some carrying bags or pulling them behind them. When we couldn't see her anymore, Dad came and got in the truck and cranked it up and we drove out of the Airport and he turned right on Valencia and then left on Palo Verde and we drove past industrial parks, trailer parks, bars, convenience stores, junkyards, used car lots, tire stores, and a few motels. All quiet on a March Sunday morning. About the only noise was the wind whipping against the truck windows.

Dad didn't say anything until we crossed over from Palo Verde to Alvernon. I turned on the radio and Dad said, "Leave it off for a while, Lim."

First thing, we went to the bus station. Dad took Mom's trunk inside and shipped it to her sister's house in Las Vegas. He gave the station agent a hundred dollar bill and when he got his change, he folded the bills and put them in his front left pocket of his shirt and snapped it shut.

When we left the bus station, we drove to the El Con Mall on Broadway and walked inside and sat on a bench. It was not quite eleven o'clock and we had to wait a while for the stores to start opening up. When Penny's opened at noon, we went in and Dad bought me a new pair of Levi's and two new short sleeved shirts. We were leaving the store and he stopped and said, "Let's go back."

He bought me some underwear and socks and we went to the shoe department and found me some good Nike high top shoes to play in. When we left, the crowds were just starting to come in. We had parked on the north side of the Mall and there were people lined up at the theater box office buying movie tickets.

When we got in the truck, I put on one of the new shirts. A blue one with button down collars. I told Dad I liked the way new clothes smelled and he laughed and said he liked the smell of a new saddle. He said, "I miss leather, and cows and horses."

I gathered up the tags and pins off the shirt and put them and my old shirt back in the sack with the new clothes. It was a windy day with a few clouds high in the sky.

We headed west on Broadway into downtown Tucson. Dad turned back south when he found 6th Street and we followed that into South Tucson. We were stopped at a light at 36th Street and Dad said, "Lim, we might as well have a steak. We need to talk."

He kept going south until we passed under Interstate 10. He got in the left turn lane and we headed back up the long frontage road to Eastbound Interstate 10.

We had went a couple of hundred yards when Dad pulled into the side parking lot of the Silver Saddle Steak House. It is a rambling old building next to an old style motel. The rooms are set back a hundred yards or so behind the Silver Saddle and the motel office is east of the restaurant parking lot.

We walked in the front door and I glanced up at a clock on the wall and it was almost two o'clock in the afternoon. There was a nice black, hand tooled, western saddle in the lobby. Silver was inlaid all on the swells and fenders and on the side and top of the cantle. The saddle had a standard Texas horn. But it had tapaderos covering the stirrups with silver inlays.

Dad knelt down by the saddle and named the parts. He told me he never saw the need for tapaderos but vaqueros he had ridden with and worked with back in Llano County, Texas had told him you need them in some of the wild Texas brush country and on the ranches down in Sonora, Mexico.

A hostess with a black skirt, white blouse, and pretty brown eyes came and took us to a booth. She smiled at Dad and asked what we wanted to drink. Dad said," I want two or three Margaritas in a row. On the rocks with lots of salt. But I got to drive back to Benson so bring us water and iced tea."

I asked him if he wanted to talk about anything and he said it can wait until we get back home. Let's enjoy our steaks now. When the waitress came back and served the tea and water, Dad said to bring him a Dos Equis Amber and a cold glass.

While we were waiting for the beer, he said, "Come up here with me, son and I will show you something." We walked a few feet and looked at the steaks being cooked on a large indoor grill filled with mesquite coals. There was a pulley that the cook used to pull the grill up when he added chips and small logs to the fire. The smell of the mesquite and the sight of the meat cooking on the grill made me hungry.

We went back to the table and looked at the menu. Dad said he thought the ten ounce New York Strip would do me fine. When the beer came, Dad took the brown bottle and poured some in a frosty mug. A nice head came up on the beer and Dad drank most of it in one good swallow.

He ordered us both New York Strips and French fries. He took me to the salad bar and when we came back, we were quiet as we ate. Dad poured the rest of the beer in his glass and sipped a little. The steaks came out on sizzling black iron platters set inside a dark wood platter.

Dad said, "Son I don't come to Tucson much. Too big for me. But when I do, this is where I wind up every time. I like the smell of the mesquite and the beer is always cold and the margaritas are just right. This ten ounce New York Strip is just right. Just right. Just enough fat on it to give it some taste. Not as much as a T-bone or a Rib Eye."

We finished eating and the waitress came and Dad told her to bring me the fudge brownie with two scoops of ice cream. While we were waiting for my dessert, Dad finished his beer and looked at me and said, "Lim, looks like me and you now. I doubt if Rose is coming back. She gave me a choice. I just could not see me in that big of a town. Dealing blackjack or poker and wearing some funny-looking shirt. What I got to do now is work on getting out of Benson. I need to get back to the land and horses and cattle. Someway, somehow."

The fudge brownie had walnuts and pecans in it and when I was through, I was starting to get sleepy. It was about the best meal I had ever eaten except for Thanksgiving and Christmas.

Dad paid the check and we walked out into a windy, Tucson afternoon. The sun was shining and it was probably in the low seventies. Just a few clouds way up high in the sky. I could smell the mesquite smoke as I climbed in the truck. Dad got us on the Interstate headed east towards Benson and we didn't talk any 'til we got back home to the trailer.

When we pulled up in the driveway, the sun was setting over the Rincons in the west. A big red and orange ball rolling over the horizon. We sat outside for a while 'til the sun was gone and the temperature started to drop.

Dad asked me to sit at the kitchen table with him. He took a can of A and W root beer out of the refrigerator for me and opened a can of Coors for himself. He kept a mug in the little freezer over the refrigerator.

When he had poured himself some beer he said, "Son let's talk for just a few minutes. You got to know a few things. First, me and you is in it for the long haul. You are my blood and that means something to me. Second, you need to know my limits. I am not meant to be the manager of Raymond's Tires in Benson, Arizona. It don't feel right. By that I mean I can do the job. No problem there. But I want to be outside. Outside on a horse. Taking care of cattle and doing the other work you have to do on a ranch."

"You remember when I took you to Tucson to watch the horse races last month. Remember when the horses were on the back rail, some would not be able to make that move and come to the front of the pack. Well, I am like those horses. Me and modern life. I won't make the effort to keep up. Always remember that. These times you need a good education and a lot of motivation. Do not get me wrong. I am doing a good job down at the Tire Store. Sales are up. Raymond likes me. He will be embarrassed when he finds out his sister Rose has left. But it is not what I want to do."

The last thing he told me was I did not need to go over to Mrs. White's anymore. He was going to ask me to stay by myself. He said he hoped it would be for just a little while. He said he did not like knowing that Mrs. White sat around in her old torn black robe in the afternoon and drank Hearty Burgundy in front of me. He said he trusted me not to do anything stupid and for me to have faith in him. He would find a way to make things better.

I went to bed a while later and was almost asleep when the phone rang. I tried to hear what was being said but all I can remember is hearing Dad say "That's good Rose, nice you are settled in so quick. The guy at the bus station said you could pick your trunk up tomorrow night."

Dad has a friend, Vern. Vern is a farrier. They have been friends for a long time. He and Dad met when Vern was shoeing some horses at a ranch in New Mexico where dad was a hand. They tried their hand at team roping at a few amateur rodeos in New Mexico and Arizona. Dad said they never could make a check to cover their expenses and show a profit, so they called it off. But they stayed friends. Vern travels a lot all over Southern Arizona shoeing horses. I heard him tell Dad he could work every day of the year if he wanted to.

A few nights after Mom left, Vern came over and sat at the kitchen table with us. We ate tacos Vern brought over and they drank beer after I left the table. I watched television and they talked. Vern is short and wide. He has a barrel chest and big ears and he is missing two teeth in the front of his mouth. One lower and one upper. His hair is black and curly. He always looks like he needs his bushy hair cut. He wears a hat except when he is indoors. He always wears a white Stetson when he is not working. A white Stetson, blue jeans and a blue western shirt.

He was strong back then. You have to be strong to shoe horses. They lean on you, step on you, and try to knock you down. Not most of them, just some of the skittish and spoiled ones.

I fell asleep on the couch watching television and when Dad woke me up and told me to go to bed, Vern had left. Dad gathered the beer cans from the kitchen table and put them in the garbage sack under the sink.

A week or so later, Vern came by in the late afternoon. Right before the sun set. He and dad went outside and stood in the front of Vern's truck and talked for a long time. Dad didn't come back until after dark. I heard Vern's truck pull off and Dad told me we needed to talk.

We were eating pork and beans and hot dogs that night. Dad cracked open a Coors and poured some hot sauce on his beans and dogs and he told me we was going to Sonoita on Sunday morning to see about a job and a new place to live. I asked Dad what kind of a job and he said ranch work.

I had a lot more questions but I left him alone. His tired eyes told me he needed some peace and quiet and besides I was just imagining where we would be. I knew Sonoita was south and west of Benson but I had never been there. I cleaned up the table and started the dishwasher and went into the den. Dad was sitting in his chair reading the Tucson newspaper.

I asked him what he was going to do with the trailer and he said, "Sell it, son. Get it out of my life and get a new start. Supposed to be a little adobe house with a kiva fireplace goes with this job. Not a big house but Vern said it sits under some big trees and has a decent porch. We can sit out and watch the stars and moon on pretty nights. But we wouldn't know how to act in a big house anyway and we just got a little bit of furniture."

He said he had put a limit on his beer drinking. Just two a night but tonight it was going to be hard to stop on two. But he did. Draining that last little bit out of the mug and putting the mug in the kitchen sink was done all in real slow motion.

He told me not to get my hopes up too high. Just put it out of my mind and we would see what would happen. When I went to bed, he was still sitting in that chair of his with the paper in his lap. Just looking out the window next to his chair. You could see the lights from the big trucks pulling the big rigs going out of Benson. The only other company we had was the wind blowing against the sides of the trailer. Mom had not called the house since that first night.

I remember going to bed and laying there thinking that Mom needed to know if we left Benson and went off somewhere else so she could find us when she came back.

I thought about how it would look. Me and Dad at the airport in Tucson, picking her up and hugging her and bringing her home to a ranch and a little brown adobe house underneath a big tree. And her walking in the house and there being a nice, warm fire in the fireplace and us together again. Living on that ranch. Sitting on a wide porch at night listening to my dad and Vern tell stories about horses and rodeos. Those kind of thoughts relaxed me and soon I fell asleep.

Chapter Two

The Circle S

Lim Couch

Sunday finally came. Dad always fixed me pancakes on Sunday. First thing I heard that morning in April was Vern coming in the door of the trailer. We just had the one door that opened on to the kitchen. Dad was frying bacon by the time I dressed and came into the kitchen. Vern had his good clothes on. Always the same when he wasn't shoeing horses. Silver Belly Stetson, pressed blue jeans, a nice blue western shirt with pearl snap buttons, a black belt and a silver belt buckle, and shined up black Tony Lama cowhide boots.

Dad always made me eat a bowl of cereal for breakfast. Today, it was Post Raisin Bran. I had a yellow bowl I ate cereal or chili out of. When I was through, Dad fried up some bacon and scrambled a bunch of eggs and we sat and ate for a while and then he made the pancakes and I got up and got the maple syrup and butter out of the refrigerator. When we finished, I scraped the plates off and put them in the sink and Dad locked up the trailer and we left in Vern's big, black Silverado. It had a king cab and I sat in the back.

Nobody was talking much. Dad looked a little nervous. We were traveling West on I-10. We got off at the Vail exit and headed south. We drove for a while and I noticed we started climbing and there was some mountains on each side of the road. Finally, we came down into a little valley and then climbed up out of it on a long grade that Vern called Biscuit Mountain.

Once we topped Biscuit Mountain, the land changed. Hardly any cactus. We had already passed out of saguaro country. Only cactus you saw anymore was a few small barrel cactus and some prickly pear and a few ocotillo. In a few minutes, we passed a sign that said Empire Ranch and Vern said, "We are almost there. A few minutes more."

Soon we topped a rise and went down into a little valley. There was a gravel road off to the left that followed a creek back to the east.

Vern pulled off on the gravel road and we drove a mile or so and then crossed the creek and drove up a steep hill. When we got to the top of the hill, there was a fence and a cattle gap. Dad said," Vern stop here and let's study this a minute."

We stopped right past the cattle gap and got out of the truck. Vern left the motor running and we stood and looked down at the valley before us. Vern said, "Whetstone Mountains way off to the East. Ranch has got good grass. Plenty of water. Two creeks that sometimes run all year. Three wells and three stock tanks. Plus the house has got a well. Trees for shade around the big house and your little place. Hay barn, horse barn, equipment shed. Calving sheds. Strong corrals and loading chutes. Fences and gates is kept up good. The buildings. They all have a good roof."

You could see a long way. Grass was waving in the wind. Red and white Hereford cattle grazed in small groups east of the ranch house. Down near a creek that ran all the way across the ranch from south to north, big cottonwood trees stood green and tall.

Dad said, "Look. He has separated the bulls from the cows. Always thought that was smart. Breed 'em in May 'til June or the first of July at the latest, then get the bulls out, put 'em in a separate pasture, and that way you get all your calving done in February and the first week or so of March."

Vern said, "Dewey, Sherman and Iris. The owners. Might take a little time to get used to them. Just be patient."

Dad said, "I count fifteen bulls. Fourteen Hereford and one I can't place. Might be a Brahma but I am not sure."

Vern grinned and did not say a thing.

I looked back the way we had driven in and I saw a Red Tail Hawk circling low. Soon, he dropped down real fast and disappeared behind a boulder. Vern saw me looking at the hawk and said, "Looks like he found his breakfast, Lim."

We got back in the truck and drove on down to the ranch house. It was a stone and adobe brick house. The window seals were all painted blue and there were curtains in all the windows. It had an almost flat red tile roof and a big, wide porch out front and a small porch at the back door. Vern parked the truck under a cottonwood at the back of the house.

We went up on the front porch and knocked on the door and a small pretty woman with thin lips and blue eyes and short blond hair came to the door. She said, "Sherman is down to the barn. Wait up and we can all walk over there. I am a part of this, too."

We waited on the porch a minute and she came out wearing a straw hat, blue jeans, a white blouse, and nice burgundy boots. We walked with her to the barn. It was about two hundred yards from the house. The doors to the barn were on the south and north ends. It was made of adobe brick and stone. The roof was pitched and there was a big hay loft full of alfalfa hay. You could smell the hay before you even got to the doors of the barn.

When we walked in the barn, Sherman Snider was sitting on a bale of hay at the back of the barn. He watched us all walking toward him and when we got within ten feet he stood up and said, "Vern, this must be Master Lim Couch and his father, Dewey."

Dad stepped up and put out his hand. "I'm Dewey Couch."

"And I'm Sherman Snider. I take it you met Iris."

"Yes sir, I did."

"You one of them wild ass, know it all, done it all better than anybody else Texans?"

"No, I wasn't raised up that way, Sir."

"You don't have to call me sir. Vern says you grew up on a ranch near Llano up in the Hill Country. That right? Some say that's good country to live in, hard country to raise cows in."

"That's probably right. Not a lot of good grass. Not much flat land. Never enough water. Not like here."

"This boy. Lim Couch. 'Bout time for him to get in school, isn't it?

"Yes sir. This fall. I hope there is a school he can go to. One thing his mother taught him was to read. He took to it real fast."

"Vern tell you the deal? You and the boy live in that house you passed on the left as you was coming to the barn. Front half of the house sits close to them two oak trees. A big hundred year old mesquite out front. They give off some good shade. Roof on the house is good. Fireplace draws good. Up early, work 'til the work is done. Don't abuse my stock. Horses or cattle. Haying in the summer. Calving in February and March. Branding, castration, and vaccination all come before June. This land. It is part of one of the last short grass prairies left in the whole world. Grama grass, side oat grama, and Blue Stem are what we have. This is what they call a fragile ecosystem. You got to watch for overgrazing. A lot of your time will be spent trailing cattle from pasture to pasture. Making sure we do not overgraze a pasture. I mean for this ranch to stay productive. And beautiful."

He looked at Iris and said, "Why don't we go on up to the house and finish this up? I was just hiding out from Iris for a little while before you come. She is always thinking up things for me to do. It is nice and peaceful down here most of the time."

We walked on back to the house. Sherman Snider was taller than Dad and his hands were big and banged up. He was missing most of the little finger on his left hand and his index finger on his right hand was bent off to the side and he could not straighten it.

He was wearing a tan straw cowboy hat with a nice Indian looking hat band with red and yellow and blue beads. His boots were dusty. Hard to tell what color they were under the dust and dirt. His shoulders were just starting to stoop some. When he took his hat off as we climbed the back porch steps, I noticed his hair was still black as a piece of coal. I figured him to be a lot older than my dad or Vern. Maybe fifty years old.

The ranch house was shaded on all sides by a stand of oaks. The house had a nice front porch with two rocking chairs on it. It went all the way across the front of the house.

Iris said, "When we brand, a lot of hands from other ranches come and help and I feed them out here on the porch. Usually beans, cornbread, and chili or some good chicken fried steak."

Iris took me back to the kitchen and shut the door. She said the men were going to talk business for a while and I could have a small piece of cherry pie and a glass of milk. I said, "Thank you, Miss Iris."

She said, "Iris is good enough. No use to make me feel older than I already do."

She was pretty and petite. She had the beginnings of a few crow's feet at the corner of her eyes but I thought she was almost as pretty as my mother and that is saying a lot. She had nice blond hair with some red in it. It was shorter than Mother's.

The pie was good. It had a good thick crust and lattices across the top and lots of cherries in the filling and when I had finished I took my dishes to the sink and washed them off and put them on the red plastic drain board.

Iris said, "Who taught you that, boy?

I said, "My mother. Her name is Rose and she is pretty like you. She is in Las Vegas now but I think she is coming back soon. If we stay here she will like it a lot better than she did that little trailer we got back in Benson."

She said, "Well, if it works out, and you do come to live here, you will have a nice house. Nothing fancy, but a good two bedroom adobe with a kiva fireplace, a decent kitchen, a nice den and a porch. Also a washer and a dryer and some good afternoon shade from some old mesquites and oaks. A big mesquite is just west of the porch and helps keep the sun away in the afternoon. Two big oaks help in the morning and early afternoon."

She asked me if I was old enough to go to school and I said I would be in the fall. I told her my mother had taught me to read and had bought me some good books to train on with a lot of pictures of animals in them.

She asked me if I could spell and write and I said just a little and she laughed and in a few minutes, Sherman, Vern, and my Dad came into the kitchen.

Sherman said, "Well, Iris, looks like we got a new hand. He has to give two weeks' notice to the tire store up in Benson and then he will be here with this boy. I am going to take them out and show them the stock. We will back in an hour or so and maybe you will feed us."

Iris said, "I got most of it cooked. An hour or so will be about right. Sherman, you be sure and explain things to Lim about Henry. He has got to be careful around him."

Sherman grinned and said, "Right," and we went on out the back door and walked down a ways to a pasture and looked out at the bulls grazing. All of the red and white Hereford bulls were blocky and solid. Short legs and wide shoulders. Some had short, stubby horns. And there was Henry up on a little rise standing near wide shady mesquite tree eating grass. A big gray bull with long, sharp horns. Around a five foot span.

Sherman said, "Lim, one thing you got to know is this. Iris is right. Henry there, is a totally different animal than those nice Hereford bulls. Two of the Herefords are four year olds. The rest are all six years old or older. They are pure bred. I bred three of them here on the ranch and the others I bought. One at an auction in Willcox and one off one of my neighbors. The rest at auctions from Marana down to South Tucson and up all the way to Gallup in New Mexico."

"But Henry I bought at a sale over in Nogales, Arizona. He was boot. You know what that is?"

I said "No, Sir," and he said, "Boot is a way you seal a cattle or horse deal between ranchers or even at a sale. You agree on a price and the buyer says, well what are you going to throw in to boot. Depending on the seller, he may say, not a damned thing, or he may try to throw in something you don't want or sometimes something you might need that he doesn't care about anymore. Or he may say, how about a T-bone steak and a cold beer."

"Well, the way I got Henry, he was the boot when I bought eight nice Hereford heifers eight years ago. I bought them from a rancher with a spread just south of Patagonia in the San Rafael Valley. He looked at me and said, well, I tell you what, I got something here I do not know what to do with. I took him in trade on a horse deal. I should have took a saddle, I'm thinking."

"So, I got Henry. He wasn't quite a year old and when I got him home and when Iris saw him she told me I should castrate him immediately so he would not stain our herd. I thought that was a little harsh. But he was ugly.

"See, he is a grade bull. No papers. Looking at him when I got him, I just could not pick any features out to say he was this breed or that. He was skinny and had a big ugly head. A color between grey and silver with a lot of black patches on his neck and shoulders.

"Anyway, I kept him around with the rest of the bulls and when I let the other bulls out with the cows in May, I kept him in the horse pasture. He had been here about a year. During that time he had grown more bones and hide and before long he got to where the other bulls could not run over him. He grew him a nice set of horns you can see but he was one gaunt animal.

"He took over that hill and that mesquite tree then and he does not stray away from it except to come down to the tank and drink water and in the winter he will come down and eat hay and some grain. When he was three, I thought about selling him to a rodeo stock man. But I didn't. I was curious as to how he would turn out. He was starting to put on weight. Not a lot, though.

"Well, about the time he was four years old, he caught his growth and started filling out. Now he is around nine. No papers on him so you cannot say exactly. He is about six foot at the shoulders and I think he would go over twenty-two hundred pounds. I bought some Criollo cattle and I have bred them to him with good results. Where my Herefords are ready for market at around eight or nine months, Henry's calves take around thirteen to sixteen months. But there is a nice benefit. I put Henry's Criollo heifers and calves out and they forage on everything. Nothing picky about them. I got around thirty now. Drought comes, I sell some of my Angus and buy Criollo and hope it works.

"Ask me what Henry is and I will tell you he has the hide of a Brahma, all loose on his neck. He has the horns of a Corriente, but I never seen a bull with that big of a frame except an old style Texas Longhorn but he has lost his ranginess and is solid. He has got a big square head. Most of those Corriente, we call them Criollo too. Same cow, really. Well, they have kind of long, almost triangular heads. Not

Henry. That head is not like that at all. Square and blocky like a good Hereford.

"Now what Iris is talking about is stay out of this pasture. Always be on the alert around him. He will charge a man on a horse if you crowd him. Most times he is docile."

They all talked for a few minutes about the other bulls but I was watching Henry and it looked to me like he was watching us. That wide span of horns ended in sharp points and they looked almost yellow in the distance.

We walked away from the bull pasture and went back to the barn. There was a nice palomino gelding in a big stall. He was wearing a red halter and had a white tail and mane. He was probably just a little under fifteen two.

Sherman walked in the stall and put his hand on the Palomino's shoulder. He was eating hay and didn't move. Sherman said, "This is Pepper. He is Iris's horse. She rides him all over the ranch. He is not much use around a cow but he is just seven and mighty easy to ride. He is good around gates and fences and he doesn't spook in the wind. Iris rides him in the Tucson Rodeo Parade with the Sonoita Lions Club and their float. A yearly tradition.

"They use the Rodeo Parade to advertise the rodeo and horse races in Sonoita. Iris and Pepper are a sight. She has a bright blue hat and a blue sequined shirt and custom made jeans and boots to match and a white belt and they are something else riding down Irvington in the Tucson morning sun. Pepper's coat is glistening all the way. Iris spends more time getting him ready than she does herself. His mane is silver and shiny. Won't let me near the two of them until after the parade is over. I ride in the back of the float on Ray. Let me show you Ray and the horses we got. Now Dewey, you got a saddle? I know you don't have a horse. Vern told me that."

Dad said, "I got a good saddle. Circle Y saddle my stepfather and my mother gave me when I got out of high school. I keep it in fairly good condition. No reason I can't use it another twenty or so years."

We were outside the barn, walking down a path that led to a small pasture with a creek running through it. There were some horses you could see grazing in the pasture. We stood by the wooden gate to the pasture and Sherman pointed to a big, brown floppy eared mule that was walking up towards the gate.

"Telling you about that Parade for the Tucson Rodeo. This is what I ride. Had this mule for eleven years. Smarter than anything on this place except Iris. He is coming up now. He knows I will carry him up to the barn and grain him. These others can stay out and eat grass. I ride him in the Parade for the Tucson Rodeo and Iris makes me ride behind the float. She tried to get me to buy a nice Palomino she found up in Pinetop but I said no. This mule suits me fine. Sure footed. Doesn't spook and can go all day."

I noticed Sherman did not have a halter or a rope with him but I did not say anything. He opened the gate and waited 'til the mule got up close to the gate and said, "Go on up to the barn now, Ray, I will be up there in just a minute."

Ray walked through the gate and started up the path to the barn. Real slow. Sherman looked at me and said, "Don't be fooled, boy. Ray has got plenty of energy when he needs it. He's just saving it."

Sherman said, "I got six horses in here and Ray and Pepper. Five of them are geldings and one of them is an old black mare out of Bull Parker. Three of the geldings is hers. There is a nice sorrel I am partial to. For working cattle and just general temperament, he is the best. He is almost sixteen hands and has a good handle on him. The rest just need riding. When I bring in hands for branding and the fall roundup, I use these horses as backups. But if the mule dies on me, I would take any of these and be content."

We went on back to the barn and Sherman put Ray in a stall and ran some water in a trough for him and gave him some sweet feed and oats and a couple of charges of hay. Iris walked up while we were in the barn and said we needed to see our new home.

We started back to the house and Sherman said, "Dewey, one thing I want you to do is ride all these horses as best you can. I think I might sell two of them. Not the old mare. That will give us the mare, Pepper, Ray, the sorrel gelding and one more gelding. That ought to be enough."

Iris and Sherman took us to our new home. It was a nice adobe brick house with a good kiva fireplace in the den, two bed rooms, a kitchen and a dining area. Plenty of room. We also had a small front porch that faced east. A nice big mesquite promised a lot of afternoon shade.

I said something about Momma would like all the room in the house and the fireplace and Iris looked at Sherman and turned away from me.

Vern said, "I will show you where I live, son." He pointed down toward the barn and there was a silver Airstream under a cottonwood tree.

Vern said," I usually make it back here at night to sleep but if I am tired or get waylaid somewhere, I have a sleeping bag in my truck and I can unroll it and sleep in the back. Most nights I make it back here."

Once again, Iris looked at Sherman. This time she smiled but neither she or Sherman said anything. We ate a big dinner a few minutes later. Chicken fried steak cut thick and not pounded out thin like you get in most restaurants. You had to cut this with a knife. Iris said this was good round steak they cut themselves and kept in the freezer. There was a big bowl of mashed potatoes and another smaller bowl of green beans cooked with bacon, and corn on the cob and sourdough rolls. And a big bowl of brown gravy.

By the time we finished our cherry pie, everyone was quiet. The men drank coffee and I helped Iris clean up. The men moved out on the front porch and when we were through in the kitchen, Iris and I went out and sat in rockers on the porch.

It was almost sundown when we left the ranch. The sun was just starting to go down over the Rincons when we got back home. Vern and dad sat inside and drank a beer and I sat with them. Dad said it sounded like a good deal to him and Vern nodded.

When I went to bed that night, I was thinking about Henry standing by himself up on that hill and Ray the mule and Pepper the Palomino and the nice way Iris talked to me and the new home for us and I closed my eyes and thought about my mother, with her long blond hair and pretty blue eyes and soft voice, sitting out on our front porch in the late afternoon waiting on me when I would get home from school. I could see it so plainly. It just had to happen.

Chapter Three

Iris and Sherman

That Sunday night after Vern and Dewey and Lim had left, Iris poured two shots of Old Charter and went out on the porch and sat with Sherman. He took one shot of the whiskey and smiled at her and said, "Thank you, beautiful."

Iris sat down and said, "If you keep telling me that, I might start believing it. You been saying that since before we were married and it doesn't get tiresome, I can tell you."

"Alright now, Iris, I think I know what is coming but you come on out with it, your way, your speed. Night like tonight, I can be a good listener."

It was dark now, but the moon was out and some stars were shining and you could hear the leaves gently rustling in the cottonwoods down by the creek. It was cool enough for Iris to go back inside and slip on an old blue sweater.

"That boy. We were down at the house and he was talking about his mother coming back from Vegas and living in the house and how she would like the fireplace and it got to me, Sherman. I know what you are going to say. They may be gone in a month. Vern says he will do fine, but you never know so I should not get attached to that boy. All that makes perfect sense. Now tell me how to do it. Not get attached to a five year old boy that helps around the kitchen and has a cow lick and brown eyes as big as silver dollars. You just tell me how."

"I just do not want to see you hurt. That deal with Dan and his wife was enough for me. Feeling unwelcome in my own son's house. Her talking down to us. But Dan made his choice. He has a nice life. His wife is supposed to be smart but I have not seen any evidence of it."

"Me either, I can understand her not wanting to eat red meat, but to lecture us on it was totally unnecessary. And Sherman, you are right. When did neurotic and histrionic become barometers of intelligence? Educated and smart are not always the same. But that is a separate problem. I know you are right. She hates the ranch. I can guarantee you we won't be seeing our grandson coming out here for the summer when he grows up. One of my dreams trashed."

"I only brought it up because I want you happy. I will say this and I will be quiet about it from now on unless you say we need to talk about it some more. Do what you want to do. But remind yourself from time to time that it might not last. You have more than earned the right to do what you want with your life. But when emotions get into things, especially when children and family are involved, things go sideways a lot.

"There is another possibility."

"What is that, Iris?"

"That this whole episode could be something we look back on with fondness in our old age."

"I hate it when you inject hope into our talks. Out here, you know better than to relax your attitude. You just have to say, I will take what comes at me and work through it. Talking about the weather and crop prices and unforeseen mishaps and busted machinery. And that attitude spills over to personal feelings. Don't expect much out of people and go on with your plans. Anything positive is a plus. Only thing in my life that has not let me down at some time or another is you, Iris. You. And that is all."

Iris laughed and stood up and put her hands on the porch rail and turned her back to the yellow full moon, the stars, and the clear night sky.

"Yes, you are right. All the hard work to do, it is hard to take a take a step back, take a deep breath, and appreciate all the good things we have around us. Sherman, we are tired all the time. Here it was Sunday and we were piddling around all day. We didn't rest and you are going to fence all day tomorrow. "

"That boy can help you some, Iris."

"Did you notice how he got up without being asked and helped me clear the table and take care of the dishes?"

"Yes, I did and I noticed no one told him to do it and his dad or Vern never made mention of it afterwards. He just came back and sat down and listened to us talk about the cattle and what needed to be done around here."

"I was planning on him helping me a lot this spring and summer. Hoeing out the flower beds, helping me with the groceries, repotting some of my flowers. Just little things. And I will slip him some cash each week."

"Don't give him the money alone. Make sure Dewey is there watching. That way, he can help the boy learn to manage."

"Speaking of managing, you think Dewey has put any thought into the nuts and bolts of that boy's schooling this fall?"

"You talking about getting him to the bus every morning? He'll get up and dress hisself. Books. Registration. All of that. I do not think Dewey is thinking much farther ahead than leaving Benson. Vern said he is one of the best with a horse. And as good a roper as you can find. But school for the boy. Men just do not think things like that through.

We just don't. You can help. Just get him in the right place at the right time."

"Yes, and me going down to the school with him and talking to his teacher and the principal and letting them know we will not interfere but we want to know if a problem comes up."

"All that, you can do that. Iris, you got tact. Me, no. Dewey, no. So in two weeks, they will be here."

"No, they will be here after lunch on Wednesday. Dewey gets off at noon on Wednesday at the tire store and works all day 'til ten at night on Saturday. He wants to start riding the fences. Get the feel of the place and get some saddle time with those two geldings. They are bred right. If he gets them going right by the middle of the summer, I can get six to ten thousand cash easy for the pair if I find the right buyer. I just don't have time to keep up with the horses like I should."

"And Sunday?"

"They will be here at sun up. Then the next Sunday, they will be here for good. The boy likes the house already. Dewey said their trailer gets a lot of wind up on that hill they live on. Coming out of Benson. The trailer is at the top of a hill on the north side of the Interstate. No trees or nothing to slow the wind down."

They sipped their whiskey and when Iris was through, she said. "Wouldn't hurt you to shower and come to bed and hold me up close for a few minutes before you drop off to sleep."

Iris liked to sleep in soft cotton gowns. Her favorites were white with flowers on them. The one she chose that night only came a few inches past her knees. She heard the shower running and turned the bedside lamp out. She listened for some wind gently rattling the windows but there was none. Things were still and quiet. She got up from bed and raised a window to let the fresh night air into the room. She waited for a breeze but none came.

Sherman came out of the bathroom wearing a blue terrycloth robe Iris had given him years ago. He took the robe off and got into the bed. Iris was in the middle of the bed and came to him.

She said, "Just hold me for a few minutes, Sherman. I opened the window to let a little fresh air in but nothing is stirring. No wind at all. Does this mean rain?"

"Could."

Sherman held her close and in a few minutes she got up and reached down and pulled the nightgown off and stood in the moonlight and grinned at Sherman.

She threw the sheets back and when she came to Sherman he kissed her on the neck and grabbed her ass with both hands and she laughed and reached and grabbed him and stroked him and said, "Well, Sherman, I see you are sitting on ready. Always a pleasant sight."

Chapter Four

Dewey Catches Up

Dewey Couch

Way I see it, after I got home from Nam and the Marines in 1972, I been trying to catch up with life. Just get back in my mind to where I was before I left the ranch near Llano, Texas. And all I mean is that, putting all that Nam stuff behind you may be something you can never do. But I do not blame Viet Nam for anything. I got a tattoo on my left shoulder. The Marine Corps flag and Semper Fi right under it. No grudges or frustrations keeping me from having a good life. No wanting to commit suicide. Most of the time, I can keep all that out of my mind.

No, the only loose end I got left from the Nam is sitting Lim down and telling him why he is named Lim. Named after my best friend in the Corps. Lim Sanders. But that will come later. I feel when he is old enough to start making some big choices on his own about his life then I will tell him about Lim Sanders and what I think it means to carry his name. Lim Sanders Couch. My son.

Our son. Rose's and mine. I remember Rose coming home from the doctor and telling me. Dewey, it is a boy. A living, breathing boy. Inside me. Gonna come out in a few months and me nineteen.

I had just started at the tire store. We had bought the trailer and were planning to live in it just a few years then buy us a starter house and go from there. Rose was sitting at the kitchen table with her hands across her belly. She was laughing and I asked her if we could name the boy Lim Sanders and she said that was two names she would have never thought of but she was not mad and asked me to tell her the story and when I got through with it, the sun was coming down fast over the distant Rincons.

She got up from the table and said, after that one, let's go somewhere and have a nice meal. Some Mexican food and a cold beer. A guacamole salad and a big beef burrito for you and some chicken tacos for me. Just one beer for me, though. The doctor said not to use alcohol much now.

I went and showered and changed out of the blue and white pin striped work shirt with Raymond's Tires on it and put on some jeans and a white western shirt and got my good black hat and came on back up to the kitchen and Rose had a sheet of yellow lined legal paper on the table.

She had written down some names. Todd Lamar Couch. James Leroy Couch. Dewey Leroy Couch, Jr. Robert Couch. Patrick Raymond Couch. She said, let me think this out for a few days and eliminate some of these and see if we can agree on this.

We drove on down to Benson to a little Mexican place called Estelle's and sat in a back booth and nursed a cold beer a piece and she studied the names. She had a black felt pen with her and she started crossing out names. The first one she crossed out was Todd. She said she just did not think we were prosperous enough to have a son named Todd. That seemed to be a name college graduates would use for their sons. Unless it was a passed down family name. The food came and Rose put those pretty blue eye on me and cocked her head a little to the side. I was eating and letting her decide.

She took a taco off her plate and bit into it and lettuce and little pieces of sliced tomato and ground beef dropped back onto her plate. I was having a beef and bean burrito and it was just spicy enough and warm enough to be close to perfect.

Now, Dewey, she said. Three things. First is, Lim Sanders ought to have a name sake somewhere sometime. Might as well be now. Right here. But if we have another boy, I want to name him. That's two things. Now the third is that if we have a girl, I want to name her Lillian. I just like that name. Classy. Name an English lady would wear easily. I do not know about out here. She might be called Lil in the first grade, but that is what I want.

I said, you got a deal. And she reached across the table and put her hand out and we shook hands which was sort of strange to me but Rose was happy and that was always enough to keep me happy.

Still, here I am on a Sunday afternoon in May in Benson sitting in an empty trailer with Rose in Vegas and Lim and me going to a new life on a ranch. Low wages and long hours. And I see that maybe now, I will have the chance to catch up. A chance to put my mind at rest. At peace. We moved everything we needed down to the Circle S today. Only took one U-Haul load in a seventeen foot trailer to get it all down.

Lim was at the ranch with Doris and Sherman and Vern was taking the U-Haul back and I was just sitting out on the empty porch thinking about where I hope my life is going. Way I saw it sitting on the porch of that trailer was that I had a chance to get back what I had missed since I had left the ranch in Llano County. Left a good red dun gelding that had been bred down on the King Ranch. Bred to handle easy and cut cows. A small, wiry horse. His line went back to Mr. San Peppy and that was some serious good breeding.

And that new Circle Y saddle built in Yoakum, Texas and given to me for high school graduation in May of 1968. And most important, my mother and stepfather. All of that gone except for the saddle. I thought when I left Llano for the Marines that I would come back and everything would be the same. I was just eighteen and thinking things through was not what I did.

Before I left Llano, things were good. I just did not have sense enough to know it. There was a war going on and me and some of my class mates in high school could not wait to get out of school, turn eighteen, and join up.

This was in May of 1968 when I graduated from High School. Martin Luther King Junior had just been shot in Memphis and Viet Nam was on the news every night and Llano and the ranch seemed so dull. I lived on a ranch just a few miles west of Llano. Texas Hill country and some good grass. My step father and mother were good to me.

I had that good red dun horse, a nice saddle, and cattle to tend. And the Texas sky and the beautiful sunrises and sunsets but I traded it all for the Marines and getting shot in Viet Nam.

When I got back from Viet Nam, the ranch had been sold, my red dun gelding sold, and my saddle stored in an old shed. My step father was always bad about borrowing money from banks and savings and loans companies. His name was Rex. Rex would see something he wanted and go borrow money and try to pay it back when he sold some cattle.

In 1970, it all caught up with him. He had a hard winter and the price of beef was nothing special and he had to sell everything. Tractors, land, cattle, horses, and the house he was raised up in. When I got back from the Marines, they were living in a little house on Buchanan Dam Lake. A great view, a small cheerful home, a boat dock, and my saddle in a shed under some boat paddles, life jackets and sacks of fertilizer.

So I got the saddle, cleaned it up, bought a used white F-150 and lit out. I had enough money left after buying the truck to buy a three year old bay gelding with some Doc Bar breeding. His name was

Tommy. I kept him until I sold him when Rose and I settled down. Sold him and my horse trailer both for six thousand dollars. Kept my good saddle.

I bounced around working on ranches and doing about as good as you can expect anyone to do with that kind of life. I met Rose at a dance at Willcox.

She was just eighteen and I was closing in on thirty and we got married and moved to Benson and she was almost twenty when Lim came along. We made our minds up to work and try to save and buy us a little house and some land. That saddle was in another shed. This time behind the trailer. But it was hanging up from a rope I had looped over a rafter.

I met Vern while I was working on a nice cow and calf spread up near Silver City in New Mexico. He was just starting out shoeing horses and he saw me roping one day during branding and said we ought to try our luck at team roping. I had the bay gelding I had bought after I got back from Nam. Tommy was one of those horses you should never sell. Never gave me any trouble and he could learn anything you could teach him. You could rope off of him and Vern had a good sorrel horse he could use. He would rent him for a few days from a rancher he knew.

Tommy only had one drawback when it came to roping and that was his size. He was just a little over fifteen two and didn't have enough muscle and weight to hold the big steers. It wasn't a problem on the ranch because you were not roping for time.

But at a rodeo, the difference in the money times and shit out of luck times was measured in tenths and hundredths of a second. Vern's sorrel wasn't his, but he worked some kind of deal out to where he could use the horse when he needed it.

We did alright for a while in some of the little rodeos in New Mexico and Arizona, so in 1981, we lit out for Tucson. My foreman wasn't real happy. It was the last week of February and we were slap dab in the middle of calving, but I begged off. Calving is always an aggravating time. You have to get up in the middle of the night and fool with difficult births. We left on a Monday and came back the next Monday.

Vern was getting known for his shoeing and he worked a deal where we could pull his Airstream to Tucson and put it on the Rodeo grounds and board our horses for no charge. So we paid our entry fees and when the Rodeo started on Thursday, we were ready to go. Vern was the farrier for the Rodeo and he shod a lot of horses that week in exchange for our space. When the Rodeo ended on Sunday, he was flush with money. From shoeing horses, not roping steers.

He sat a little tarp out over a table and I wound up sleeping on that table at night. Better than sleeping on the floor in the Airstream. Our first go around, we were in the money. Almost thirteen hundred dollars in prize money for us to split.

Next go around was our chance to qualify for the good money on Sunday. We were all amped up. Just excited, no pills or anything. Just adrenaline. And the steer comes out and I got a great jump and a good catch and my good bay horse dug in and I turned the steer right where Vern could put a loop on him and Vern hesitated and then made the throw and we had him down but the flag man took his time. Just a little slow we thought.

Me and Vern wanting a chance to bust out of our lives and get a start on the Rodeo Circuit. You draw a check in Tucson, you can draw one anywhere. Good cowboys, good stock. So we had the steer stretched out and the announcer called out our time and all we had to do was wait and see. Our two day time was just fourteen and one tenth seconds. First day time was six and seven tenths seconds.

We sat back on the chutes on our horses and waited and Vern said that goddamn flag man was just indifferent to us. A pair of nobodies. If he had paid closer attention, he could have chopped off close to a second. One of the other riders said we was right but not to worry because we was going to make the cut and be back on Sunday.

Didn't happen. Not only did we miss out on the check that day, we was three tenths of a second away from riding on Sunday. Three tenths of a second. I did not blame Tommy or Vern. Tommy held his ground with each steer. He dug in as deep and hard as a horse that size can be asked. And Vern got his loop on and it was a good pull down. Just a rough break. Riders who pulled checks in the National Finals got bucked off or missed a catch with a rope. Happens to them all.

But we had the thirteen hundred. Minus entry fees, food, beer, and a new shirt I bought after we won the thirteen hundred. Plus I knew they was gonna dock my pay back at the ranch for the time I was gone. I dreaded facing the foreman.

Sunday at the Rodeo was a long day. Watching the other fellows get good rides and knowing they was going to cash a nice check went down hard. Vern stayed back at his Airstream. Shoeing horses. Mainly just tacking on loose shoes. But he came out way ahead.

When the Rodeo was over and Vern was through shoeing, he took his tip jar down, emptied it, and put the money in his left front pocket, and said, let's go to the Silver Saddle. Just about enough money in here to pay for a decent meal and some margaritas. The Silver Saddle was full. We had to wait almost an hour for a place to stand in the bar.

We stood up and drank Margaritas and each ate a ten ounce New York Strip and baked potatoes and a salad and a little bowl of beans. When we were through, the place was thinning out and we settled up and took our drinks over to an empty booth.

Vern took out a pencil and got a clean paper napkin and started toting up our mutual expenses and came up with a total. We both got just a little over four hundred dollars after expenses. Vern was still mad about the flag man but I just let it go. He might of thought the steer wasn't still enough for him to drop the flag.

Anyway, Vern said he didn't think this borrowing horses and roping part time was going to get it. I had a horse but the trailer I pulled the horses in was borrowed. I saw what he was talking about and I said, You are right Vern. We could make it if we had some backing. I got no one going to bat for me. I may get fired for leaving the ranch for eight days during calving.

And that is what happened. I got back to the ranch late Monday and the foreman didn't say a word except to tell me there was a few more calves on their way but I had missed the worst of it. In a few days, it was the first of March and most of the calving was over so the owner came down to the bunk house and gave me my money in cash and told me, First thing in the morning you clear out. And then he walked out of the bunk house and got in his truck and drove off. Probably going into Silver City to have dinner and a drink since it was Friday.

Me and Vern kept up with each other all these years. He got me a job on a spread near Willcox up near the Chiricahua Mountains two weeks after I got fired for going to the Rodeo and I stayed there until I married Rose and moved to Benson.

Me in a tire store. A salesman and manager with what Raymond called an easy smile and a slow way of talking that people trusted. Rose and I did real good until I went into Tucson one day and picked up a load of tires and brought them home. Lim was three then. I stopped and bought me a nice pair of black lizard Dan Post Boots and they was just $99.99 plus tax. On sale.

When I got home from unloading the tires, it was almost nine o'clock and Rose had already fed Lim and he was down in the floor playing with some little cars we had bought him for Christmas. And supplying some sound effects to go along with the playing. One car in each hand and sliding them across the carpet.

When I walked in, Rose saw the package under my left arm and said, What did you bring me from Tucson and I told her I had bought me some new boots and I pulled them out of the box and showed them to her and she stared at them for a few minutes and then got up and got my supper off the stove and went and sat down on the floor with Lim while I ate.

She stayed up in the den after she put Lim to bed and waited me out. When she was sure I was asleep, she come to bed. I was still awake. I had to go to work the next day and I looked at the clock by our bed and it was after midnight.

I didn't say anything but I knew she was mad and the next morning at breakfast she said there was more important things that I could have done with my money than buy a damn new pair of boots. You could have resoled the old ones and worn them for another five years. They look fine.

I got up and went on out of the trailer and went to work. I borrowed three hundred dollars from Raymond on Saturday and took Rose and Lim into Tucson on Sunday and we shopped at Penney's and Sears and some dress shop. All in that El Con Mall on Broadway.

Rose got a new blue dress and a yellow sweater and some new black shiny shoes and I got Lim a new pair of Nikes and a Dodgers baseball cap. We were walking out of the mall and Lim asked if we could go eat dinner at the Silver Saddle but Rose said we have spent enough of your daddy's money today. I'll make us some tacos and a guacamole salad when we get home.

I was hoping that would be the end of it. In a way, it was. She never brought it up again but from then on, she slowly pulled away from me. We still had sex and sure it was still fun, but she stopped making any moves or giving me signals. It always had to be my idea. I could tell. Not a lot of money and raising a child was discouraging her. Married too young with too little money. Simple as that.

When Lim was four, she started teaching him to read. The television stayed off at night until she was satisfied with his progress. I didn't mind. I was always tired from the tire store and I liked the idea of Lim getting a good start in school. I would help around the kitchen at night after supper while she was in the den laying on the floor with Lim. Helping Lim learn to read. Sounding out words and teaching him the alphabet. And some numbers.

She started in on me about moving to a bigger town where there would be more opportunities. When she left, she left the gate open for me to come to Vegas. I was going to the Circle S and taking my boy with me. Vegas was somebody else's town.

When Vern came back from the U-Haul place, we drove on down to the Circle S. I could see Henry on his hill. It was late in the afternoon and Henry's wide horns were catching light from the setting sun. Maybe an hour of sunlight left. Tomorrow Sherman wanted me to ride with him and get to know the whole place.

I thought I would take both of the geldings. Ride one 'til about noon and ride the other one 'til dark. Get them both used to being trailed. Both horses needed a lot of riding before you could do much with them. Back on the ranch in Llano, one of the old cowboys had said you had to knock some of the bark off a horse that had not been ridden much for the past few months.

Before I did anything toward really shaping these horses up, I needed to get them used to being ridden again. Get their minds back on the business of working cows and long hours. I noticed real fast that first Wednesday afternoon I went over and rode that I needed some shaping up also. Takes a while for your legs to get used to being back in the saddle.

But it was fun to be back riding and working on a ranch. I knew it was not going to be a lot of money. But the only people I really had to deal with from now on was Lim, Vern, when he was around, Sherman, and Iris. Not a lot of noise.

There was a long list of things I would not miss. Phones. Delivery men with orders you had to check. Customers. Most customers not knowing anything about tires. Just wanting to get in and get out. Everybody in a hurry. Filling out the deposit every day from the prior day's receipts. Credit card receipts. Cash to be counted. Checks that sometimes bounced. The main thing, the phone. No secretary or receptionist to help screen the calls. Most all of them went straight to me.

Vern and I stopped on the way out of Benson and I bought us a beer a piece. A Coors for me. Bud Light for Vern. He told me if I could get those two geldings ready for sale by the middle of the summer or Labor Day at the latest, it would put me way up there in Iris and Sherman's eyes. A little extra cash 'til the fall when we would start selling some stock.

Vern said Sherman and Iris were doing fine financially but a little extra cash for the summer months would be good. Vern thought if I got these horses lined out and got them sold, Sherman would probably take on some colts and coming two year olds and get me started on getting them ready.

Of course, then he would need another hand but during the summer he could get some high school kids to do a lot of the work. Setting out irrigation pipes. Fence work. All to keep me in the saddle. I liked that idea. And Vern also said that Lim would be tagging along behind Iris most of the time. Couldn't hurt. With Rose gone it would be nice to have a woman looking after Lim some. Not like she would be drinking Hearty Burgundy in the middle of the afternoon.

Vern said the thought of that could almost turn you against drinking. We turned into the road leading into the ranch buildings. I got out and opened the gate and looked out west toward the Whetstones and I saw Iris and Lim. They were standing at the bull pasture fence. Lim was pointing up at Henry. Henry was looking east toward the mountains. The old bull was standing alone on top of the hill. The younger bulls were in small groups down toward the creek with their heads in grass. The setting sun cast soft light on Henry's black and white speckled shoulders. The sunset was all orange and red. A broad and sprawling red and orange and gold Arizona sunset spread across the western sky.

Chapter Five

Sherman and Dewey

Sherman Snider, Circle S Ranch

That first Monday Dewey and Lim were here, I got up at 4:30 and by five, I was drinking coffee and watching Iris cooking breakfast. She was wearing something she called a wrap. A nice white and blue floral looking knee length cotton dress that she wore over her pajamas. It was still cold outside and the sun would rise over the Whetstones around five forty five. It had not started getting light just yet.

I could smell the bacon frying and the biscuits cooling on top of the stove. Iris had two paper sacks on the table. I asked her why she had two sacks. I knew one was my lunch. She said, you know Dewey ain't thought of lunch with all he has got to worry about. You two will be gone all day. I will check on that boy. I need to get him some sort of routine. Helping me and doing little chores around the place.

I looked in one of the sacks. Leftover chicken fried steak in a sandwich. Sliced into two sections. And an apple and a little box of raisins. Looked good to me. I got up and got me a warm up for my coffee and sat back down. We ate breakfast together almost every day of our marriage. To me, the most essential meal of the day was breakfast. Hands down. I ate my bacon and eggs after I ate a small bowl of oatmeal with brown sugar and butter. Iris was eating oat meal, with Splenda, and raisins. No butter. I ate two of her biscuits with butter and some store bought strawberry jelly. She ate a biscuit. Slowly. No jelly and no butter.

She said, "More carbs than I should have for the whole day. Right here in this biscuit. But it sure is good. I will eat me a salad for dinner and try to get by on a banana and apple for lunch."

"You are going to use up a lot of calories running after that boy, Iris."

"I know."

We sat for a few minutes more and talked about whether we needed a few more bulls or not. We had eleven counting Henry. I knew I could do some swapping and get me two more. That should be enough. Iris agreed. Our calves had all come in. No real problems and we had done it all with borrowed help. I was up most every night in February either helping one of my neighbors or one or more of them helping me. They would send over a cowboy to help if I called.

The way we got things done. The cowboys worked when they were told for as long as necessary. That was understood. Calving and branding and gathering. You worked until the work was done.

Iris didn't hardly weigh over a hundred and fifteen and she was solid. No stomach and a nice slim waist. I knew she was thinking about that boy.

Wondering when he would get up, if he had breakfast food, what Dewey had told him to do during the day, and whether there was any real food in their house.

I left the house and headed to the barn. There were no lights on in Dewey's place. Vern's truck was gone. I never heard it pull out. There were lights in the barn. When I walked in, Ray was in cross ties and one of the two geldings was saddled. The other gelding had a halter on. Both were haltered up and waiting to go. There was a bridle with a d-ring snaffle bit draped over the saddle horn.

Dewey said, I would'a saddled Ray but I didn't know what saddle and blanket you used.

Lim was steady brushing. I noticed he had a sandwich in one hand. Looked to be wheat bread, egg, and sausage. Ray looked asleep. He had his head down and his feet set wide apart. Lim was talking to him. Saying, "You better get your nap now because my Dad said not to expect ya'll back 'til dark."

Ray is a little over sixteen hands and Lim could not reach all the way up to the top of his shoulders and back. I took the brush and told Lim to eat his sandwich. Lim asked me if he was a smooth ride and I said yes he was or I would not have him.

I saddled Ray and we started out heading east. The sun was coming over the Whetstones. The Whetstones are low mountains. Nothing majestic. But when the first orange and red fingers of the new day crept over the horizon, I felt at peace. I had a good feeling about Dewey Couch.

Vern shod our horses and we let him park his Airstream under some of our mesquite trees and eat at our table sometimes when he got in from his work or carousing early enough to make it to supper. Vern went to just about every ranch in Santa Cruz County and some in Pima and Cochise. A valuable man to know. He knew every horse of any consequence in Southern Arizona. And their owners.

You want to pick up a gelding to work your stock. Vern knew where to go and what you could expect to pay. Brood mares. Same thing. Colts. He could find you a good one. Tell you what horse had been trained by some mouth ripper, or spoiled by an indulgent owner, or just did not have the right instincts.

We rode east and followed the main pasture fence on the north side of the property. Dewey had a little note book and a yellow pencil and when he saw something he thought was significant, he would stop and write it down. He did not get in a hurry and did not rush his horse. The bay he was riding this morning was a coming four year old with a nice high hip and strong wide shoulders and a short bull neck. His trot was smooth and the other bay followed at a trot.

When it was noon, we had just turned back south in the main pasture. Dewey said he thought he would switch horses. He saddled the second bay and said, "This one should be easier to work with. Bob is a little ahead of Stevie. He already is worked down some. It only took a few minutes to get Stevie working behind the bit. Flexing at the poll and gentling down. I want to start Stevie on some figure eights this week. Bob is already doing them. When I can back a horse through a figure eight without him throwing his head or acting up some way, then that tells me he is ready for whatever you want him to do."

He passed me Stevie's halter rope and said, "Watch Bob. He rode him off in the pasture fifty yards or so and backed him up and then raised the reins and short loped him in a figure eight once then brought him down to a trot and turned him and made another figure eight at a trot, then stopped him, and backed him up a good ten yards and stopped him. Bob stood quietly as Dewey twirled a rope out and spun it over his head."

He turned him back up to where I was and said, "He will be ready in two weeks. I am going to rope off him this afternoon. If that goes well, then I will work with Stevie more and back off Bob. No reason to sour him. I want him fresh when we sell him. I say three weeks from yesterday, you can sell them. Good finished horses for ranch work. They are both good on gates already. I like the way Bob digs in with his back end when you pull him to a stop out of a trot or short lope."

I was hungry and we rode on some more until we find a mesquite tree with some shade. Dewey and I ate our sandwiches and looked out over the Cienega Creek at some Hereford cows with calves grazing near the creek.

I told Dewey, "We have close to three hundred mother cows, counting the Criollos, and about that many calves. Our Herefords came to us from the Empire Ranch seventy five or eighty years ago. The Empire bought their first Herefords from the XIT over in Texas. The XIT was one of the first to have pure bred Hereford. Our bloodlines are as good as you can get."

The rage now is Angus. Some say that Angus calve easier. 'Specially, the first calves. We do fine with our Herefords. Some problems calving. Not many. What the Angus breeders have done is market their beef more aggressively. You see it in all the stores. Angus beef. Truth is you can not tell an Angus steak from a Simmental or a Beefmaster or a Brangus or a Hereford. Good beef all tastes the same. The Angus gets a little better price and preferential treatment from the cattle buyers.

But I ain't changing. I just like Herefords. And I sure ain't gonna sell all these cattle and start over. When the grass is good and we get some rain and the prices are up, we make good money. One of those factors is missing and we have hard times. Trick is not to spend too much when you do have a good year. And stay out of banks unless you are putting money in.

Dewey laughed and told me about his stepfather. Rex. Always borrowing money and finally losing their ranch.

There was an apple in each of our lunch sacks and we sat watching the cattle and the silver water in the Cienega for a while as we ate our apples. I asked Dewey if he had any questions and he said he didn't. He was just glad to be on a horse again and out on a ranch with good water, high grass, lots of cattle, and good horses.

That was about all I ever got out of Dewey. He mainly talked about the horses and the cattle and the fences and the work to be done.

Around the first of July, I made some calls and some people came and looked at the two bay geldings. We sold them both to a rancher from over near Willcox named Rand Phillips for twelve thousand and eight hundred dollars cash and no boot asked for or given. He paid top dollar and asked for me to call him when we had a horse for sale in the future. I knew Iris was fixing a nice meal for Rand before he left for his ranch.

Iris said she would fix us some spaghetti and garlic bread. After she went up to the house Rand and Dewey and I sat on hay bales in the barn and talked about stock 'til after dark. Dewey did not know Rand Phillips. But I did. The man was a fifth generation rancher and raised Herefords like me. He was a big man with a long red beard and a red flat top. He had wide shoulders and no extra weight around his waist. He usually had to stoop a little to get through most doors. In his late forties. Had a reputation for good stock and paying cash for most everything. He wore custom made black cowhide boots with fourteen inch tooled shafts from Paul Bond over in Nogales, Arizona. He carried his cash in a pouch specially sewed in the lining of the shaft in his left boot.

About the time we had the deal firmed up, Vern drove up. He had been shoeing some horses at a ranch over near Tubac. Vern came over and Rand told him he was right about those horses. Seems Vern had been at Rand's spread shoeing his horses a few weeks back.

Iris called us in to eat. She told Lim there would be plenty of spaghetti and for him not to worry about Vern. He had some safe houses he stopped in and ate at. Vern told her he would just have a small plate to be polite.

Rand laughed a lot and ate two plates of Iris's spaghetti. He sopped up the last of his sauce with garlic bread. I asked him if he ever worried about being robbed carrying that much cash and he said Not hardly and I left it at that. I gave him an envelope with the papers from AQHA and bills of sale and he grinned at Iris and asked if she still had her good Palomino gelding and she said yes and we walked out to his truck and trailer and he loaded Bob and Stevie into his trailer. Lim stood with his father and watched the truck and trailer pull off into the star filled night. Dewey did not say anything but he had a mighty sad face when Stevie and Bob was leaving. I liked that about Dewey. He made the effort to know his horses and he took the time to find out what it took to make them handy around the ranch. Dewey said horses was nice to look at but they were hands just like him and had to work long and hard or be sold or swapped. He never liked to sell a good one.

Iris made us all come back to the house and we sat out on the front porch. There was a soft breeze and Iris went inside and fixed us some coffee. Vern pulled a pint of Jim Beam out of his jacket. He had already gotten into it. Couldn't tell when he had cracked it open but there was at least one healthy shot gone. When we got our coffee, he poured about a third of a shot into me and Dewey's coffee. Lim sat on the steps and looked out at the sky and listened to us talk.

Vern asked Iris if she wanted a taste of good whiskey and she asked him to pass the bottle and when she got it, she walked in the house and fixed herself a highball. What she calls it. A little whiskey, sugar, water, a lot of ice and one of those maraschino cherries stuck down on the bottom of the glass. She came back out on the porch and asked Dewey why he looked so sour and Dewey said he was worried that Rand would go from a D-ring snaffle to another bit and get the two horses confused.

Vern laughed and said, "Rand ain't stupid and he's got over twelve thousand dollars in those horses. You don't worry."

We sipped on our coffee for a while and then Iris asked Vern about Rand's wife and family. Way Vern told it, Rand and his wife had met at New Mexico State when they were in college. Rand playing football and doing some steer wrestling. His wife, Josie, was a little petite woman with a soft voice.

After they married and moved back to the ranch, Josie lost a child. Still born. Vern said there was about a two year period there where you did not see Rand smile. He spent a lot of time drinking at a little bar in Willcox. Off to himself in a booth in the back of the bar near the old juke box. Then they had a little red headed boy and the drinking stopped and a little red headed girl came along a couple of years later. Vern said Rand's father was dead but his mother still lived on the ranch and helped with the branding and castrating and vaccinating in the spring.

Vern said Josie was scared of horses and mainly stayed in the house and took care of the children and cooked and read Romance novels. Vern always made a habit of shoeing Rand's horses late in the day. Timed it where he would get a meal at Josie's table. He had eaten there many times and she cooked everything from beef stroganoff to chicken marsala to thick cut pork chops to eggplant parmesan.

But the best was the pies and cakes. Vern said the first time he ate supper there, she brought out a big old black chocolate cake. The icing was black and the cake part was yellow. He named off some more of her desserts. Cherry pies with thick homemade crusts, and coconut meringue pies, and strawberry short cakes. Then he raised his voice and said, "A good piece of pie and cake sure does set a meal off."

Iris said, "You are right. Why don't you make us one of them pies or cakes. Best I can do is blackberry cobblers or banana pudding. Sometimes a lemon icebox pie."

Vern laughed and said, "I ain't seen none of that tonight."

Iris said, "Might be a while before you see any of it again. Man makes as much money as you do sure ought to drink a little better whiskey than what you bring around."

Vern laughed and said he had some Wild Turkey he kept hid in his trailer for special guests.

Iris said, "I better not see any of your special guests around here. And Lim, I will practice on you tomorrow. A banana pudding with a lot of vanilla wafers and whipped cream and the rest of this crew can wait on Josie Phillips to send some food over."

I said, "Thanks Vern. Appreciate your help in my domestic matters."

Vern said Rand was so big he did not usually ride a horse. He had a mule uglier than Ray and about a hand taller. Then Vern got to talking about when he was a kid and he used to go to the mule races in New Mexico. No one else had ever heard of a mule race but Vern swore it was true. He said folding money would change hands on a mule race just like a horse race.

Vern said Bob and Stevie were probably going to be ridden by Rand's children. The boy was almost fifteen now and the girl was twelve. That made Dewey feel better.

I told Dewey the big sorrel gelding was his to ride now. He was seven and good with cows and easy to rope off. Called him Shadey. 'Cause he always stayed off in the shade of a tree when he was out in the pasture.

Dewey said we had sold some mighty good horses and he was going to miss both of them. Then he told us about Tommy. His good roping horse he had bought after he got out of the Marines. Said he missed him and a man was crazy to sell a good horse. He should of just leased him out to a decent hand. He told Lim how Tommy would come alive when you put him near some cattle and when you got your loop around a steer, he would set down hard and keep the rope tight. Hauled good and had stamina. I wondered if he missed Rose or Tommy the most. But I never asked.

Iris finished her highball and asked Vern where he got the idea Jim Beam was as good as Old Charter. We all laughed and then Iris sat down on the top step with Lim. She ran her right hand through his hair and pulled him to her. He asked her when he could start riding and she told him his legs was still real short even though he was going to be tall like his daddy. He did not say anything else and after a while she said Pepper could use more riding than I am giving him. Let me think about it and we will talk about it tomorrow.

I knew what that meant. She was going to teach that boy how to ride. Gentle as Pepper was, he was the best horse on the ranch for Lim to learn on.

I went back in the house and got Dewey, Vern, and me a nice cigar each. When Iris saw us firing them up she said she was going to bed and for me not to bring that thing back in her house. Alive or dead. Said for us to crumble the butts up and scatter the tobacco in her flower bed.

Dewey told Lim to go on home and get in bed. As soon as he was gone down towards their house, Vern poured us another small shot of Jim Beam. Dewey asked if it would be alright if he went over to Rand's ranch in about six weeks and checked on Bob and Stevie. Just to be sure. I said it would be fine.

Vern said, "Leave about midday and take Lim with you. And stay for supper."

I did not tell Dewey I was going to sweeten his check next month to the tune of three hundred and fifty extra dollars as his bonus for getting Bob and Stevie ready.

What I asked him about was buying a couple of weaned colts this fall and putting them to halter when they were a year old and then to saddle when they turned three. Dewey said he thought he could handle training four and keep up with his work.

Vern and Dewey and I sat out on the porch 'til around midnight and when the Jim Beam was gone, I brought the coffee urn out and Vern told us about some new folks that had bought some land down south of Sonoita near Parker Canyon and were going to raise Arabians.

I asked where they were from and Vern said somewhere in Wisconsin. Owned a dairy farm there, sold the dairy farm, retired and bought two hundred and thirty acres of land here. Dewey said he never could get an interest up in Arabians. Too damn jittery and complicated. He liked Quarter Horses. Bred to work cattle and race short distances. Easy to train and well mannered. Dewey believed in Ford pickups and good Quarter Horses.

Vern asked Dewey if he wanted to go down to Nogales, Sonora Saturday night and see some of the girls over on Congress Street. Dewey said that could wait and Vern laughed and said, "How long, Dewey?"

Dewey said, "'Til I am sure Lim has got the right clothes and other things he needs to fit in at that school he will go into in the fall."

Vern said, "Well, you can go with me and drive me back and I will buy you some supper at La Roca and you can sit at the bar at one of them joints on Congress Street and I will come and get you when I am through."

Dewey said, "Naw, I think I'll just stay around with Lim. Maybe take him into Tucson. Eat a guacamole salad and a New York Strip at the Silver Saddle and go to a movie and then come on back home. Whores can wait a while. Besides, I am scared off of whores. In the Nam, some of those guys picked up some doses without a cure. Rumor was they got sent off to Guam and put in a special ward in a hospital and was not heard of since. Don't know if it is true. May not be. Just something that sits in the back of my mind."

Vern said, "You are right. Lord knows, you are right. But that is one thing makes it more fun. A little danger. A little excitement. Negotiations. The strangeness of it. Getting off of Congress and back across the border without being stabbed or shot is always a challenge."

Dewey said, "I know I am probably wrong about this, but I am still holding out for Rose. Might be a day she has her fill of Vegas and comes on back to Arizona and Lim and me. I know what you both are thinking. Don't put no money on it. The odds are long. But I went all in with Rose. All my chips in the middle of the table on her. Way I see it."

That was a week's talking for Dewey. Nobody said anything for a while. We just sat there and enjoyed the night. The sound of the wind rustling through the trees. A cow lowing off in the distance. And a calming and restful silence. A clear sky with a big yellow moon and some stars. No clouds. Just a big sky and the Whetstones low and black and far away on the Eastern horizon.

Vern said, "Another story Rand tells. He was playing football in college and doing pretty good and then one summer he comes home and is helping his dad around the ranch and doing some steer wrestling on the Turquoise Circuit and some of the local rodeos and he is talking to his father one night at the supper table."

Vern laughed and took a drag off his cigar and a sip of Jim Beam. Dewey and I sat and waited. We knew he would get back to the story when he was ready to.

"Asks his daddy for some backing. Front money to help him get started on the rodeo circuit. Said his father sat his fork down, took his napkin off the table and wiped his mouth, leaned over the table and pointed his finger at him and said, Son, I had just as soon shit and go blind all at the same time as do anything to encourage you to be a full time rodeo guy. All but a few wind up broke or crippled or both in body, in spirit and financially. That's a hell of a trifecta."

Then he told Rand he had all the chances he needed to kill, maim, or permanently injure himself within a five mile radius of where he was sitting.

Rand said the thing that surprised him was his father's language there at the supper table. Anyway, he said he started to say something, but knew it would not do any good so he just shut up. Nothing was said for a few minutes and then his father said, "Son, whatever you do, don't do like I just did. Leave your swearing outside. Never swear in the house or in front of your wife and children. And pray you have girls. Boys just wear a father out."

Rand said, that was the best advice he ever got. Sure enough, right there on the ranch, he had busted his knee when he got throwed from a horse, broke his wrist trying to gentle a colt down, and banged his left eye up one time when he was drinking in Willcox and miscalculated where his truck door was and banged it into his eye.

Dewey said, "That's all true. I know. But a team roper can go on into his forties or further. Mostly they quit because they get tired of living out of a suitcase and being lonely. Not because they get hurt."

I said, "That would get old. About the second or third year. And if you lose your good horse and have to buy another one, you may never find another one. Some of those boys have three or four horses so if one goes down they can keep going."

Vern said, "Dewey remember when we were just three tenths of a second off of being honest to God full time team ropers on the circuit? Drawing a good check at Tucson would a done it."

Dewey said, "Might have been for the best. I got Lim and a good place to work and you got more business than you can handle. Tell you something else. I would just as soon take an ass whupping as having to pack up and go from town to town all the time. Don't even like to leave the ranch 'cept to go to Tucson with Lim. Down to the feed store and back is enough traveling for me. I been half way around the world. I seen some pretty girls in Australia and Thailand but I don't need all that anymore. Always in a hurry. Catching airplanes. Big cities. You can have it all."

Vern said, I am getting the same way. I hate leaving in the morning. Wish I could get everybody to come here and let me shoe their horses under that oak tree by my trailer. Life on the road gets more tiresome every year.

Wasn't long after that, Dewey went on back to his place and Vern and I sat there and enjoyed the night breeze and Jim Beam. After Vern got up and left, Iris came back out on the porch and sat down. She was wearing a white nightgown with spaghetti straps. She was drinking a glass of chocolate milk.

She asked me, "Now that you sold those two horses, you are going to go out and buy some colts, aren't you?"

I said, "Yes."

She handed me her glass and said, "Take a drink of this. Might settle your stomach down after that sorry ass cigar and that mediocre whiskey we been drinking."

I said, "I like Jim Beam. 'Specially when it is free."

She said, "Me, too. I just don't want Vern to get the big head. Now back to these colts. Why not hold one back, this year or next year. Hold him back for Lim. He will outgrow Pepper. Pepper is a good riding horse but not much around cows. You watch. When he is around ten, Lim will need a good horse. One he can ride 'til he gets out of school."

"Keep it between us," I said. "By the time he is ten, Dewey may have drifted off to another spread. Might be living on a ranch in Utah or Idaho. Who knows."

Iris said, "They will stay. You watch and see. I heard Dewey. He won't even go to Nogales for a whore on Saturday night. He wants to set down roots. Get some peace in his life. But Rose. She has not even written to that boy. I check the mail every day hoping there is something. A card or a letter. Something. And not a thing."

"Lim ever say anything about getting a call from her? They got a telephone down there. But there have been no long distance calls made from it. That is the deal. I pay the phone bill except for the long distance. I told Dewey that first thing. I never talk to him about Rose. He never has brought it up except tonight. Hoping she will come back."

"Lim would say if she had called. It would be something he could not keep to himself," Iris said.

I silently agreed with Iris. I thought Dewey was settled in for the long haul. But I did not want to say it. Just keep it unsaid.

"Them spaghetti straps on that gown."

"Yes, dear."

"I like them because they do a poor job of keeping your night gown up."

"What if I just throw it on the back of that chair in our bedroom and take some of the mystery out of your life?"

We left the porch and I closed the front door and followed her back to the bedroom. She took her nightgown off and never missed a stride. When she was at the foot of the bed, she turned around and smiled at me and held her arms out to me.

The soft moonlight streamed through the window. Iris was fragile. Her barbwire attitude with Vern was gone. She was a small, fragile woman with thirsty eyes, warm, but small, probing hands and a soft, enticing voice.

She pulled me to her and asked me to hold her tight.

Just for a minute, she said. Then, I can tell, you have some business you want to attend to.

Chapter Six

The Middle Years

Iris Snider

The next morning at breakfast, Sherman looked up from his cornflakes and blueberries and asked me if I was sure I could share Pepper with Lim.

A fair question, I said. And I left it at that. A horse like Pepper stays with you long after he is dead and gone. Hard to give any part of him up. We had bought him a few years ago from Davey Waddell. He owns a spread down near the border. South of Bisbee. North of Douglas. Short on water and grass. But Davey always hung in there and one way he kept the bank away was to raise, swap, and sell horses. Nowadays, he is swapping horses he has trained up for some of our good Hereford yearlings.

Davey and Sherman were about the same age but ranching had been harder on Davey. Years back, he had married, but it had not lasted and most people, including Sherman, had forgot the reason or reasons for the breakup but Davey was a loner now. You would see him at the Rodeo in Tucson, at Las Vigas in Nogales, Arizona, the Steak-Out in Sonoita, La Roca in Nogales, Sonora, or Jack's in Patagonia. Only on a Friday or Saturday night.

Always the same. Hunkered over a glass of beer at the bar. By himself. A pressed shirt. Clean jeans and a nice Stetson. Had a straight answer to a question. Ask him if he had a horse to sell that you could rope off, he would give you an answer you could carry to the bank.

One time he told Sherman, I got a nice horse to rope off, but once the loop is set, he loses interest and he might sit down and get it taut or he might start walking to the side. Let me have another six or eight weeks and if I can get it cured, I will call you. If you don't have that much time, you better look somewhere else.

He and Vern were friends. Did some drinking together and Vern shod some of his horses. Not all of them. Davey did most of his own shoeing. He was one of those ranchers who called on Vern when he had a problem. Ranchers knew if a horse came up with a quarter crack or was cross firing, you needed to call Vern. Or if you were tired of shoeing your own horses and also needed somebody to share a bottle with. And somebody to tell you what was going on everywhere from Tubac to Benson, down to Douglas and even over to Willcox. Vern knew. And Vern carried a bottle and a set of four shot glasses in his truck.

Davey was a slow talking, ordinary looking fellow. He, Sherman, and Vern were having a beer at Jack's one cold November day a few years back and Davey told Sherman he had a horse for me. Sherman said Davey told him, "Now Sherman, I got a horse that Iris would like. He is out of some good stock. Cutting horse stock you can trace all the way back to Doc Bar and some good King Ranch mares. But Sherman, he ain't nothing around a cow. Almost worthless. But you put a nice black saddle with a lot of silver on it and Iris in one of her outfits riding in the Parade at the Tucson Rodeo or the Rodeo in Sonoita and you then have a winner. Perfect confirmation. And a Palomino. A mane and tail I got all bleached out. Long mane and a tail that drags the ground. And a deep gold color. Gentle as a puppy dog. Keep him in a stall during the day so that gold color doesn't fade on you and you got a nice horse. Tea cup nose. High hip and shoulder. Fairly short back.

Straight legs. No stifle problems. Manners like an English butler. Horse don't mind being rode a lot. Won't spook out on the trail. Wind and dust don't faze him. Just not interested in working cows. A riding horse. That's what I got for you."

Sherman telling the story. Saying how Davey never raised up from the bar and never raised his voice. So we went over to his ranch on the next Sunday and I rode Pepper out on the pasture and up in the gently rolling hills and when I got back, Davey said, "Ride him out a couple of hundred yards away from us and the barn and get him to back up for you and do a figure eight at a trot and then bring him down to a walk and do a bigger figure eight at a short lope and turn him and make him change his leads."

I did all of that and when I got back Davey said," Not bad for a coming four year old. He will only get better. Flesh out some more and get more gentle the more he is used to you. Twenty years of riding pleasure. Yes Sir, way you take care of horses, Iris, you got a horse that will make you proud." I got off and walked up to the fence and Sherman looked at me and I nodded and he said how much and Davey twisted his head, paused, looked off into the hills, and said," Well, I told you he is no cow horse and no roping horse but what I was thinking of doing is keeping him around for a little while in case I find somebody with a kid that might like a pleasure horse to show in the AQHA shows. But I would take eight for him. Cash money today. Papers is right here."

Sherman said, "That is a lot of cash. 'Specially with the price of beef going down. Turn on the radio. I stand to lose twenty five thousand dollars off my yearlings from last year's revenues in the fall if the market projections hold up."

Then it was Davey saying it was hard to measure in dollars the feeling Sherman would have watching someone else riding Pepper. He told Sherman he would wear a set of tires out on his pickup riding all over the country trying to find a nicer horse.

Both of them were enjoying the back and forth. Truth was we were doing pretty good with the ranch and could afford to pay more than what Davey was asking. Both of them knew Pepper was going home with us. Just a matter of time. Nobody in a hurry.

Davey told us to come up to the house with him. He took the bridle off Pepper and slipped a little red nylon halter over his head and tied him up in the shade of his old faded red barn. We all walked up to his little adobe. There were fresh red and white petunias in a fruit jar sitting on his kitchen table.

The house was neat. A brown leather couch with a matching leather chair, a heavy oak coffee table and a little television on a stand were about the only furnishings in the living room. There was a dark stain on the back of the chair. Davey probably napped there sometimes. A Vanity Fair magazine lay open on the coffee table. There was a nice citrus smell in the house.

"New woman in your life, Davey?" I asked.

"A nice one, too. But not as pretty as you. If she was here right now, she would say the same thing. She is working now. Probably drop by a little before sundown."

That was as far as I felt I should go with that. Davey was smiling and I felt it was his place to tell us more. His mind was on selling a horse. He had good stock. Horses and cows both. But he was probably short of cash. Way short.

Davey brought a bottle of Herradura Reposado and four glasses to the table. He poured us each a splash and turned to Sherman and said, "Now, Rachel, that is the nice lady that comes around some and keeps me company, she will be sad to see Pepper leave this ranch. She was mighty sad this morning when she left knowing he might be gone by the end of the day. So I got to have a nice chunk of cash to show her or she is going to be mighty regretful."

Sherman said, "I tell you what you need as much as cash, Davey. That is two good Hereford heifers. Already weaned. You can breed them in the spring. You come to the ranch in the morning and pick out the two you want and bring Pepper. And I throw in twenty one hundred dollar bills."

"We close now." Davey said. Make it four thousand, three heifers and one of those bull calves you kept to swap for breeding stock. I could use an upgrade in my breeding stock and you got some mighty fine Herefords."

"Make it thirty five hundred cash, two heifers, and a nice bull calf."

"Deal!" Davey said. He and Sherman raised their glasses, toasted the deal, and finished off their tequila. Vern looked at me and smiled and we drained our glasses, also.

Sherman said, "You come on by tomorrow in the morning and bring Pepper and his papers and we will make the trade."

We were driving home and had just turned off 90 onto 82 going west to Sonoita when Sherman said, "You know. In the short run, I beat him on that trade. Saved some cash. Forty five hundred dollars. Horse was probably a good buy at any price under seventy five hundred. But in the long run, he got me. Upgraded his herd big time. Two good purebred Hereford heifers and a good breeding bull for him. Of course that is all a year or more away. He should get twenty calves out of the deal over the course of time. But we got a nice horse. A real nice horse."

Everything Davey said was right. What he didn't know was that Pepper responded best to a woman or a child.

Before I let Lim get on and ride, I made him lead Pepper down a fence row with a halter. Lim on the right or left close in talking some but moving him down at his walking pace down the fence row. He had to do this for two days then I put Lim on Pepper and walked them down the fence row one whole afternoon. Just helping Lim learn to sit balanced on the horse. And making him sit still. He was so excited he was a little wiggle worm on Pepper's back the first day. But he learned fast. What to do and what not to do.

Finally, I let Lim ride him down the fence line a hundred yards or so and turn him around and walk him back. In two weeks he was trotting a little and turning him with his reins and knee pressure.

I laid the law down to Lim. No jerking the reins. No moving around. Balance. Balance. Your leg pressure telling the horse what you want to do. And Lim listened. That's the way it is with kids. You got a tight window of time where they will listen to you and carry what you say with them the rest of their lives. With Lim, the window was bigger than with most kids. By the time he went to school in late August, he was riding all over the pasture closest to the barn.

Lim would get up in the morning with his daddy, eat a little breakfast, go up to the barn, feed and water Pepper, do any chores Sherman or Dewey had for him, and then come on down to the house and help me if I had some thing for him to do. I gave him twenty dollars a week. Every Saturday was pay day for him. He told me he was saving for the day he could buy his own horse.

Sherman hired a hand named Charlie Webster in the fall after Lim started school. Charlie was in his late twenties and worked hard. He had a pot belly and he was maybe five six. Said he was from Utah. His parents owned a ranch near Round Valley and Bear Lake in the north east corner of Utah near where Wyoming, Utah, and Idaho borders all come together. He did the fence work, hassled with the irrigation pipes, and helped cut and gather the hay.

Dewey was on a horse most all day every day. But when it was time for cutting, gathering, and stacking hay, he was there to do his share. Calving in February and branding in April. Dewey did his part. Rest of the time, he was on a horse most every day.

Charlie stayed around but most of the other hands hardly ever lasted over a year. Work was hard and pay was low. But Charlie said he was just waiting a while 'til it was time for him to go back to his folks and get ready to take over the family ranch. His parents were in their late forties and he had two sisters still in high school.

Charlie bought his own horses down with him. He mostly stayed to himself and watched a lot of wrestling on cable television in the bunkhouse. He stayed until Lim was in the fourth grade. He left the week after Thanksgiving. Came up to the house on Friday night, drew his pay, thanked Sherman for the job, loaded his horses, and left to go back to the family ranch. We never heard a word back from him once he left. Not a word.

Right after Lim got started in the first grade, Sherman bought some colts and hired other hands so Dewey could have enough time to spend with the horses. Then after about two years, he bought some mares and a nice young two year old stud and we were in the horse business.

I was all for it. Sherman said the profit margin was mighty slim but he just loved horses. Some men played golf. Some bought boats. Some chased younger women and got divorces. Some did worse. Sherman just liked horses. After the first four years, we never lost money on our horses, we just never made an awful lot.

Ranches and the horse culture were dying out. The whole West was getting chopped up into little small ranchettes that were just rich men's playgrounds. Grandiose homes, wonderful vistas, and no stock. Drive around Sonoita, Prescott, Sedona, Cottonwood, or Tubac. All those places. See a new house on a lonely hill with an expensive fence, a little nickel ass barn and a horse or two standing around doing nothing. Swatting flies and trying to stay out of the heat or the cold wind. Bored and rendered useless by their owners.

Men like Vern and Sherman and Dewey took a horse and kept him busy or sold him. No abandoned pets on the Circle S. And this not from a lack of sentiment. Listen to us talk and you think our horses are part of our family. We mistakenly give them human attributes all the time. But feed costs money and the profit margins and fixed expenses on a ranch are things you had better watch constantly or a For Sale sign will be on your front gate before you know it. A ranch is just not a place for nonproductive animals. Give a mother cow a year without a calf. Then if she doesn't catch that second year, she's gone. And some folks do not wait for a second year if the cow is over eight years old. Has to be that way. We grow our own hay, but there are labor and machinery costs tied in with that. Grain. All from the feed store. Buy something at the feed store, get a bill on the 25th and pay it on the first. Turn into a slow pay or a behind on your bill customer and the only way you can get any feed is cash.

School days came in late August. Lim did fine in school his first four or five years. In the sixth grade he started to lose interest. Lot of C's on his report card. I talked to him about it. He said he was going to grow up to be a cowboy and maybe his daddy and him could find a little spread someday. He said all he needed was basic math and reading. So he didn't get cheated. He made A's in History and Math and B's and C's on the rest.

In the summer after his sixth grade, we went over to Davey Waddell's ranch one Saturday afternoon. Davey sent word through Vern, he had two nice colts he wanted us to see. For sale, of course. By this time, Lim had a lot of his growth. He was coming on twelve years of age and he was almost six feet tall. Slender and gawky. Long arms and legs that did not always look like they belonged on the same person. Until he was on a horse.

Sherman sat in front of the king cab of our Silverado and Vern, Lim and I squeezed in the back. Dewey drove so Sherman could drink a Coors on the drive over. When we got to Davey's ranch, he met us at the barn. We had seen three horses in the corral next to the barn. A nice looking sorrel with a lot of chrome, a big boned, rangy dun, and a sleepy looking, bony black horse with a big head and long, long legs.

The black was tied up to the fence away from the other two and had a old rope halter on. He was not a colt. He was a young horse. He had a ratty, long black mane, a long, big head, a bob tail, and a long, skinny neck. Prominent rib and hip bones added to the dismal picture.

Sherman and Dewey went into the corral and looked at the colts. Lim went over to the black and picked up a bridle hanging on the fence. He slipped the bridle on the black and asked Davey if he could ride him and Davey said, "Sure, but I got to warn you, he is rough as a cob."

Lim climbed on bareback and rode the black out of the corral into the pasture. There were some cows grazing a few hundred yards away. As they left the corral, the black was shaking his head, bowing his neck, and prancing sideways. After Lim had ridden him a few hundred yards into the pasture, he turned around and came back into the corral and jumped off the black.

Sherman and Dewey were talking to Davey and Lim had to wait a few minutes before he could ask Davey if he could change bridles. Davey again said sure. The bridle Davey brought out of the barn had a D-ring snaffle bit. This was Dewey's favorite bit to start our three year olds on. The first bridle Lim had rode the bay on had a curb bit with a long shank and a high port.

Lim rode off and soon he was over the hill and out of sight. It was a beautiful, spring day in Arizona. Orange blooms of globe mallow and golden Mexican poppies were scattered over the hillside. The sky was a perfect blue with a few passive clouds hanging on the distant horizon.

The hills were green with new, almost knee high grass. An ocotillo near the corral gate had new, red flowers blooming on the ends of the tall, gently swaying stalks. The wind would pick up later in the afternoon, but, for now, there was only a gentle and comforting breeze from the south.

Sherman and Dewey had eliminated the dun colt and were dickering with Davey over the price of the nice, flashy, sorrel colt. Dewey had walked him out of the corral and turned him around after a hundred yards and trotted him back. The colt had been frisky but he had stayed close to Dewey's shoulder on the way back in.

Vern and I were catching up on some gossip about a history teacher at Patagonia High School when we saw Lim ride back over the hill. He rode in the middle of the grazing cattle and cut out an old red and brown brindle cow with two long menacing horns and hazed her slowly back towards the corral.

She made a couple of attempts to get back to her calf that had been grazing with her. On the third attempt, she barely slipped past Lim and the gawky black. Lim let her pass when she swung her head and horns near the black's right shoulder. After she had run a few yards back toward the other cows, Lim headed her and turned her back towards the corral. She gave up after another futile try to get back to her calf.

Lim shut the gate to the corral, then backed the black up and turned him and opened the gate. He walked the old brindle cow out of the corral and came back in the corral and put the halter on the ugly black. The big horse was not looking sleepy now. His eyes were alert and his ears stood straight up. Lim walked him out of the corral into the pasture. He walked him almost to the top of the distant hill before he turned back toward the corral.

Vern and I followed Dewey, Davey, and Sherman into the house. There were two rose bushes blooming in a bed to the left of the front porch steps. Purple petunias, orange marigolds, and yellow lantana grew in a bed to the right of the porch steps.

We saw Davey several times a year. He was always the same. Slow and even tempered. A few years back, Dewey, Sherman and I were eating at Las Vigas in Nogales, Arizona when we saw Dewey eating alone.

Sherman invited him over and he came over and sat down and I could tell something was wrong. It took me about a minute to figure it out. Rachel was gone. I never mentioned her name but when we got home that night, I went down to Vern's trailer and left him a note to come up to the house if he got home before eleven.

Vern came trudging up to the house later that night. He was bone tired. I fixed him a plate of food. Some chicken fried chicken, green beans, and some candied sweet potatoes. And a glass of Bud Light. I bought it special for him. Sherman and I drank Dos Equis Amber and Negro Modelo when we drank beer.

Vern said Rachel had lost her job working in a doctor's office in Benson. The doctor retired and moved up to the Deschutes River country near Bend Oregon.

He sold his medical practice to a bunch of doctors in Tucson. Rachel went to Phoenix to live with her brother and his family until she could find a job. This was the first time I had been back to his house since she had left.

The house was clean. No dishes in the sink. No old newspapers on the floor. No disgusting smells. No food on the table. Everything was neat. Davey's jeans were clean, his shirt was washed and pressed, and his hair was neatly cut.

While I was doing my silent inspection of his home, Davey was giving it to Sherman and Dewey.

"Now fellas, I think you are giving up too early on that dun colt. A little training and some good food. I say six months and he will start to fill out. Now the sorrel. Maybe I was wrong to even let another colt in the corral with him. Lots of chrome and style there. Could go AQHA halter classes or any one of a dozen other classes. Got good pleasure history on his dam's side and also going to have the size and chrome to turn some heads whatever you decide to use him for."

Sherman said, "You are right, but you probably want too much. I can see using him on the breeding side. 'Specially if I could put him with a trainer and get some AQHA points. Just one problem and that is this economy. How about giving us a decent figure to work with. Right now, I got three extra horses eating me out of house and home. Three I want to sell or swap. Why don't you bring the colt over to the Circle S tomorrow and Iris will invite you to a nice Sunday dinner and maybe we can work something out."

Davey said, "The colt's name is Socks. Two nice white socks on the front end and two white stockings in back and a nice symmetrical blaze. Lot of chrome and great confirmation. Price of gasoline being what it is, I bring that colt over there, I want to be able to bring back some cash. Eight thousand is my low ball price. Offer me 7,950 and I am coming home. Soon as I get fed. Of course."

"Eight thousand for a colt is some serious business for poor folks like us. But he is a nice colt. No getting around that."

"Well, I am sorry but I have nothing to offer you to eat except some posole a nice friend dropped by the house. Some posole and beans and corn tortillas. And I got some good tequila for you to sip on while I get the food warmed up and set out on the table for you."

Davey was warming up the posole and the beans when Lim came to the door. I saw him motion for Dewey. Dewey went out on the porch and shut the front door. In a few minutes, they both came back in the house and Dewey said," Lim wants to talk to you, Davey. About that ugly ass black horse."

Lim said, "Mr. Waddell, give me a price on that black."

Davey said, "Let me get this food on the table and we will talk."

When we were all seated at the table and eating, Davey said, "Lim, let me give you just a short history of my dealings with that black and then throw in my philosophy on horse trading.

"First of all, the black. I was at the sale barn last month in South Tucson. Looking for some nice Hereford yearlings. I had been asked to share a pint of Four Roses single barrel bourbon by a cattle buyer out of New Mexico and his girlfriend. I had a few pops. I did not plan on driving home. Anyway, I am walking back to my truck and I see the black leaning against an old rusted out stock trailer. Anyway, the long and short of it is I drink some mescal with two fellows that owned the black and I give them seventy five dollars and a pretty new saddle blanket and I was the somewhat reluctant owner of the black. I knew better. Why? I figured he was going across the border then to Europe or to some slaughterhouse in Mexico and I figured I could save him from that. Sell him to somebody or throw him in on a deal and at least keep him alive for a few more years. The way the ranching business is now, he is probably going to be across the border in a few years. He just is too big and gawky to be a ranch horse. He is never going to be able to make the quick, sharp cuts you need from a horse who is working cattle. His legs are too long. His head is too big and I can't get any weight on him."

Davey got up from the table and opened a cabinet under his kitchen counter and pulled out a short, round bottle of mescal.

Davey said, "Now Iris, before you start protesting that this is nothing but kerosene with a little vanilla flavoring added for color and flavor, I want you to taste it. Just a teaspoon. All I ask. Those two fella who sold me that black threw the rest of the mescal into the deal. This is pretty good. Eighty proof. Anejo Reserva. Aged two years in oak barrels."

Davey handed me a teaspoon of the mescal. It was not bad. Something to sip at the end of day. Sitting out on the porch watching the doves settling in for the night in the cottonwoods down at the creek. It might do on a cold day when the sun was just a weak, white ball in the sky and you were out of bourbon.

"Tell you what, Davey. You work this horse deal out and you can bring this bottle over with you. I'll have green chile enchiladas, a guacamole salad, and a fresh banana pudding. Afterwards, we can all sit out on the front porch and watch the sun go down over the Santa Ritas and the doves coming home to roost in the cottonwoods down by the Cienega."

"Oh, we gonna work this horse deal out. Sherman Snider won't let a deal like this pass him by. Naw. He is way too smart for this. You looking at a nice sorrel with lots of chrome, a good, easy disposition that he can sell for twenty five to fifty thousand in a year or so."

Sherman said, "Before we get to this sorrel, we need to get this resolved about the black. Lim has the money to pay for a horse of his own. Up to a point. He has been saving money since he came to the Circle S. Money he has earned doing work that freed all of us up to do other things. Cleaning out stalls, moving irrigation pipes, helping Iris with the yard and flowers. Calving, branding, castrating, and anything else we have asked. I sure don't want to hoe out flower beds or set out petunias after a day's work or on Sunday. So give me a figure"

Davey leaned back and said, "Lim, if you want to ever make part or all of your living selling horses, there are a few things to remember. First is be honest.

"Tell the truth about your horse to a customer. For one reason, that was the way I was raised. The other reason is this. You think there is a lot of country, say, between Tubac and the New Mexico line. But news travels mighty fast. If someone thinks he gets cheated on a horse deal, you can guarantee it will be all over Southern Arizona real fast. Bad news travels faster than good news. And gossip travels the fastest."

The posole was in a big, olive green crock pot. Davey stood up and spooned out second helpings to Lim and Vern. Vern had his yellow napkin tucked into his shirt. He was drinking a Dos Equis Amber out of the green bottle.

Davey said, "Now of course you want to highlight the good qualities of your horse. No question. But remember the old saying. My dad told it to me a long time ago when I asked him why he told a customer that a horse was a pain in the ass to load. My dad said, "Pigs get fat, son. And hogs get slaughtered." Point being that an honest profit is always best."

"Now this black. First off, you ain't heard me bragging about his Doc Bar breeding, have you? Reason, he is a grade horse. No papers. I got a bill of sale. Seventy five dollars. One black gelding approximately three years old. Of indeterminate origin. How you like that phrase, Iris? I read it in the Wall Street Journal in the doctor's office when I got my yearly physical. I was there an hour waiting to see the doctor and I seen two articles I could read."

"I quarantined the black when I got him home. Got the vet out and made sure he did not have Coggin's disease or something. No telling where he has been and who owned him. I asked the two fellows at the sale barn for a copy of the Coggin's test and they said it was in the barn back home. They never said where home was. That was why they didn't run him through the sale. No vet papers. So he is sound as far as I know. No foot problems except he cross fires sometimes. By that I mean his back hooves will come up and catch the opposite front foot when he turns fast. Probably my fault. All I have done is put some old used keg shoes on him."

"I tried to put some weight on him. That son of a bitch eats more than any horse I own and will not put on weight. Look at his front end.

Too damn narrow. His neck is pitiful. Ewe necked they call it. Like a mangy, neglected sheep. His hips are totally lacking. Not any depth and his back legs are too long. Also, his head is just plain out ugly. Too long. With almost a parrot nose. And I can't set his head. Used martingales, tiedowns, everything I could think of and he just fights it. Head up and nose out. Only thing he is good for is eating."

Dewey said, "Lim wants a price."

Davey said, "Tell you what. I'll forget about the vet bill. And the money for feed and hay. Give me one hundred dollars."

Lim said, "And the old rope halter you had on him and that bridle I rode him with. That a part of the deal?"

"Son, that is fine. But one more part. Since this is not a horse I can vouch for, you bring him back and you can have your hundred dollars back. Up to six months from today. I hope it works out because I will be saving a lot of money on grain and hay with him gone."

Dewey counted out a hundred dollars in tens and twenties and Davey wrote out a bill of sale. Dewey looked at the bill of sale and asked Davey why he didn't put the horse's name on it. Davey said he only called the black whatever obscenity came to mind and Lim would have to give him a proper name.

Lim left the house running. His dad's words, Lim you know better to run in the house, trailing him out the door. I got up from the table and watched him run to the corral by the barn and worm his way through the old gray board fence. He untied the halter rope and walked the black out of the corral, grabbed some mane, and vaulted up on the skinny horse's back.

Lim rode off slowly into the pasture. The gawky, seemingly uncoordinated black, shuffled along in a gait somewhere between a walk and a trot. A gait that was unfamiliar to me. I called Vern over. Sherman, Dewey, and Davey were eating Doritos and dickering over the sorrel colt.

I asked Vern if he had ever seen a horse move the way the bay was moving and he smiled and said, in almost a whisper, "Iris, I have. And we will talk about it in the truck. But let me tell you this. If we can put some weight on that horse, Lim will have out swapped a pretty good horse trader. We will just have to wait and see."

We went back to the table and I started to clear the dishes. Davey told me to sit down. He would do it later. I went ahead and cleared the table except for a bowl of Doritos. The spicy kind. His dishwasher was empty and it didn't take long to get things cleaned up and the dishwasher going. It started with a slow growl followed by an ominous whining noise. Finally, the noise settled down to a low drone and I sat down at the table and listened to Sherman and Davey go at it.

Sherman said, "Davey, look, me and you been doing business for a long time. I am just looking out for you. You say you need cash, well I say that is correct. But who doesn't? What you need more than cash is to improve your herd some. You still got too many grade cows chewing up your grass. Those little Mexican steers forage good but they take longer to flesh out and once they get to the feed lots up around Amarillo, they don't put on weight fast enough. So you get low prices in the fall. I got a couple of nice bull calves and some little heifers already weaned off. Breeding goes all the way back to those bulls was brought over to the XIT from England."

Davey said, "After that speech, I need a half shot of that mescal. How about you, Iris? I ain't askin' these fellows. I ain't never seen the day, they wouldn't drink me out of house and home. Not that I don't do the same."

I said, "No thanks, it looks like either me or Lim will have to drive home and since he is unlicensed, it will be me. He drives a truck and a tractor all over the place when we need him to. How about me starting a pot of coffee?"

Davey said, "Thanks, I might need some after this here negotiating session is over and I am out a good horse and still cash poor."

Davey pushed his chair back and said, "First thing, I was planning on bringing both the black and the sorrel over tomorrow morning about breakfast time. But Lim may want to ride him back this afternoon. Might want to discourage that thought. It is a good two day ride and those road shoulders are far from safe."

Dewey said, "Going to be hard to put weight on that horse with all the riding he is going to get. School will be out soon."

Sherman swirled the amber colored mescal around in his shot glass and waited for Davey to swing the conversation back to the sorrel.

After a few minutes, Davey said, "I love to smell coffee. 'Specially in the morning. Coffee brewing and bacon frying. What you need to get started."

I said, "Now Davey, since you do not seem to want to sell your sorrel colt today, why don't you at least answer a question for me? I know it is absolutely none of my business but I sure would like to talk to whoever made this posole. It is mighty tasty. Pork cooked down to just the right grade of tenderness. The broth is mighty good. Spicy, but not too hot. Hominy blends in nicely."

"Let me have your offer, Sherman. Let your conscience be your guide. Remember, you are dealing with an almost destitute Arizona rancher. Grass is scarce this year."

"Looks mighty green out this window. I guess you did not hear me asking about the mystery chef," I said.

"We will talk about the mystery chef after a while. I need to hear this offer."

"Tell you what, four thousand cash and two good heifer calves. You pick the heifers. You know that colt is mighty thin on top. Now he does have some good stock on his dam's side but on top. The stallions are not impressive going three generations back."

"I picked the stud. And you are right. Only paid a three hundred and fifty dollar stud fee. So I do not have to pass a two thousand dollar or higher stud fee on to you. But do like the Bedouins. They put more emphasis on the dam than the stud. Can't say they are not right most of the time."

I was restless. The afternoon was slipping away. A beautiful spring day in Southern Arizona. Davey looked tired and he had an edge to him today that I had not seen before. He was saying all the right things but there was a desperate tone to his voice. You could tell he wanted cash. Sherman's offer was good. Two good heifer calves would wind up giving him twenty or more calves over the years.

I left the house and stood on the front porch and looked west. The sun would be down soon and I was not going to miss the sunset today. Davey had roses trellised against the front wall of his house. I recognized Tropicana and Mr. Lincoln blooms. He had some white climbers and some lemon yellow floribundas in the flower beds next to the porch.

I walked up to the old stone horse barn to check on Lim. As I walked past the open end shed Davey used for a garage, I saw his old truck, a John Deere tractor, and an empty space. There were tire tracks in the empty space.

In the horse barn, Lim had his horse in cross ties and was running a curry comb over his neck. He had a brush in his other hand. There were several green molded plastic chairs down near the feed room so I got one and sat down and watched Lim. He had been talking to his horse when I came up but he was quiet now.

I said, "Lim, why this horse? You know you can ride Pepper or some other horse of ours anytime you choose."

Lim said, "I can't really say. I just like the way he moves. He is a little clumsy right now but Vern can shoe most of that out of him. He feels like he can not really get his true balance. You know how Pepper is. Just automatic. Always smooth and easy. Well, when I brought him back over the hill and got him in the middle of Davey's cows up on the slope, he perked up and I could feel the energy from him in my legs. He was ready to work. He just ain't been taught how."

"He needs some weight on him, Lim. We will work on that, but you got to know Davey has been feeding him. You heard him say the horse was eating him straight into the poor house."

"I ain't saying he is a finished horse. All I am saying is when he got in the middle of them cows, he perked up. As long legged and rangy as he is, he is never going to be a top cutting horse. I know that but I just want to try. And for a hundred dollars I can not go wrong. "

"It is going to take a lot of patience, Lim. I just do not want to see you get disappointed and discouraged over something that can't be helped. That's all."

"All Dad said was give it a try if you think you can get him going in the right direction."

I left it alone. The boy had his mind set on the horse and I needed to butt out and let him alone. I took the brush from Lim and brushed where he had curried. When we were through, Lim pulled up a chair and we sat and looked out the front door of the horse barn. The barn was up on a small hill and you could see for a long, long, way. Grey mountains in the East, rolling hills running South all the way past the border, and a broad red, purple, and blue horizon in the West were all set against a backdrop of a powder blue sky. No clouds for as far as you could see.

The sun was starting to set and I was showing Lim all the colors on the horizon as the sun turned to a bright orange and reds, purples, blue, and orange filled the vast Western horizon. Something I tried to do as often as possible was watch the sunsets. A simple, but unbeatable, pleasure.

Before the sun disappeared over the horizon, I saw a car coming down the long, sloping hill from the highway to Davey's house. The car pulled up in front of the house and a woman got out and went to the back passenger door and took some groceries from the car and turned towards the house. Davey was out the front door and met the woman and took the sack of groceries into the house. Vern and Dewey came out and brought the rest of the sacks into the house.

I turned to Lim and told him to put his horse in his stall and give him some hay and grain and then come on up to the house. I knew we would be leaving soon. As I walked to the house the sun ducked below the horizon. I stood for a moment and looked at the broken pink and orange strands on the horizon as they gradually begin to fade away into darkness.

When I went inside, Sherman was telling the woman he would have helped with the groceries but he was wore out trying to work a deal with Davey. She was shy. You could tell that, but she liked having all the men around her. Davey introduced us all. Her name was Lynn. She was tall and rangy with long legs and plaited brown hair that hung down past her waist.

She was wearing a denim skirt and a white blouse. I figured she was four months along. Maybe five. A woman like her could fool you. Whatever weight she put on was almost all baby. I helped Lynn put up the groceries and she poured us some iced tea and we went back out to the porch.

The sunset was almost gone and a soft breeze was blowing in from the South. I asked Lynn when the baby was due and she said July or early August. She told me she taught math and accounting at the high school in Sierra Vista. She had six years working at the High School, but she and Davey had decided they would tough it out and let her stay at home until their son was old enough to do for himself.

I told her about my degree from the University of Arizona in finance and accounting and how I used it keeping the ranch afloat. Lynn did not have on a wedding ring and neither did Davey. I had looked while we were all in the house.

It had been a beautiful spring day. Lim had a new horse. A new chapter in his life. Lynn and Davey were starting a new adventure. I told Lynn about the impasse in the negotiations about the horse and Lynn said Davey wanted cash because having a baby coming this summer frightened him. She would lose her health insurance after the baby was out of the hospital and private insurance was too expensive for a small rancher like Davey.

Lynn said they were rolling the dice, having a child in this expensive world with so little cash set back. She and Davey both wanted to keep the sorrel but a quick profit was more important. They did not have the money to hire a trainer to campaign the sorrel in the AQHA circuits. If he could get enough points they could stand him to stud and cash in for fifteen to twenty five years.

I asked her how she met Davey and she said she did some individual and small scale tax work on the side and Davey had come to her to help him and she had tried to get things straight but it was hopeless because he never kept receipts and she said she got so mad at him, she drove out to the ranch and yelled at him about his irresponsible ways and he had ducked his head and let her have her say.

When she was through yelling at him, he poured her a glass of iced tea and he sat down at his kitchen table and looked at her for a few minutes and then said, "Well, what about this? A good solution for us both." And I said, "Does this solution include paying me the two hundred dollars you owe me?"

He got up and pulled his billfold out and counted out two hundred dollars cash and I put it in my purse and told him that was a start and just what was the rest of it and he said, "You move out here, show me on a daily basis how to do all this record keeping, and we let the rest of it play itself out its own natural way."

Lynn said she picked up her tea glass and poured it out in the sink and told him he was the farthest thing from a man she wanted to have a relationship with and then she left the house. She was almost to Sierra Vista before she turned around. She drove back to his house and he was on the front porch listening to the quail call and the lonesome wind rustling through the trees.

She walked up on the porch and he asked her if she wanted to see her room because he knew she would not want to rush into something and she opened the door and went inside and there was a spare bedroom with a small bed and the cheapest looking dresser she had ever seen in her short and mostly, uneventful, life. No curtains on the windows, no chair. A nice enough closet. And a clean oak floor.

Lynn said she moved her furniture into the spare bedroom and sent the bed and cheap dresser to Goodwill and got a receipt and explained the concept of personal tax deductions to Davey.

When Lim came up to the porch, I introduced him to Lynn and he took his straw hat off and smiled and went into the house. His shoulders were drooping and his boots dragged across the porch floor.

Lynn asked me how old Lim was and I said, "Eleven," and she laughed and said, "Well, some woman has got a nice treat coming to her in a few years. You just watch."

I knew she was right. He would never be movie star handsome. Especially with those big ears, but he was going to be slender and tall and he had a shy grin that was disarming. Relaxed you. Wholesome is the way I saw him growing up. And shy.

In a few minutes, Sherman came out of the house, cussing softly and shaking his head. He went to our truck and took the check book ledger out of the cab and walked back to the porch.

He shook his head and said, "Eight thousand and he will throw in a halter. I at least got that much to boot."

Lynn went to a small desk in the den and brought a Mont Blanc pen to the kitchen table and Sherman started to write the check. He turned to Lynn and said "How do I make this out."

Lynn said "Waddell Ranch, Inc."

Sherman said, "I bet you had something to do with that Inc. part. I been making checks out to just plain old Davey Waddell for a long while."

He handed the check to Lynn and put the Mont Blanc in his left shirt pocket. I stood up and took the pen from his pocket and gave it to Lynn. Sherman looked over at Lim and said, "Well, Lim, it looks like I may have to put you in charge of my future horse buying chores. Here, my own wife has turned on me. I ought to get that pen complementary to the sale, Iris."

Davey said, "Lim, now have you thought of a name for that jug headed, un-coordinated, clumsy, and over-all ugly horse I sold you."

Lim said, "Yes sir, I got one. Fits, too."

"What you gonna call him, Lim," Dewey asked.

"Davey." Lim said it real soft but it was obvious he did not want to take any more ribbing over his horse.

We laughed and when we got up to leave, Dewey said, "This boy has been riding Pepper all these years, so he will have some learning to do."

I asked Davey if he and Lynn would come over tomorrow in time for breakfast. The deal was for Davey to trailer the two horses over tomorrow.

Lynn said, "Davey will be at Mass in Benson at eight o'clock with me. He will probably be over around noon and be back before dark so he can feed the horses and then spend some time with me."

"Noon, it is," I said. "Knowing Davey, he will be hungry and I will feed him."

I drove on home. Sherman had drank enough for the night and he slipped off asleep before we got home. No one talked much. I asked Lim when he decided to name his horse, "Davey," and he said, "When he started razzing me about my horse. I like him and if Dad and you and Sherman and Vern will help me get him started right, I will do the rest."

The night was clear and a big yellow moon lit up the whole valley all the way back to the Circle S. When we got home, Sherman, turned to Lim and said, "I heard you asking for help. I can damn sure tell you what not to do. I have ruined a few horses in my day. We all have, so you listen to what we say and then do what you think is best for the horse. Davey. Good name for that horse. Make you remember when and where you bought him."

We all started walking away from the truck and Sherman said, "Come to think of it, Lim, Davey is a little gawky and awkward looking until he gets on a horse. You nailed him. We won't let him forget this day."

When Sherman and I were settled on the front porch and were sharing a shot of Herradura Reposado , Sherman started writing some figures down on a yellow legal pad. I asked him what he was doing and he said he was trying to figure out how much he had to shell out to make a profit on the sorrel.

"A trainer and his fees. AQHA advertising, air fare for us to go to some of the big shows. Insurance. Big cost but we got to do it. You want the stud fees, you have to campaign him. Get his name out there. I will insure him for at least 75,000 for now. At least."

I took a small sip of the tequila and filled the shot glass up to the top. Sherman laughed and said, "It is spring time and Saturday night and I am sitting across from the prettiest and smartest girl you could ever want. Yet I am worrying about a horse. A colt. He ain't even a horse yet."

I looked to the east and I could see the dark outline of the Whetstone Mountains against the moonlit sky. Bright stars, a big yellow moon, and a coyote's lonely moan relaxed me. Around midnight, I left the porch and went inside and showered. I had been in bed for a few minutes when I heard Sherman turn the shower on. When he came to bed, he pulled his warm body close to me. I turned to him and asked him if he still had his mind on that colt and he laughed and threw the covers from the bed and I rolled over on top of him and his hands found my breasts and I guided him into me. I took one last look at the big yellow moon shining high in the spring sky, reached behind me, grabbed his knees, and rocked back. His hands moved to my hips and soon we found the right pace and when we were finished, I rolled off him satisfied and lay beside him and listened to his short, hurried breaths for a few minutes until he went to sleep.

I sat on the side of the bed for a few minutes, but I was thirsty, so I went into the kitchen and drank a glass of orange juice. The only sounds were the steady hum of the refrigerator and the lonesome call of a coyote down near the creek.

Chapter Seven

The Best of Times

Vern

When we came home that night after Lim had bought Davey, Dewey and I sat out in front of my Air Stream and drank a beer. There was a soft, summer breeze that kept things cool and we could see all the way to the Whetstones in the East and the Santa Ritas in the West. A beautiful, late spring night, complete with a big yellow moon and silver stars in the distance gave me comfort.

I had seen horses like Davey back years ago in Dallas. At a Tennessee Walking Horse show. They had an exaggerated gait called a running walk where the horse reached way out with his front legs and his back end was low to the ground and his back legs over-strided. The horses carried their heads way up high. They arched their necks and nodded their heads.

Leather pads were stacked on the front feet to add height to the long, reaching gait. Small chains were looped across the front ankles of the horse. This gave them more animation and action to the gait. The horses wore brightly colored ribbons in their manes. They had long tails that sometimes drug the ground.

It was an impressive sight. As long as you could forget the horses had probably all been sored. Trainers applied mustard oil, used too heavy chains, anything to add action and reach to the gait. Some of the gait was natural. Most of it was artificial. I watched about an hour of the show and went to Joe Garcia's down by the Fort Worth Stockyards and ate enchiladas and drank Pearl beer with some friends.

I do not believe in spoiling a horse. But I do not believe in hurting one either. Especially, just so you can achieve an unrealistic gait. The Walking Horse gait that made them famous came from the old single foot gait. A smooth gait that has evolved into a rack or a running walk. The running walk accents a reaching, high stepping, showy, front end. The rack is a faster gait with the accent on high stepping, and not a reaching stride. The challenge in shoeing a horse is to find the shoes that will let him move naturally. But do not get me wrong. The Walking Horse people are not alone in mistreating show horses. It goes on at all levels. Drugs to calm a horse down. Drugs to jack him up. Drugs to make him run faster. Drugs to make him more relaxed. Overtraining. The list is endless.

Associations for reining horses, cutting horses, trail horses, and, most specifically, the American Quarter Horse Association all look for a performance horse that is sensible, works easily under the bridle, and can perform tasks relating to ranch work.

Confirmation and handling ease are the main guidelines in halter classes. I got no clue as to what they want in those English classes. No clue and no interest.

Before Davey brought the horses over on Sunday, Dewey and I went up to the barn and talked to Lim while he was feeding and cleaning stalls. Dewey told him not to listen to any bullshit about his horse. The horse needed to be looked at by a vet to see if his teeth needed floating and to see if there was anything we could do to put some weight on him. Dewey told him he was going to have to learn patience or he was going to lose his horse's confidence if he crowded him and confused him early on by asking him to do too many things.

And I told him the patience was going to start today. I had looked at horse's feet. He had on simple keg shoes on the front and the back and his toes and heels had both grown long. First thing I wanted to do was to take his shoes off and get Lim to walk him down a fence line, turn him, trot him back up the fence line, and then turn him back to me and trot him to me. All with Lim on him bareback.

Dewey laughed and told Lim I was right but it wouldn't hurt to ride him some real easy at a walk for a few minutes each day just to give him some exercise. Twenty minutes, Dewey said. And I agreed.

I told Lim it would take me a few days to find out what I wanted to know and then it might take months of tinkering before we got his shoes right. Lim sort of set his jaw but he did not say anything. We helped him finish his chores and then went down and drank coffee in front of my trailer and waited on Davey to bring the horses.

It was crowding noon when Davey drove up with his truck and stock trailer. He had three horses in the trailer. Davey's nephew, Jimmy Dale Scruggs, got out of the truck and went to the back of the trailer and started to unload the horses. He brought the sorrel out first and Sherman took the lead rope and walked him around some while the other horses were unloaded.

Jimmy Dale brought Lim's horse out next. He held out the lead rope and said, "I want to see who bought this ugly ass horse."

Lim walked up to him and hit him under the left eye with his right fist and before any of us could get between them they were passing some pretty good licks. Soon, they were rolling in the dust and kicking and gouging away.

Jimmy Dale was a head taller and twenty pounds heavier than Lim but Lim gave as well as he took. Jimmy Dale got on top of him and was going to hit him and Lim threw a handful of dust and dirt in his face and got up and kicked him in the ribs.

Dewey and Sherman just stood there. Sherman was laughing. Dewey did not move. He looked shocked and confused. I heard the front door to the ranch house slam and Iris was running towards us, hollering all the way from the porch to the trailer for Sherman to stop the fight.

By now, they were both running out of gas and had started wrestling and punching each other on the ground. I looked at Davey and he nodded once and I grabbed Lim and he grabbed Jimmy Dale.

Jimmy Dale said, "You little shit ass, I was just kidding you. Not my fault you bought an ugly jug-headed son of a bitch for a horse."

Lim got away from me and was going after him again and Dewey came up behind him and said, "Leave him alone son. I don't think he wants anymore anyway."

Then Iris started in on them. First she told Jimmy Dale he could start walking back home to his mother's spread if he said anything else or started anything or cursed or took the Lord's name in vain.

She asked Lim if he was hurt and Jimmy Dale laughed and they tried to start it up again.

Iris said she would have lunch ready in a few minutes and she expected to have a nice, peaceful Sunday. I thought she had teared up but when I looked to be sure, she was stalking off from us.

She walked away a few more feet, turned and told Lim she was ashamed of him, and walked on back to the house.

Sherman said, "You boys take those two horses up to the barn and throw 'em some hay and make sure they have fresh water in their stalls and come on back and wash up. Iris made a pot roast and a peach cobbler and there are some nice ranch beans to go with it."

Jimmy Dale and the sorrel followed Lim and his horse up to the barn.

When Lim and Jimmy Dale were in the barn, Davey said, "Fellows, I am sorry for that. Jimmy Dale can be one continuous source of aggravation. He is my sister's boy and since his daddy died, I have tried to teach him some things and give him a little money for helping me around the ranch, but the truth is, he is more trouble than help. He works good, but my sister calls me all the time wanting me to take him off her hands. For her being a mother is an afterthought. At least that is what Lynn says and she has some facts to back it up with."

Sherman said, "That's all forgotten. You could say Lim started the fight when he laid that first lick across Jimmy Dale's cheekbone or you could say Jimmy Dale provoked it by his smartass mouth. Either way, nothing for anybody to apologize about or hold a grudge over."

Dewey and Davey shook hands and Davey went in the trailer and brought out the big red dun colt Sherman had passed on yesterday.

Davey said, "How about I leave him here and let you all work with him until branding time. When it comes time to brand, I will come back up and Jimmy Dale and I will help you and maybe we can swap the dun for a couple of bred heifers and a bull calf."

Sherman said, "Let me talk to Lim and Dewey. They will be the ones that is doing this extra work. Davey, you can think up a lot of ways to get over on me, you know that. Dewey and Lim will get your horse lined out and halter trained and then you set your price up too high and you get a better horse back. I can tell you right now, you ain't getting no two bred heifers and a good bull calf. Naw, that ain't happening."

Davey said, "Let that horse have another year, put him to saddle and you will be thanking me. Count on it, Sherman. He just needs some attention and I ain't got enough time to do everything I need to do. Hard enough to keep the place going. I got me a couple of nice brood mares, you got to give me that, Sherman."

Sherman looked at Dewey and Dewey nodded and Sherman said, "'Bout six weeks to branding. If he don't work out, I will put him out in one of the pastures and let you take him home when you and that hellion come to help me brand."

Dewey took the halter rope from Davey and dropped it on the ground. The dun didn't move. Dewey ran his left hand up the dun's face and between his ears. He stood still. Dewey kept his left hand on the dun and walked around him and came up on his right side. He ducked under his head and stood at his left shoulder and ran his hand down the dun's back. He still had not moved.

Dewey picked each hoof up and then nodded to Sherman.

Dewey said, "Who's been schooling this horse, Davey. You are the worst pore mouther I have ever seen. I am going to guess Lynn and maybe Jimmy Dale. Mostly Lynn."

"Well, truth be known, fellas, if Lynn was not pregnant, I would hold on to the dun and maybe the sorrel too, but I don't have the cash to hire a trainer and campaign a horse on the AQHA level. Breed 'em and sell 'em. That's my plan. Lynn says if the sorrel does like we hope he will, we can breed back to the same stud and then use the colt as our stud. Own brother of the sorrel."

I knew from listening to Davey talk, he and Lynn were not going to take Jimmy Dale Scruggs into their home and raise him. They had a child of their own coming soon and Jimmy Dale was already a hand full. Davey told us his sister, Nancy Joyce Scruggs, brought Jimmy Dale over right after we had left yesterday afternoon.

Her story was that she was going to the Desert Diamond Casino in Tucson and gamble for a little while and then come on back and pick up Jimmy Dale. The last part never happened. Not even a phone call.

Davey said Jimmy Dale stayed at the ranch while they went to mass and when they got back, he had hitched up the trailer and backed it up to the barn door. He has just turned thirteen. He has already been put on probation by the Juvenile Court in Cochise County for fighting.

He slugged one of his teachers who was acting as a hall monitor. This was two years ago. He was off probation now but had been held back a grade.

His father, Ray Scruggs, had been down to Douglas one night a few years ago and gotten in a fight and left the bar in a big ass hurry after he had broke a bottle over a fellows head.

On his way home, Ray ran off the road and rolled his truck over several times before it stopped in a rocky wash just off Highway 80. The truck and Ray were both totaled. They took Ray straight to the morgue and the Deputy Sheriff who handled the wreck called for Nancy at the ranch and it being Friday night, she was not there.

So, of course, Davey wound up going to the morgue and handling everything that cold morning. Identifying the body, tracking Nancy down, finding a funeral home, and driving back to the Scruggs spread to tell Jimmy Dale his father was dead. The boy was nine or ten when his father died.

There was some insurance money but Nancy has just about run through it by now. Word is she is supplementing her modest ranching income by selling dope. Mainly weed. None of this new found financial success has made it Jimmy Dale's way.

I do not know what was said up at the barn, but soon Dewey, Lim, and Jimmy Dale came into the ranch house and sat down for lunch. Iris gave both of the boys big frowns but she did not say anything else to them. She was wearing some black blue jeans and a pretty emerald green blouse.

After everyone was seated, Iris asked Sherman to say grace. After Sherman was through, we had a mighty quiet lunch. Mashed potatoes with good, thick beef gravy, asparagus, green beans, sourdough rolls and thick slices of tender pot roast. Iris said she had changed her mind about the chicken enchiladas and the avocado salad and tacos because she was afraid it would set us men off to drinking tequila.

When we were through eating, Sherman asked Iris if we could have some cobbler. She said she was thinking about it but right now she was mad at the whole idea of having to live in a universe with men in it. No one had anything to say to that.

She poured us some coffee and sat down. Jimmy Dale and Lim were slumped over their plates with their heads bowed. Finally, Jimmy Dale said, "Miss Iris, I enjoyed my lunch. You made those mashed potatoes from scratch. I do not get that at home."

Lim said, "Thank you for my lunch. It was mighty good. Will you come up to the barn with me later and see my new horse?"

Iris went back to the counter in the kitchen and started spooning out cobbler for us. Fresh peaches, not canned. Cinnamon and nutmeg laced all through it. And a brown crust that was buttery and soft.

Iris pointed her long wooden spoon at Lim and Jimmy Dale and said, "We are going to do some flower planting as soon as you boys are through eating. I got four Lantana bushes. And a whole bunch of petunias. They need to be in the ground. Now, eat up."

I looked over at Jimmy Dale eating that cobbler and something grabbed me in my gut. Yes, he was a certified juvenile delinquent. A smart ass. But there he sat. Probably eating the best meal he ever had in his life outside of what Davey or Lynn might have prepared. And no way Lynn at her early age could compete with Iris in the kitchen. Takes time and practice. And a knack. Iris had it all.

She loved to cook us up a good meal and then harangue us as we sat at the table, her willing captives. She would chew on Sherman about his manners. Me about my clothes and my gut. She usually left Dewey and Lim alone although anytime any of us reached across the table and grabbed a pot of beans or a platter of steak, she would let us have it. Ask for food to be passed, this isn't a boarding house was one of her favorite sayings.

Jimmy Dale had trouble cutting his roast beef and I saw him looking around and trying to handle his knife and fork the way we did. You could tell he was uncomfortable. He kept his head down all through the meal. I wanted to tell him to sit up straight and to quit strangling that fork but it wasn't my place.

I sat there drinking my coffee and thinking about the hard row I had to hoe when I was a kid. I had stayed out of trouble but I had been right on the edge of it so many times, I knew better than to feel sanctimonious.

When I was in the second grade my father lit out for Florida one cold Texas February morning. We were living in a little house near Amarillo and he had run out of money and whiskey and we were living on my mother's wages. Slim wages. She was a cashier at a grocery store in Amarillo.

In a few months she shipped me off to Aunt Mamie in San Antonio. Aunt Mamie was nice but she was living on Social Security. Her husband worked at a convenience store. If he wasn't working, he was sprawled out in front of the old Philco television set in the front room. 'Bout all he ever said to me was "Get me a beer, boy. Make yourself useful."

One time I walked between him and the television and he swatted me on the ass. Hard enough to knock me down. Then he cursed me. I ran away the next morning and the police picked me up a block away from the bus station. I was going to Los Angeles. I had seventy-five cents on me. Mamie's husband's name was George and I never called his name. The whole three years I was there.

Then I got shuttled off to Ash Flat, Arkansas. It is just north of Texarkana. I stayed there a couple of years with my Aunt Addie and her husband, Uncle Pat. They were mighty nice folks and Aunt Addie was always sewing me up a new shirt. With pearl buttons. Imitation, I am sure. They ran a nice little farm and we always had a lot to eat. Aunt Addie did not weigh a hundred pounds and she had a plain face but I guess I loved her as much, if not more, than my own mother. She was my mother's middle sister. Mamie was the oldest by at least ten years.

Only thing I did not like about living with Aunt Addie and Uncle Pat was the Pentecostal Church they belonged to. Hell and damnation. Uncle Pat and Aunt Addie telling me if I played with my tallywhacker, I would run the risk of going blind and being shut out of the gates of Heaven. Well, I proved 'em wrong on that prophesy.

One bright, sunny, and cloudless summer morning when I was thirteen, my mother showed up at the house. I was working in the garden behind the house when I saw this big red Oldsmobile driving up the long gravel road to our place.

My mother got out of the passenger's side and her new husband got out of the driver's side. This was all a big surprise to Aunt Addie, Uncle Pat, and me. Mom had a pretty yellow blouse on and she was wearing blue jeans and black, shiny boots. I left my hoe in the garden and ran up to her and she gave me a big hug and started crying and saying she was sorry things had not worked out better but she was on her feet now and she wanted me to come back to Texas with her if I wanted to.

Aunt Addie came out of the house and she and Mom was calling to each other and crying and sniffling and hugging each other. The fellow standing behind her and looking mighty uncomfortable was her new husband. His name was Terrell Sims.

He stepped past Aunt Addie and Mom and stuck his hand out and said, "Terrell Sims. You will be welcome in our house. Your momma has already set up a bed, a dresser, and a nice chair and desk in your room. You got a closet. We live on my ranch. Down near Stephenville, that's east and south of Abilene and west of Fort Worth and Dallas."

We shook hands and the next day we left Arkansas for Texas. I have good memories of Aunt Addie and Uncle Pat, but my tallywhacker has not fell off, I ain't blind, and I have not been back to church since I left Arkansas that day.

Terrell ran a good ranch. He was like Sherman except Sherman likes to be around people and Terrell was a loner. Big time. Outside of Mom and me, Terrell stayed off to himself. Sherman likes to dicker over horses and cars and farm machinery and cattle. That gives him a lot of enjoyment.

Terrell would need a horse and show up at a ranch, pick out the horse he wanted, look out over the corral fence for a few minutes, reach in his left back pocket and pull out this little tablet he carried, fish a little stub of a yellow pencil he carried with him from his left front pocket, write down a figure on a little sheet of paper, tear it out of the tablet and hand it to the owner of the horse. While the owner was looking at it, he would say, "Cash, my hand to yours. One time offer."

If the deal went through he would tell me to go to the trailer and get a halter for the horse. The one time someone said, "Shit, Terrell, you can have the goddamn halter. Pure Texas courtesy is all that is," Terrell said, "Naw, I just paid for the horse."

I never saw him sit down and eat with any of his neighbors. The minister of the local Baptist Church knew better than to come on our place. Mom went to church most Sundays but Terrell told Mom I was old enough to make my own mind about that sort of thing. We usually worked a half day and then rested in the afternoon when Mom came home from church.

I guess I did alright around the ranch. Terrell never said one way or the other. I thought I was a pretty fair roper and I sat a horse fine but I was just really getting all of the ranch chores down to where I had some confidence in my ability when Lonnie Davis asked Terrell if I could help him out some during the summer months.

Typical Terrell. He said, "His business," and walked off. Lonnie Davis was a farrier and a damn good one. He was built like me. Wide and low to the ground. He had a big chest and his arms and shoulders were too big for normal shirts. He usually ripped the sleeves out of his shirts to give him some room to move around. He had short, spindly legs, and very little hair. He looked like he was going to topple over whenever he was walking around. He wore old brown boots made of rough out leather that were worn down at the heel. He always had a nice white straw hat that he somehow kept clean.

I helped him all summer. Mainly tacking on shoes and taking shoes off horses before he shod them. We traveled in about a hundred or so square mile area. Sometimes we stayed overnight at a ranch and shod horses the next day. We traveled in a little dark blue Toyota Tacoma. Lonnie would tell me at least once a week that most people in Texas had too much truck for their needs. Lonnie lived southwest of Stephenville near a town called Bunyan.

Lonnie lived alone on an eighty acre spread and he told me he had a small house by a pond. He had a small grove of pecan trees around his house for shade. The pecans brought in a little cash in the fall.

He paid me four dollars a day for the first two weeks and then raised me to seven. Our routine day started with him picking me up before daylight and driving to the ranch where we had horses to shoe. Lonnie liked to get started early.

We would park the truck and I would unload. First the forge and then the anvil stand. The anvil stand had three legs on it. One was adjustable and when I had it level, I would wrestle the anvil out of the bed of the truck and get it balanced on the anvil stand. I would set out Lonnie's old wrinkled brown leather apron and then arrange his hammers, rasps, hoof picks, nippers, pull off tongs, hoof knives, clinchers, and hoof gauge.

Lonnie and I would bring four horses out from the barn or corral they were waiting in and tie their halter ropes up to a fence. Lonnie said horses do not get as skittish when there are several being shod at the same time. He liked to shoe outside. A barn is my preference. I would take the long handled pull off tongs and take the old shoes off the horses.

Lonnie would look at the shoes to check for uneven wear and then throw them in a black wooden box in the back of his truck. He would later sell them for scrap iron or use them in trade with some hard up rancher. He never put old and worn shoes on a horse.

After I had all the shoes off of the horses, I would take a wooden handled hoof pick and a hoof knife and clean the horses' feet. Lonnie would be sitting in the bed of the truck watching me.

When their feet were clean, I would take the nippers and trim each horse's feet. Lonnie would be watching me and tell me when I had trimmed off enough.

I would then take the rasp and use the rough edge to smooth the hoof out. When I was through with the first horse, Lonnie would come over and start shoeing. He used the hoof gauge on most horses. The good ones that were used out in the pastures to gather, drive, and rope cattle. His rule was fifty degrees on the back and fifty two on the front.

Brood mares usually got their hooves trimmed. Lonnie would trim them at an angle of fifty degrees on all four feet. Most ranchers did not bother to shoe them. Lonnie had four small note books he kept in the glove compartment of his truck. He had notes about horses he shod for every ranch he worked.

Later in the summer, I got my learners permit and he started letting me do the driving. The little Toyota did not have any power but it was easy to handle. While I was driving, Lonnie would put his wire rimmed glasses on and study his notes about the horses he would have lined up to shoe.

Lonnie was easy to get along with and he helped me learn my trade. He told me flat out. "Son, this is a hard business. You get to move around and you can turn down any shoeing job you want to, but it is hard on you once you hit fifty. A long time between fifty and sixty five when you can draw Social Security. Between fifty and sixty five is when you are most likely to get hurt and laid up for a while and lose half your business."

Sometimes the rancher would feed us lunch. Usually chicken fried round steak, beans, and rice and either corn bread or tortillas. And iced tea. Lonnie would eat slow and pace himself. When we didn't get fed by a rancher, we would sit in the bed of the truck and eat sandwiches. Usually peanut butter and Welch's grape jelly on white Wonder bread.

What Lonnie hated was having to go to the local ranchettes in the area. Small properties with new barns and skittish horses. Horses that seldom got ridden and were sometimes spoiled and a little hard to deal with. Lonnie said he charged the rich guys who did not really live off the land more because the chance of injury to him was more likely.

Most of the old ranchers would come out and sit on a hay bale or a bucket and talk to Lonnie while he was shoeing their horses. All Lonnie did was listen. He told me never to repeat what was said because it would come back and bite him in the ass.

When we went to the ranchettes, roles were reversed. The new owners wanted to know all about the old guys. How many calves did he brand this year? Does his wife really have cancer? Lonnie would shake his head and say he did not know about that and keep on shoeing.

The real ranchers paid by a check or with cash in an envelope but the new owners of the weekend farms would be slow to pay sometimes. Asking if he took credit cards or some other bull shit. But Lonnie got his money. He would not leave until he was paid in full.

Jimmy Carter was President of these United States that summer and Lonnie hated his guts. He said we had to be a bunch of pussies to elect a peanut farming liberal hick to the Presidency. He was mad because Carter let all those Cuban criminals come over and take over Miami. And he was pissed about the Panama Canal, also. He told me it made him so mad to think about it, he had stopped reading the newspapers except for the sports pages and the TV schedules.

He would not listen to the radio either. He said, since Bob Wills, Earnest Tubb, Patsy Cline, Hank Williams and Webb Pierce were all gone, all he saw were a bunch of dudes with fancy blow dried hairdos and he would just do without all of that.

But the way I saw it, Jimmy Carter was just from a different part of the country and had a different point of view from us. When Reagan came into office, Lonnie was happy again. He told me, "If those cheap crooks over in Russia and Iran fuck with Ronnie, he will bomb their ass off the planet."

When that first summer was over, I asked Lonnie if I could work for him full time. He said he would give me twenty dollars a day, but I ought to stay in school. I was tired of school. I did not have any friends to speak of. Boys or girls. And I could read and do figures enough to where I would not be cheated by some car salesman or fast talking customer so I knew if I stayed in school, all I would be doing is sitting behind a school desk waiting for my eventual release.

I expected a fight from my mother but she said she would not fight me over it because she saw how happy I was working and how bored I was in school.

Terrel said, "Stay with Lonnie until you have learned all you can and then strike out on your own. You can come back here and live and finish school if you change your mind."

I stayed at the ranch and worked for Lonnie until the last year of Reagan's first term. One day Lonnie said he knew I was ready to go out on my own and he would sell me his old truck and most of his tools.

Terrel loaned me some money and I struck out on my own. Lonnie said Willie Peel, a black farrier, had died a month or so ago and his territory would be wide open. I moved to Deming, New Mexico, rented a trailer in a small trailer park and went around asking for work at the local ranches. Somehow Lonnie got a list of the ranches Willie Peel had worked. Most of the ranchers were already lined up with some other farrier, but I got enough business to get me by.

It was tough at first but I gradually got accepted by ranchers all the way down to the border and east to Columbus and west to Willcox and north to Silver City.

I had my feet on the ground and was making good decisions with my life. I bought me a new Airstream and stopped living in trailer parks. Most of those little trailer parks, there was someone watching your trailer to see when you came and went. I lost two televisions to burglars before I figured it out.

After a few years of scruffing around, I wound up at the Circle S. I asked Sherman one day about parking my Airstream at his place. My business was gradually moving West to Interstate 19 that went from Tucson to Nogales. I had ranches and ranchettes all the way to Tubac and Rio Rico and up to Green Valley.

When I asked him about it, it was late in the afternoon and I had shod all of his horses. We were sitting in the horse barn and each of us were drinking a cold Dos Equis Amber and sitting on the tail gate of my old truck.

He told me he would have to study on it and check with Iris. We finished our beers and a few days later when I got home, there was a message to call him.

We worked a deal. I shod his horses for rent and also helped with the branding and calving. He let me have a nice spot near some mesquite and oak trees and I guess I will stay here for as long as I can. I get a good breeze when the wind blows softly through the trees and when the rain and wind act up and storms lash the countryside, the trees knock off a lot of the hard rain and mean winds. I am safe.

Best of all, Iris Snider is in my life. I suspect every man in Cochise, Pima, and Santa Cruz County who has come into contact with Iris Snider has got some kind of a crush on her. She does not flirt. She is just naturally warm and friendly.

I was thinking of all of this as I looked across the table at Lim and Jimmy Dale. After Iris told them they were going outside and plant flowers, Jimmy Dale pulled his napkin up to his face and said something to Lim and then they both started laughing.

Iris asked what was said that was so funny and Lim said he could not repeat it at the table and Jimmy Dale got up and went to the door and said, "Show us where these flowers are going."

Iris asked if we would clear the table while she got Mr. Ali and Mr. Frazier working and we laughed and Sherman said we were going to drink just a little coffee and we would take care of things.

Iris had this big ass Panama sun hat she had bought down in Nogales, Mexico and she stood in front of the mirror in the hall and fitted it just right and went out the door. She stood on the porch and got the boys started on planting the flowers and came back in the house. We were still drinking coffee.

"I heard what Jimmy Dale said", Dewey said. Jimmy Dale said, "We are fucked now." You got to work on his indoor manners some. But those boys are working now. Just a few hours after the big fight."

When the flowers were planted, Davey and Jimmy Dale went on back home. As they drove away, I thought I had it pretty damned good when I was growing up. I always knew where I was going to sleep and I was always welcome. Jimmy Dale might have to sleep on the floor at Davey's or his mother might be home and hung over. Or worse. Either way, he was going to have a tough row to hoe for a long time.

Lim, Dewey, Sherman and I walked up to the horse barn and I got Lim's horse out and put him in the cross chains. The horse had a kind and intelligent eye. He wasn't skittish or dull. Just confused. And who could blame him.

Dave had shod him and each shoe was different from the other. Each one a scrap. The shoes on the front had worn kegs on them. One was aluminum and one was regular metal. One back shoe was a slider you put on roping and cutting horses and the last back shoe was a worn out and heavy old iron shoe I would not put on any horse. Davey Waddell was not going to put any money into a seventy five dollar horse unless he had to. New shoes and a farrier were certainly never in the picture.

None of his feet were cut to the same angle. Front shoes should be cut to the same angle. Back shoes can be cut to a different angle than the front but the back shoes should have matching angles. I took all the shoes off and told Lim we were going to start from scratch with his horse.

I took the hoof knife and cleaned all four hooves. He was sound anyway. No quarter cracks or thrush to deal with. Then I took the nippers and cut the excess hoof from each foot and took a rasp and smoothed each foot out. I cut his front at a fifty three degree angle and his back at a fifty degree angle.

I told Lim I thought his horse had some Tennessee Walking Horse blood in him because he had such a natural long stride, high bobbing head, and a long head. The way he was shod, his front end could not get out of the way of his over striding back legs.

What I did was cut his heels lower in the front and let the front of his hooves grow longer. For his back shoes, I did the opposite. I left his heels long and shortened the front of his foot. This cut down but did not eliminate his natural overstride. With his front feet shod for a longer stride and his back shod for a shorter stride, he needed slow work under saddle until he could get collected and work in a natural way. The easiest way to do this was have Lim ride him slowly up the long drive leading out of the ranch.

I told the story about the time when I was just starting out and Lonnie and I went to a Walking Horse barn over near Dallas. Not many Walking Horses in Texas, but there were a few and they even had enough to have a show in Dallas-Fort Worth every year.

The regular farrier for the barn was stove up from a horse kicking him or getting the worst end of a bar room fight in a beer joint outside Dallas. Lonnie said he had heard both stories as being the gospel truth.

We walked in the long barn and the trainer was working a horse the whole length of the barn. We stood against a stall and let him pass. The horse was a big chestnut stud and he was nodding his head and throwing his front feet way up in the air and his back end was striding way up under him. There were chains around the horse's front pasterns.

When the trainer was through with the big stallion, he dismounted, gave the reins to a barn boy and told him to take the chains off the horse, unsaddle him, and cool him down. The trainer was a short, barrel chested man of around fifty. He walked with a limp. His left foot was turned in and his left shoe was built up.

He said, "All I want you to do is reset two horses and check three more for me. I got a show in Oklahoma City this weekend and I do not want to throw a pad in the middle of a class. I pay in cash. I never stuck a farrier in my life. I appreciate you coming on such a short notice."

The horses were put in cross ties and the trainer, his name was Mack Strong, stood by as Lonnie reset the shoes. It took a while. The horses all had leather pads and wedges between their front feet and the shoe. This was done to give them more action and more reach. The pads made the horse raise his feet higher and the wedges gave him reach.

Lonnie reset four horses and left one alone. All of the horses were healthy and full of pep. When Lonnie was through, he gave Mack Strong a price and Strong paid cash and thanked Lonnie again. Lonnie said, "Sure thing, Mr. Strong. Good luck at the show."

When we were outside, Lonnie stopped by his truck as I was loading his anvil and tools back into the truck. His jaw was set hard and I knew to be quiet. We drove a few miles down the road and Lonnie said, "You notice that smell. That funny smell. That is a combination of mustard oil and a heavy petroleum based grease they use to keep the chains from rubbing all the hair off a horse's ankles They tell me you take a little tiny bit of that mustard oil and put it on a horse's pasterns and he will drop his back end and then throw that front end out and nod his head at the same time.

We drove on down the road a ways and as luck would have it, we found a beer joint that made good cheeseburgers and had some homemade tamales in the shuck. Lonnie ordered us beers and we each ate a big cheeseburger and a couple of tamales. The tamales were made just right with a heavy corn taste to them and spicy shredded pork. The cheeseburgers were thick and each one had a thick, dark red, tomato slice, an onion slice, lettuce, and some sweet tasting American cheese.

We was drinking Pearl on draft and Lonnie was saying how he had got to where he liked Coors a lot better than Pearl but his real favorite was Dos Equis Amber. We had skipped lunch to squeeze

Mack Strong's horses in and the mug of Pearl on draft was mighty pleasing to me. We ordered another and Lonnie asked the bartender if he had any pie and he said naw, but he had some chocolate cake and Lonnie said, well get it out here, then.

We set the beer mugs aside and ate the chocolate cake. White cake with chocolate icing. It must have been baked that morning because it was about the best thing I had eaten in a long, long time.

Lonnie pushed his plate away and leaned back and said, "I just do not like to have anything to do with soring a horse or hurting him in any way. It is just not right. We are the masters of their fate. I think that carries with it some responsibility. But it's money, Vern. Lots of money. That big chestnut stud is probably a six figure horse. A competitive life. That of show horses and trainers. Doesn't matter what breed."

"A horse that don't perform costs his owner and trainer money. Owner takes five horses out of a barn because the trainer displeases him and puts 'em with another trainer, grim times is on the trainer with the empty barn."

Lim asked me if Davey looked like he had ever been sored and I said "Naw, he is clean. Look at his ankles and pasterns. Nothing to show any mistreatment. I think he is part Walking Horse and part something else and since we do not even know who Davey bought him from, we will never know."

I held no ill feelings towards Davey Waddell. He was just spread too thin. I had shod his other horses and Davey never griped about the price. But he figured this horse wasn't worth the price of shoeing. He got him away from a trip to the soap factory but then he did not know what to do with him.

Sherman went in the tack room and we could hear him shuffling things around. Finally, he came out and handed a bit to Lim. He said, "Lim, this is a Waterford bit. It is mounted on D-Rings so what you have is a variation on the regular snaffle. Look at the bit itself. The chain links are all round. For some reason, this makes some horses relax and they won't pull on it. The key is hand pressure. You pull hard on him and you will lose him. I can guarantee you that. Try that once he is shod and if he likes it, fine. If he doesn't, we will try something else. In the meantime I want you working Socks and the gawky new roan with a halter. Socks is your number one priority. He gets the most attention. Start them off easy. Walk 'em down the fence row. Dewey knows what I mean. I want you to work with them an hour each when you get home from school and then you can ride Davey if there is any day light left."

We sat in the barn for a while. Lim put Davey up and threw some hay in the rack in his stall and grained him. Half oats and half sweet feed. He came back and sat down with us. We were each drinking a cold Coors and Sherman told Lim to go in the tack room and bring out the bottle of George Dickel and four shot glasses. When Lim came back out, he gave the shot glasses and whiskey to Sherman.

Sherman poured a half a shot for Dewey and me and handed them to us. He poured about a third of a shot and handed it to Lim. Lim's upper lip was swollen to about twice its normal size and his right eye was starting to close up a little. Then he poured himself a half a shot and stood up.

He raised his shot glass toward Dewey and said, "Makes me proud to see Lim cares about the stock we have, Dewey. A man that will fight for his horse's honor is all right with me. Now, I better head on back to the house or Iris will be up here and you know she would not like to see this young man taking his first drink of whiskey. This is your first, I hope, Lim?"

Lim laughed and said, "Yes sir."

Sherman said, "Now Lim, this is not bourbon. Bourbon is made in Kentucky. This is Tennessee Sour Mash Whisky. George Dickel. They make it up near Tullahoma, Tennessee. Them Walking Horses Vern has been talking about was first bred up around Shelbyville and Tullahoma in Middle Tennessee. They were an off shoot of pacers and trotters from Kentucky and Indiana and what made them popular to plantation owners throughout the South was that flat foot walk. A long striding front end, a nodding head and a reaching back end. They could cover ground faster than a trot and smoother than a lope or canter. A natural gait they have is called a rack or a single foot. This can be a real fast gait or an easy gait that is just a little faster than a lope. First time they had a Walking Horse Celebration in Shelbyville, this old horse named Strolling Jim won. The Celebration is the big Walking Horse Show. Strolling Jim was a big headed bay horse. Then a lot of years later there was a big black stud named Ebony Masterpiece who won. He was the best stud to come out of the Walking Horse world. He stood at stud for years a few miles out of Shelbyville. He's dead now.

"After World War Two all of these shows and trainers and breeders started springing up and of course people had money invested in the horses. So people eventually started to forget about the Walking Horse as just a pleasurable riding horse. No, ribbons and trophies and silver platters and big stud fees and high prices for colts changed the old Plantation Horse into today's Walking Horse. Interesting to see how Davey works out."

Sherman still had some George Dickel in his glass. He reached and got the bottle and filled his shot glass full. He looked at Lim and said, "Young man, don't forget to turn these barn lights up and lock that tack room door so Vern won't be tempted to come back up here later and get some more of my good whiskey. A shot a night is enough. I am going to share this with Iris."

After Sherman left, we all three sipped whiskey and looked out over the Whetstones at a big yellow moon that looked like it was dancing drunkenly across a beautiful clear Arizona spring sky. It was so clear you could see Herefords grazing down by the creek almost a mile away.

In the next few months, Lim and Dewey got the three new horses all lined out and Sherman gave Lim a nice bump in his wages when school was out. We put light toe weighted shoes on Davey and I squared his back shoes off and cut his back feet at a forty nine degree angle and he looked loose and comfortable to us.

Once I got Davey shod right, I would usually beat Dewey and Lim home at night. Sherman had called Doc Siegfried to check on all three of the new horses and he had floated the red dun's teeth and left the other two as they were.

But Doc Siegfried gave Lim a white, tall plastic bottle of the vilest smelling stuff I had come across. It was an iron supplement and Lim measured out a bottle cap of it every time he fed Lim. By the Fourth of July, his coat was slicked out and his neck and shoulders were muscular. He had probably put on over a hundred pounds.

Lim bought Davey knowing he was not built to be a cutting horse, but damn if he didn't do a passable job out in the pasture. Lim had started him off with the Waterford bit and worked him easy for a few weeks. Davey's head was longer than our other horses and Dewey took a hole punch to a headstall and fitted the bridle for Lim. The Waterford bit was a snaffle with an old copper mouthpiece.

Dewey told Lim the reason Sherman had not thrown the old bit away is that some horses like the feel of an old rusty bit more than a brand new bit. Davey's bit was not rusty but the round copper balls in the mouthpiece relaxed Davey and he and Lim started out fine as soon as I got his shoes right. With his back feet squared up and cut at a lesser angle, there was less chance of him cross firing.

After Lim worked Socks and the red dun, he would saddle up Davey and they would go out in the pastures. Lim said if you put some pressure in his mouth and squeezed him with his knees he would get into that slow rack and nod his head some. When Lim brought him back to the barn he would let him pick up the tempo in his rack and come on home. It was a pretty sight. You could just barely see Lim's head over Davey's head.

Many a night I would come home and Lim would be riding Davey real slow in a rack up that long hill on the road that leads out of the ranch. By the end of the summer, Davey was stronger and he worked his front and back end in harmony.

I would stand out by one of the fences and watch Lim bring Davey home in the late afternoons from the pasture. He sat up straight and he was deep in the saddle. The rack was not much faster than a lope but Lim said he had let him loose some and he would get too fast and lose the gait. Davey would nod his head some and his back end was lower than his front end and it looked like he was walking in the back and running in the front. It is a fascinating gait when the timing is right.

The red dun was a good find. Lim put him to saddle in August and he was just as natural a cow horse as you could find. He had the same fault as Davey. He was just a little too big to make the sharp turns you see the top cutting horses make. Dewey and Lim both rode him while he was being trained in August. Dewey said one rider was enough for any horse when he was being trained, but Lim had good hands and he did not see where it had hurt the dun.

He was a handsome horse. Good confirmation and a big star in his forehead. The red dun coloring was unique. Iris named him Johnny and when Sherman asked her why she picked that name she said because he was a handsome and friendly animal and Johnny fit the bill.

Davey came over around the first of July. Ten weeks or so after we had taken Johnny in. Jimmy Dale was with him. Jimmy Dale brought a buckskin with him named Skeeter. Skeeter had been his father's horse. He had just started him under saddle when he tried to straighten that curve out down near Douglas.

Jimmy Dale and Davey Waddell had finished training him. He was just barely fifteen hands and could and would turn on a dime. I liked shoeing him. I would go to Davey's to shoe his horses and he would have Skeeter off in a catch pen eating hay when I drove up.

He said Skeeter would fight any horse around and probably wind up crippling them. But with people, he was as gentle as you could get. Jimmy Dale rode Skeeter with a hackamore. Not my favorite way of handling a horse but that was the way Ray had started him and it worked so there was no way Davey was going to let Jimmy Dale change anything up.

Lim and I went out to the trailer to see Jimmy Dale. I had already heard Sherman tell Davey he owed him for four weeks and two days board on Johnny. We all knew better. Dewey and Lim had already ridden down to the creek and picked out a nice bull calf and a young heifer for trade. They were hid from Davey in a catch pen behind the horse barn.

Sherman told Jimmy Dale that Iris had already told him there would be no fighting today. Jimmy Dale laughed and said, "I want to see what Lim has done with his horse. He has had ten weeks. He ought to show something by now."

"Well, I tell you what. Go out to the far pasture and gather and drive the cattle to the pasture on the Cienega and next to the Empire. There is about a hundred head scattered over that far mesa. Probably a few over." Sherman said.

I did not want to sit around all day and listen to Sherman and Davey fuss and tell whoppers. I went up to the barn with the boys and saddled up an old sorrel mare that Sherman kept around. She was about the same size as Skeeter, but her coat was beginning to fade some since Sherman ran her on the pasture most of the time. He grained her in the morning and sent her back in the pasture.

Jimmy Dale went down to the horse pasture and threw a loop over her head and brought her on back to the barn. The old mare's name was Little Molly. As soon as I had her cleaned up, I threw a saddle and blanket on her and we were ready to go. Little Molly had one white stocking on her back left leg and a white star on her forehead. You could not keep her in a stall or around other horses. She would tear everything up in a stall. Feeders and hay racks all wound up torn off the wall. She bit other horses with no provocation. She was kept in a turn out and fed in a stall with the door to the turn out open so she could leave when she was though eating.

She had been a good brood mare for a few years and she was a good dependable cow horse with a smooth slow trot and an easy, relaxing short lope. Trick was to keep her away from other horses.

The far pasture was a good hour away. We could have put the horses in a trailer and been there in a few minutes but we did not have anyone to bring the truck and trailer back so we just rode on over. Lim opened the gate to the next pasture. We would have to drive the cattle through it. The creek ran through it and I knew the cattle would be troublesome since they would wade into the creek and mill around under the cottonwoods near the shore of the creek.

Little Molly was rough coming out of the barn. She wasn't being ridden very much. She had thrown a few good colts in years past and Sherman just let her stay in the pasture and live an undisturbed and easy life. She had a little grass belly on her but it was not something that could not be worked off in a week of riding. But that was not going to happen.

Sherman just rode his mule. Iris rode Pepper. Lim and Dewey rode the other horses. Lim was busy with his new horse and the two new horses Davey Waddell had sold us. Dewey switched off between three geldings. So Little Molly stayed out in the pasture. I was the only one who ever rode her nowadays.

We were out about a mile before she started to smooth her trot out and from then on she was a pleasure. I stayed back about twenty yards from Lim and Jimmy Dale. They were talking and laughing. A good horse like her will always come back to you if you ride them enough. That usually cures most problems with horses. The old wet saddle blanket saying. I know it has been overused until it is a cliché but it is still true. It is certainly not an answer for all horse problems. Some horses get started out wrong and stay confused their whole lives. Some just flat do not like being ridden. But Little Molly was content riding down the pasture a few yards behind Lim and Jimmy Dale.

Little Molly had a nice slow trot she could keep going for a long time. It was smooth and she covered a lot of ground but we could not keep up with Lim and Jimmy Dale. Davey was doing that flat walk his breed is famous for and Skeeter was trotting to keep up.

That first mile out I don't think Jimmy Dale and Lim stopped talking for a solid minute. I was glad to see Lim with a friend his own age. He never brought home any friends from school and never asked to go to anyone's house to visit. I figured Jimmy Dale was the same.

We were headed east towards the Whetstones. They sat low and gray on the endless blue horizon. There were no clouds today. We had gotten some good rain in June and Sherman cut hay late in June and he said he had one of the best hay crops of any year he could remember. After he cut and baled his hay and put it in the barn, Sherman said he knew he was being greedy but he wanted a good rain so he could get a nice late July stand to cut. The rain did not come and it looked like he might not get but one more stand to cut and that would come in late August or around Labor Day. He tried for three cuttings a year but he had plenty saved and he could get by with two cuttings.

I had stayed around the ranch and helped with the hay. That was part of my deal with Sherman. When it came time to load the bales on the long trailer and off load them into the hay barn, Lim said he wanted to help. He was eleven and he told Sherman he was strong enough to throw a bale of hay up on the trailer. Sherman said he could help some but he still had to work Socks and Johnny in the afternoon.

What Lim didn't know was that hay in the field weighed a lot more than hay that has been sitting in a barn for a while. A bale weighs less as it gets older. Since you always feed the oldest hay first, Lim had not had to fool with any of the new bales.

He tried to throw the big alfalfa bales up on the trailer by himself but it was a battle. The trailer bed was about even with Lim's shoulders so it made for a hard throw. Sherman told him to partner up with me and I was glad because I was using a whole set of muscles that had not been used much since the September hay crop of last year.

Lim and I worked together that whole week, loading hay and stacking it in the barn. Lot easier to throw hay when you had somebody on the other end of the bale. Lim was tired after the first hour of the first day. I could tell. He pulled his hat down low on his head and he was breathing hard. But he kept at it and after he started helping me, he learned to pace himself a little and I watched him to be sure he was drinking enough water. Iris drove the old Farmall that pulled the trailer and she was always embarrassing Lim telling him not to get too hot and to drink plenty of water.

When I thought he needed water, I would just tell Iris to stop the tractor and let us get a drink. There was a big old orange Styrofoam cooler with a white top that was filled with the coldest water I had tasted. It was strapped onto the back of the tractor and there was a tin cup tied to the handle of the cooler with a piece of rawhide. The tin cup had a long handle on it. I asked Iris why didn't she have another cooler with Coors and she laughed. I think Lim had all he wanted of bringing in a hay crop in just that part of a week. We started on Monday and finished Saturday right before noon.

Sherman would run him off at three and tell him to go rest 'til five and then work Socks and Johnny. Socks was doing great. Lim said he would meet him at the stall door in the afternoon and let him slide the halter over his head. By now Lim was working them both an hour a day for five days a week. Work Monday and Tuesday. Rest on Wednesday. Work Thursday, Friday and Saturday. Rest on Sunday.

Dewey and Sherman did not like to train horses in round pens. They both said too much work in a round pen soured a horse and made him restless and bored. When we came in from the hay field, it would be almost dark and Lim would just be starting to feed the stock.

Sherman had bumped him up to one hundred and fifty dollars a week for the summer work. The week of the haying he gave him two hundred and told him he ought to see if he could get some money out of me since he had done half of my work. But I got no money. The haying, branding, calving, and gathering was all in trade for my spot under those nice shade trees.

When we got to the far pasture, we saw a bunch of cattle crazing in the meadow near the gate to the pasture. I told Lim we ought to get them first because three riders were going to have a hard time driving a hundred head. We made a long, wide turn across the top of this first meadow. I dropped off first and started heading cattle toward the gate.

Lim stopped in about the middle and started down the slope and then Jimmy Dale went on towards the far fence and soon we had them started. They moved slowly. The mix was half cows and half yearlings. The yearlings were almost six months old and had never been driven before. Some were troublesome but the horses were all good and it was fun to be in the saddle driving cattle.

I rode ahead to the gate and counted the stock as they moved through. We had almost half the herd in that little short drive. I told Lim I had counted forty nine head. He said, "That leaves about sixty or so."

We rode on through the pasture and got them in the new pasture and I looked up at the sun and I could tell it was past noon and we still had more cattle to find, gather, and drive. There were some foothills to the east of the first meadow we had found cattle. There were scrub mesquite, acacia, and palo verde trees all growing up on the little hills and the washes between them.

After we came out of the foothills, there was a nice meadow that stretched for miles. This was where the National Forest Land started. Sherman had a long part of the meadow. Above this meadow were some more rolling hills that were at the base of the Whetstones.

We got to the edge of the last hills and I told Lim and Jimmy Dale to hold up a spell and we got off the horses and sat out on some big rocks and ate. I only bought three Hershey Bars and three little bags of peanuts. Lim had some jerky and Jimmy Dale had made up four peanut butter and jelly sandwiches.

We took the food out of our saddle bags and piled it all up and ate. There was a spare peanut butter and jelly sandwich left and Lim and Jimmy Dale told me to eat it and maybe it would help me keep up. I ate it and we sat there and watched a Red Tail Hawk circling in the clear sky.

I just happened to look south and I saw a black line way off on the horizon.. It could have been a front coming our way. Right now, it looked like it had just left Mexico heading up north. A very light breeze from the south started up. I told Lim and Jimmy Dale we had to go up in these hills a ways because there was a meadow up there. About a two thousand acre piece of sweet grass. I knew there would be cattle up there and I knew they would not be happy about leaving. That little area up there and in fact all of this pasture got a little more rain than the rest of the Circle S graze. Grass was knee high in a lot of places in this pasture but it had been eaten down in some other places.

We had to ride single file up a narrow and rocky old game trail the cattle used. It had gotten a little wider but it was still too narrow for three horses to ride side by side. Little Molly was as sure footed as a mountain goat and we took the lead up the trail. Skeeter and Davey would stumble every once in a while but Little Molly had her head down just above her knees. She slowly picked her way up the trail. I let her have her head. She would stop sometimes for a few seconds when the trail was full of ruts or rocks and then she would find her way and keep climbing. We soon left Skeeter and Davey behind.

The trail was almost a half mile up to the meadow and it was mainly straight. There were some nice pines and mesquites growing up this high but the pines were not the real tall pines you see in the Rockies. These were maybe twenty feet tall.

When we were at the meadow, I got off and loosened the girth so Little Molly could take a breather. We sat and let the horses rest. Jimmy Dale pulled a pack of Winstons out and lit up. He took the open pack and motioned to Lim and me. We both passed. I asked him if Lynn was doing alright. The baby was due sometime in late August or in early September. Jimmy Dale said she was fine but Davey was nervous and fidgety every time he saw him. He said Davey came up to his place three or four times a week and helped him with whatever needed doing and he was not any fun to be around anymore.

I knew part of the help Davey was giving was bringing some feed up for the three horses on Jimmy Dale's spread. His mother had her credit shut off at most feed stores and the truth was she had the money, she just would not take the time to pay the bills.

Jimmy Dale said Davey would catch up with her from time to time and show her the receipts and she would give him a check on the ranch's account. Jimmy Dale had told me while I was shoeing Skeeter and his other horses that the checks usually cleared but sometimes Davey had to run them through a second time.

Before Ray Scruggs died, I had shod their horses. He was easy to deal with and always paid cash up front but sometimes when I got there, he would meet me with blood shot eyes and whiskey or beer on his breath. As I watched Jimmy Dale smoking that Winston, I wondered how he would wind up. He was already a good hand.

Today, he was wearing an old pair of brown boots that were worn down at the heel. Someone had done a lousy job of sewing up a rip in the left sleeve of his plaid shirt. He carried that pack of cigarettes in his left front pocket.

When the horses were rested, we circled the pasture and started the cattle down the narrow trail. It took a couple of hours because we had to check in the trees above the pasture. We found a few ornery cows with calves laying up under trees. They were hard to get down to the meadow.

We were moving the cattle down to the pasture gate when I took a minute to look at the sky south of us. The breeze had picked up. I saw dark black clouds marching low in the sky towards us. There was rain spilling out of the clouds onto the thirsty land. The cattle were getting more restless by the minute. I was riding drag and Little Molly had worked up a lather. There was a steep and rocky ridge on the left so we jammed the cattle up against the base of the ridge and Jimmy Dale and Lim kept them bunched up.

I could see two more hours of work and maybe an hour of good daylight. I didn't like driving cattle after the sun went down. I figured the extra hour we needed would be an hour after the sun set when there was still light at dusk.

We only had a mile or so to go when the first rain hit us. It was cold and the wind was bending the ocotillo stalks growing up on the top of the ridge. The ridge played out and Lim and Davey took the left flank. The rain was steady but the wind was what bothered me. It had started slanting the rain some and I was worrying about Little Molly catching a chill out in the storm.

We had one last long hill to drive the cattle over when I looked up and saw two riders at the crest of the hill. It was Sherman and Dewey. Dewey was riding his good bay gelding. The same one he had ridden since his first day on the Circle S. Sherman's old mule was ambling down the hill with his ears flopping. He looked like he didn't have a care in the world.

Sherman went to the right and helped Jimmy Dale and Dewey took Lim's side. The cattle picked up their pace now that we had more riders yelling at them and challenging them when they slowed down or meandered off to the side.

Davey held his own with the other horses. They were all good at keeping the cattle bunched up. The other horses made sharper and shorter turns than Davey but he made up for it with his long stride and quick start. Sherman's mule looked like he never got in a hurry but he had a good long stride and he got the job done. He knew when Sherman said, "Get on up, you big eared sonofabitch", it was time to pay attention.

When we got the cattle over the hill, they seemed ready to get in the new pasture. The big double gate was open. I saw Sherman's big black Dodge Ram truck and his stock trailer on top of a small hill about three hundred yards from the pasture gate. Iris was sitting under a green umbrella on the hood of the Dodge. She had a tan duster on and the wide brim of her big sun hat was flapping in the wind.

We got all of the cattle through when dusk was ending and night began. There were no stars and no moon would shine on us tonight. The wind was high now and the horses stomped nervously as we closed the gates and waited on Sherman to give us the tally. He had sat by the gate and counted the cattle as we walked them through. His tally was sixty three. That put us over a hundred and ten. That was a lot of cattle to be moved in one day.

While we were waiting for the final tally, Jimmy Dale leaned back in the saddle and fired him up another Winston. I asked Sherman where Davey Waddell was and he said he had left around four and said Sherman could keep Jimmy Dale for a few days if he had work for him.

I looked up the hill and Iris had moved into the cab of the big truck. We loaded the horses in the trailer and Jimmy Dale, Lim, and Dewey rode in the back of the trailer with the horses. I sat in the front between Iris and Sherman. Iris drove the truck on back to the barn. We had to cross a narrow bridge across the Cienega. Water was coming up close to the top of the little bridge and the creek was running fast and hard.

It was cold in the truck and no one said anything 'til we were close to the bridge and Sherman said, "Be careful going over this bridge. I built it a little narrow."

Iris had her head near the steering wheel and she was lining the truck and trailer up with the bridge. She said, "Any somebody that don't like my driving is welcome to walk on back. But I ain't holding supper up for you. I can tell you that right now."

That was the last said by anyone for a while. We made it across the bridge and the creek fine. The big truck had something extra in it and it pulled the trailer and horses up the last hill with no trouble. Iris backed the trailer into the horse barn, shut the truck motor off and walked on down to the house to get our supper ready.

I unloaded Little Molly and unsaddled her. She was not cold but I was worried about any moisture on her so I rubbed her down good. I gave her some oats and some hay and made sure she had fresh water in her stall. I knew Sherman would turn her back into the little horse pasture tomorrow but she needed to stay out of the weather tonight since she had worked so hard. It was a shame someone did not have the time to ride her about a half day for the next week. She would lose that grass belly fast.

Sherman and Dewey went on down to the house first. They left the truck and trailer where they were. You could still see and hear the rain through the open door of the barn. Rain was splashing hard on the hood of the truck. The wind had started to die down some and I gave the storm another hour at most. When it rains in Southern Arizona, you get short intense spurts. Some last seconds. Sometimes you have big, black clouds that stretch across the horizon and you get less than a five minute spurt of rain.

You just do not get the long, back to back, days of rain you get in a lot of the country. This was a big rain and I called it a storm. There was lightning over the Whetstones and you could hear distant rumblings of thunder. And the wind was strong enough to blow the high stalks of the Ocotillos almost to the ground. Of course, they sprang right back up. And it was all over in less than three hours.

When we left the barn to go down to supper, it had stopped raining. There was water dripping off the barn but the air was still as we walked to the ranch house for dinner.

Iris had on black jeans and a white blouse with red and yellow embroidery across the front of it. Her hair was all in place and her lipstick was a wonderful shade of pink.

We didn't even get in the door before she started in on us.

She was standing in the door when we walked up to the porch. She said, "Sherman Snider, and the rest of you, especially you, Vern. Take them muddy boots off before you even think about coming in this house and eating at my table. And you boys, I sure hope you did not catch a summer cold. They are aggravating and hard to get rid of. "

Jimmy Dale said if she would fix him a hot toddy, she would not have to worry about him catching a cold. Iris told him she was not going to even think about him drinking whiskey in her house.

Lord, that woman looked so pretty. A yearning came up in me that I knew was wrong but I could not help it and did not care to suppress. My yearnings for her were my secret. You do not have to tell the whole damn world your every thought and desire. I got my faults. I can attest to them but being a gate mouth was not one of them.

Our hats were all wet. I tried to knock some of the water out of mine by slapping it against my leg a couple of times. I knocked a little off but not much. That was all right. It was a cheap brown felt hat I had worn for a few years. It was damn sure not a John B. Stetson. I had several but I was careful when and where I wore them. We all hung our hats on the oak rack inside by the front door.

The windows rattled some in the wind but the storm was passing us. I could see lightning up north of us. I knew we would have a big swollen creek for the next few days. But tomorrow morning would be great. You could count on a clear sky and soft breezes and a big, red sunrise and a colorful sunset. The big western sun would be back. I had to drive almost all the way to Tubac tomorrow to shoe some horses for a rancher that lived high in the hills north of Rio Rico and south of Tubac.

Iris had the food all laid out on the table by the time we all got our hats off and resting on the oak rack. We sat down and there was a white soup bowl sitting on each of our plates. She asked us to pass our bowls to her. She ladled out big bowls of posole. You could smell the spices and the meat before your bowl got to you. When we were all served, she passed around corn bread sticks. This was Lim's favorite meal. Posole and cornbread sticks.

After the posole came chicken enchiladas and green corn tamales. There was not a lot of conversation except for Sherman telling Lim he thought he had him a three thousand dollar horse who would be worth more if he was registered in some breed association. But we did not even know if he was bred in Mexico and brought here or bred back east and swapped all across the country.

Sherman also told us that Davey Waddell had left around three that afternoon with his new Herefords and a little cash he had squeezed out of the deal. Jimmy Dale was going to stay with us for a week and help around the ranch and Davey Waddell was going to be sure all of Jimmy Dale's stock was cared for while he was gone. His cattle were all scattered out on a single pasture.

Jimmy Dale's father had set up a winter graze on some National Forest land. That just left two horses that needed to be checked on and grained once a day. They stayed in a small green pasture by a thin creek during the day. Jimmy Dale was going halves with Davey Waddell on the hay crops he got off his place. Davey provided the equipment and helped get the hay cut, baled, and stacked. Jimmy Dale only had around a hundred cows but he had a good calf crop this year and he knew he could keep the place going.

Sherman said, "First thing tomorrow, Monday, I want you boys to ride the creeks and be sure we don't have any cows or calves that have slipped off in a bog. With all this rain, there is no telling what they could have done. Cows are stupid. Number one rule of ranching."

"Tuesday, I want you to get the old truck, not my new Dodge Ram, and hook it up to the old flatbed trailer and move the irrigation pipes up to the last pasture on the southeast side of the spread. That is my other hay field and it will need some water in a week or so."

"Wednesday is fence day. Up early and Jimmy Dale I want you riding Little Molly. Give her some more work. And Wednesday, I want Lim riding Dewey's other bay gelding. I will have something for you to do on Thursday, I can guarantee it, but for now that is it. And you boys stay out of devilment. Lim, you still got Johnny and Socks to work with so get on home in time to get it done before dark. And leave that irrigation pipe on the trailer. Dewey and Lim and I will set it up later."

Iris said, "Thursday might be a good day for these two boys to help me move some of my bigger flower pots and to repot some of my flowers. Plus they can clean out the beds and do some trimming around the yard."

Jimmy Dale put his head down and Lim started laughing.

Iris said, "Jimmy Dale, you have disappointed me."

Jimmy Dale said, "Miss Iris, I have not said or did one bad thing since I been here."

"Well, I thought you would have already asked me about dessert. I hid it way back in the refrigerator so Sherman would not get into it."

Iris got up and opened the refrigerator and poked around for a few minutes and then brought out a big square cake. A three layer with white icing and cocoanut and small yellow pieces of pineapple sprinkled over the top of the cake. The actual cake was yellow. Iris said she added a few extra eggs to the batter and poured some pineapple juice on each layer to keep it soft. There was bits of pineapple and cocoanut all through the icing of the cake.

Iris cut a big corner piece of cake and passed it to me and said, "That is not for you. Give that to Jimmy Dale. He is a guest in our house."

When she cut the next corner piece, Sherman reached for it but she handed it to me and said, "I am thinking about not giving you anything but a cold shoulder and some lukewarm coffee for a while, Sherman. For distracting me and making smartass remarks while I am driving a truck and pulling a trailer full of horses and hands. All during a driving rain."

I passed the corner piece to Lim. When Iris had served everyone else, she cut a thin piece and passed it to Sherman.

We were all tired and cold and wet when we came to supper and the cake just didn't stand a chance. We finished it off and when she was handing out seconds, she finally gave Sherman a nice corner piece. There was strong, hot coffee. No one had drunk any alcohol at dinner. Iris had pink nail polish that matched her lipstick and that yearning feeling came back to me.

I left first. I went down to my place and opened the windows and the door and let some air circulate through the trailer. There was no need for a fan or the window air conditioner I had. I poured a small glass of Old Charter and sipped it and listened to the wind and distant thunder. There was still some lightning in the north and east up on the Whetstones but it was clear in the south. The storm had passed.

Jimmy Dale told me a few weeks later that Sherman gave him a hundred and fifty dollars for his week's work and an extra fifty for moving that herd on the Sunday of the big storm.

Jimmy Dale worked hard. Sherman never complained about his work. He wouldn't let him smoke in his barns or in the ranch house. He slept in the old bunk house and he and Lim stayed up a many a night playing hearts or spades. Jimmy Dale stayed at the Circle S about half of the time during the next few summers and during the school year, he would be around most weekends.

Lynn had the baby and she and Davey got the ranch to going on a profit making basis. Everything around their place looked brighter. Davey planted some new rose bushes in big pots in front of the porch. Davey bred the mare that was Socks' dam back to the same stud for several years and advertised the foals in the local stock journals and when Socks started getting points in AQHA shows, the price for the yearling colts went up to fifteen thousand dollars. Then she had a colt that was almost the spitting image of Socks and the price went all the way up to twenty thousand.

I tried to keep track of Jimmy Dale's mother. Nancy was hardly ever around when I would go over and shoe Jimmy Dale's horses. If her blue Lexus was there, she was always piled up in bed. I never asked Jimmy Dale or Davey about her. I knew it embarrassed them to talk about it. But every once in a while they would both let something slip.

What I could piece together was that Nancy was in and out of jail because she had gotten caught Driving Wild, that's what we call DUI, in Tucson and had done a few days in jail and been placed on probation and violated her probation by coming up positive on a drug test. She had tested positive for marijuana and tried to tell the judge it was secondary smoke that showed up on the test.

Jimmy Dale said the judge told her that was worse than if she had just had an unguarded moment and smoked a joint in the privacy of her home. He said not only was she smoking dope, she was consorting with a bunch of dopers to boot. So he put her in jail and she was supposed to do almost a year.

That was when she switched lawyers. Word was she still had some cash hid from everyone. Her new lawyer was Randall Price. We all called him Randy. I shod his horses and had been for a long time. Sherman and Iris used him as their lawyer. He represented a lot of ranchers and a lot of miscreants. That is a word I picked up from him one Saturday morning while I was shoeing his horses and he was drinking a vodka Collins.

Randy had bought a spread near Tubac in the late eighties and had built up a small, quality herd. He only had around a hundred head of cows. He raised Santa Gertrudis cattle and practiced law in Tucson and the outlying counties. He was almost sixty and he had a twin brother who lived up in the Williamson Valley north of Prescott. They owned a family ranch that had been left to them by their father and mother.

His brother was fourteen minutes older than him and his name is Jim. They called the ranch up near Prescott the High Meadow Ranch.

Everybody liked Randy. He said he was scaling back on his law practice and spending most of his time ranching. He got Nancy out of jail, and had her probation reinstated. Only problem for her was she had to submit to random drug screens and report to a probation officer in Tucson every week.

We all thought that would stop her or at least slow her down for a short period but she just switched back to alcohol. She passed the drug tests but she put her drinking in high gear. She might not have been taking dope but the word was she was selling it hand over fist. Meth and Marijuana both.

Randy told me he thought she would crash and burn sometimes in the near future. He said when she came to his office in Tucson to settle his fee, she left a big headed steroid daddy out in the lobby. He had tattoos up to his chin, a shaved head, and big arms. Randy said he made everyone in the office nervous without saying a word. Nancy said he was from up near Stafford and had just got out of Florence Prison. Randy never asked what he was in for and Nancy never said.

I worried about Jimmy Dale but there was nothing I saw to do. Jimmy Dale was two years older than Lim but he got held back a grade so when Lim was going into the eleventh grade, Jimmy Dale should have been a senior at Sierra Vista. But he quit before the year even started and turned all his attention to running his family spread. By this time, Lim was still fifteen pounds lighter than Jimmy Dale but he was up to six one and Jimmy Dale was just a little taller.

Jimmy Dale was over to the Circle S most weekends. Especially on Sunday. Iris had told him there was always a plate for him if he got hungry so he took her up on it. Lynn helped him with the bill paying and accounting and Davey Waddell was always around to lend a hand. Gradually, Jimmy Dale and Nancy's little spread started to stabilize.

Jimmy Dale was selling older grade cows and buying young registered Herefords. He told me that Nancy would give him a chunk of cash every once in a while and tell him to put it into the ranch.

Jimmy Dale told me his mother had a wad of hundreds in her left boot. She had a special pair of boots with a pouch sewn into the shaft. Just like Rand Phillips. But I never told anybody about where Rand kept his money. From time to time, Nancy would have some people over to the ranch and Jimmy Dale would pack up and come to the Circle S and sleep in the bunk house and eat with me or Dewey or Lim. He left Iris alone except on Sunday.

The Sunday meals we had at the ranch house were some of the best times I have had in my life. Especially when Jimmy Dale and Lim were growing up together. Jimmy Dale and Lim would swap horses a lot. Jimmy Dale liked to bump Davey up into a full rack the last few hundred yards to the barn when they would finish their work on the ranch and head on home. Davey was something we had not seen in that part of the country. He could rack as fast as a lot of horses could run. Lim said Jimmy Dale would call Davey a jug head but he loved to ride him. Lim rode Little Molly a lot. He would ride Davey in the morning and switch off to Little Molly in the afternoon when we were driving cattle from pasture to pasture. That way, he always had a fresh horse.

After Sherman bought Socks and Johnny, word got out that Lim was a patient and steady hand with colts and young horses. Sherman put Socks with a trainer the fall after he bought him from Davey. We kept Johnny and Dewey and Sherman rode him after Lim finished him out. When Lim was through with him, he could do just about everything you wanted a ranch horse to do. Sherman sold him the next spring for eleven thousand dollars and gave Lim five hundred dollars for his help in training the young stallion.

The year he turned thirteen, ranchers started bringing colts by for Lim to halter train and start under saddle. He never took more than three at a time and everything went through Sherman. All the money went to him and he paid Lim his cut on the fifteenth of each month.

Lim was saving for a pickup truck. He worked his young colts and two year olds after school and during the summer he was usually off on Davey in the morning about the time I would pull out to shoe for the day.

Things were changing. The bigger ranches still had wranglers who would work the horse herd all year. They would break the horses in the old style way in a round horse pen. The smaller ranches could not afford a full time wrangler and they usually bought their horses already broke and finished off.

Sherman and Dewey's way of handling colts and young horses was becoming more popular. Top colts never even saw a large open pasture at some of the trainer's facilities. They were kept up in smaller pastures and many spent most of their young lives in stalls. Show horses were hardly ever turned out to pasture because the sun light faded their coats and the grass diet led to unattractive grass bellies.

Sherman and Davey taught Lim to start a colt with a halter at an early age. Lim would be the only one who would feed and water the colts when they were brought to us. Every morning he would be the one to change the buckets in the stalls. The one who tossed the hay in the stall and poured the grain in the aluminum corner feeder.

In the afternoons after school, Lim would take each colt out of the stall, put him in cross ties and groom him for a few minutes. They all would get used to his voice and his touch. They learned to give him their hooves when he wanted to clean them. He would take a hoof pick and clean each hoof and talk to the horses as he did it. He would run his hand between the colt's ears and scratch and rub them between the ears.

He would take them down to a fence row in the horse pasture and walk them down the row at his shoulder. Soon he had them trotting, loping, and changing leads. When it finally came time to put a young horse under saddle, Lim would get him used to a headstall and a snaffle bit first. He would do the same routine with ropes for reins.

When he felt the horse was comfortable with the bit, he would ride him a little bareback and then put him to saddle. The old round pen bronc busting days were over at the Circle S and most of the smaller ranches.

The summer Lim turned sixteen, he bought a used black 1998 F-150. It was a basic pickup. It had a radio but the CD player did not work. The truck had a regular cab, not a big king cab. The seats were gray cloth. It was low mileage and Lim put new tires on it.

We bought the pickup in Green Valley from a widow woman from Iowa. Her husband had died just a year or so back and she had held onto it for a while but her children told her to sell it while it was still worth some money. I remember the day we drove up to her house to look at the truck. She had not put an ad in any of the papers. She told me she was scared someone would answer the ad and see she was alone and rob her and knock her in the head and kill her.

Dewey, Sherman, Lim, and I went to see her. Randy Price had handled her estate matters and she had called him to tell him about the truck. He had called me and told me it sounded like a deal for Lim. The Widow Thackery was a small fragile woman. She lived on a high hill in a nice adobe home. You could see all the way east across the Valley. The Santa Ritas were on the not so distant Eastern horizon. She made us sit down in the living room and it was obvious she was nervous and lonely.

She was in her eighties and probably did not weigh over ninety pounds. She poured us coffee and we settled in to listen for a few minutes. We surely did not want to get her scared and upset. We had just settled in and Dewey had told her the truck was for his son and he expected to pay a fair price when she got up and said, "Wait. Just wait a minute."

She went back into the kitchen and soon she returned with plates of store bought sponge cake and fresh sliced strawberries. I looked at Sherman and he had his hat in his right hand and was shifting around nervously in his chair.

While we ate, we also listened. She told us her husband had been stationed in Hawaii all of World War Two in a hospital where he was a doctor. An orthopedic surgeon. She said when he came back from the war in 1946, she was a pretty cheerleader at Council Bluffs High School. Of course, she showed us the pictures to prove it. And she had been a pretty girl.

She said she had no trouble getting Jimmy Thackery to marry her. He had practiced medicine there in Council Bluffs for a long time and they had come to Green Valley in 1985. She said this was when Green Valley was just getting recognized as a top retirement site. She said Jimmy Thackery had played a lot of golf and they had hiked every trail in the Santa Ritas. Green Valley is west of the Santa Ritas and the Circle S is east of the Santa Ritas.

Jimmy had been diagnosed with pancreatic cancer not long before he died. She said she was all alone now but she could handle it. She was not going back to Iowa because she would miss all the sunrises over the Santa Ritas and the constant sunshine and the peaceful solitude that came with not having a lot of family around you all of the time.

Finally, after a few minutes, she got up and said, "Well, you come to see the truck. Not listen to me. We followed her through the house. In the mud room, I saw a pair of old black cowboy boots. They had nice red, green, and blue stitching on the shafts. They were lying on their sides. There were also some hiking boots, a fly rod, and some coats and flannel shirts still hanging on a rack.

She gave the keys to Dewey and he asked her to open the garage door so we could back the truck out and look at it. He let Lim drive it down the street and back it up some in the driveway.

Dewey opened the hood and the engine was spotless. He asked Lim to let it run a few minutes. He looked at all the hoses and the radiator to see if there were any leaks. He got on his back and crawled under the engine and looked for any leaks. There had been no oil or transmission fluid on the garage floor.

He went to the back of the truck and crawled under it and checked to see if the frame looked bent or the tail pipe or muffler were loose.

He said, "Ms. Gladys, I think I can make you an offer. Have you checked with anyone to see what your truck is worth. It only has twenty seven thousand miles on it and you do not look like the type who would roll the mileage back so I will make you a fair offer."

Gladys said she would call her son-in-law if she had any questions but he had told her the price range she should demand. Dewey made her an offer. It was about two thousand more than what Lim had saved up. She thought about it for a few minutes and said, "That is about what my son-in-law told me I could expect to get. I will take it. I am tired. I used to exercise all the time when Jimmy was here. We liked to hike together. But now, I don't have anyone to go walking or hiking with so I have let myself go. I guess selling this truck is just another way of letting Jimmy go."

She cried a little and then got up and went out in the kitchen. When she came back, she had coffee for us and a nice tall root beer float for Lim. I tried to trade with him. Gladys said, "You just let that boy alone."

Dewey and Gladys settled on the price of the pickup after Dewey upped his offer a hundred dollars. Gladys went to a an old oak roll top desk and got the title to the truck and Dewey took a check out of his top left pocket and filled it out and gave it to Gladys. Sherman took a blank bill of sale out of his bill fold and filled it out. Gladys read it over and then signed it. Dewey just signed it, folded it, and put it in his brown leather bill fold.

We let Lim drive the truck back to the Circle S. We stopped in Nogales and ate at Las Vigas. They have a model train that runs on a track that is suspended from the roof. It runs around the edges of the restaurant and the engine whistle gives out a sharp warning whistle when it rounds a corner.

We were sitting in a booth in the back drinking a pitcher of beer and I told Dewey I would like to throw in a thousand dollars on the truck deal because I knew Lim was shy two thousand and one hundred dollars of having enough.

Sherman said, "I can, too. Just do not tell Iris. She will have me buying the whole goddamn truck, putting new tires on it, and paying the insurance."

Dewey said, "I got this. I got some money saved."

Dewey never drank much, but tonight I think he was enjoying the machacha sonoresne and the beer so I backed off and told Dewey to drain the fucking pitcher if he wanted to. Machacha sonoresne is thin strings of dried beef that have been marinated in a chili sauce and deep fried. It is a hard dish to get right. Fry it too hard and it is tasteless. The only two places I will order it is Las Vigas in Nogales, Arizona and La Roca in Nogales, Sonora. Some of the best eating you can find if you wash it down with some cold beer. I told Dewey and Sherman I would drive home. Then I poured the rest of my beer back into the pitcher.

Dewey said, "Look, I got this meal and the truck, too. You can drive us on home, Vern, but I tell you I would of paid another three, maybe five, hundred for that truck. That old doctor took mighty good care of it. Eight cylinder, 351 clean engine."

Sherman said, "I got to take Iris some of this machacha sonoresne home with me. And it looks like Dewey has everything covered. Lim has a good horse, a job even during the school year, and now a nice truck. Next thing will be girls. Girls. A whole new set of problems, Dewey."

We all laughed. Soon Dewey settled up with the waiter and I drove us on back to the Circle S. When we got home the sun had just gone down. Lim and Iris were sitting on the front porch of the ranch house. Lim was eating a big piece of chocolate meringue pie. The new truck was sitting in front of the ranch house.

Iris ate her food on the porch and we all sat around listening to the south wind blow through the trees around the house. There was a big yellow moon in the sky. Dewey told Lim that in Texas, out in the Hill Country, folks called a big summer moon like that a Comanche Moon. Because when the moon was full and the nights were clear, the Comanche would raid. There had been a lot of Comanche in Llano County right after Texas won its independence from Mexico.

We were having a nice peaceful night, drinking coffee and eating chocolate pie and then Jimmy Dale drove up in his red Chevrolet Silverado. It was two years old. Nancy gave it to him on his eighteenth birthday a few months back. He parked his truck in the driveway and walked up to the Black Ford. He looked all around it, kicked the tires, took the tail gate down, and opened the hood.

He walked on up to the porch and said, "Now, Lim, I was wrong about your horse a few years back, but I just wish you had checked with me before you went and bought a Ford. You know Ford means Fix or Repair Daily or Found on the Road Dead. And one thing you need to know. Once you let that truck start to unwind, when it gets up to around eighty-five, it will start shimmying all over the highway."

Lim laughed. No fistfight tonight. Jimmy Dale was his closest friend and he was always giving Lim a hard time but since Lim had trained Davey and gotten some confidence, he just let Jimmy Dale have his fun.

Iris said, "Well, there is no reason for that truck to ever go eighty-five miles an hour, I can tell you that right now, but if I ever hear about it, you can forget chocolate pie and all other desserts. Both of you. And Jimmy Dale, I believe you have been drinking beer and driving up and down the highway."

Jimmy Dale was a lot of things. He had his faults, no question about it. He had already been out of school for a year. He had quit before he finished. Said he had a ranch to work. But he was not a liar. Especially not to Iris.

He took his old brown hat off and ducked his head and said, "Well, I had a Coors with my dinner and I drank two more coming over here."

Iris said, "Well, that is a shame. I know with all that beer in you, a piece of chocolate pie would make you sick, so I will put this pie back in the refrigerator."

When she came back from the kitchen a few minutes later, she had a big mug of coffee and a big piece of pie. She gave it to Jimmy Dale. He sat on the top step of the porch and ate his pie.

The night was clear and bright. You could look off the porch and see cattle down near the grassy banks of the Cienega.

There were two old oak rocking chairs on the porch. Iris and Sherman each had one. Iris's had a blue cotton covering for the seat and the back. Sherman went in the house and when he came back, he had three small glasses with maybe a half a shot a piece of Four Roses Small Batch in each one.

"Feller up at the Cattleman's Association meeting last month up at Pine Top said this was mighty fine sipping whiskey. I never cared for the regular Four Roses."

The three of us sipped some of the bourbon. It went down mighty easy. Hard to tell Sherman it was not as good as Elijah Craig. So I just sipped and enjoyed the night. You sip a good bourbon and you can pick up some vanilla and grain flavors. A few minutes later, Jimmy Dale stuck his coffee cup in front of Sherman and asked for a little taste.

Sherman laughed and said, "No to the whiskey, but how about you helping me and Lim and Dewey move some cows tomorrow up to that far pasture next to the Whetstones. You can ride Little Molly since you didn't bring one of your own horses."

"That is good for me if I can call Davey and get him to feed for me tomorrow."

"That has already been taken care of. Davey Waddell called and talked to Iris and said you were on your way and you had been drinking a little beer and could we keep you the night and Iris said we could use you tomorrow gathering and moving cattle from pasture to pasture."

Jimmy Dale had some clothes he kept in the bunk house. Lately, he had been wearing some nice black smooth ostrich boots around the ranch house when he wasn't working. He kept an old pair of roughouts in the bunk house for work. Some of his shirts looked almost new and every once in a while it looked like someone had ironed his jeans. Probably Lynn.

I was beginning to think Jimmy Dale had a chance of making it. A chance to rise above his family's shortcoming. We had all tried to keep him in school. Except Lim. He said he did not blame him. He said 4-H was the only place he thought you learned much that would help you on a ranch. Lim said after math and some English and a little History, it was wasted time.

When he got up to go to the bunk house, Jimmy Dale went by his truck and got a paper bag from the front seat. I could see part of the Coors Label on the six pack sticking out of the bag as he was shutting the passenger door.

Dewey, Lim and I left shortly afterwards. I stopped at the bunkhouse and went inside. Jimmy Dale was sitting in an old brown leather chair that had three wooden legs. A red brick and several white pieces of wood held up the fourth side of the chair.

He had a pot of coffee brewing on the stove and a cold can of Coors in one hand. He was stretched out in the chair. He told me to get a beer out of the refrigerator. I sat on an old oak kitchen chair and I asked Jimmy Dale how things were at his spread. He had not asked me to shoe his good horse, Scooter, in about eight weeks.

He said things were not that great with his mother and he did not see how they would get any better but the cattle were all healthy and he had enough spending money to buy his own food and put gas in his truck with a little walking around money left over. He had three hundred dollars saved up but he figured that and some more would be needed for a new set of tires in the spring.

He was living in the bunk house there on his place. He had a stove and an old Sony 27 inch television that he said would last forever. He and Davey had patched the roof and replaced one window. He said it was dry and warm. Jimmy Dale was sleeping on a bunk bed and relying on an old corner red brick fireplace with a ramshackle hearth for heat in the fall and winter and a small window air conditioner for cool air during the summer.

We split the last beer. Jimmy Dale said he had been with Davey one day a few months ago at a ranch north of Greer and just south of the Navajo Reservation. They had went there to deliver a horse to a rancher. Jimmy Dale said he had noticed a colt grazing in the horse pasture and he had bought it for five hundred dollars. It was not a registered colt, but he liked it and he could not put words to what he had been attracted to.

The colt was almost eighteen months old. He was a paint. He had a white mane and tail and lemon yellow and white markings. His face was solid yellow and he was a small horse. He was not golden like a true palomino. He was getting darker now that Jimmy Dale had him in a stall.

Jimmy Dale asked me not to tell anybody about the paint. He said he was copying what he had seen Lim do with colts and young horses. Ground training with a halter and lead rope was where he started. He said he was going to wait until the horse was almost three before he put a saddle on him. He never told me his name that night.

When we finished the last beer, Jimmy Dale said I needed to come by one day soon and trim Scooter's feet and reset his shoes. When I left the bunk house, Jimmy Dale had lit a Winston and was sprawled out in the old chair blowing smoke rings. I never asked him why he moved out of his house into the bunk house. I just figured he did not like to be around his mother when she was drinking or stoned on weed or pills or worse.

The paint turned out pretty good. Of course, Lim found out about the paint and he helped Jimmy Dale ground train him. The paint took a while to catch his growth. By then, Lim had his mind on a lot of different things. Jimmy Dale and Davey broke the paint. No one knew what to name the ugly colt until Dewey told Jimmy Dale to name him Dan.

Dewey said Dan was a lucky name for a horse. Dewey had owned an old ugly grade horse when he was young and his name was Dan. Dewey said he was ugly but dependable. So Jimmy Dale named him Dan and he was just that. Ugly and dependable. He had quick feet and could turn a cow faster than most expensive horses. Dan never got over fifteen hands but he worked hard and earned his keep. He was mighty ugly, though. Mighty ugly.

Lim's horse, Davey, had filled out nicely and was almost sixteen hands tall. His black coat was full and rich and he had a strong shoulder and hip. He could not make the sharp cuts that Scooter and

Little Molly could make, but he could cover a lot of ground fast with his long stride.

That is the way things went during those years. Both boys growing up and staying around the Circle S most of their spare time. All of us knew when they started driving, things would change. It was the natural way of things.

Chapter Eight
Carrie Ann Shelton

Lim Couch

I was sixteen and it was the first day of high school in late August when I first saw her. I got to school early that day and parked my shiny truck near the side door of the school building where everyone in high school would have to see my truck as they walked into school and went to their lockers. There was around fifteen or twenty guys hanging around my truck.

I was never the most popular boy at Patagonia High School. That was fine with me. About the only thing I really felt a part of was the 4-H trips and I was on the Judging teams. We would take trips in a school van and judge hogs, horses, dairy cattle, sheep, and beef cattle. We judged the animals on confirmation. I loved it. Especially, the beef cattle and the horses.

I did not really have any enemies and since I did not have a truck until I turned sixteen, I did not really have much to do with girls. Not by choice. I was shy and I had not been on a date yet. Jimmy Dale told me it was time for me to get me some. He had a girlfriend who lived in Benson. I had been with them a few times. Her name was Sara and I did not cotton to Sara very much. She was just a year older than me and had a mighty fine set of tits but she cussed more than me and Jimmy Dale and she smoked Salems in Jimmy Dale's truck and drank vodka straight out of the bottle. And smoked a joint most nights I was around her. That was all her business but I did not want to see Jimmy Dale going down the same old road Ray and Nancy Scruggs had traveled.

Sara was a senior at Benson and was a cheerleader. Jimmy Dale went to all the football games and brought her home from the games. Sometimes they stopped in Benson and stayed in a cheap motel. Jimmy Dale was always worried about getting her pregnant. He told me he did not know what he would do if she wanted a baby but it worked out because Sara started dating this guy in Benson that drove a three year old Lexus and managed a liquor store. He was about twenty five years old and had been in the Army for a while in Iraq.

Jimmy Dale said he did not know whether to go kiss the guy or try to beat his ass. He said he was glad to be rid of Sara. He was beginning to think he would have to marry her and buy a trailer and be stuck out at the ranch for the rest of his life taking care of a kid and Sara.

I told Dad about Sara and he said it sounded to him like Jimmy Dale might be hooking up with someone who was a lot like his own mother.

Nowadays, Jimmy Dale was around the ranch most weekends picking up a little cash from Sherman for helping us move cattle, fix fence, stack hay, or move irrigation equipment.

The Boyce brothers came up to the truck right before the bell rang for us to go to our home room for an hour of study hall. Jeremy Boyce was my age and was the right tackle on the football team and played first base on the baseball team. He was Patagonia High's best athlete. His brother Don was in the ninth grade and he was a computer nerd. He was taller than me and I was six foot two when I was sixteen. Jimmy Dale was six foot even. A fact I constantly reminded him of.

Don was already talking about going off to the University of Arizona and studying calculus and physics and such. Everybody in school tried to get Don to play basketball but he said he was not interested. He wanted to design computer games. Jeremy and Don lived on a cow and calf ranch just south of Patagonia in the San Rafael Valley.

They would come up and give us a hand at branding time. Jeremy had to have a big mule to ride since he was already over two fifty. When Jeremy got to be a two hundred pounder his father found him a big red and brown mule that was around seventeen hands. Don rode a nice chestnut gelding with a white star in his face that he had been given when he was eleven.

Jeremy was like Jimmy Dale. He liked Chevys and he was giving me grief in front of everyone about my cheap ass truck when I saw this girl get out of a maroon Jeep Grand Cherokee. Her father was dropping her off in the parking lot.

I asked Jeremy and Don if they knew who she was. Jeremy shook his head and Don said, "I will tell you in a minute when she is inside .We shut up and gawked at her as she passed us and went into the building. She gave us a withering glance as she passed us.

She had red hair that hung down past her shoulders and freckles across her nose and cheeks. She was wearing blue jeans and a long sleeved white blouse that was buttoned up all the way to the top. She had on black Reebok sneakers. I watched her walk into the building. She had a swimmer's tight body. Long legs, muscular ass, and well formed, but small breasts and alert brown eyes that could stare right through you or make you want to reach and grab her and hold her close.

Don told me her name. Carrie Ann Shelton. He said her father had made a ton of money in investment banking in California and had bought the old Selby place near Elgin and retired, then moved here to raise Angus cattle. The Selby ranch had been tied up in estate litigation for several years. The cattle and horses had been sold several summers ago and the land had lain empty of cattle or crops for the last few years. Sherman had tried to lease the Selby land for grazing but the relatives were all fighting and nothing got resolved. Carrie Ann Shelton lived about six miles from the Circle S. I figured they could run five hundred cows comfortably on the graze they had.

The Sheltons had moved into the old adobe Selby ranch house in early June. I asked Don how he knew all of this and he said his father had sold some Angus to Grant Shelton, Carrie Ann's father, back in July. Don said Carrie Ann's father was originally from Kansas and had moved off the family ranch years ago because he had two older brothers who were living on the ranch. They raised wheat, corn, and cattle. Grant Shelton had a diploma from Harvard hanging on his den wall. Don had seen it when he went in the Shelton home with his dad to pick up the check for the Angus back in July.

Don said the diploma was all in hard to read Latin words but he was sure it was Harvard Business School because the school name was in bigger and easier to read letters.

Don did not know what Carrie Ann's mother's name was but he did tell me Carrie Ann had an eleven year old brother who was just learning to ride. His name was Danny.

First period was a study hall for eleventh graders. All fifty three of us. I sat at a desk next to Carrie Ann. No one had anything to study yet, so we were all talking and catching up with what had happened during the summer. I asked Carrie Ann if she had learned to ride and she told me she knew how to ride before she could spell Arizona. She spent a few weeks each year on the ranch in Kansas and had been riding before she started school.

She asked me if I had a name and I said, "Yes, I am Lim Couch."

She said some of the other girls had warned her about me because I was so bashful and never dated.

I guess I was blushing because she asked me why I had such big red ears and I ducked my head and did not answer her. Jeremy was sitting behind her and I was on the next row of desks right beside her on the right hand side. I asked her if she was a swimmer and she asked me how I knew and I said, "Because you have a nice figure and no body fat."

Jeremy laughed and said not to pay any attention to me. I was just a cowboy and did not know any better. She asked me if I was a real cowboy and Jeremy said, "Why, hell yes, he is. He ground trains colts and is a good hand unless you want him to rope something and then you are shit out of luck. Ask him about Socks."

Carrie Ann said, "I will save that for later. If Socks is one of your old girlfriends, I am not interested in hearing about your escapades."

Jeremy was laughing and so were some of the people around us. Jeremy said, "Socks is a horse. A stud horse and a AQHA Champion that Lim started out. Halter trained him and got him to change leads and back up. Then when he was close to two the Sniders took him to a real trainer over at Tubac. Name of Lamar Tisdale. Tisdale is a top trainer. Most people can't afford him. Socks done real good in AQHA. Then the Snider's sold him for a ton of money and he is standing stud somewhere."

Mr. Crawley was our monitor for study hall. He was a slight, older man who taught history and was ready to retire and move to Panama City, Florida. He only had two more years. I liked him. He said he wanted to smell the ocean every morning and walk the beach every day when he retired.

He came over and told Jeremy if he didn't quiet down he was going to make him do twenty five pushups.

Jeremy said, "Will that be two hands or one hand?"

We were all laughing except Carrie Ann. She was looking at Jeremy as if he was a stranger from outer space. Jeremy made a big show of doing one hand pushups. He got to number twenty three and could not quite make it.

He fell out in the floor and we all laughed. Mr. Crawley and Carrie Ann, too.

I did not see Carrie Ann any more that morning until noon. She was eating lunch with Mary Siegfried. Mary's dad was our vet and the vet for most of the ranches around Sonoita and Patagonia. Mary was our class president and she was the one you went to if you needed to know something or get something done with the faculty and administration.

We had been in the same class ever since I started in school. Her mother had run off a few years ago. My dad had told me last summer that when I was seven, he had come home for lunch one day from riding fence and found the divorce papers from Rose stuck in the doorway. I can remember Randy Price coming out to the house one night and Dad showing him some papers out on the porch. I was inside doing my homework and Dad had told me to stay in the house until he got through with his business with Randy Price.

Dad finally told me last summer that the divorce papers had been signed and sent back to the court in Las Vegas when I was still seven years old. He said he had started to call Rose one last time but thought that was a bad idea. He said a divorce was a severing of all ties. Randy Price had told him it was a final and complete end of his marriage to Rose.

When he had told me about the divorce, we were sitting on the porch on a cool June night and we were watching some low black clouds march slowly across the valley from the South. He told me I should never think bad about Rose. Truth was I could not remember much about her. She was pretty and talked softly to me. I tried to remember while we was on the porch that night if she had ever yelled at me and I swear I could not and I think it would have stood out in my memory if she had.

And Dad could talk all he wanted to about a divorce being a final severing of ties but any fool could look in his face when he talked about Rose and tell he had not stopped loving her. I asked Vern about it a few weeks after Dad told me and he said it tore Dad up something terrible and his private feeling was that my Dad was a one woman man and he could not see anything wrong with that. Especially if the woman was Rose. Vern said she just got bored with her life and my Dad would not go to Vegas and be something he could not stand.

Vern said it had to do with being cut off from the land and the sunsets and the mountains and the horses and the cattle and the smells of old leather, Alfalfa hay drying in the field, and wet sage the morning after a rain. Those were things my Dad missed when he was selling tires in Benson.

Vern was drinking some rye whiskey out of a jelly jar when we were talking about this. We were sitting out in front of his silver trailer on a clear summer night. There was a calf bawling for his mother somewhere off down by the Cienega.

Vern said he knew he lived in an Airstream trailer but he had some money put back and he could work his own schedule. He could shoe four horses next Wednesday or trim the feet of twenty brood mares or go to Jack's in Patagonia and eat cheeseburgers and drink beer and watch a baseball game. It was his choice. He was slowing down a little as he got older. He only worked a half days on Saturdays a few days a year and very seldom worked all day Saturday. He helped around the ranch on the weekends but he said he did not consider that work unless he was in a hayfield.

He could turn down work and he could help people who were jammed up by a bank or bad luck or some combination of the two. He usually asked for his money up front but he let some people slide until they could sell their yearlings in the fall. Sometimes he would take hay instead of cash and stack it in Sherman's barn and sell it in the winter for a small profit.

He liked the fact he could see the country, listen to people's stories, do his job and be free of any ties when he got home. He told me he liked the smell of the coal burning in his forge in the mornings and the feel of cash in his left front shirt pocket at the end of the day.

Mary Siegfried's mother left Sonoita when Mary was eleven. She just hauled off and left, according to Mary. She lived with a sister in Tucson for a while, got a divorce, and then married a retired CPA in Tucson. She lived in one of those big mansions up north of Sunrise in the Catalina Foothills. Mary said her mother made a tiresome, half-hearted effort to patch their relationship up. Mary said it was all too awkward and unnatural for her, so she resisted any effort by her mother to see her.

Mary did not have curves. All of her features were sharp edges. She was too skinny but she was the number one student in our class and she was thoughtful. She nagged me a lot about my grades. My dad never did. But with Mary, it was always, you can do better and you need to be thinking of college. She turned sixteen a few months ago and got her driver's license before me and she drove me and Jimmy Dale to Tucson one Saturday and we went shopping at the Tucson Mall and ate hamburgers and drank milkshakes at the Steak N Shake. Jimmy Dale was nice that day. He did not cuss or smoke in front of Mary. And he picked up the tab for our meal. He tried to get Mary to go by this bar that he thought would sell him a few beers to drink on the way home. He was eighteen and was going to have to wait until he was twenty one before he could buy liquor legally. Mary said no and Jimmy Dale let it pass.

Mary was driving east on Broadway and Jimmy Dale said he was still hungry and Mary Ann pulled into a Lucky Wishbone and went inside and got some more food. We ate fried gizzards and livers on the way back down to the Circle S. It was some of the best food I had ever eaten. Jimmy Dale saved some of his. He said he had some beer at home to go with the chicken and that would be his supper.

Mary was almost as tall as me. Her hair was brown and she wore it cut short. Too short for me. I can tell you that. Jimmy Dale said she was going to be gay or an old maid or both, but I could have cared less.

She was my best friend outside of Jeremy. I could call Mary late at night if I had trouble with my homework or if I just had any question about school. That fucking Jeremy. He would even call me with questions about his homework. He was just lazy in school. He had that dream of being a rich athlete. He told me he wanted to see a little of the world, play some ball, stash away some money so he could have a new pickup every year, marry a pretty girl, and come on back to the San Rafael Valley and raise cattle with his father. Mary and I kept telling him he would have to pass some subjects in college in order to keep his eligibility but he said he would find a way to get by.

Mary had been asked by the principal, Ms. Stevens, to show Carrie Ann around since our school was new to her. Jeremy and I sat across the table at lunch from Mary and Carrie Ann. Jeremy said, "Get Lim to tell you about his hundred dollar horse. That is the only way you can get anything out of him. Don't ask him about his dumbass friend Jimmy Dale."

Jeremy and Jimmy Dale were not friends. I never figured out why. Jeremy said you got to be dumb to drop out of school after the tenth grade. I told him you had to be dumb to call me with questions about homework. Carrie Ann said, "Well, did anyone bother to ask him why he did it? And what did his parents say and do about it."

Mary said, "His dad is dead and from what Lim has told me, his mother is not around enough to have any real say in what he does. Looks like she does not have any interest in what he does."

Carrie Ann said, "Okay, then tell me about your hundred dollar horse.

I looked her in the eye and said, "I got a better idea. You let me take you home from school and we can swing by the Circle S and I will let you ride him."

Jeremy jumped up and reached in his billfold and pulled out three one dollar bills and started waving them around and was asking everyone in the cafeteria to pay attention. When everyone was quiet he said, "This is an historic day. Mr. Bashful, two years running at Patagonia High School, has asked the new girl for a date. Right out in front of witnesses. I got three dollars that says she won't go. Any takers?"

Most everyone was laughing and some people were trying to get in on the bet. Before anyone could finalize any of the bets, Carrie Ann stood up, reached across the table, snatched the three one dollar bills out of Jeremy's hand, and said, "You lose, gate mouth. You lose." We all laughed. And maybe Jeremy laughed the longest and hardest. He was my friend. He and Jimmy Dale could say anything they wanted about me.

Jeremy liked to kid people. I only ever heard Jimmy Dale kid me. I was the only friend in his age group he had. But I noticed Jeremy only kidded people he liked. He called Mary, Sticks, but we were all friends and Jeremy was who she called a few weeks ago when her blue Camry slid off in a ditch late at night on the winding road going south to Parker Canyon Lake. Jeremy got up and came by the ranch and got me and we went down and hooked up a chain to her front bumper and pulled her out of the ditch with Jeremy's truck.

Jeremy got on his back and crawled under the Camry and cleared away some grass and dirt that had stuck to the frame and the front fender. When he got out from under the car, Mary thanked him and Jeremy said, "Look Sticks, one of these days you will be a doctor and I will be hunting you up for some free medical care. You need two specialties. Heart and Orthopedics. That will be just enough to take care of me. "

I brought my own lunch most days. I would usually eat an orange or an apple, a boiled egg, a peanut butter and jelly sandwich, and a couple of Fig Newtons. I could eat a package every day of my life. Only thing better than a Fig Newton is Iris's cakes and pies. I drank a Dad's Root Beer over ice every day with my lunch. I would watch the schedule for the lunches and when they had meat loaf, tacos, fried chicken, or roast beef and mashed potatoes, I would buy my lunch.

I started eating my lunch. Jeremy grabbed half of my sandwich and gave me half of one of his ham sandwiches and then traded me some Oreos for Fig Newtons. A trade I only made because he was my best friend in school. Mary and Carrie Ann ate salads and apples they bought in the cafeteria. No desserts for either one of them. Jeremy had three sandwiches of his own and one he got from a little tenth grade girl named Jody who Jeremy had told me already had the prettiest body and sweetest smile of any of the girls in school.

Mary was telling me to sign up to take one of those college eligibility tests. I told her I was not thinking of going to college and Mary said to take the test anyway so if I changed my mind, I would not have a big hassle at the last minute. Mary said the U of A had some Agriculture classes that I ought to look into and I told her I would think about it.

I asked Carrie Ann where she wanted to go to college and she quickly said, "Stanford for undergraduate and then to Harvard Law. I want to be an environmental lawyer."

I had never met anyone my age who was so certain about their plans for the future. Mary was already getting brochures from colleges all over the Southwest and California. She said she would probably wind up at the U of A and then go off somewhere out of state for medical school.

Jeremy said he wanted to go to the school that had the best chance of getting him in the pros. He said some college coaches could pick up the phone and bump you up into the first three rounds of the pro draft if they thought you were worth it. He said you had to watch and see which coach was probably going to get fired if he did not win in one or two years. He said there was nothing worse than to be a junior with a new coach because when you were a senior he would probably start playing his own recruits over the old left over players he had inherited from the fired coach.

Jeremy said it was complicated if you did not get an offer from Oregon or USC or some other team you knew was going to be good most every year. He said he had letters from twenty or so schools but he was hoping he could go to Texas A and M because they had a lot of classes in Agriculture and he would be serious about his studies if he was learning about drought resistant grasses or protein supplements for calves. He just did not give a good goddamn about symbolism in the works of Lord Byron.

He wanted to learn something he could bring back to the San Rafael Valley that would make cattle raising easier and more profitable. I agreed with him and Mary told me I would have no trouble getting into college but there was no getting around it. You had to take some required courses.

I did not tell anyone the other fact that was keeping me from thinking about college. Money. I had some and Dad had some. Enough for us to have a decent second hand truck a piece. Enough for clothes and food. A new pair of boots every once in a while. We had a comfortable life on the Circle S. But it was a working ranch hand's life.

There was no money left over to pay the high dollar tuition at a school like the University of Arizona or Texas A and M.

And I was not going to get a scholarship. I never played sports that much. And like Jeremy said, I was not too wonderful a calf roper and I sure didn't want to hook up with any bucking stock so I could not get a rodeo scholarship. I would have to borrow money. Thousands of dollars would have to be repaid at the end of my college career. And for what? I was not going to be a doctor, a dentist, a pharmacist, a vet, an accountant, or a lawyer. So what was the point? Did the world really need another Art History or Sociology graduate.

We finished lunch and went on back to class. When school was out for the day, I found Carrie Ann outside near my truck. She had called her mother at lunch and told her she had a date after school to go see a horse named Davey. The one Davey Waddell had told her about. I heard her tell her mother I was the best looking boy at Patagonia High but that was not saying much.

We were in my truck leaving the parking lot when I asked her how she knew Davey Waddell and she said her whole family had ridden over to his spread one day in June to look at a horse for her. Davey had shown her a nice three year old gelding I had halter broke and put to saddle. His name was Jax and he was a grey that I had wanted to keep for a while longer and smooth him out some but Davey had said he was close enough to being finished to where he could sell him for a nice price.

Carrie Ann said Davey really put the hard sell on them. She said she rode him and did not like him. He was too young and skittish for her. And Davey wanted seventy five hundred for him. She wound up buying an eleven year old bay broodmare named Jackie. Jackie had not thrown a colt for two years and Davey sold her cheap. Carrie Ann said Jackie handled fine and did not ever get in a big hurry or shy away when it was windy.

Carrie Ann thought it would have stupid to pay that much money for a three year old horse that she could tell needed some training. Especially when she was going to Stanford in two years. The horse would stand in a stall or be resold in all likelihood after she went off to Stanford if she had asked her dad to buy him.

After Davey and her father had agreed on a price, Davey took them up to his house and they sat around for a few minutes drinking coffee and eating pound cake while Davey filled the papers out to transfer ownership of Jackie. And this is when Davey had told her about me buying a horse from him for one hundred dollars and then naming him Davey because he was gawky.

She asked me if I was a Horse Whisperer and I said I did not know what that was and she said it was somebody with psychic powers who could communicate with horses in special ways. I told her I had a hard time spelling psychic. Psychic and rhythm. Two words I always had trouble with.

I told her I just like horses and there was no secret to anything I did. You just fed and watered them first. Got them used to you and let them make the connection that you were the person who took care of them. Simple first step.

Get to know them first. Find out if you were dealing with a shy, skittish horse or a well behaved horse or a spoiled horse. Then get them used to wearing a halter in their stall and out in the pasture. Introduce them to a lead rope and a fence line after that. Walk them down the fence row and teach them to relax and stay with you and follow your signals.

Carrie Ann rode Davey and I rode Little Molly. We left the barn and headed east towards the creek. The sky was as clear and blue as it could possibly be. I looked to the south and then the west and I could see no rain clouds on either horizon.

Carrie Ann looked at ease on Davey. It looked to me like the old horse was strutting a little more than usual. He did that when a woman rode him. When I was thirteen, Rhonda Smith from a ranch down near Parker Canyon had been named Tucson Rodeo Queen. Her parents and her oldest brother ran a nice cow and calf spread. Rhonda was a petite blond and a good rider. She wanted to ride barrels on the PRCA circuit but she was still in high school and had not found a horse she thought was good enough for the big time rodeo competition.

She and her father came up to the Circle S and asked if she could ride Davey in the Grand Entry at the Tucson Rodeo and the big parade before the Rodeo on Friday. She was slated to carry the Stars and Stripes and make a pass around the arena after the National Anthem.

Vern pulled Davey's regular shoes off and put some heavier toe weights on his front feet and cut his heels back some. Rhonda brought up one of her nice little mares named Lou for me to ride until after the Rodeo. With the heavier toe weights and his heels cut back, he was best suited for a racking gait. I did not want to risk bowing a tendon or aggravating a stifle joint on the range with him carrying those heavy toe weighted shoes on his front end.

She trained him for the Grand Entry by riding him up the long hill leading away from the ranch house up to the main gate. She rode him all five days of the Rodeo and I went Sunday with Dad and Vern and Jimmy Dale and watched. Davey really put on a show. When the other horses had left the arena and the National Anthem had been played, Rhonda walked him out to the gate and then turned him around and pushed him into a full rack as he passed in front of the chutes and the east stands.

His head was high and his nose was tucked in and his strong neck was arched. He was over striding with his back feet and his head was nodding in rhythm with each stride he made with his front feet. His tail was almost dragging the ground and Rhonda had put red, white and blue ribbons in his long, wavy, mane. When he made the turn at the north end of the arena and passed in front of the big west grand stand across from the chutes, he was stepping higher than I had ever seen before. Rhonda and Davey got as much applause as anyone that day.

I went to Rhonda's trailer after the Grand Entry and Jimmy Dale and I walked Davey down. I complained about the ribbons in his mane. Rhonda laughed and took the halter rope and walked with us and asked me how much I would take for my horse and I said he was not for sale. She said she could probably send some film of the pass he made in front of the west stands out to all of the rodeos and make a little money with him. Enough to pay her expenses if she ever found a decent barrel horse.

I laughed and said Vern was going to take those heavy toe weights off of him tonight and I would be riding him in the east pasture checking fences after school tomorrow. Rhonda's father came over and gave me two one hundred dollar bills for letting Rhonda ride Davey but I would not take the money.

We were at the Silver Saddle after the show eating steak and Vern told me some horses just did better for a woman. Something you could not explain. Jimmy Dale said he would sure enough change some of his ways for a nice girl like Rhonda .Rhonda was a nice blond who never made it to the big time in rodeo. Her parents could not bankroll her. You have to have at least one good horse, a reliable truck and trailer, and some cash to live on if you want to try to be a barrel racer on the Rodeo Circuit. Seems every high school in the rural west has at least one girl who wants on the barrel racing circuit. The ones that make it have to have some cash behind them to pay expenses, and a lot of luck in finding a horse. Rhonda is in Pharmacy School at the University of Arizona in Tucson and every time she sees me she asks about Davey. She wants me to sell him to her.

She still comes home from college in Tucson and helps around the ranch during the summer. Hard for me to imagine Rhonda in a white coat in CVS filling prescriptions. But there is no way her family ranch can support the two boys and her and the families you know they will eventually acquire. Her younger brother, Jimmy, is in the Marines stationed somewhere in the Far East and the oldest, Kirby, is helping run the ranch. Kirby has already started a family and I expect Rhonda and Jimmy will wind up living away from the ranch and probably away from Arizona.

Carrie Ann and I stopped down near the creek and sat on an old cottonwood log that was starting to rot. It was still strong enough for us. We had gotten nice rains three times in the last two weeks and there was a splash of summer poppies on the hillside across from the fast moving creek waters. They had reddish orange centers and dark yellow flowers

There was a barrel cactus a few feet from our log that had red flowers. Carrie told me she had been a pretty good competitive swimmer until she was fourteen and she had just burned out. She was tired of the travelling and the training and she had told her parents she just wanted to quit. She had thought her parents would explode, but her father had said it was her decision and if she did not want to make the commitment, there was no use in spending time training and traveling all over the state.

She said she had not been in a pool until she moved out here this summer. Her father had built a nice lap pool and a cabana behind their house and now she swam for fun. Usually a leisurely one mile swim in the early morning. She loved to finish her swim as the sun rose over the mountains.

Carrie Ann said she was going to have some fun now before she went off to Stanford. I was hoping that would include me but I did not have a car or a lot of money to carry her places. Just a used F-150 and a few dollars to spend. I did not tell her any of this. I would just let things happen. We rode across the creek and checked the fences on one of the east pastures. The cattle were grazing in almost knee high grass and a soft wind came up out of the south. It was just a few months until we would sell off this year's crop of calves.

I was hoping to see one of the red tail hawks that hunted the Circle S pastures. We had seen a few quail. And some doves were starting to fly west to their roosts in the cottonwoods and mesquites that lined the Cienega Creek.

We headed on back home and I could see some black clouds over the Santa Ritas. Little Molly picked her trot up and raised her head after we crossed the Cienega and headed west towards the ranch house. Davey was strutting around just like he did when Rhonda rode him in the Rodeo.

When we were about half a mile away from the horse barn, I told Carrie Ann to tell Davey, "Come up," squeeze her legs, and pull gently on his reins, and he would shift into a rack. I told her to hold him back and not let him go too fast because the ground was uneven and rolling most of the way back to the barn.

Little Molly was not happy when Davey and Carrie Ann pulled away from us. I kept her in a slow trot and she wanted to stay up with Davey. She threw her head and switched her tail around some and started to break into a gallop but I held her back and she calmed down and reluctantly got back into her slow trot. No horse likes to be the last one in the barn. But after she settled down she held her trot and when we topped the last hill, I saw Carrie leading Davey out of the horse barn.

He was unsaddled and she had put his old red nylon halter on him. I could see the sweat glistening on his lean, black body. Little Molly wanted to hurry on in when she saw Davey but she settled back into her slow and easy trot. Some horses have a hard, rough trot. Sometimes you can smooth the trot out with corrective shoeing if the farrier is good and he is lucky. Little Molly just had a nice, smooth way of going. I pushed her up into a short lope and she settled into it and we went on back to the horse barn.

I unsaddled her and slipped her bridle off and haltered her. We walked out of the barn and went back up the road towards Davey and Carrie Ann. Davey had stopped his strutting and prancing around and lowered his head. Sometimes he would nudge Carrie Ann with his nose. He never did that with me.

As we were returning to the barn, I looked out over the Santa Ritas and the sun was almost ready to leave us for the day. Already shades of pink, reds, orange, and dark blue were forming on the horizon as the sunset began to form over the wide western horizon.

Sherman and Dad rode up as we were taking Little Molly and Davey back into the barn. Sherman came up and introduced himself to Carrie Ann. Dad hung back and Sherman said, "This is Dewey Couch. He is quiet like his boy."

Dad took his hat off and grinned and shook hands with Carrie Ann. His old blue shirt had a small rip in it right over the left front pocket and his smile was friendly, but tired.

She said, "Your father is handsome and shy. You are just shy."

Sherman laughed and said, "How did you like riding a hundred dollar horse?"

Carrie Ann said, "Davey Waddell told me all about this horse. He is great. The smoothest horse I have ever ridden. The first Tennessee Walker I have ridden."

"Lim could sell that horse and pay for most of a year in college, but he ain't gonna do it," said Sherman.

Sherman and Dad left the barn and Carrie Ann and I fed and watered the horses. As we walked down the hill to my truck, Carrie Ann asked, "Where do you live?"

I pointed out our house. I could see my dad in the kitchen. He was starting supper. I asked Carrie Ann if she would stay for supper since she liked my dad and she said yes and pulled her cell phone out and called her mother.

We sat down at the kitchen table and talked to my Dad after I set the table. Dad said we were not having anything fancy and Carrie Ann said that was fine with her. She said she did not know why sitting on a horse for a few hours wore you out and made you so hungry since the horse was doing all the work.

Dad was boiling spaghetti and warming up some meat sauce Iris had given us a few weeks back. Iris would go on a cooking tear about once a month and cook chili, meat sauce for spaghetti, and chicken soup and freeze it in bags just big enough for two people. She would knock on the door of our house and give half of the packages to us. She would then commence to fuss at Dad for not having enough vegetables and fruit in our diet.

Vern said she fussed at him for eating too many carbohydrates and sweets. We just took the food and thanked her. She would take the other half of the food to Vern.

Dad took a can of tamales out of the pantry and opened it and started heating them up in a pan. He opened a can of Hormel's chili with beans and poured it over the tamales and turned the heat down on the stove.

He had just put some fresh ears of corn in a pot to boil when Iris knocked on the door. She had a big, clear glass bowl with salad in it. She introduced herself to Carrie Ann and then started in on Dad and me. Me first.

"You, Lim Couch, you should have brought Carrie Ann by the house and introduced her. I could have called her mother and had everyone over to the house tonight for supper. Carrie Ann, welcome to the Circle S. You are welcome anytime. I hope you had a nice ride. I saw you and Davey coming back to the barn. He was showing off, I can tell you that."

Before Carrie Ann could say anything, Iris started in on Dad. "Dewey Couch, I hope you are not going to serve those tamales and chili and beans straight out of a can to this young lady. Straight out of a can. I do not see how you can live on it. Sherman is just as bad as Dewey, Carrie Ann. I brought a nice salad with avocado, grated cheddar cheese, fresh sliced tomatoes, and spinach greens. Already got the oil and vinegar on it. I know there is nothing even approaching salad dressing in this house. Beer, canned tamales, pork and beans, hamburger meat, chili and beans, pork chops, sirloin steak, bacon and eggs is about all you buy and this boy needs to put on some weight. He needs fresh vegetables and fruit every day of his life."

Dad said, "Yes, Ms. Iris."

Iris said, "Carrie Ann, I hope you come back to see us soon. And tell your mother, we should go to Tucson for lunch. And soon. I will call her next week. Oh, and I know I have just been wasting my breath with you, Dewey Couch, but you mark my words. You will regret not eating fruit and vegetables. You just wait and see."

After that last blast, she was gone.

Dad laughed and we started eating. Carrie Ann and I ate salad, corn and spaghetti. Dad picked at his salad and ate about half of it and started in on his canned tamales and chili. He ate canned tamales and chili at least once a week. He drank a Fat Tire out of a cold mug with his supper.

Carrie Ann asked him where he grew up and he started telling her about the ranch in Llano County and swimming in the Llano River during the hot summer days after he finished his ranch work.

She asked him why he named me Lim and Dad told her I was named after a black Marine Dad had served with in Viet Nam. He was from somewhere in the Mississippi Delta and was a sergeant. His name was Lim Sanders and Dad said they got to be friends because they both liked horses. Lim had grown up on a cotton farm near the Yazoo River. He told Dad he had always had some sort of horse to ride from the time he was eight years old until he joined the Marines.

Lim Sanders was a sergeant and Dad was a private. Dad got shot one night while his platoon was on patrol. Dad said he was gut shot but he knew he would live if he could just get to a hospital and get the bleeding stopped. Lim Sanders got the bleeding slowed down and helped carry him back to the company base on a hill but it was raining and no helicopter could land until morning.

Lim Sanders stayed with him and kept changing the compresses and making sure Dad could get through the pain. The helicopters came in the morning and Dad said he barely made it because he had lost so much blood. When he finally got well, he tried to find his unit again and thank Lim Sanders but their company had been sent back to the jungle and Dad was sent stateside to fully recover.

Dad told her about going back to Llano County and everything being different after he came home from Vietnam and how he drifted around until he got married and moved to Benson and ran a tire store for Rose's brother before he came to the Circle S. And now it was August of 2001 and we had been here for just over eleven years.

Carrie Ann looked over at the pictures we had framed and set on a cedar bookshelf. Dad went over and brought a couple of them back. He showed her a picture of Rose in her white wedding dress. She was holding a small bouquet of white flowers and she had a big smile on her face and looked happy.

Carrie Ann asked me how long I had called Rose by her first name and I told her she was my father's former wife. I had stopped thinking of her as my mother a few years ago. Carrie Ann frowned at me and told me that was some wrong thinking on my part.

There was some peach ice cream in the freezer and we finished it off. We sat at the old kitchen table talking for an hour or so after dinner was finished. Mainly, my father talking to Carrie Ann. Talking about team roping with Vern. Horses he had owned. Swimming in the Llano River.

Carrie Ann said she was glad she swam for fun now. She would get in the lap pool and swim different strokes and different distances and if she felt like missing a day or two, she did it without feeling guilty.

When we got up to leave, she told my father she was glad she got to meet him. She had never sat down and talked to a real cowboy before. She told him I did not count because I was too young and she had heard from Jeremy that I could not throw a rope worth a darn.

Dad said ranching was changing and you could get by fine nowadays without being a great roper. He said I was as good a hand as any. He told her what set me apart was that I was good with colts and young horses.

When we left to go home, Dad followed us out of the house with three Fat Tires. He said, "Now, Carrie Ann, two of these are for Vern. More than two puts me to sleep real fast."

I took Carrie Ann home. We sat in the truck and talked for a few minutes but I was way too shy to try to kiss her. She told me I needed to change my attitude toward Rose. She called her "my mother" instead of Rose. I knew she was right. I still resented her not even coming back and trying to make it with Dad and I on the ranch. Carrie Ann said I could resent it all I wanted to but Rose was still my mother and by my own accounts she had taught me to read before I was five and she had been a good, gentle person with me. I did not argue with her about any of that because I knew she was right.

I started bringing Carrie Ann home from school most days. Sometimes she would change and drive over to the Circle S and ride with me in the afternoons.

Things were pleasant. I was a junior in high school and had a pretty girl and a nice home life and a few friends and some good horses to ride. I even had seven one hundred dollar bills rat holed in a pocket of my bill fold. Savings from money I earned. No one had to give me money. Things were easy with Carrie Ann. I knew she was going to college in less than two years. There was never any doubt about it. She would be gone off to Palo Alto in late August of 2003. But it just worked out between us.

Simple as that. She liked to ride horses with me and we talked a lot. I showed her how to recognize all the cactus on the ranch. Cholla, prickly pear, ocotillo, saguaro, barrel, hedgehog, beehive, and fish hook. When I was just starting to ride, Iris Snider would take me out for a ride after school and point out all the plants and animals she saw.

Iris had night blooming Cereus plants in pots near the front porch of her home and a climbing white rose bush near the front gate. Yellow jasmine grew on a lattice on the east side of the ranch house. Iris showed Carrie Ann her flowers and plants. And she pointed out all the ones I had planted for her. She kept rose bushes in pots that were tall and heavy. It took two people to slide them around in the yard when Iris took a notion that the roses were not getting enough sun or were getting too much sun. The two people who moved them most of the times were me and Jimmy Dale.

Iris told Carrie Ann about Jimmy Dale and me fighting. Our punishment had been weeding her flowers and planting new flowers. We all laughed and I told Iris and Carrie Ann I missed seeing Jimmy Dale and Iris said he was trying to run his ranch at the age of eighteen and he was not getting much help from anyone except Davey Waddell and that was a hit and miss deal at best since Davey couldn't hire enough help to run his own spread the way he wanted it done.

Carrie Ann wanted to know everything about the ranch. The plants, the animals. She called it the flora and fauna. I said plants and animals.

The second week in September, Dad held me out of school. We had had some nice rain during the late summer and a third hay cutting was waiting to be harvested. I threw hay bales on the long trailer. I stacked hay bales in the hay barn. I slept hard each night. I would drive the tractor that pulled the trailer for the first hour or two of the day until Iris came and took over. I still weighed a little less than a hundred and fifty pounds. I was six foot one and almost six foot two.

Iris walked the mile or so to the hay field every day. One morning, I saw her topping a rise and walking toward us. When she saw us, she started trotting toward Sherman who was on the ground throwing hay to my dad and a hand we hired just to help with the hay. I stopped the tractor and got off and she ran right past me. She was crying and I got scared. I had never seen her cry before.

She ran to Sherman and buried her head in his shoulder. She was shaking and sobbing. I just stood there at the front of the trailer. Dad jumped off the trailer and took his hat off and started to say something, but we both just stood there.

In a few minutes she quit crying and turned to us and said, "They crashed two planes into the twin towers at the World Trade Center in New York City. Thousands of people are trapped and dying or are already dead. Thousands. It was a terrorist attack. It had to be. Who else would do it?"

The tractor was still running. Sherman asked me to turn the tractor off. Then he said, "Now, let's finish this load. Iris, if you feel like it, drive. If you do not you can ride on the back of the trailer until we finish this load and then we will go back to the house and see what this is all about."

Iris drove. I threw bales on the trailer. Dad and Sherman stacked. The extra hand was from Nogales. His name was Raul and he threw bales. More bales than any of us. He was barrel chested and strong. He was stronger than me. He threw more bales up than me and he never broke a sweat 'til around two in the afternoon. He did not talk. Sometimes he whistled a few bars of a song I was not familiar with. Raul was just a few years older than me. He was stronger and more efficient. The heavy bales got the best of me sometimes. I was almost six foot two and weighed about a hundred and fifty pounds but it was mainly arms and legs. Sometimes I would let the heavy bales get me off balance and I would lose my timing when I was throwing them on the trailer. The result would be an off balance lunge.

Raul moved in an economical way. He bent his legs when he picked a bale up and used his lower body to give him power when he threw the bale on the trailer. I tried it but I could never get the timing right.

When we had the trailer stacked high with hay, Sherman said, "That's a load, let's go on back."

After we unloaded the hay, we all walked back to the ranch house. Raul hung back. He did not know what to do. Sherman turned around and said, "Come on, Raul, you need to know about this just like the rest of us."

Sherman led us all into the den. Iris had stopped crying and was fixing iced tea and ham sandwiches for us. Raul and I stood. Dad and Sherman sat on the couch. The TV networks had the whole thing. Slow motion and real time shots. Both planes and both towers. The estimates on the casualties kept going up. It was obviously a well-planned attack.

After an hour or so, we went on back to the hay field. Raul told me he had a brother a few years younger than him that he knew would enlist the next day. He said he was too old for the war and his family needed his brother to stay in Nogales and work. Nothing much was said for the rest of the day.

We finally got all the hay out of the field and stacked in the hay barn. No more haying for me until next June. Sherman told Raul he could use him some more since I would be in school until late in May. Raul said he would be back the next morning. By the end of the week, Sherman told him to move into the bunk house. He was full time.

The morning after 9-11 I went back to school. Carrie Ann had called me early and asked me to pick her up. She said she was nervous and did not want to drive. I picked her up and we went on to school. No one was showing out in the halls or flirting with girls. People gathered in small groups and talked or just went straight on into their first period class rooms. On the ride to school, neither Carrie Ann nor I had much to say.

The first period was study hall. Mr. Crawley called the roll and then said he wanted to talk to us today and he wanted us to talk to him. Not as a teacher but as a fellow American citizen. He said he was sad today. Not for himself, but for the people who had died in New York and Pennsylvania and for their families.

Then he said when he was walking down the halls this morning, he started worrying about us. The students. He said he knew there would be reprisals by our government and he understood the necessity of it. He just could not help hoping that none of us would lose our lives in future years. Or any members of our families.

He said he had no military experience but he could see yesterday's events as the starting point of a protracted military involvement by our country. He said that the United States had a voluntary military now. No draft. Men and women served side by side in many instances.

Mr. Crawley asked for a show of hands for everyone who had thought about entering military service after they had heard and watched yesterday's tragic events.

All of the boys and most of the girls raised their hands. Carrie Ann raised her hand. I was surprised. When I asked her about it later, she said military service was compulsory in Israel and she thought it would be a good idea here but she knew it was impractical and unworkable in our country.

He then told us about how our government had rounded up the Japanese families in California after Pearl Harbor and put them in camps until after the war ended. He said he mentioned that only to caution us about jumping to conclusions and being part of a mob mentality.

He leaned against his desk and was quiet for a few minutes. He was my favorite teacher. He wore old scuffed up black ropers, tan khakis, and a dark blue golf shirt.

He said, "I noticed that Mary has been very nice and considerate to our new student, Carrie Ann. I also know that the principal asked her to do this. A simple act of hospitality. Now, I want all of you to think about this hypothetical situation. Suppose this morning, the principal called you into her office. And asked you to show a new student around. A gifted and intelligent student. You all would agree to do it, right?"

We all nodded or said yes.

"OK, so now you are on the hook to do it. And suppose the principal introduces you to the new student and he is a nervous, and not overly friendly Arab. From Palestine. Or Syria. Or Jordan. Or Iraqi. Or Philadelphia. A second generation American. Yet an Arab. An Islamic. A Muslim. "

"Take it further. A girl. With her head covered. Nervous eyes and little to say. A long flowing dress."

"Just think about it for a few minutes. You, the principal, and this new student. Today. September 12, 2001."

"Jeremy, what about you? Gonna invite the new student to sit with you and Mary and Lim and Carrie Ann for lunch? Maybe give him half of your sandwich. What would you tell the principal, Jeremy?"

"No. That is what I would say and no I wouldn't give him or her part of my goddamn sandwich or the sweat off my balls if he or she was burning in a fire."

"Would you harass them? Call them names? Knock them down in the halls? Throw things at them?"

"No, I wasn't raised to do that sort of thing. And the rest of us wasn't either, but I can pick who I associate with. And that is my business."

"Even if you later learned the student's parents fled Iraq to avoid being killed by Sadaam Hussein?"

Jeremy just looked down at his desk and would not answer.

"And now, Mr. Lim Couch. What about you?"

I said, "Not today, not today. I woke up last night thinking about people jumping out of a burning building. I could see them in my sleep. But I am like Jeremy. I would not harass them. I just would not have anything to do with them. There are people in school that look down on me and call me a shit-kicker because I am a cowboy and want to stay one after I leave here. That is their choice. Fine with me. But I should be able to make my choices, also. But if I learned more about him and found out more about his family, I would probably be subject to change. I just can not think clearly today. I can tell you that. This was the first morning in my life I have seen my Dad mad at the breakfast table. Not ever before. But today, he said he was still angry and needed to get on a horse and move some cattle and get all of this out of his mind."

Mary raised her right hand. Her eyes were moist and she stood up and put her left hand on the back of the desk in front of her.

Mr. Crawley said, "Alright, Mary, what is it?"

Mary said, "How fair is it of you or anyone to expect us to think clearly this morning? I am like Lim. Let me have some time."

Mr. Crawley said, "When I was leaving this morning, I heard a preliminary report that said among the dead were American Muslims. People of Arabic descent. Think of the irony. Some one escapes from Saddam Hussein's atrocities, takes his family to the Land of the Free, settles in Patagonia or Sonoita, Arizona and is ostracized by his neighbours. And blamed for the crimes of those he fled from. There is no Arab student in the principal's office. We are as we were yesterday. But none can ever be the same again. None of us. Mr. Lim Couch has returned, with a sun burn, from the hay fields of the Circle S and we all have this tragedy, this attack, to deal with. Now despite Jeremy's bluster, I suspect if he was confronted with a situation like this and an Arab student came to our school, Jeremy would gradually adopt an attitude of tolerance as I think almost all of you would. But as Mary has said, today is special. A time to grieve. But in subsequent days, I only ask that you think through your decisions on all matters that will come up relating to yesterday's heart rending tragedy. Do not get caught up in hysteria. Listen to your heart but use your minds. As Jeremy said, he was not raised up to be a bully or a bad citizen. And with that, I will let you have a few minutes of peace and quiet to reflect on what has been said this morning and what happened yesterday."

Mr. Crawley sat down at his desk and opened a book and began reading. He did not look up again until the bell rang for second period.

At lunch, Carrie Ann, Mary, Jeremy and I sat together and no one ate much. Carrie Ann asked me if she could come home with me and ride Davey out in the pastures by herself. I said sure.

Sherman had asked me to ride down to the pasture we had the Criollos in and check on some steers. He wanted me to count the ones I felt were ready to go to market. My dad, Sherman, and me were going to drive them up to a holding pen on Sunday and next week, they would be taken to Marana to be sold.

When school was out, Carrie Ann and I went on back to the Circle S and she saddled Davey and rode west through the pastures toward the Cienega Creek and the Whetstones. There was a breeze out of the northwest bringing cold air and low, dark clouds to the ranch.

I saddled Little Molly and let Carrie Ann and Davey get out of sight before I left the barn. I headed south at an angle across the nearest pasture and when I hit the Creek, I looked around north but I could not see Davey and Carrie Ann. I followed the creek south. Little Molly was hitting a good, smooth lick. A nice slow trot. My reins were loose and I let her have her head.

Sherman kept the Criollos in a big pasture at the south end of the ranch. The cattle had plenty of water from the creek but the pasture was hilly with few grassy meadows. A small canyon, barely a mile long, lay west of the creek near the southern boundary of the ranch.

It was not a wide canyon. At its widest, it was probably three hundred yards across and at its narrowest, maybe a hundred. It was home to some of the older cows and their calves. It seemed that when the Criollo cows got past the age of six and had calved a few times, they got more ornery.

The most contrary of the whole bunch stayed up in the canyon and were reluctant to leave. I rode slowly up an old game trail to the end of the canyon. Molly picked her way. I kept the reins slack and leaned over the saddle horn. Molly kept her head down. She needed her head free to help her keep her balance on the narrow and rocky trail.

I only saw a few steers and a bunch of old cows. Once I was out of the canyon, I found some nice steers that Sherman would want to carry to market next week. It had taken me a long time to go up the canyon and back, so it was getting late when I closed the last pasture gate and headed on back to the barn.

As I was closing the last gate, I looked up at the sky. The wind had died down and the clouds in the west had turned from black to red. It looked like the sky was on fire. Orange, red, and pink clouds formed a sunset to remember. I looked for Carrie Ann as I approached the barn but I could not see her.

Sherman was in the barn. He was feeding Ray. He told me Dad had rode out to find Carrie Ann. There was still a few minutes of light left. I unsaddled Little Molly, fed and watered her, and told Sherman I had counted eleven steers that I thought were ready to go to the sale barn.

I asked him about the old cows that hung back in the canyon most of the time. He said they were harmless but he knew they should be sold. A cow gets past the time she can calve and it is time she goes to the sale barn. Sherman knew that. He and Dad were the ones that had taught me that rule. But Sherman had a soft spot for the old Criollos with their long horns, bad dispositions, and lanky builds. He said they reminded him of when he was growing up and most ranches still had not switched over to Angus or Hereford purebreds.

The sun had just gone behind the Santa Ritas when Dad and Carrie Ann rode into sight. As she was unsaddling Davey, I noticed her eyes were red and watery. Dad was quiet as usual. He took the saddle off Davey's back and hung it up in the tack room.

Carrie Ann sat on a hay bale after she brushed Davey and put him in his stall. I had already put his feed and water out. Dad came over and said, "Son, Carrie Ann is eating with us tonight. Her special request. Tamales and chili. Vern will join us, I am sure. I can see him sitting down in front of his trailer. I have a nice piece of sirloin marinating in the refrigerator. How about you going on down and light the coals for the grill for me. I got to talk to Sherman a few minutes. Carrie Ann, can you set the table for us? Might as well put a plate out for Sherman. Iris is in Tucson for the Symphony and she will be back tomorrow."

We went on down to the house and started supper. Sherman, Vern, and Dad came down a few minutes later. Dad grilled a big piece of sirloin. He, Sherman, and Vern stood around the grill and drank Dos Equis Amber. Carrie Ann and I warmed two cans of tamales and two cans of chili with beans on the stove. We had everything ready when they brought the meat in.

Dad sliced the sirloin and then we all sat down and ate. Carrie Ann said, "I invited myself to dinner. Tamales and chili just seemed right after my ride. It is turning cold. For sure."

Dad went to the refrigerator and brought me a Dos Equis.

"Won't hurt you none to have a cold beer with your meal, son."

Carrie Ann and I were quiet during dinner. The men talked about the price of beef, football, buying a new and bigger tractor for the ranch, and whether Iris would call before supper was over. She called a little after eight.

We had just finished supper and Dad was spooning out strawberry ice cream for everyone. I answered the phone and Iris asked me what I was doing and I said eating supper and told her who all was there and she asked if we had any vegetables on the table and I said beans and she laughed and told me to tell Sherman to come home early for supper tomorrow no matter what he was doing because she was going to stop by Tucson Tamale Company on her way out of Tucson and buy some beef tamales and some green corn tamales. I said yes ma'am and she told me to tell him to lay off the beer and booze tonight. I told him about the tamales and lunch tomorrow but I left out the part about laying off the booze.

When we were through eating, Carrie Ann and I cleared the table and put the dirty dishes in the dishwasher. I turned the old Sears dishwasher on and it shook for a few seconds and then settled down to a low, calming drone.

The others were in our small den. Dad was building a fire and Vern and Sherman were both trying to light cigars off the same match. Vern was holding the match and Dad was breaking up kindling and laughing at them. Soon the mesquite logs caught and red and orange flames flickered in the fireplace.

Carrie Ann said she needed to get on home, so I started for the door. She went over to my Dad and hugged him and said Thanks and when she caught up with me on the porch, I could see her eyes were red again. She still did not want to talk much but we kissed hard and for a long time when we got to her house. She held onto me and hugged me when we were on her porch.

When I was driving home, the wind picked up and the clouds were dark and low in the sky. As I walked in the house, I could not smell any rain but the wind was rattling the windows in the house and one of Vern's lawn chairs in front of his trailer had blown over. The big mesquite tree that stood near our porch was low and wide but there were branches dipping in the wind.

When I was inside the house, I sat down on the floor next to the fireplace. Vern and Sherman were still smoking their cigars and drinking Evan Williams bourbon. Vern had brought a pint down with him. His contribution to dinner. Sherman was giving him a hard time about his whiskey not being as good as Dad's. I had snuck a sip out of a bottle of Evan Williams Vern had left at the house a few months ago and I thought it was mighty good. Dad was grinning and sipping his whiskey.

Sherman said he would be polite and finish his shot of Vern's whiskey but he wanted to cap the night off with a shot of Dad's good whiskey.

I hung around the fire for a while and nodded off for a little while. Vern woke me up saying, "Lim, get up. Look out the window."

It was snowing. In September. I had never seen snow this early on the Circle S. It only snowed for two hours or so. The clouds drifted south and the sky was clear again. It was only a light dusting. It would be gone by noon tomorrow. Not enough to shut school down. Most years you would only see snow on Apache Peak or French Joe Peak in the Whetstones.

Sherman said, "No use in putting a horse out in this tomorrow. It will melt by noon or early afternoon and the ground will be slick and a little soupy for a day or so. We can go into Nogales and eat lunch and then go to the feed store. That will be enough for tomorrow. By the time we unload the feed, I will be ready for supper. Bet it did not snow in Tucson. Maybe up on Mr. Lemmon. But not down in Tucson."

Dad told about how he and his mother had went into Austin one cold December day to buy Christmas presents and they had been caught in a snow storm coming home. He said the snow came down so hard they had to stop in Burnett. That was about a hard hour's drive from Llano. Finally, when they got home, they had to park the car down at the foot of the driveway because their ranch house was on a hill and his mother was scared to drive up the hill. He and his stepfather fell down bringing packages up the hill. He said his mother made snow ice cream that night. He said it was thinner than regular ice cream but it was good and you could taste and smell vanilla in the ice cream. He said he wished his mother was still alive and could make us all snow ice cream tonight. He had never figured out how she did it.

He laughed and said they had a white Christmas. On a ranch just outside Lllano, Texas. The only one he had ever had. He said

Christmas in Vietnam was just another day since he was on patrol for his first two Vietnam Christmases and in the hospital his last year in the Nam.

He said, "Enough about Vietnam" and went in the kitchen and spooned out some strawberry ice cream and poured himself some coffee. After Sherman and Vern left, we sat by the fire and drank hot coffee. I asked Dad if the World Trade Center tragedy was what had upset Carrie Ann.

He poured a half a shot of Wild Turkey in a glass and sat it down on the arm of his chair. He took a while to answer my question. The fire was dying down and I put three small mesquite logs on the embers of the fire and punched the embers with the old, long black poker and watched the new fire take hold.

He said, "First of all, what we said was in confidence. She trusts me. For some reason. The way it is with kids. They have things to say that need to be said and listened to. But they do not want to tell their parents. You talk to Iris about things that you do not tell me about. So, I will try to break it down for you without betraying her confidences. Carrie Ann is carrying around a lot of guilt. She knows she is rich. At least her parents are. She remembers going to Kansas during the summer or at Christmas and seeing the people on the ranch who worked hard and drove old ratty cars and drifted from job to job. She wants to give back to society. Her way. Going to Stanford and then to Harvard or Yale Law. Her goal is to help save and preserve the rivers in our country. We got some scenic ones. The Llano was nice. The Little Colorado down near Marble Falls is beautiful. The Frying Pan. The Deschutes in Oregon. The San Juan. And there are a lot more. A lot more.

"She doesn't understand what happened yesterday. The evil being done in the name of religion. Throwing God's name into the mix. The mix being death, shattered dreams, attacks on innocent citizens. The mix. Add politics. Add scare tactics. Add indecisive politicians all over the world. And add just mean ass ignorant people. And they are everywhere. It is hard for a good person like Carrie Ann to confront evil. Most folks do not talk about it to their children. You can recognize and identify it, but how do you explain it. Ignorance, poverty, and hatred all play a part but ignorant and poor people are not evil. So I can't explain evil."

He took a sip of whiskey and a healthy slug of coffee.

"I did a piss poor job of explaining things. I left Vietnam out of our talk. I am trying not to ever talk about it anymore. It does no good and serves no purpose. But tonight I let it slip into my thoughts and conversation. I told her to concentrate on her goals. And one more thing. She loves it here. The mountains, the pastures, the horses, the cattle. She has had her mind set on Palo Alto and Stanford for the last few years and now she is here and happy. She described herself as a spoiled rich kid.

"She says she wants to blot yesterday's tragedies out of her mind. Ignore it all. But she said she knows when she goes home tonight, she will sit in front of the television with her father and mother and watch CNN until she falls asleep."

I told my dad I did not want to see any more of the news about 9-11. I knew those people died for nothing at the hands of a bunch of cowardly terrorists. What else was there to know?

The Arizona Daily Star was on the kitchen table. Dad got up and brought it to me. He said, "Son, I think it is time you started reading this. Might not be the best newspaper in the land but it is a good place to start. You need to keep up with what's happening in this old mean ass world. A lot of it will sicken you. Sometimes I just give myself a vacation from the newspaper. But you got to try to keep up. Vern helps me. He has the Internet up there in that little Airstream. A personal computer is what he calls it. He says I should get us one."

I told him I did not care one way or the other. I just wanted to train horses. Start colts at halter. Break 'em to saddle. Make a good using horse out of a two or three year old.

Dad said, "When I got back from the Nam, I just wanted to find a peaceful part of the West to live in. I found it. But Lim, you are young. A lot of country out there. I think a man that can handle a horse will always have a chance to make a living. But Lim, look around. Ranches being sold off and made into ranchettes. The west is gradually getting chopped up. Absentee owners fencing in land and not growing nothing or raising cattle or keeping horses. Like Vern says, "The billionaires is buying out the millionaires. They buy the land up, get bored with ranch life in a few years and sell it and buy a big condo in Maui."

I said, "I will take my chances. It is worth the gamble. To live out here and work outdoors year round. It is worth it. Now if I was in Wyoming or Montana where the snow is four feet deep at times, then I might want out. But I want to stay around here. I would like to learn from a real trainer for a year or so and then come back here and help you and Sherman around the ranch and train colts and young horses."

We stayed up until the fire was down to coals. I read the paper and Dad watched CNN and Fox News. He kept switching back and forth between the two channels. He had sprung for DirectTV a year or so ago. We had put the satellite dish on the roof together and Vern had stayed in the house and helped us line it up. Between the paper and CNN and Fox News it was a somber end to a long day.

I forced myself to read the paper every day after that night. I would read it right before I went to bed. At first it was all so random and it was hard for me to get excited when oil in Venezuela went up a dollar a barrel. Or Tom Cruise had a new girlfriend. But gradually, I saw the sense of what my father had said. Carrie Ann said I needed to connect with the rest of the world.

During the week, I would get up early, feed the horses, come back to the house, eat some breakfast, and then pick up Carrie Ann and carry her to school. She always burst out of her front door. Pretty red hair streaming behind her. Long legs striding sexily towards me. Her face always so soft and inviting in the early morning light.

She would get in the truck, kiss me on the cheek, put her left hand on my right thigh, and smile at me. She always asked about my Dad. She would say, "So how is Dewey Couch?" She liked saying his full name. Some nights she came over and sat outside with Vern, my Dad, and me. Sometimes, we would sit in front of Vern's trailer.

Vern always had a story. You didn't need a television with Vern around. He always dressed his stories up a little, I am sure. But he had such an earnest manner, I always took his stories for gospel. He cleaned them up when Carrie Ann was around.

The stories were about our neighbors. Our friends. Ranchers. Beauty Parlor owners. Café cooks and waitresses. Lots of running off to Phoenix and Tucson in the middle of the night stories. Always told slowly. Once he got home, took his first drink, ate his supper, and sat in his lawn chair outside his front door, he was calm. And his voice was deep. You just trusted what he said. I still remember a lot of his stories.

Mike Sprole's wife over near Benson caught him with his eight year old's Sunday School teacher in the old run down motel next to the Silver Saddle in Tucson. Mike was a rancher and a school teacher in Benson. His spread was south of Benson and he ran a bunch of grade cows on a poor stretch of land. Vern said he was ready to quit shoeing his horses, but his wife talked Mike into paying up his bill. Mike's wife was Pearl. Vern said when Pearl got through with Mike, he would not be a rancher any more unless he won the lottery after the divorce. The Sunday School teacher took Mike in for a while and then run him off.

Now Mike was living in a rental trailer up near where Dad, Rose, and I had lived when I was a kid.

Jim Landis was in the first stages of Alzheimer's and his wife and his grown children were debating about putting him in a home or trying to care for him on his ranch over near Rio Rico. Jim was right at eighty and was known for being one tough guy when he was young. He had come back from the Pacific in 1946 and hung his Marine Uniform up and put his jeans and boots on and followed the rodeo circuit for a few lean years. He was a roper and a steer wrestler. But the money was slim. Even when you won. Not like now. Now you can make a nice check at any decent rodeo. So he came on back to the family ranch and kept it going all these years. At a profit. Vern said. He had some good grass and enough water and he could fix any engine on his place and ride any horse in Southern Arizona. And now he was not able to say his kids' names. Or remember where he kept his car keys.

Davey Waddel and his wife were leasing some more land and had just bought two young Hereford bulls and a nice young sorrel brood mare with Doc Bar breeding. They stopped having kids after the second one. Davey's place showed signs of making a profit each year. Vern said every time he went to shoe Davey's horses, there was a new piece of machinery, a new brood mare or bull, or a new truck. He had even fixed up the bunk house and hired a full time cowboy. Vern said the new cowboy had just retired from the Air Force after twenty five years and he worked hard for a fat man and drank a lot of tequila at nights. Sitting up in the bunk house watching wrestling on television and drinking tequila. Vern said that was the life he had chosen. Drinking up his retirement in a bunkhouse.

One night, Carrie Ann told a story. I already knew about it but Carrie told it better. She said one school night in October, Jeremy showed up at Mary's house. Old Doctor Siegfried answered the door with a glass of scotch in his hand. Mary was in her room. Jeremy asked to see her and Doc Siegfried said that was fine. He called out to Mary that the football player was here and wanted to see her. Mary came out and Jeremy stammered some. He does that when he gets nervous. Which is seldom.

Jeremy and Mary went out on the front porch and sat down in rocking chairs. Jeremy asked her if she would go out with him. She asked about Jody. Jody was hands down the hottest girl in Patagonia High School. Jeremy said she was nice but she was boring. And he liked to talk to Mary. Then he said if she went out with him, she couldn't nag him like she did now in the lunch room every day.

Carrie Ann said that Mary had told her that Jeremy talked so low she could barely hear him and she realized how shy and unsure of himself he really was. She went out with him but she was making sure he kept up with his studies. He came over to the Siegfried place a lot of nights and they would do school work and just talk. Talk about school. 9-11. George Bush. Iraq. Israel. And Texas A and M.

And Tommy Crumby. Tommy was nineteen. He was a teammate of Jeremy's on the football team. He played all the special teams and was a strong safety. And a good one. But he had been held back twice in school. He was not going to college. So he joined the Marines on the Saturday after 9-11. He was Jeremy's best friend on the football team and now he was gone to somewhere in North Carolina for combat training.

Carrie Ann said she thought Jeremy got scared after 9-11 and needed somebody to talk to that had some sense. Someone his own age. Somebody who would help him understand things. Now Jeremy and Mary are both talking about going to Texas A and M. Mary to get ready for Veterinary School and Jeremy to play football and get a degree in Agricultural Studies.

I said that Jeremy had told me he wanted to go to Texas A and M and then play pro football. After the third year in pro football, most contracts are up and are either renegotiated or the player is released. He can sign with another team or his first team. Depending on the terms of his first contract. Jeremy had told me he wanted to invest his money so he would never be poor. If he could be a first round draft choice, he would get a decent signing bonus.

He was going to plow some of it back into the family ranch. Buy his dad a new hay baler. Four or five good young bulls. New furniture for his folks. A couple of good cutting horses for his dad. Michelin tires for his dad's truck. A Lexus for his mother.

After I said all of that, I shut up and listened to Carrie Ann. Vern was asking her about how she planned to save all of those rivers when there was so many new people crowding up the whole country and so much money to be made from mining copper and drilling, and finding, oil.

Carrie said, "You sue the bastards. Fight 'em hard in the courts. Get injunctions. Try to get in Federal Court. Ask for punitive damages. Put your case in front of a jury and tell them it is their planet and they can sit idly by and let it be polluted and ruined or fight to keep the rivers pristine and beautiful. Be the best fucking lawyer in the courtroom. The very best."

Vern laughed and said, "Sue the bastards. I like that."

Then he asked Carrie Ann if she thought Jeremy and Mary would make it. A solid, good marriage in the future. Carrie Ann smiled and said, "Yes. Yes, I do. If Jeremy knows enough to trade up from Jody to Mary, I think they will make it."

Vern took a drink of whiskey. He and Dad were drinking Old Forester. Dad only drank a shot or half a shot a night. Vern drank too much sometimes. He would stumble when he got out of his old green lawn chair and stepped up into his trailer. He would always grab the door and steady himself. He never fell. But it scared me. Iris worried about him. I heard her tell Sherman and Dad one night that Vern was a functional alcoholic. He would drink too much but he always got up and went to work.

Seeing weakness or vulnerability in someone you looked up to was part of growing up. I knew that. But Vern lived alone. By choice. Dad and I were about his only friends. Sure, he shod a lot of horses and had lots of stories he told about his customers and their friends, but in the end, it was Dad and me that sat out in front of his trailer in rickety lawn chairs and talked about the weather, baseball, football, horses, and life on the Circle S. Vern made a lot of money but he never used any of it to buy some false teeth. He just let the gaps where he had lost the two front teeth stay there. Neglected and forgotten.

Carrie Ann and I spent a lot of time together. Driving back and forth to and from school. Riding horses in the afternoon when I had time. Eating dinner with Dad. I had some colts I was starting under halter and one two year old I was riding. The money helped. I saved most of it.

On the weekends, we usually got together on Friday and Saturday nights. Her father said Sunday was for family and she usually spent part of it with me and then went home in the middle of the afternoon.

In October, one Friday night when her parents and her little brother were in Phoenix to see an art exhibit at the Heard Museum, I spent the night at her place.

We swam in the pool and drank champagne and ate fried chicken and later on we went to bed together. I was nervous and I remember the moon light shining through the bedroom window. Her bedroom was almost as big as our house. When it was over and we were lying in bed together, I will always remember her talking soft to me and saying,

"Lim, my Lim." All the time she was talking so soft, she was running her nails across my chest and kissing me on the neck and mouth.

I went back home the next morning and helped my dad and Sherman take down some irrigation pipes and move them to a shed so they would not get damaged during the winter. That afternoon, I rode a new grey gelding Sherman wanted me to get started under saddle. The horse was just past two and was skittish. After about a half hour we crossed the Cienega and headed east along the pasture fence. He settled down and started paying attention. He caught his leads and I would take him off the fence and ride him in circles and get him to change leads. He was still not ready to back through a figure eight. That has always been my big test. If you can get a horse to consistently back through a figure eight, you can teach him most anything. But you had better not crowd a young horse. It is easy to forget that a young horse is just over or around two years old. It just takes time for them to take in everything you may want them to do. If you do crowd him, you will have a sour horse. And a sour horse is useless.

I took a break and sat down on a rock that was atop a little ridge and looked east. I ate some Vienna sausages and crackers and a slice of cheddar cheese I had found in the refrigerator. A fine lunch. Topped off with a warm Barq's Root Beer, a bag of salty peanuts, and a few Fig Newtons.

I rode the grey on back to the barn. Just a walk and a slow trot. That was all I asked of him. I could tell he was getting used to me and was settling down. I would need to start him on opening gates and backing up soon. It just took time and it would take more now that the winter was coming on. Best thing to gentle a new horse down was ninety degree weather.

Heat takes a lot of the spunk out of a new horse. Now and for the next few months, there was going to be chilly days. Some with a lot of wind. Wind distracts horses. Especially young horses. Sometimes they panic in high winds. Mostly, they just don't pay attention.

I liked the grey a lot. His owner was Lacey Rand. She lived in Tucson and had bought the grey when he was a weanling. Ms. Rand was in her late forties and was still a looker. Brown, short hair, big green eyes, and a warm smile and when she looked at you, she kept her eyes on you as she talked. She was in real estate sales. She heard about me from someone in Tubac who knew about me starting Socks under halter.

Lacey had a nice black Dodge Ram pickup and a good two horse trailer with a dressing room and good tires. She brought the grey down one Sunday in August. She told me his name was Gus. He was a short coupled horse and he had a short strong neck. She wanted me to get him trained to be a good using horse.

She said she had a forty acre lot at the east end of Speedway in Tucson that was a quarter of a mile from the Saguaro National Forest. She wanted a gentle, easy to handle horse. She went on trail rides all over the west. Her last horse was a sorrel gelding that was twenty two. She had kept him through two divorces. And now he was retired. She said she still rode him but she did not want to take him on any week long trail rides in the Sawtooth Mountains.

With his short, muscular neck, it would have been wrong to try to set his head in the classic western pleasure way. I did get him to quit nosing out. I used a curb bit and a long shank on it and he would tuck his nose in. It took a while but the curb bit had a low port and I did not try to outmuscle Gus. Once he got the idea and was comfortable moving with his nose tucked in, he was fine. Took a few hours, though.

He was strong. Heavily muscled in the shoulders and hips. He would have probably done well with cattle but I just rode him in the pastures as much as I could and got him to change leads and stop and back up. He was barely fifteen hands tall.

Sherman came up to the horse barn one night in November, just after Thanksgiving and told me he wanted me to clear the colts out that I had under halter by the end of the year. He said he was going to get me more two year olds to start under saddle after the first of the year. He could charge more for the two year olds under saddle and we would both make more money. That was fine with me but I would miss the colts.

Lacey Rand came to get Gus right before Christmas. She and I rode out in the pastures, crossed the Cienega, and went up the long climb to the far mesa on the Circle S. She had good hands. And she listened and asked good questions. When we were coming home, it was getting late in the afternoon. I asked her to back him up through a figure eight.

Gus did it perfectly on the third try. I told her to rest him a minute or two then ride him out a hundred yards at a trot and turn him and bring him back at a short lope and stop him when she got to where Davey and I were. Things went smoothly. When she got back to Davey and me, I told her to neck rein him in a wide circle.

After a few tries, Gus was fine. I asked her to back him through one more figure eight. This time, it was tighter and he went through it a little faster.

We rode on back to the barn and she unsaddled him and put a halter on him and we cooled him down by walking out in the horse pasture and back to the barn. I told her I hated to see him go and I asked her if she could ride him at least four times a week. She said she could. I told her not to lunge him in a round pen. I feel that is the easiest way to sour a horse.

She and I walked him down to her trailer and she loaded him with no trouble. We walked back up to the barn. Dad and Sherman were drinking beer. Lacey got a plastic can and turned it up and sat on it. She wrote out a check and handed it to me. It was made out to me and it was for two hundred dollars. She said, "A little bonus. Christmas is coming up but I think I got my money's worth. I might bring him back for you to tune up from time to time if I know I am going to be busy and can't ride him."

She looked at Dad and then looked back at me. She told my Dad, "I assume this is your son. Don't you ever feed him? "

Dad said, "Why sure I feed him. He eats more than I do and doesn't put on a pound."

Lacey said, "Well, it is obvious he got his looks from his mother."

Dad laughed and said, "You are right about that."

She said, "Well, I would ask you two rude bastards for one of those beers you got in the cooler but I need to get on back to Tucson with my horse."

Sherman said, "Send us some business. Lim is going to be starting two year olds from now on. And if you want him to tune your grey up, you can have two weeks free a year if you send us some of that Tucson business. 'Cept, I got to charge you just a little for board. Lim likes young horses. You got to watch these horses that have been started by someone else. Lots of 'em are ruined. Just plain ruined. Either by the owners or trainers or both. There is little you can do for them. A waste of our time and their money."

Lacey Rand sent us some business right after Christmas. We got two young horses from two of her friends in Tucson. Davey Waddell sent me one of his two year olds and I took one more from a rancher near Sierra Vista. I had four horses to train, school work, and Carrie Ann. I was busy. I started leaving school early some and not going at all some. I did not get behind in my school work but I had some late nights spent reading, doing homework, and writing papers.

I would stay out of school and ride two of the horses for three or four hours out in the pastures. It paid off. All four got plenty of riding time. I hit it lucky with those first four horses. They were all out of good stock and had not been spoiled as a colt.

I was real busy during calving season in February and early March. Sherman had traded for some nice new heifers last year and the first calves were due. Most of the trouble you have with a cow birthing a calf is when the cow has the first calf. We had about twenty or so cows birthing their first calf that year and Dad, Vern, Raul, and I did most of the work. And a lot of it was at night and some of it stretched into the first few hours of the day. One calf took almost six hours to finally show its head. One foot was turned under his stomach and one foot was stuck out in front of his head. Dad and I stood on opposite sides and pulled the cow's vulva apart as best we could and Vern got his hands inside and pulled the calf out. Vern was the oldest but he was also the strongest.

Once calving was over, I could concentrate on the two year olds. I thought they were just about ready by the end of April. We branded the first week in May. It was a lot easier now than it had been in the recent past. The big change was the use of a calving table. Instead of having to rope and tie each calf, you drove them in a chute with their mothers and ran them through a long chute.

The calving table looks like part of the chute except it is metal. It has two sides and when the calf steps between the two sides, you squeeze the two sides and then flip the calf. You can brand, castrate, vaccinate, and tag the calf in just a few minutes. Some ranches use an electric branding iron. The Circle S just gets Vern to fire some coals up and keep the branding iron hot.

I helped do about every job except branding. Nobody touched the branding iron except Vern. We branded on the left hip. A circle with an S inside it. The brand had been registered with the State of Arizona by Sherman's grandfather back before World War Two.

School was out in the middle of May. After branding, I went back, took exams and then did a final tune up with my horses. They were all gone before June rolled around. Carrie Ann and I had more time together. We spent most of it riding Davey and Little Molly in the late afternoons. The weather was perfect. A big clear blue sky, gentle breezes, temperatures in the mid-eighties during the day and the low sixties at night.

One night right before the new bunch of two year olds came in, I went up to the ranch house one night after supper and talked to Sherman. He handled the business end of my horse training. I had been thinking about a nice bay I had started for one of Lacey Rand's friends.

I had really wanted to keep the bay for another few weeks and ride him most days, but the owner had called Sherman and asked if he was ready and Sherman had told him to come and get the bay. I told Sherman I wished I had spoken up and said something about keeping him two more weeks.

Sherman told me that starting young horses meant just that. Starting them and not finishing them. He told me I could ride a horse every day and he would come around and reach his potential between the ages of five and seven. I knew that.

He said, "There comes a time when the owner has to step in and ride his own goddamn horse. He paid for four months. That is what he got. Lim, these ain't our children. Look at what you did with that horse. When he left, he could stand still while you saddled him up, stand still while you got on. Accept a bit. Neck rein. Do that damn backward figure eight with ease. Change leads. Load in a trailer. Stop when you asked him to. That is a lot to ask of a two year old and he did all that and more. Oh, and help opening gates. All that. "

Iris was in the den. She was reading a magazine and drinking a cup of tea.

Sherman went over to his desk and found the big manila folder he used to keep all the records of my horse training business. He said, "Iris, will you talk to this guy, Jack Noble. Lives in Tucson. Lacey Rand sent him and that nice bay to us for Lim to us. Just a follow up call. Lim, I usually make these calls myself but I was going to wait another month, but let's see what he says."

Sherman dialed the number and Iris took the phone and went back into the den. She talked for around ten minutes and then came back and gave the phone to Sherman.

She said, "He will send you another colt the first of the year. He said he was spending some time every day with the bay. He said he would not let him stand in the stall all week and ride him an hour on the weekend. He took him on a short trail ride and opened and shut gates with him and he is doing those god awful figure eights. They make me nervous. A horse doing all that backing just isn't natural, Lim."

Sherman said, "You know, Lim, we all live by the old wet saddle blanket school of training a young horse. That's fine 'til you have one bow a tendon because of overuse. So you need to get rid of these guilt trips you are giving yourself. Small doses are what a young horse needs. So if you miss two days riding a young horse, that might be the best thing you have done for him. I think a lot of young horses are ruined because they get sore and then turn on riding and their trainer."

We sat and talked for a while longer. I was getting ready to leave when Iris set a big bowl of vanilla ice cream and a small bowl of sliced strawberries in front of me. Dad and I had chili dogs for supper. Good sized franks, soft fresh buns, Hormel Chili without Beans and diced onions. I had three. Dad had two and Vern had three. And of course a couple of Fat Tires to wash em down. I just drank a root beer over ice. Alcohol was just a sometime thing with me.

By June 1st I had four two year olds to start under saddle. They were all nice, but one of them was a big chestnut I could not get to pay attention. He just would not do anything right. I tried everything I knew. I rode him off by himself in the pasture. I got Carrie Ann to ride Little Molly with us and nothing worked.

Finally, I told Sherman I felt bad about taking money from the rancher when I wasn't getting anything done.

Sherman said, "Let's get Doc Siegfried out here and see what he says. He don't have any wolf teeth, I know that. But, let's see if something is wrong with him. Some horses just ain't worth a shit, Lim. That's just the long and short of it. They might have all the best breeding pedigree you could want. Both sides, dam and sir. And still not be worth feeding. Happens all the time."

Doc Siegfried came late in the afternoon the next day. There was not much light left and the sunset was going to be full of orange, blue, and red streaks. A gentle breeze drifted through the horse barn. The big chestnut was in the cross-ties.

Doc Siegfried said he could find nothing wrong with the horse. He asked if he was listless.

I said, "No, he has got plenty of energy, he is just not interested. And he isn't mean."

Doc Siegfried ran his hand up between the chestnut's ears. He dropped his head and let him look in his ears and then scratch him between the ears.

"Nice and gentle. I don't think he has been mistreated. Sherman, as hard as it is for me to say this, I do not know as how I can charge you for this call. But don't worry. I'll make it up to you."

Sherman said, "You could stay for supper long as you leave me enough to eat. You little sons of bitches always eat more than your share. Iris has got a nice chocolate cake she made. I started on it this morning while she was primping in the bed room. Just the way I like it.

Really dark icing and nice yellow cake. And I think we are have chicken marsala and a salad. Maybe I will open a bottle of Chianti Classico. That is, if you are interested."

Before the Doc and Sherman left for the ranch house, Sherman said, "Lim, rest him for two days. Put him out in the horse pasture. Then bring him back up to his stall and turnout and give him a try for a week. If that does not work, I will call and give the owner his horse and money back."

I sat down on a hay bale and pushed my hat back. I was mighty discouraged. Dad and Vern were in the tack room. I could hear them moving things around.

I just sat there and looked at the chestnut. His name was Max. Perfect confirmation. Strong and muscular with a perfect neck, an alert eye, and a pretty chestnut coat.

Soon Dad and Vern came out of the tack room. Dad handed me a hackamore headset. Vern had about twelve feet of a thick cotton rope in his hands. Vern sat down and attached the rope to the headset. His glasses were down on the bridge of his nose. He was breathing steady through his nose. He looked tired. Real tired.

When he had the rig ready, he gave it to Dad.

Dad said, "Son, this is a hackamore. I shy away from 'em. You can really hurt a horse with one of these if you put too much pressure on him or if you do a lot of yanking trying to get him to turn. Now, I will get him out of the horse pasture on Saturday afternoon when I finish for the day and try him out with this. The heavy rope helps get his attention. Max is going to fill out to weigh around twelve hundred pounds. You watch and see."

When Saturday came, Dad worked 'til a little after noon. I had put Max in his stall and turnout the night before. Dad saddled him up and I saddled Little Molly up for Vern. They rode out into the pasture. I could see Dad was letting Max trot along and throw his head whenever he pleased. I worked another colt and in an hour or so later I saw Vern and Dad heading back to the barn. Max was trotting alongside Little Molly. His head was not perfect but the contrary son of a bitch was paying attention. Dad had his own head ducked low and his hands were set wide and low.

When I was through for the day, Carrie Ann was in the horse barn with Dad and Vern. Carrie Ann was drinking blue Gatorade out of a bottle. Dad and Vern were working on a couple of bottles of Dos Equis Amber. They were passing around a big sack of Fritos.

The next day, Dad rode Max again and I rode Davey. Max was starting to pay attention. Dad still kept his hands wide and low. We turned around and started back to the barn around lunch. Dad pulled up down near the Cienega. You could hear the water running in the creek. We stopped on a hill and ate ham and cheese sandwiches. The creek was silver and glistening in the midday sun. We sat on rocks. Eating ham sandwiches, munching on Fritos. Splitting a nice green Granny Smith apple.

We had just sat down and Dad was unwrapping his sandwich, when he pointed north. I looked in the next pasture. There were twenty or so Pronghorns drifting west. Their heads were down for a few minutes. Eating up Sherman's pasture. He said it was one of those things that just went with living here. We did not shoot them and Sherman and Iris would not let anyone else hunt them. We also had deer, doves, and quail. Sherman said, "Let 'em be. We got good Hereford beef to eat."

Dad said, "You up for tamales and chili tonight? I sure would like some tonight. With a cold Fat Tire and one of those cobblers I got stuck up in the back of the freezer. A cherry. And some ice cream. That do it, Lim?"

I said, "Sure."

We were almost ready to go when he said, "Lim, back on the ranch in Llano, there was a fellow worked there that used a hackamore. Used it like a torture instrument. His revenge against horses. Every horse he ever rode had calluses across his nose. You can shut a horse's breathing if you misuse a hackamore. He used a wire across the horse's nose that was very thinly covered by rawhide. His horses always had sore noses. Wide and raw sores sometimes. Not a way to treat a horse. But there are plenty of folks who use them the right way. With just a little gentle pressure, Max is starting to pay attention. The wire in our hackamore is wrapped with a lot of rawhide. He is gradually learning to pay attention. I think he is a horse that just never will get over his displeasure with a bit in his mouth. He is improving. Not as much as I would like to see for a horse with his potential, but we got a start."

I rode Max for two more months and I could see he was coming around. When it was time for me to turn him back to his owner, he was handling gates, lead changes and stops fine. I had not even tried to get him to do the figure eights the way I liked to do them. Backing through the pattern with no head tossing.

Sherman surprised me. He called Max's owner and said we would give him forty five more days free of charge. It took me most of that time to get him to do a figure eight the right way.

The day Max left, Sherman let his owner take the hackamore bridle with him. Between horses and Carrie Ann, I was always on the go that summer. When my senior year started, I noticed time was sailing by faster than it ever had. I know what they teach you in school. Sixty seconds in a minute. Sixty minutes in an hour. Twenty four hours in a day. But it sure looked to me like time was going by so much faster.

Jeremy committed to Texas A and M in October of his senior year. He got a full ride and Mary got an academic scholarship to A and M also. Jeremy was All State. First team. Jeremy was a Parade All

American and wore his silver belly Stetson to New York for the group pictures.

Carrie Ann went to Stanford twice during the fall. Both times, her mother went with her. They were bickering. Lots of slammed doors and exaggerated sighs.

I was taking off from school some to help at the ranch and work my two year olds. I took the ACT Test. One day, I came home from the barn and I saw Mr. Crawley's truck down at the ranch house. Sherman came up and asked us to come down to the house when the chores were done. Us being me and Dad. I thought I was in trouble. I had left school at noon one day the past week and forgot to sign out or get a permission slip.

When we were all together, we sat around the dining room table. Vern had not made it home yet.

Mr. Crawley started it off. "I usually do not interfere with my students plans. If they ask for advice, I certainly will give it. I am not the school guidance counselor, but I would like to say my piece. We got the results of the ACT Tests yesterday. Lim was third in his class. He made a 29. Mr. Couch that was only behind Mary and Carrie Ann. Not many in his range. Most incoming freshmen will have lower scores. He has told me repeatedly he does not want to go to college. I would like to talk about it for a few minutes and then I will leave and not interfere further."

Mr. Crawley drank some coffee. He looked at me and said, "Lim, you have told me you want to train two year olds and work on a ranch. Have you thought this all the way through. The money. The danger. The risk. You got the same risks as a rodeo rider. Only yours is not compressed into eight second segments. Yours is constant. All your life.

"A two year old horse is going to outweigh you six to eight hundred pounds. He can roll on you. Sideswipe you. Throw you. All of that and more."

I said, "I know all of that. You are absolutely right. I just want to be able to get up in the morning and see the whole sky. Not just what shows over some buildings. I do not want to look at the ass end of cars for two or three hours a day. For five days a week. I like horses. I like being around them. This right here is what I want. And I do not want to get out of school with six figures of debt. A busted leg will heal. Debt does not go away. My dad has taught me if you can't pay cash, you don't need it."

Mr. Crawley said, "Mister Couch. I believe it is Dewey. What do you say?"

"Lim is mighty good at what he does. He still has a lot to learn, sure. But he is way ahead of most folks. And people trust him. Clients of his can see the way he feels about their stock. He has to turn work away and he won't be eighteen until the summer after he graduates. I just am not going to push him into something he does not want to do and does not believe in."

Sherman said, "I'd get him set up in school. He could learn some things and help the ranch. New and better grasses. Accounting. Herd management. Breeding strategy. They got college courses on all that. I would let Iris jerk a knot in his neck and we could get him to go if he could just take those courses. But hell no, he has got to take college English. More math. More bullshit that he won't use, so I have a solution that I think will work.

"First of all, he will make his own mind up and do what he wants to do. Second, he is seventeen and susceptible to a mighty lot of changes in his life.

"What I want him to do is help around the ranch for a while after school is out, then find work with one of these top notch AQHA trainers."

Mr. Crawley said, "Now, exactly what is AQHA?"

Iris said, "The American Quarter Horse Association based up in Amarillo. They keep breeding records, register new colts, sponsor shows and sales. They set the standards for confirmation and performance for the whole breed. They are constantly expanding the classes in the shows. Reining, trail, English Pleasure, and ranch horse classes. They operate under a point system. Your horse earns points if he wins or places in an approved show. The goal is an AQHA Championship. We had one. An AQHA Champion. Guess who started him out. Halter trained him as a colt. Lim Couch. Right here on the Circle S. After school and on the weekends. Before he was in high school. You have to have enough points in a performance class like Western Pleasure or Reining and in halter classes which judge the horse on confirmation and handling. Our horse, Socks, got his in Halter, Western Pleasure and Reining.

"So, let's say Lim is asked to start a new horse. He can tell the owner after the training period if he thinks he is best for a trail horse, ranch horse, cutting, reining, or whatever. If he gets experience with a real trainer and goes to the shows for a few years, he will establish contacts that will last him the rest of his life," Iris added.

Sherman said, "A lot of these old boys scruff around for years and get that one horse that puts them on the front page of the Quarter Horse Journal and then you can't get a horse in his barn to save your soul. A tough life. Breaking colts. Training and showing horses. But it can be rewarding and I think with Lim, people will be loyal to him and keep sending him horses."

Iris said, "Lim is like a ring sour horse. He has no interest in school. No curiosity. No faith in the system. School for the most part equals drudgery and boredom. He wants to stay as independent as he can. In a couple of years, I will get him to take online courses in the subjects Sherman and I think he needs. What Sherman and I see in the long run, ten, maybe fifteen years down the road, is Lim coming back and running the Circle S. Training horses on the side. In fifteen years, we will be past sixty five and crowding seventy. So will Dewey. We are not turning over the running of this ranch to some stranger. I can promise you that."

I asked about the online courses. Would they be like a regular class where you had to be there at a certain time?

Mr. Crawley said, "Lim, you can take some of the same classes Jeremy will be taking at A and M. You can log on at five am or eleven pm. You still have semesters and grades but the times are flexible."

I thought about that. That might be fun. Actually learning something about a subject that you were interested in.

Mr. Crawley stood up and said, "I just wanted you folks to know that Lim has got it in him to excel in school. Ms. Iris, I am afraid you may have nailed it. He needs a few years away from school. Good luck, young man. In whatever your try to make of your life."

Before he could leave, Iris said, "Now Mr. Crawley, before you leave, let me give you a nice piece of this chocolate cake I baked just this morning. A nice piece for Lim also. You know, he never would have told us about how well he had done on this test. Why, we did not even know he took it. So thank you. And Lim, I am going to send some of this cake with you. It is Sherman's favorite. A big, moist three layer yellow cake with chocolate icing. And Sherman Snider, you can just get that pained expression off your face. There is plenty to go around. Lim, let your conscience be your guide as to whether you share with Dewey and Vern."

Vern was in his trailer when we left the ranch house. I built a fire while Dad warmed up some beans and franks. Vern came down and brought four Dos Equis Ambers. Dad gave me one to drink with my supper. I saved it for the weekend and drank a root beer over ice. The cake was moist. Dad told Vern about how I had done good on the test and Vern said for me to take some more of those tests if it meant Iris would be sending us chocolate cake.

Iris had it just about right. I was soured on school. It wasn't that I was against learning. I was all for learning. I just wanted it to be about something I was interested in. How about the history of the American Quarter Horse? How to train a reining horse. Or a cutting horse. The origins and traits of modern day cattle breeds. Santa Gertrudis, Simmental, Charolais, Red Angus, Black Angus, and a breed or cross that was catching on. New ideas on grazing.

My senior year was choppy. Something going on at school all the time. Dances, banquets, parties. Between Christmas and calving time, Carrie Ann told me her mother had been nagging her to go to summer school after graduation.

We had planned to have a nice summer together. Both of us knew it was probably going to be our last summer but neither of us ever said it. She said she finally gave in. It was not worth fighting her about. Her father stayed out of it. He and one of his hands were building new calving sheds and Carrie Ann said he would come in at dusk, take a shower, eat something and fall asleep in his black leather recliner. She did not have the heart to get him involved. She had just started to notice age starting to creep up on her father. Mainly in his eyes. And he talked slower. Sometimes he seemed to be reaching for his words.

When she told me all of this, I was grooming a new little sorrel gelding I was just starting under saddle. He had a nice blaze and two white stockings. His name was Louie and I was being careful not to get him sore from too much exercise. He was barely fifteen hands and he needed to put on some weight. Some muscle weight. I liked the little horse. He stood still in the cross chains while I brushed him. No fidgeting. No head tossing. No foot stomping.

A friend of Davey Waddell owned Louie. Tommy Kurtz. Tommy lived in Tucson and had bought Louie from Davey as a colt. Tommy was a CPA but he had grown up near Davey and they had been high school friends. Tommy had a home off River Road just west of Craycroft. His house was set way back off the road. He planned to ride Louie on some trail rides. Louie was out of the same mare that gave birth to Socks. A different stud, though.

Tommy planned on riding Louie down in the Rillito River Wash. It was right behind his house. Most of the time, the Rillito was a wide glorified wash. It even had some small trees growing in it. The Rillito River only had water in it a few days a year during the monsoons in late summer and when the snow runoff from Mr. Lemmon made it down in the spring.

Tommie had a seven year old daughter and his plan was to give Louie to her when she was ten. I thought it was a good plan. Louie was a fast learner and in three years he would be a five year old. That is about the time most horses settle in and become consistent and reliable. That's how long it takes for the training to really take hold.

When she had finished telling me about Summer School, Carrie Ann asked if I was mad and I said no. Which was a lie. But I did not stay mad. That night after supper, I sat by the fire and drank a half shot of good whiskey Dad had bought. Russell's Reserve. Mighty fine. There was no use being mad. Summer school made perfect sense. I knew that. She could get ahead of the fall crowd and relieve some of the pressure on herself. I would have plenty to do. I was sure that as soon as Sherman found out she was gone to Stanford, he would add another horse to my summer string.

I got to thinking about my Dad. He never pushed me into things. I knew to keep my room up, help with the few chores around the house, and go to school without complaining. After that, I guess there were not a lot of rules. He did not talk much. If he had problems of his own, I never knew about them. He did date and he never talked about any women.

I couldn't see him nagging me or pressuring me to do something. 'Course, I was not going into the super competitive academic world. Stanford. As good as a school can be, according to Iris and Mr. Crawley. Hard to get into and hard to keep up once you were in.

Dad told me I could have half a shot of whiskey at night as long as I did not make a habit of it. Damn. Russell's Reserve was relaxing. Smooth. Made me sleep easier.

Anyway, when I saw Carrie Ann the next day at school, I had a smile on my face. We shared lunch. She brought me a piece of custard pie and a pastrami sandwich her mother made for me. After school, we went off and parked down south of Elgin on a gravel road. We were a mile west of the old Canelo School house. We were on an old abandoned ranch road and I parked my truck on a rise and I took an old green and blue checked blanket out from behind the seat of my truck and spread it out under a mesquite tree. We could see a long way. The Whetstones loomed low and gray in the east and the Santa Ritas were closer and loomed higher.

We talked some, but mainly we started making up for the time we knew we were never going to have together that summer. That afternoon, I gave the horses a rest. We watched the red and orange sunset over the Santa Ritas and we folded the blanket and got ready to leave and Carrie Ann reached and held me and buried her head in my left shoulder.

When I got home, dad was grilling hamburgers in the front yard. He had a nice new grill. He and Vern had made it from a fifty gallon drum. Vern had cut it into two long pieces, Dad had painted it silver, and they had added handles, legs, a metal grill, hinges, vents, and an oak side board.

Vern was sitting in a lawn chair drinking a Fat Tire. Dad had a whole bunch of hamburger patties ready to grill. I asked him if Vern was that hungry and Dad stammered a little and said, "Well, I think we are going to have company."

Vern was laughing and I noticed Dad had on his nice white shirt with pearl snaps and a nice yoke in the back. He had his good black boots on and fresh jeans.

He looked like he had shaved. He asked me to go in the house and slice some tomatoes, onions, and to break up a head of lettuce. And to set the table for four.

I was almost through setting the table when I heard a car pull up and park behind Dad's pickup. I went outside when I finished and Lacey Rand was standing by Dad drinking a Fat Tire. She had on a nice blouse and tight jeans she had stuck down inside her red and black boots. Vern stayed just long enough to eat. Lacey brought what she called a pretty fair tres leches cake she had stopped to buy on her way out of Tucson.

After dinner, I went up to Vern's and we sat inside his trailer and played dominoes and ate peanuts. Lacey left a little before midnight and Dad came up to the trailer and told me to go on to bed.

After Christmas, Dad started spending most Saturday nights in Tucson. Lacey came down to our place a couple of times a week. She and Dad started sleeping together and he would get up early and fix a big breakfast and the three of us would sit and eat. She would look over her coffee mug at my dad and he would blush and grin. It wasn't hard to get used to Lacey. She did not try to boss me around and I thought it was nice someone like her would hook up with my Dad.

Calving was easier that February because we only had five new heifers. Only one had a hard time with her calf and Vern and I handled everything on a Saturday night. I was over at Carrie Ann's watching "Sleepless in Seattle," when Vern called and told me he needed help. Dad was in Tucson. The calf chain, pulling the calf out, cleaning up the afterbirth, all came easier. We finished before two a.m. The calf had a bright red color and a red ring around her left eye. She found her mother real fast and when we turned out the lights in the calving barn, she was pulling hard on one of her mother's teats.

We cleaned ourselves up in the horse barn and went on back to Vern's trailer and played dominoes and drank some J.W. Dant bourbon and ate Doritos and Oreos. About four that morning, I got up to leave and Vern said he was going to sleep 'til noon. I slept for a few hours, got up, ate some raisin bran, fixed me some peanut butter and grape jelly sandwiches and went up to the barn and took care of my horses.

I was just fixing to leave the barn on Louie when a nice, red Toyota Tundra pulling a silver two horse trailer came past the ranch house and stopped in front of the horse barn. It was Jimmy Dale Scruggs. He got out and unlatched the trailer door and backed a nice, young buckskin stallion out.

He walked the stallion down the road a ways and then brought him back and tied him to the trailer. He said, "I have ridden him some. Just a little. He is still skittish but he is going to have some size on him in a year or so. You know me, I like a big horse. I called Sherman last night. We worked a deal. I got a nice heifer I will give him in partial trade and the rest will be cash. I got cash here but I don't want to knock on his door this early on a Sunday morning. House looks real quiet."

He handed me the halter rope and said, "I want a using horse. One that will stand still when I open a gate, ground tie, change leads, and if you get time, start him trailing cows. And I want him to have a good head set and pay attention when you ride him. You know I do not have a lot of patience."

He brought a saddle and bridle with him. A snaffle bit and long, soft brown leather reins offset a nice new leather headstall. The saddle was old and looked comfortable. I hung his gear up in the tack room and unsaddled Louie and put him back in his stall. I asked Jimmy Dale if his horse had a name and he said, "Steve."

I said, "Why Steve?"

And he said, "Hell, Lim, he just looks like a Steve. Just fits him."

I did not go any further with it.

I put Steve in a stall and Jimmy Dale reached in his front left shirt pocket and pulled out eight one hundred bills. He gave the cash to me and asked me to give it to Sherman. I asked him to come down to the house. I was hungry. Raisin Bran did not keep me going long. I fried bacon, scrambled eggs, and fixed some toast. While we were eating, Jimmy Dale told me about some big changes in his life. His mother was gone. Out of his life. He was bitter. And relieved. And confused.

He told me in bits and pieces as we ate our breakfast. It had all started to unravel a year or so ago. He had went up to Davey's house to borrow a hundred dollars to buy groceries and gas. He had credit at the feed store but had to pay cash for everything else. He had to chase his mother down for money. Davey gave him two hundred dollars to tide him over and told him he had just about enough of Nancy's way of doing things.

Jimmy Dale had not seen her in ten days. Lynn told Davey to call Randy Price and see what he thought could be done. Randy listened to Jimmy Dale's history and said he would check some things out at the courthouse and get back to him. What he found out was that Nancy had never done anything about Ray's estate after his death. Randy filed a motion in court to probate the estate and a motion asking for an accounting of all monies spent after Ray's death.

When Nancy was served with the motions, she went up to the bunkhouse and started screaming and cussing at Jimmy Dale and he got scared and went to stay with Davey. When the motion day came up, Randy had subpoenaed the ranch bank records and Nancy's credit card statements and her checking account records.

On the day of the hearing, Nancy did not show. Randy, Davey, and Jimmy Dale sat in the courtroom until it was almost lunch and then the judge said he was going to appoint a guardian for Jimmy Dale and set another date for a review of the financial records. Randy Price asked that Lynn be appointed guardian since she had an accounting background and was familiar with ranching. The judge agreed and Jimmy Dale moved back to the ranch.

He said Nancy was gone. She had cleared out. Her clothes were gone and the house was bare when he got back from court the day Lynn was appointed his guardian. There was trash in the floor and spoiled food in the refrigerator and torn up family pictures on the old dining room table. Pictures taken when Jimmy Dale was a kid. Jimmy Dale and his dad sitting on their horses. Taken when Jimmy Dale was nine. Torn up. Pictures of his father and mother when they were married in El Paso. All torn up. School pictures of Jimmy Dale. All torn up.

Jimmy Dale said he just sat there in one of the mismatched chairs at the dining room table for a long time. He did not know what to do with the pictures. He said he left them there and after he told Davey and Lynn, they both came up and brought some cheeseburgers and sat around the table and pieced the photographs together with scotch tape and glue as best they could and mounted them on white typewriter paper.

When they went back to court, the judge reviewed the financial records and listened to Lynn tell what she thought had happened. Lynn told the judge Nancy had emptied the ranch bank account a few days before the first hearing. Then she had cut a trail. Apparently to Vegas first and then to LA. She had kept using the ranch credit card in Vegas and LA. Lynn had taken the order appointing her Jimmy Dale's guardian to the Wells Fargo Bank in Sierra Vista and had the credit card cancelled. It had over fifteen thousand dollars in recent and unpaid charges. A hotel room bill in Vegas at Rio Suites. Cash advances at The Mirage. A three thousand dollar charge for clothes.

All of this happened about the time I had met Carrie Ann. He said things were coming around now. He had sold steers for good money and the judge had let him trade his old truck in for a better used truck. He would not be a minor in less than two years. He had two hands working for him and they were living in the bunk house. They were from the state of Sonora in Mexico and were honest and hardworking. Jimmy Dale said he put a DirecTV dish on the bunkhouse roof and gave them a flat screen. He had fixed up the bathroom and shower and put a new refrigerator in the kitchen.

Jimmy Dale was going to buy some decent bulls when he sold his cattle next year. He asked me not to tell anybody about what he had told me. Vern had carried him last year until he sold his cattle in the fall. But he was paid off now. Vern had not told anyone at the Circle S about all the changes. Jimmy Dale said he was not proud of how things were when his mother was running things, but he did not want the whole of Southern Arizona to know about it.

He left around noon and I rode Louie that afternoon for a while and came back to the horse barn and saddled Steve. I rode him down past the Cienega. The late afternoon sky was full of fast moving black clouds. They were headed north. I rode east for a while and turned Steve on back. The wind was picking up. I looked south. The last of the clouds was passing by and you could see it was going to be clear, windy, and cold very soon.

Steve was a decent horse. He was not athletic like Louie. He was muscular and strong, but he was too slow to be much of a cutting horse or reining horse. His trot was fine, though and you could tell he would go all day. Just what Jimmy Dale wanted. He had a short black mane and a full, thick tail. When I got back to the barn, Carrie Ann was talking to my father. He had just got back from Tucson. She had brought half a chocolate meringue pie. We went on back to the house and Dad grilled hamburgers and hot dogs in the cold and wind.

Lacey started coming around more. A couple nights a week, she would show up around eight and stay the night. A few weekends, she came over around noon on Saturday and stayed until early Monday morning. She cooked some and when she came from Tucson, she always brought something good to eat.

Jimmy Dale came back and got Steve right before branding time. I had fattened him up a little and he looked good. Jimmy Dale used his horses. He did not pay a lot of attention to grooming his horses or fattening them up. He rode Steve down to the creek and back a couple of times and I saw him out in the pasture stopping Steve from both a trot and a short lope. He had him do a reverse figure eight. Steve would do it, but he was awkward and was not as agile as Louie or Little Molly.

Jimmy Dale loaded Steve in his trailer and came on back in the barn and told me he was cool with the way Steve had turned out. He said he might bring him back once a year and let me tune him up. Then he turned away, got in his truck and drove away slowly.

I still had Louie all the way into May. Tommy had come by one Sunday afternoon in March and told me he was so busy at work, he wanted me to keep riding Louie until June 1st.

Things were moving too fast for me. I still had three horses I wanted to have ready by May 1st and I wanted to spend as much time with Carrie Ann as I could. I had no illusions. I knew when she left the slow pace of Sonoita, Patagonia High School, and the Circle S, she would be entering the fast paced, techno world. Stanford was on the cutting edge of everything academic and that was where Carrie deserved to be. But that did not mean I would not spend a lot of time missing her.

She wanted me to get a PC, but I just did not see the need for it. But late in the spring, Lacey brought one down and set it up. She used it for business and she would sit in the den and pay bills and send e-mails while Dad and I watched TV. I really liked having her around. She set me up an e-mail account and showed me how to get on the Internet. Lacey told me I could keep up with Carrie Ann at Stanford. We could exchange e-mails.

But I knew. When Carrie Ann left for Stanford, it would be over. A few stale e-mails would not keep us together. Our interests were just not going to be the same. But for now, we were having fun together and we were both determined to cram everything we could into the few remaining months. But then branding time came and went and it was just weeks before she would leave for Palo Alto and the beautiful Mission buildings with red tile roofs at Stanford.

Mary heard about Carrie Ann going to Stanford for summer school and she decided she and Jeremy should go to Texas A and M for summer school. They were both leaving for College Station at about the same time as Carrie Ann was leaving for Palo Alto. Mary wanted Jeremy to get a head start in school. She was worried he would be overwhelmed with classes and football.

We finished branding ten days before I graduated from high school. Relatives from Kansas came down for Carrie Ann's graduation. Cousins, uncles, and aunts. All over at the Shelton Ranch. Everybody at the Circle S was invited over the Sunday night before graduation on Wednesday. Mr. Shelton did it up right. Roving Mariachis with deep and emotional voices, a big bass, two guitars, and three trumpets. Grilled sirloin. Potato salad. Slaw. Green corn tamales. Beer iced down in an old wash tub.

What I will remember most about that night was Carrie Ann taking Vern and my Dad around and introducing them to all of her relatives. Smiling and laughing with both of them all proud and dressed up in clean jeans, nice boots, and ironed shirts.

And then it was all over. My diploma in a drawer in my bedroom. Carrie Ann gone. Mary and Jeremy gone. And, just a few weeks later, Tommy came and got Louie. Of all the horses I had started out, Louie and Socks were the best, so far. Tommy rode Louie out in the pasture and when he came back, he had a big smile on his face. He was happy and gave me three one hundred dollar bills. He said it was in appreciation of my professionalism. I folded them up and put them in my left front shirt pocket and shook his hand and thanked him.

Louie belonged on a ranch. A working ranch. Not some fucking rich man's toy. But a real ranch. With cattle and chores. Trailing cattle. Sliding stops. Opening gates. Cutting cattle. And most importantly, just being used. Having demands made on him on a daily basis. Not being something pretty just stuck in a stall and a turnout for the rest of his life.

I knew Tommy would do what he could to treat the horse properly. That was not the problem. The problem was just the world that horses lived in now. They got great medical care and superior dietary regimens but they still mostly were idle. The worst fate a good horse like Louie could suffer. A long, drawn out and boring existence. An inactive but safe existence. When tax time came, Tommy would be working sixteen to eighteen hours a day and Louie would be standing idle in the Tucson sun all day.

The weekend before I graduated from high school, Dad and I went to Paul Bond Boots in Nogales, Arizona. It is a large, barn like structure on a hill on Mariposa Street near Interstate 19. I had a nice pair of black lizard Dan Post boots, but Dad said Paul Bond and Lucchese made the best boots. He ordered me a pair of brown goatskin boots from Lucchese and we picked out a pair of black calfskin boots at Paul Bond. They took my foot measurements and made the boots to my specifications. No toe stitching. No stitching on the shafts. Just leather boots. With a fourteen inch shaft and a snip toe. Dad said they would last me forever.

It was after July 4 before the boots were ready. The Lucchese's came first and toward the end of the month the folks at Paul Bond called. I only wore the boots when I went out or Lacey came over.

The summer went slowly. I worked my new horses. They were all good. No spoiled brats. My social life was playing dominoes with Vern, talking to Lacey, going to Tucson with Iris. Eating dinner with Lacy and Dad at Las Vigas. Sunday or Saturday barbecues with Dad, Lacey, and Vern.

I made a halfhearted effort to connect with Jody. She looked great. Nice long blond hair. A tight body. Big tits. I took her to Las Vigas and I was bored all night. She was fine but we just did not fit. Now, Carrie Ann. We just fit. No better way to say it. Once I was with Carrie Ann, I knew it would be hard for me to connect with anyone else. I sure as hell was not going to burn the tires up on my truck running up and down the highway chasing girls I knew I would be tired of in a month.

Vern told me Steve was working out for Jimmy Dale but he wished he would give him some supplements with his feed so he could bulk up. I went over to see Jimmy Dale a few times and he came over a time or two and ate with us. He looked tired all the times. He said he had met a new girl. Her name was Estrelita Reyes and her folks lived in Sierra Vista and owned a convenience store, a dry cleaners and two coin operated laundries.

He called her Lita and he brought her over one Sunday afternoon. It was the cleanest I had ever seen Jimmy Dale. A nice shiny pair of brown smooth ostrich boots, clean jeans, a brown Ranger belt with a nice buckle, a green and blue plaid shirt, and a brown felt hat.

Lita was quiet. She talked to Dad and Vern while they were grilling steaks, but her voice was so soft, it took a while for me to get used to it. She was a small woman. Her hair was long and black. Her eyes were big and brown. Her face was narrow and she was nervous. She still had rosy cheeks and high cheekbones. She was just out of high school and was going to Pima Community College at the Sierra Vista branch in the fall. When I looked in her eyes, she was like a skittish horse. She looked away quickly. I liked her. I told myself if Jimmy Dale messes this up, I am calling her up and asking her out.

She worked in the dry cleaners and at the convenience store. She met Jimmy Dale in the convenience store and she said she told him she did not go out with customers. Especially customers who came into the store dirty and half drunk. Jimmy Dale sent her some roses and showed up at her house wearing clean clothes one night and knocked on the door and she let him in the house but he had to sit on the couch in the den until she had eaten supper with her parents and youngest sister and helped clear the table.

I told Jimmy Dale he needed to put some weight on Steve. He said, "I like 'em lean. He ain't a show horse. He is a using horse. He gets plenty to eat."

By the end of the summer, I had four horses ready to turn back to their owners. They all were ready to ride and just needed polish. About the time school started in late August, Sherman asked me to come up to the Ranch house at seven p.m. He didn't say why. When I got through that day, I went up to the ranch house. I got there a few minutes before Tommy drove up. Sherman had a grim look on his face and Iris was in the kitchen cleaning up after supper. She looked sad.

Tommy came up to the door and Sherman suggested we sit out on the porch. He brought a bottle of Jim Beam, three shot glasses, some ice, some cocktail glasses, and a pitcher of water. He left the bottle corked while we talked.

The sun was just now settling down over the Santa Ritas. A little breeze was blowing. I could not tell from which direction it came. I figured the south. There were doves lighting in the Arizona sycamores and the mesquites down by the creek. Iris had switched over to her fall flowers. Some red geraniums were still healthy and blooming. She had red and white pansies, gold and red daisies, yellow marigolds, and some purple nightshade in the flower beds. She was already fretting about the temperatures at night. She was afraid she would lose her flowers to a hard freeze before Thanksgiving.

Sherman took his time starting things off. You could tell he wanted to use the right words. And just the right words. And just as few as possible.

Tommy looked broken down and tired. He had no color in his face.

Sherman said, "Lim, looks like Tommy is in a situation. One that will take a few years to resolve. His wife and daughter moved back up near Pagosa Springs and Durango in Southern Colorado. Looks like they might not be coming back. Divorce papers have already been served. None of this is our business and what is said here tonight needs to stay on this porch. Except for Dewey and Vern. They will keep it here on the Circle S. Now, Tommy, you tell Lim what you need and want from us and we will reach an accord and then we can knock the bottom out of this pint of Jim Beam. Iris will help on that part."

Tommy said, "No way can I give Louie the attention he needs in the next few years. I want you to get him back in shape and keep him here until I can get this divorce out of the way."

Sherman opened the Jim Beam and sniffed the cork. He poured us a shot each. Tommy poured some ice in a glass and poured water in it. I took mine straight. Sherman poured his shot in a glass and put a few ice cubes in it. I sipped mine slowly. Sherman swirled his around in his glass and downed about half of it in one swallow. Tommy looked out at the Santa Ritas and the fading orange, red and blue sunset and left his glass on the porch rail in front of him.

Tommy said, "I hate to waste that horse. But with all of this in front of me, I do not trust myself. I have to simplify my life. Keep my business life stable and learn to live without the two people I love the most in this world."

I took a big sip of whiskey straight out of the shot glass and poured me a little glass of ice water and drank that. The Jim Beam was good. It had a few rough edges, I'll grant you that, but it was still smooth enough going down.

Tommy said, "I got a little over six thousand in Louie. I was hoping to get seventy five hundred. That way, you could make some money and I could get back to even. Or, at least, close to it."

Sherman said, "Look, from what I have seen in passing and what Lim has told me, you do not need to be selling that horse for that kind of money. I say, give me a hundred and fifty a month for taking care of him and we will just let Lim round him into shape. The right kind of supplements in his feed and he will be slicked out and ready to sell by spring. Asking price would be fifteen grand. A pretty firm fifteen. He will be doing a sliding stop, good reverse figure eights, and changing his leads smoothly by spring. His head is already set and his trot is smooth."

"Lim, I am cutting you out of a training fee. But when a man is down, it pays off in the long run to help him. Is that alright with you?"

"I tell you what, Tommy, fifteen might be too low. I will get him doing some trail patterns from the AQHA trail classes and by the end of spring, you may have things worked out and you may just want to take him back to Tucson. I'm telling you, Louie is a horse of a lifetime. When he is five, he can be as good a horse as you can find in the country. You may not want to sell him. I can get him to work cattle some. Nothing spectacular. No advanced cutting training. I do not know that side of the business well enough to go very far with it, and if you take him back to Tucson next summer, you are not going to need a cutting horse. Just a good riding horse."

Tommy took a sip of Jim Beam and leaned back in his chair. He said, "I got guilt enough to deal with. My sin was simple neglect. Too much work and not enough attention to my marriage. I sure do not need to add ruining a good horse to the mix. I will do what you say, Sherman. You and Lim know best."

In a few minutes, Iris came outside with some pound cake and a coffee pot and four cups. The pound cake was moist and had fresh crushed pineapple on top. Tommy did not finish his shot of whiskey. He and I sat quietly while Iris fussed at Sherman because he told Tommy the pound cake was nice and moist but it would have been better if Iris had put some crushed pineapple on it then drained the can of pineapple juice over the cake.

Tommy and I let them go at it. We knew it was all for show. Iris stormed off the porch and went back inside. Sherman did not say much else. Soon, Iris came out and gave Tommy some cake and gave me about half of it to share with Vern and Dad.

Tommy brought Louie back to the Circle S the week before Labor Day. Labor Day, we worked trailing cattle from a pasture on the south end of the ranch all the way up to a pasture with fresh, knee high grass that was right at the border of our ranch and the big Empire ranch.

But at the end of the day, Dad grilled some carne asada he had marinated overnight. Lita and Jimmy Dale, Lacey, Vern, Iris and Sherman all came over. Jimmy Dale brought Lita and some tamales her mother had made. Lacey made potato salad. Dad grilled some corn and asparagus. Iris bought some guacamole and a big chocolate cake.

Vern. Well, he came up with a six pack of Fat Tire in his right hand and a six pack of Dos Equis Amber in his left hand.

There would be some new horses to start in the next few weeks. We would have to get some cattle ready for fall sale. Cut them out from the rest of the herd, trail them into the holding pens, and load them in big tractor trailers when the buyers and Sherman agreed on a price. That was still six weeks or so away.

When we were lining up to fill our plates, I looked west towards the Santa Ritas. The sun was fixing to go behind the mountains. The horizon was full of color. Red, orange, and dark blue streaks for as far west as you could see. The air was calm and peaceful and it was starting to cool down some. Lita was talking softly to Jimmy Dale. He was clean again. He had a fresh haircut and was wearing a nice white Stetson and a blue western shirt with pearl buttons. Dad and Lacey were talking to Iris and Sherman about Sedona. Where to stay. What to eat. What to do.

Me and Vern, we sort of stood off a ways from the rest. Vern said, "This is all might fine, Lim. Mighty fine."

I took a swig of Fat Tire and said, "Yes, it is. Mighty fine."

Chapter Nine

Pile Up on AZ83

Jack Fant had never lived more than a hundred miles from the Concho River. All three forks of the Concho River got together near San Angelo, Texas and from there the Concho flowed south until it merged with the Colorado some sixty miles south of San Angelo. Jack lived on Farm Road 1692, south of San Angelo. He liked the Concho and it forks north of San Angelo.

Jack could see the Concho slowly twisting through the back part of his spread. Jack was almost seventy. Sixty seven and counting every day. When he was seventy, he could sell his struggling truck line, collect maximum Social Security Benefits, and take leisurely canoe trips down the Concho. Most places on the River, you could throw a rock across it, but when Jack needed to sort things out, he would walk to the River, sit on an oak bench he had made in his shop behind his house, and listen to the soft river sounds. He especially liked the River at sunset. There were always birds coming in to roost in the nearby mesquites and cedars. Teal and mallards in the fall. Some geese in the winter.

They never stayed long. The Concho was just a stopover. The rest of the year, white wing doves and quail were always around.

The last weekend in October of 2003 had been planned out in advance by Jack. He was going to stay home with his wife Francine, drink beer, smoke a brisket, watch football, and see if he could get some action out of Francine. They had been married over twenty years. Francine was just twenty six when she married Jack. He was forty five when they married. He had just got the truck line going and Francine was his first hire. She had two years of college and a sweet voice. Put her on the telephone with your customers and things got smoothed out.

She was good with numbers and soon they were staying after work and slipping down to the Del Rio Lounge. She told him she was a good Christian girl but she had never read it anywhere in the Bible that a girl could not enjoy sex. She told him that one Wednesday night. She went to dinner with him instead of going to Prayer Meeting at the Logan Street Baptist Church. She sang in the choir and was the bookkeeper for the Church.

Jack knew he was not a good looking man. His nose was too big and it was not exactly centered on his face. Jack had moved around a lot as a kid. His mother was a waitress and they lived in a lot of towns while he was growing up. Del Rio, down on the Border, Pecos, Fort Stockton, Uvalde, and then back to the place on Farm Road 1692. His mother had moved back when his grandfather died and left her the small ranch. A little parcel of land that would not even support fifty head of cattle.

He had played football in high school, but he was slow of foot and uncoordinated. They tried him at tackle but he could not handle the speed rushers. At guard, he could not pull as fast as the coach wanted, so he became a center. One Friday night, he got his nose broken in a game against Big Springs. He told the coach he would wait to get back home before he got his nose looked at.

He got back home and his mother was in the living room of the ranch house drinking Old Crow and Coke. She was between waitress jobs and was always drinking and nagging him. She took him back to town and the doctor in the Emergency Room set his nose and referred him to a plastic surgeon. The plastic surgeon took the splints off his nose a few weeks later and recommended further surgery but the school board was balking at authorizing the surgery. They wanted him to go to another doctor and get a second opinion.

Jack never got around to it. After football season was over, he dropped out of school and started working for his Uncle Bob. Bob Tolliver. Bob drove a big rig all over West Texas and into Arizona, Nevada, New Mexico, and California. Jack would spell him driving and help with the loading and unloading when necessary. Jack was six foot two and weighed two hundred and fifty pounds. Not a lot of it was muscle. He never thought it was worth it to spend a lot of time either in the gym or on his personal appearance.

He was ugly. Plain and simple. The first woman he ever had, he paid for. Down across the border in Piedras Negras. Across the Rio Grande. He and Bob together. His uncle telling him not to carry much money across the border and to try to pick the girl that looked the neatest and cleanest. That way you could guard against catching some bad disease. They had left their truck outside their room in the Days Inn in Eagle Pass and caught a cab across the Rio Grande. Jack had taken a shower before they had left the motel. He had put some Vitalis on his hair and some Old Spice on his face.

Uncle Bob was a little sawed off runt, but he thought he was something with the girls. He told Jack, "Son, with these girls, you take the shower after you see them. "

When he said that in the cab on the way over to Piedras Negras, Jack noticed the cab driver turn his head toward Uncle Bob, but all the little sad faced driver said was, "Senor, the girls at the café I recommend are all very clean and muy guapo."

Jack and Uncle Bob sat down at a table in the back of the café and ordered cervezas. Jack hooked up with a woman in her early forties. She was black and had gold in her teeth. She was slender but had nice legs. When they got in the room, she told Jack how much she wanted and he gave it to her and she held the two twenty dollar bills up to the unshaded light bulb that hung down in the middle of the room.

Then she turned the light off and Jack was through in less than twenty minutes. The whole thing. Taking his clothes off, helping her off with hers, watching her fold her black panties and yellow bra and place them on the dresser, him exploring her body. Mainly her breasts. And then her guiding him into her and she straddling him and getting him off fast. Jack wanted to ask her how a black woman wound up whoring in Piedras Negras, Mexico. He was out the door before he got up nerve to ask her.

Jack picked the right one. He did not catch anything. Uncle Bob got the clap a few months later in Juarez. Jack was making some money driving trucks as a back up driver for a local truck line. Then he got the break he did not take advantage of. Driving a beer truck for the Budweiser distributor in San Angelo. He drove to all the little convenience stores and the grocery stores and bars all around San Angelo. Benefits. Retirement. No overnight stays. Raises from time to time. A sweet deal. Jack figured that out when he was around forty and he could feel age creeping into his bones and joints and he was writing checks each month to pay off his own trucks. And insurance. Rent. And wages. He had saved a little money, but when he was thirty, he quit and bought his own truck and worked as an independent. The work was spotty at times but the money was good.

He had just built his business up to six trucks when he met Francine. He finally worked the nerve up to ask her out to his place. They had been drinking Coors and eating cheeseburgers and watching a rerun of Ironsides when he got the nerve up to stick his hand inside her blouse and search for her left nipple.

Francine stood up. Ironsides was over and Francine turned the television off and took her blouse off. She had nice long blonde hair and a lot of it hung down over her breasts. She was short but she had a nice waist and a wonderful ass. She was wearing a white see through bra. He reached up to grab her breasts and she moved his hand and said, "I got a little surprise for you, Jack."

She slid out of her jeans. She had pink panties on. Hip huggers. She strutted some and Jack was getting frustrated. He stood up and she pushed him back on the couch. Then she took her bra off and walked to him. He reached for her. She pushed his hands away and said, "This is my show, roll with the flow." She put her hands on his shoulders and moved her breasts back and forth across his face. She left him sitting there and stepped back and took her panties off. Real slow. Then she took her right foot and put it in his crotch. Her feet were small and muscular. She had pink toenail polish on. She unzipped his pants and found his tool and touched him slowly. Up and down his shaft. He fought the urge to come but knew he did not have much longer before he would blast off like one of those space rockets down at Cape Canaveral.

She pulled his pants down, stretched him out on the couch, and mounted him. She worked up and down slowly and he knew he was going to disgrace himself and come too soon but he held out for a while and finally he grabbed her and mounted her. He pounded as hard as he could and soon it was over and she was laughing and running her finger nails up and down his back in long, slow strokes.

Francine gave him confidence. He drank less. She moved in. And she brought her eight year old daughter. Claudia. Even when she was young, Jack could tell little Claudia was a walking fuck up. Everything was a crisis. Church. School. Friends. She was a pretty little girl. Short like her mother. It might have helped if Jack had known Claudia's father. But he was gone. Some five years back. He was a Marine sergeant. Stationed in the Middle East. Francine got a check each month. But this was from the government for Claudia. No letters. No phone calls. Nothing from Sergeant Ralph the Marine.

Jack started going to church on Sunday. Just the one service at eleven o'clock. No prayer meeting or Sunday School. And no church if the Cowboys played one of the early games. Jack married Francine and adopted Claudia. His child now. She called him Jack. Not dad. Just Jack. Jack Fant. Newly married. Now a major check writer to the Logan Street Baptist Church. Not a deacon. He told the minister, an Irish lad right on the edge of obesity, "I'll give money, but no offices or titles. My checks don't bounce. Send that message on up to the Lord."

Jack did not care. Francine never slacked off in the bedroom. She liked it as much as he did. Jack lost some weight. Forty pounds. He got down to two hundred and ten. He couldn't go any lower. It was all he could do to maintain. Keeping it level at two ten. Eating steaks and eggs and ham and pork chops and meat loaf and green vegetables, eliminating the carbs, and keeping busy on his off days around the little ranch. Keeping the fences up. Cutting some hay for a little extra money. Bush hogging the big yard. Used to be, Jack could eat a half gallon of Blue Bell strawberry ice cream during Sports Center and go to sleep on the couch. No more of that for him. Now it was church, the truckline, and Francine.

Now he was closing in on seventy. He wanted to move to Florida. Some out of the way place down near Tampa. Buy a little boat, fish some, eat a lot of seafood, and walk the beach at night and early in the morning with Francine. But it was not going to happen. Claudia had graduated from high school a few years back and promptly married Danny Boy Stokes. His real name was Daniel Stokes, but when he was in the sixth grade a girl called him Danny Boy one day and it stuck. The way most kids said Danny Boy, it was like one word. He was the point guard at Claudia's high school. The backup point guard until his senior year. His senior year he got kicked off the team for smoking dope and selling it. He graduated and started a series of poorly paying jobs. He and Claudia eloped and after a few months, word got back to Jack that he was bragging at the pool hall that Claudia had the biggest tits in West Texas. It just might have been true but Jack did not see how you could put your own wife's name out like that in a dusty old pool room with a bunch of hard tails for an audience.

Jack did not say anything to Danny Boy about the pool room remark or much of anything else. You could be around Danny Boy five minutes and see he was bogus. Anybody could see it. Anybody but Francine and Claudia. Francine said he would find his way. Claudia and Danny Boy had three children in four years. All pretty little doll faced girls. Slender little blondes. Claudia said she was going to try to raise them as vegetarians so they would not be plump like her.

Danny Boy had five jobs in the four years. He was such a fuckup he lost a job as a meter reader for the county. He lost his ledger with all his meter readings recorded in them and said somebody must have stolen them out of his county truck. A few days later the records showed up. A barmaid at the pool hall went to the county building and gave them to a deputy sheriff waiting to testify in court. The deputy got them back to Danny Boy's supervisor and Danny got a call that afternoon. He was canned.

Francine and Claudia said he should have gotten a probationary period to prove himself but Jack thought that he would have fired him. Jack did not say anything. He kept his mouth shut and walked out of the house down to his bench on the Concho and watched the sunset and listened to the doves call.

The way Jack saw things, he would be loyal to Francine. She never complained when things were tight years ago. The closest he ever got to losing his temper happened that night when he came on back home. Francine was at the stove. Cooking fresh pole beans and frying chicken. He could smell fresh sour dough rolls in the oven. And he knew the chicken would come with mashed potatoes and gravy. All after Francine had worked all day helping at the truck line. He would have to work around the place a little extra so he could take the potatoes and gravy off his waist. He knew that. Maybe once a month, he would back slide and eat some potatoes and gravy or maybe a pint of Ben and Jerry's Cherry Garcia.

He was sopping up the last of the gravy on his plate with a hot sourdough roll when she said, "Now Jack, I been praying about this situation. This Danny Boy problem. I want you to put him on. Down at the Fant truck line. He drove a truck for five months before he got laid off. That was a few years back. You would not have to teach him anything. And best of all, Jack, you could be his mentor. His example. His teacher. Claudia and I were talking tonight and I told her if he was around a good Christian man like you, it would stabilize him."

His thoughts were different. The worst idea he had ever heard. A great way to jeopardize the morale of his other drivers. And a drain on his profits. Just when he was able to lease Francine a new Cadillac every two years and charge it off to the truck line. He knew he could forget about Florida. He was going to spend the rest of his life propping that worthless son of a bitch Danny Boy up.

What he wanted to do was take the worthless son of a bitch behind the house and beat the living shit out of him and put a thirty eight to his head and tell him to straighten his worthless ass out. But he did not. He hired him and he did a half assed job. He was fine on the short runs. In state. Down to Del Rio and back in the same day. The long runs were another story. Always complaining to Claudia about not being at home to help take care of the kids. Truth was that when he was home, he was drinking beer and watching TV. Danny Boy never missed a wrestling Pay for View. He swatted the girls on the butt if they walked between him and the TV. All the complaints from Danny Boy came right back to Jack at the supper table. Francine always taking up for him. Jack would endure all of it. Jack knew the real problem. Jack had no confidence in his ability to keep his wife. Jack was plain and simply pussy whipped. No way he could say no to Francine. No way.

He remembered the way he was brought up. No father. A mother who was seldom home. A mother who was a decent person who liked to drink her Old Crow when she was not working. So he just shut up and let it play out. Francine had a whole closet of negligee and night gowns and a couple of drawers full of pretty panties and bras. And they all looked good on her. Francine prancing out of the bathroom with pink panties and bra. Oh man, Jack thought. He still had it made. He would just have to find a way out of this without jeopardizing his life with Francine. All that strutting around the bedroom in high heels and black, lacey teddies was what he lived for.

A question in the back of his mind troubled him. He could never get around it. It lingered and he had no answer for it. The question was one of simple math. He was sixty seven now. If he sold his business for the three million dollars it was worth and he was drawing social security, just how long could he keep Claudia and Danny Boy going. He knew a new owner would fire Danny Boy inside of a year. Probably less than six months. You buy a business for a couple of million dollars, you can't lollygag around. You got to get your investment back. Hard to do that with Danny Boy on the payroll.

An idea had been coming into Jack's head a lot lately. But he knew it was wrong and he was not going to do it. He just wouldn't. But then things changed one Friday morning. Jack went to work and noticed that Danny Boy's truck and trailer were outside on the lot.

When he went into the office, Francine said, "Claudia called and said Danny Boy was having severe stomach cramps and was going to be out today."

Once again, Jack did not say anything. But the idea he had pushed aside came back to him before he even got out of the lot in Danny Boy's rig. He knew Danny Boy had a sweet trip for today. Odessa and back. One stop. So Jack made his trip for him. On his way back to San Angelo that afternoon, he had that same old idea come to him again. And this time, he thought it was his only choice. He would take a picture of Danny Boy down to the White Stallion Bar in Alpine and ask the bartender if Al was around. The picture would have Danny Boy's address written on the back.

Al would be around. Al was good about showing up. Al owned the White Stallion. He loaned out money on the side. And fronted some dope deals. Al was just shy of fifty and he was five eight and around a hundred and sixty pounds. The routine was you gave Al a picture and some cash and your problem was gone in a week or less. Jack had some cash no one knew about. When he got back to the office, Francine and Claudia were in the break room.

Jack sat down. He knew already what was coming. Danny Boy had a run to Nogales, Mexico to a maquiladora plant. He was taking some parts for assembly in Nogales. Jack knew who was going to be leaving in the early morning hours and driving across West Texas, Southern New Mexico, and Southern Arizona. All the way to Nogales, Mexico. Yes, sir, he could answer that question easily.

So he let it all play out. Francine making the excuses for Danny Boy and making a pitch for Jack to call in another driver to make the run. And Claudia just sat there waiting to get her say.

Jack said, "Francine, I sure am not going to ask another driver to cover for Danny Boy. I do that and I lose a driver. They are hard enough to find, anyway. But don't worry. Danny Boy is family. I will take care of it, myself."

Francine said, "Now, Jack, that is not right. You are spoiling those drivers. Spoiling them. You stay here and watch your football games. I know you want to see your Cowboys on Sunday and LSU and Ole Miss down in Baton Rouge on Saturday night. So you stay home. I will call the other drivers and line this up."

Jack said, "Francine, I will be back Monday afternoon. No problem."

Claudia looked at Francine and smiled. Jack thought it was a smile of triumph. He did not bother to ask Claudia what the smile meant. It probably meant she was happy because she and Danny Boy could stay up Saturday night after the football games were over and the children were in bed and watch porn together. And Wrestle Mania was coming live from Toronto, Canada on Sunday afternoon.

Jack drove to Alpine the next morning. He knew the White Stallion opened early. Al used to live in San Angelo and Jack had carried some questionable items to California for Al. Questionable items like guns. And hand grenades. Just a few here and there. A couple of hundred dollar bills here or there for Jack the transporter.

Now Al's cover was the White Stallion Bar. Jack cut south from San Angelo just after the sun came up and went southwest on 67 until he got to I-10. He went west through Fort Stockton and cut south on 67 again until it ran into 90 and he went west into Alpine. He pulled into the parking lot of the White Stallion before eleven. The front doors to the bar were open and a big white guy was mopping the floor. The guy looked mean. But he had a limp and his right eye wandered and would not focus. He told Jack to help himself to a beer. He would settle up with him when his mopping was done. Jack asked for Al. The bartender with the mop pointed to a back room and went back to mopping. Jack had been in before. Usually to pick up some cash. Or some guns. Or both.

Al was sitting behind his big oak desk. His feet were propped up on his desk. Jack noticed he was wearing shiny, brown alligator cowboy boots. With a square toe. Jack hated cowboy boots with a square toe. But the young kids. They said they fit better. Danny Boy wore square toed cowboy boots. Jack let it pass. No way was he getting cross ways with Al.

Al stood up and said, "Big money. What you got for me?"

Jack handed Al the photo of Danny Boy. Danny Boy grilling steaks. Jack remembered the day. The grill was Jack's. In Jack's back yard. The steaks were Jack's. But Danny Boy, he had this special marinade and he was going to show Jack how to grill steaks. Big thick rib eyes burned on one side was the end of that story.

Jack said, "I need this guy out of the picture for good. Gone. The sooner the better."

Al said, "A nice looking young boy, Jack. Tell me a little something about him. I see his name is Danny Boy. That for real?"

Jack growled and said, "Take my word for it. He is bogus. A big problem to me."

Al said, "I bet you brought ten. All hundreds. Since I may need you down the road, I will get it done for that. Within a week. Is that soon enough?"

"I got the ten. Just like you say."

Jack reached in his jacket and pulled a white envelope from the inside pocket and tossed it across the desk to Al.

"Within a week is what I told you. Don't be calling me if it is longer. No phones. Trust me. It will get done."

Jack nodded and got out of his chair and left the office and walked to the bar and asked for a Bud Light to go. He gave the bartender a ten and left the bar and crawled into his truck and headed west. He followed 90 through Marfa and got back on Interstate 10 at Van Horn. Lots of folks did not like this part of the country. Desolate. Yes. But Jack liked the wide open spaces and the little bars that popped up in the little towns. The old tough ranchers who still wore Silverbelly Stetsons and drove dirty old pickups with guns in the gun racks. Now some of them kept their walking canes in the gun racks while they drove their last miles down these lonely, dusty roads. Jack had kept it at eighty five most of the way between Marfa and Van Horn. The steady drone of the engine relaxed him. And the thought of having Danny Boy out of the way.

No remorse. Claudia brought Danny Boy into the family. After all the money he had spent on her over the years and she just called him "Jack" like he was the clerk down at Safeway. Danny Boy had life insurance. Good life insurance. Enough to pay the house and cars off. With some left over. He knew he would have to make up the slack. That was fine. He just did not want to go through his life being made a fool of by Danny Boy.

Jack went right on through El Paso. Still West on I-10. He had drained his beer before he had even passed through Marfa. Now he wanted to get into Arizona by night fall and have a few and watch Sportscenter and catch up on the games he had missed. LSU and Ole Miss in Baton Rouge. Always a classic. If he could just get up early in the morning, he could make Nogales before noon , deliver his load, cross back over the border and get a motel room in Nogales, Arizona and kill a six pack watching football in his room or go to a bar and drink the afternoon away. He wondered if he would get a tearful call from Francine on Sunday informing him that dear Danny Boy had been shot to death.

He figured that call would come later. He was glad he was not going to have to buy a new suit for the funeral. He had plenty of church clothes. He knew who would pay for the casket and the burial and the headstone. That was all on top of the ten grand.

Jack drove hard the rest of the day. It was almost eight that night when he pulled into a Holiday Inn Express in Willcox, Arizona. Hell, it was Saturday night. He wanted fresh sheets and a quiet sleep. He checked in and asked for a four o'clock wakeup call and paid in cash.

After he had everything set up in his room, he walked back down the frontage road to a bar a few hundred yards west of the Holiday Inn.

The bar had a big red neon sign. It said Bar. There were nine pickup trucks parked in front of the bar. And a ratty old yellow Jeep Cherokee was parked by the side of the bar. Jack went in and sat at the bar. The LSU-Ole Miss game was just finishing up. Jack was wrong. The game had been played in Oxford and LSU won 17-14. LSU was ranked third in the AP Poll and Ole Miss was ranked fifteenth.

Jack sat and drank a draft beer. Coors Lite. And he ate two cheeseburgers and an order of French fries. The beer was cold. The cheeseburgers were greasy and thick. Cheddar cheese slices and sliced pickles and a thin slice of fresh lettuce and a big dark red slice of tomato on each burger. He had them hold the onions. The fries were hand cut and fresh and hot. They had been dashed generously with salt and pepper.

Jack was on his second beer when the bar maid came over and said, "You been sizing me up since you got here. How far away from home are you, big boy?" Jack had not realized he had been staring at her. She was way too young for him. About Claudia's age or maybe a few years younger. She had nice long black hair. Done up in a ponytail. Jack just smiled and went on back to his room after his fourth beer. He got up at four and his head felt fuzzy. He had some pills in his old brown shaving kit. There were only two left. He took them both.

That will keep me awake and alert long enough to get through this day, he thought. He pulled out of Willcox onto I-10 and soon he was making the climb to the Texas Summit in the Dragoons. Almost five thousand feet in altitude. Then he went through Texas Canyon. The big boulders that lined the road were dark. The sun would not be here for another half hour. He passed through the Canyon hitting a steady eighty miles an hour.

He slowed down just a tad as he came down the big hill on the East side of Benson. He turned off on highway 80 going south to Tombstone. He picked up 82 north of Tombstone and headed west. He had less than two hours to drive until he would be in Nogales at the maquiladora factory. He started getting light headed right after he turned west on 82. He stopped on the side of the road near Whetstone and threw up.

He stumbled going back to his truck. That was the trouble with amphetamines. They could cause different reactions. He probably should have just taken one of the pills. That would have done the job. He could tell he was a little disoriented and it scared him. Driving for all these years and he had never had an accident or been arrested. Never was caught carrying weapons into California.

He rolled his driver's side window down and turned off the heater. It was probably close to fifty five degrees anyway. The fresh air would keep him alert. He thought. It had worked before. You get drowsy and let some fresh, cold air into the cab and it could get you through a few more miles until you got to the next town with a decent truck stop. He was on the final push. Not long and he would be grabbing a nap before the Cowboys kicked off.

Jack slowed down. He knew something was wrong. He was dizzy and he could not hold a thought in his head for more than a few seconds. And his eyes were not focusing right. He was going less than fifty when he came into Sonoita. He passed the feed store on the right and slowed down some more. He was less than an hour away from dumping his load in Mexico.

He just did not understand it. He had slept a good six hours uninterrupted last night. He had forgotten to call Francine last night and his cell phone was switched off now. He just did not think he could deal with anymore family news this morning. He would call her after she got out of church. She would probably have the kids at her house and Claudia would be shopping in San Angelo and Danny Boy would be watching Wrestle Mania. Steve Austin and The Undertaker in the Main Event.

When Jack neared the intersection of Westbound 82 and Southbound 83, he nodded once and when he looked up he saw he was headed right toward a white SUV in the turn lane of Highway 83. In a flicker of clarity, he saw an older, clean black, Ford 150 stopped in the right southbound traffic lane. There was a young boy behind the wheel. The truck was pulling a silver two horse trailer. Jack saw a black horse in the trailer and then it all came together in a clash of brakes and metal as his truck drifted slowly but surely into the white SUV.

The truck was slowing down but the force of the collision knocked the white SUV into cars in the right southbound lane. It was all noisy. Jack tried to focus his eyes and his mind but it was too late. His truck glanced off the SUV and hit the black F-150 right behind the left rear wheel. Jack's truck kept going and turned the truck on its side and the trailer snapped away from his truck and hit the F-150.

The horse trailer turned on its right side and the big, black horse was impaled on a broken piece of the trailer's side moulding. The side moulding was penetrating his stomach. Blood gushed from the wound and the horse was on its side. He screamed. A loud and mournful and desperate sound.

Jack never heard the horse scream. He had not put his seatbelt on when he had gotten back into his truck after throwing up near Whetstone. The impact of the crash threw him through the front windshield and his neck broke when he hit the rocky ground on the west side of the highway. Jack Fant dead at sixty seven on the side of the road at the junction of 83 and 82 in Sonoita, Arizona shortly after dawn on an overcast Sunday. Tragedy his legacy.

A woman and her two children in the SUV were hurt badly. But they were conscious. Crying and comforting each other and listening to the horse scream. Ambulances were called. The Sheriff's department sent three cars. Jack Fant's trailer was lying on top of the Ford 150 and no one could see if the driver was dead or alive.

Iris Snider was eating a buttered biscuit and drinking orange juice when the phone rang shortly after the wreck. A neighbor called and said there had been a bad wreck and she thought Lim Couch was trapped in his truck and that black horse of his was making a god awful noise. He was hurt bad and somebody needed to take care of him. Iris and Sherman went and told Vern and Dewey. Dewey was drinking coffee and eating breakfast when Sherman told him. Lacey was in San Diego at a sales meeting.

Soon they were all at the scene. They could not see much of Lim's truck. But they heard Davey and Dewey went to Sherman's truck and got Sherman's forty five out of the glove compartment and walked over to the trailer and knelt beside it and tried to comfort Davey but he saw his left front leg was snapped. A clean break. Bone showing near the foot. Dark blood was dripping from the side of the horse trailer.

He knelt beside the trailer for a few minutes then stuck the revolver inside the trailer and shot Davey in the center of his forehead. He put the revolver back in the glove compartment. Davey was dead. No more suffering. At least they had that. The deputies would not let them get close to Lim's truck.

Lim heard the shot and knew what it meant. He was pinned in the cab of his truck. He had pain in his head, his ribs, and his legs. He thought his left leg was broken. And his left collarbone. He was scared to touch it. He knew it had to be broken to hurt this much. It was throbbing and throbbing hard. But his right ankle was busted too. When he tried to move it, it hurt as badly as his left leg. His head had hit the cab door hard in the crash. He was laying on his right side. He had undone his seat belt after the crash. There was no airbag in his truck. He knew some ribs were broken. He was having trouble breathing and there was not a lot of air in the truck.

He knew he should call out for help. Yell as loud as he could. But he was hurting so bad he could not find the strength to yell. His head hurt and this scared him the most of all. A deep throb came and went inside his head. He passed out some, but he always came back. He knew he must be in shock.

He could not hold a thought. Could not make a progression from one thought to a logical conclusion. Could not reason. Thoughts came into his head and left. He thought he heard Iris call his name. The next instant he was thinking about potato chips.

But the worst of it all was the shot. He knew what it meant. His good horse Davey was gone. Davey had never let him down. Davey at the Tucson Rodeo strolling down the west rail in front of the big cheering crowd at a full rack. His head nodding. High proud head. Davey coming home to the barn in the soft afternoon light with Carrie Ann riding him. His neck arched, showing out for Carrie Ann. Davey in the early morning light, nickering when Lim walked in the barn. Davey his good horse. Bought with his money. Trained by him. Now dead.

The deputy sheriff in charge came over and talked to Dewey, Vern, and the Sniders. She was a sad faced woman in her late forties. She had lived in this ranch country most of her life. Not much she had not seen. She knew the Sniders by reputation. They were decent ranchers who kept to themselves and raised good cattle and horses. That was all she knew of them.

Her name was Mary Riley. She said, "You will just have to be patient. We have ordered a crane from Nogales, Arizona. It is being loaded on a flatbed trailer right now. Then, it will be and hour or so getting it here."

Dewey said, "I know my boy is gone. I just do not want a lot of people looking at him when we get his body out from under this mess."

Iris said, "Dewey Couch, you just have some hope. Am I right, Ms. Riley?"

Officer Riley said, "We just do not know. No one has heard a sound and you can not see anything."

Dewey stood as close as he could to the truck. He tried to listen for a sound. A groan, a wail, a cry, or anything. Just a sound. None came. People started to leave the scene. Bystanders and curiosity seekers and friends of the Circle S. A TV crew from Tucson showed up. The pretty blond reporter wanted to talk to Dewey. She tried to stick a microphone in his face. Dewey walked off. Iris told the reporter, "Now is not the time to ask us questions." Iris walked back to Sherman's truck and put her arm around Dewey. He was sitting on the tailgate. His head was down and he did not want to talk.

When the crane came, it took almost an hour to get it in position to move the trailer. Finally, the crane moved the trailer slowly upward. The trailer shifted and resisted upward movement. But eventually it did move. It moved upwards and away from the cab of Lim's truck. The EMT's brought a stretcher and reached inside.

One stood up and said, "He's alive, but he's in shock and we have got to get this cab off of him. The crane driver came over. He had a long, heavy iron pole. Probably twelve feet long. He stuck it inside the cab and he and the EMTs and Vern all pushed upward and the cab moved enough so they could slide Lim out.

His eyes were open but when the EMTs and his father and Mary Riley asked him questions, he just stared back. He was laying on the stretcher. The EMTs gave him an IV and put him in an ambulance. Iris climbed in the back with Lim. She did not ask permission and no one challenged her. An EMT also got into the back of the ambulance.

Sherman told Dewey to follow the ambulance on into Tucson. Sherman said to put his flashers on and stay right on the ambulance's tail. No one would stop him. He said he and Vern and Raul would take Davey back to the Circle S and bury him on a hill overlooking the Cienega Creek. The tall hill before you got to the first east pasture. There was no shade on the hill but you could see the ranch to the west and the Cienega to the east if you were standing on the hill.

It was slow getting Davey back to the ranch. Sherman borrowed a forklift from a lumberyard in Sonoita. Then Sherman went down to a welding shop just south of the intersection and someone came up and cut the top of the trailer off and Raul took the fork lift and got Davey out of the trailer. There was a sheet of three quarter inch plywood on the ground next to the trailer. Sherman had brought it with him from the lumber yard. Raul sat Davey down on the plywood and then scooped the plywood and Davey up and started back north to the Ranch.

Vern brought the ranch tractor and backhoe up to the top of the hill and dug the grave. He had brought a couple of shovels. One was a long handled shovel and one was a short handled sharpshooter. Vern and Sherman stepped into the grave and smoothed out the sides of the grave and scooped out the loose dirt.

When Raul came up the hill with Davey, it was already midafternoon. A dull, winter sun was slowly creeping westward. They dropped Davey down on the ground at the top of the hill and left Vern to watch over the body while Raul and Sherman went down to the creek and loaded rocks from the streamside into the bed of Sherman's truck. When they were back on the hill, Sherman had Raul drop Davey's body into the hole. They stretched his body out and placed dirt on it for a few feet and then covered the dirt with the piece of plywood. They shoveled the rest of the dirt on the plywood. They finished it by stacking rocks on the grave.

When Raul stacked the last rock on the grave, Sherman said, "I'll get him a nice headstone. Put his name on it. Bring it back out here when Lim can come. Horse deserves that. Damn fine animal. Helped raise that boy. Helped a lot around the ranch. Only fine gaited horse we ever had on the Circle S."

They were tired when they finished. Davey weighed more than a thousand pounds and it was hard work to get him stretched out evenly on his side. Plus loading and unloading rocks from the Creekside.

After they had put the tractor in the shed, Sherman pushed his hat back and said, "Rather than run around all over Tucson trying to find Lim, I think we ought to go back to the house and sit on the porch and rest. I will scare us up some dinner. We can just sit tight. Iris will be in the middle of things and she will call me when she knows something."

They watched the gold and pink sunset with cold Fat Tires in their hands. Not a time for talking. When the sun had passed over the Santa Ritas, Sherman said, "Hope hamburger helper is okay with you boys. The cheeseburger and macaroni is my favorite. Won't take long."

They were just settling down to dinner when the phone rang. Sherman answered it and listened to Iris talk for a few minutes and then he said, "You go to the Arizona Inn, get a room, get some food sent to the room, and then sleep. Raul and I will start sorting out the cattle tomorrow. The buyers will come the week before Thanksgiving. We will be out all day. Call me tomorrow about this time. We buried Davey. High on a hill near the Cienega."

When he was through talking, Sherman listened for a minute and then said, "I love you, too." He came back to the table and sat down and then got back up and went to the refrigerator. He came back with three more Fat Tires. In the brown bottles.

He said, "My last one tonight. Three beers does me in these days. Used to could drink all night and up into the morning."

He poured half of the beer into a glass and leaned back in his chair. He said, "Iris said they won't be through with him for a few hours more but what she knows from talking to one of the intensive care nurses is he has a concussion, four broke ribs on his left side, a broken left leg, and a broken right ankle. And the most painful of all. A broken left collarbone."

They drank the last beer slowly. Raul and Vern were fixing to leave and the phone rang again. It was Dewey. He said he would stay in the room with Lim tonight and come on home tomorrow night if that was alright with Sherman.

Sherman said, "That will be fine, Dewey. That will be fine. We buried Davey up on a hill near the creek. I will order a headstone as soon as we get these cattle sold."

Raul and Vern helped clear the table and stack the dishes in the dishwasher. When they were gone, Sherman turned on the Encore Western Channel and watched Red River for a few minutes. He kept nodding off so he turned the TV off and poured himself a taste of whiskey. Elijah Craig 12 year old. He did not even pour a shot. He sipped it until he fell asleep in his leather recliner. He did not want to sleep in his bed without Iris there beside him.

The next day, Dewey and Iris talked to a doctor. A young man. For a doctor. Probably in his early forties. He sat with them in a little office near the nurses station in the Intensive Care Unit. They were at the University of Arizona Medical Center on Campbell. The doctor told them that the prognosis was excellent. All breaks should heal in time. Main thing to do was keep his spirits up. And keep him trying to improve. Rehabilitation would take almost a year. At least. The ankle was the worst but only because it would take more time to heal. The ankle was broken close to the foot and would have to be in a stable cast for a long time. He would need personal care. The broken collarbone would make it difficult to move and to sleep. He would need a nurse to look after him.

Iris was writing on a small tablet. Dewey said he was glad he was alive. He knew he could pull through this. The doctor said, "I am recommending some psychological intervention by a specialist in traumatic work injuries. She will talk to him and get him focused. Right now, he does not want to talk, he doesn't want to eat. Only thing he asked is that I tell you to get a red bandana out of the truck. It is on the rear view mirror. It belonged to Carrie Ann. I assume that is his girlfriend. I am limiting his visitors to you two people. Ms. Snider, I understand you have been like a mother to him since he came to your ranch. And Mr. Couch, you certainly can see him. But that is enough. He needs to concentrate on getting over this. No distractions."

Dewey went back to the Circle S later in the day after tracking down Lim's truck at a junk yard in Nogales, Arizona. He found the bandana tied around the rear view mirror. It had blood and grime on it. Dewey remembered the bandana. Carrie Ann tied it around her neck when she rode Davey. He took the bandana and the papers in the glove compartment home with him. He ate some cold pork and beans for supper and went up to the Ranch House and told Sherman he would see him in the horse barn at five in the morning. Before he went to bed, he put the bandana in the washer and waited on the old creaking machine to finish the last cycle. He took the bandana out of the washing machine and checked to be sure it was clean. He put it in the dryer, turned it on, and went to bed.

The next night, he took the bandana to Lim. Lim asked him about the horses. Dewey told him about Sherman and Vern and Raul burying Davey on the hill overlooking the Cienega. Lim did not say anything but Dewey could tell he was gritting his teeth. His eyes were full of water but he did not cry. In a few days, they moved Lim out of the

Intensive Care Unit. Dewey drove from Sonoita to the Hospital every night and drove back to the Ranch about sunup every day.

A kind faced woman who looked to be just past sixty came to see Lim after he had been in the hospital a few weeks. Her name was Dr. Jill Arthur and she was a psychologist who specialized in traumatic work injuries. Lim liked her. They talked up on the roof of the Hospital. Lim liked it up there. It was open and you could see all the mountain ranges surrounding Tucson. The Rincons to the east, the Santa Ritas to the south, the Tucsons to the west and the Catalinas to the north.

Dr. Arthur had a soft and soothing voice. They talked about a lot of things. Carrie Ann and Jeremy and Mary leaving, his mother, Davey, his father, Vern, Sherman, and Iris. And Jimmy Dale. And the horses. Louie, Little Molly, and Socks. She came for several weeks. Not every day. One day she asked Lim a question. The question was, "Lim, if you could be anywhere this morning, where would you be? And what would you be doing?"

Lim said he would be on the Circle S riding Davey up the long hills that led to the mesa at the foot of the Whetstones.

She asked him who he would like to be with him.

He said, "That little son of a bitch, Jimmy Dale, and Carrie Ann. Well, scratch that. That is stupid to wish for. She is not coming back. So just make it Jimmy Dale."

Dr. Arthur said, "And what would you do on the mesa?"

"Gather the cattle and start them back down the long hill and trail them to another pasture. And go home and take care of my horses and go down to the Ranch house and eat steaks and drink a beer with my father, Raul, Sherman, Vern, and Jimmy Dale. Talk about cattle, and horses, and what had to be done the next week. And have Iris fuss at Sherman some for not appreciating her cooking. And have her bring out a peach cobbler and tell Sherman she was not sure he could have any. After supper, go up and play dominoes with my dad, Raul, and Vern. Maybe finish the day off with a shot of good whiskey."

Dr. Arthur said, "You can do all of that. Now Lim, tell me, do you regret anything. Something you are ashamed of or just something you are not proud of?"

Lim dropped his head and Dr. Arthur had to coax him to speak. When he did, she could hardly hear him.

What he said was, "That morning, the morning of the wreck, I did not eat much breakfast and when I was leaving, I stopped by the house and fixed me two peanut butter and jelly sandwiches and found an apple. If I had just went straight on to the Boyce ranch, Davey would still be alive. Just think. Three or four minutes either way and this would never have happened and Davey would still be alive."

Dr. Arthur said, "Lim, I knew you had been blaming yourself for the wreck and Davey's death. That is typical of people like you. People who willingly take on responsibility. People who care about those around them. And that is good. Some people blame other people for everything that happens to them. But look at it, Lim. Look closer. You did nothing wrong. The woman driving the white SUV is probably thinking the same thing you are today. Was it her fault she and her children were hurt. If she had left ten minutes earlier, she would not have been hit and the truck would not have come over and hit you."

Dr. Arthur came a few more times. On her last visit, she gave Lim one of her cards and told him she was satisfied he was making good progress emotionally. She told him to call her if he got depressed for longer than an hour or so.

The cattle were gathered, sorted, and the current year's calves and some of the Criollo steers were sold. Dewey worked during the day. He ate his fast food suppers in Lim's room. Lim kept the red bandana in his room. Lim told his dad, "I know it is over between us. She is where she should be. But that don't mean I can't miss her if I want to."

Dewey did not say anything. He slept on a cot in the room with Lim. He would leave before five to go back to the Circle S until the cattle were sold. When the cattle were sold, Sherman said, "Dewey, you set your alarm for seven. Iris will look in on him most days. The worst is over. If you oversleep, don't worry about it. Raul and I can handle eighty percent of what needs to be done around here now. A slow time 'til the middle of January when calving starts again."

A lot of the time, Lim just felt a dull pain in his leg and ankle. If he moved too quickly, he sometimes would feel a sharp pain in his ribs and collarbone. His appetite came back in a few weeks and the hospital served him a decent Thanksgiving meal. He was working on coming home for Christmas. Just to be up in the horse barn again was his goal. Even if he was in a wheelchair.

Randy Price showed up a few days after the wreck. Dewey asked Iris to call him. Dewey had insurance on Lim's truck. Good insurance. But he did not know if it would cover all of the hospital and doctors' bills. Randy came and had Dewey sign papers of representation. Lim was just eighteen. Dewey signed them, also. Randy told them not to worry about anything right now. He was looking into Fant Trucking's insurance coverage already and he would find out if Jack Fant had owned any real estate back in San Angelo.

Back in San Angelo, Francine had been babysitting her three grandchildren on Sunday afternoon when she got a call from a Sheriff's deputy in Arizona. Jack was dead. Killed earlier that morning when his truck crashed. She called Claudia on her cell phone and Claudia left Macy's and went to her mother's house. Claudia called Danny Boy.

When the phone rang, Steve Austin was just being introduced at Wrestlemania. The Undertaker was coming down to ringside. Danny

Boy said shit and answered the phone. He had to turn the TV off and leave. $49.99 for the pay for view down the toilet.

They buried Jack Fant near the bench where he would go and sit and watch the Concho River flow by. Before the burial, there was a closed casket service at the Concho Baptist Church. Reverend Craft praised Jack for his generous gifts to the church and told a few stilted stories about Jack. They were not funny. He did not mention the amphetamines in Jack's system. Nor did he talk about guns and hand grenades going to California in Jack's trucks. And Al and the White Stallion and ten thousand dollars and a photograph of Danny Boy were all part of a secret Jack took with him to his grave.

They buried Jack on the Thursday after the accident. Danny Boy and Francine both went to work on Friday. Francine had changed the routes around so Danny Boy could be back at the terminal by four thirty. Before he left that morning, Francine told him she had prayed last night and asked God's guidance in running Fant Trucking and an idea had come to her this morning while she was eating Frosted Flakes and sliced bananas.

Danny Boy wanted to tell her if it did not have anything to do with pussy or money, he was not interested. Danny Boy saw the potential for big, unreported profits with Fant Trucking. Problem was that Jack and now Francine were both too stupid to do it. Danny Boy could see the trucks rolling all over the Southwest with drugs hidden in rocker panels, door panels, and false bottoms. Massive profits to be made.

Danny Boy and Riley Darnell had talked about it some down at the pool room. Off at a corner table with a pitcher of Coors Lite and a platter of nachos and two cold mugs sitting between them. Riley had the connections. He drove a truck for a commercial laundry and uniform service and his brother Wynn had just got out of Huntsville and knew some heavy hitters. Wynn had been a stick up man down in San Antonio but he had told Riley that was too dangerous. Running dope and guns was where the money was. A fortune was there to be made.

When Danny Boy got back from his run that afternoon, he went up to the office to pick his check up and talk to Francine. He told himself to keep a straight face. What Danny Boy wanted most was to make a lot of money, hide it from Claudia, and then walk away from her and the three kids. And now she was talking about having a fourth. A boy. Just what Danny Boy needed.

When he was in the office, Francine and two of the girls were in her office. Claudia had taken the oldest daughter to the dentist to be fitted with braces. Not covered by his insurance at the Fant Trucking Company.

Francine said, "Danny Boy, on Monday, I want you to come inside and help me. You can have my old salary. Eighty five thousand a year. 401K.But not my Cadillac. You can have Jack's company truck. The red Dodge Ram. Same health benefits. I will take Jack's salary. I want you calling on customers, supervising the drivers, hiring and firing. In a year, you will be running the place. Well, less than that if you apply yourself. You are smart, Danny Boy and you have a pleasant personality and you are super nice looking. Trust in God, Danny Boy and apply yourself and you will make a lot of money. Jack would not get out and wine and dine our customers. You are a natural. What do you think? If you would like to go home and talk to Claudia and pray on it tonight, I will understand."

Danny Boy paused for a few seconds and then he said, "Francine, If you think this is the Lord's will, I will do it. I can come in tomorrow. Saturday. And you can start showing me how all of this works. How we get our business. What we charge. That sort of thing. "

Francine was happy. Danny Boy had such an earnest look when he talked about his future. And he was such a handsome young man. She just knew things were going to be fine. The phone rang. She waved at Danny Boy as he left. He did not take the kids with him. He was on his way to the pool room. He was hoping Riley would be there. He was going to start the ball rolling by hiring Riley to take his place as a driver. He would then gradually replace the other drivers with people he and Riley handpicked. Knock down a pitcher of Coors Lite, split some wings with Riley, and plan his future. His plans for the night. Come home after the kids were put to bed and see if Claudia would give him some.

When he pulled up in front of the pool room, Danny Boy reached for his door handle and he noticed a pretty red head standing by his door. She was trying to light a cigarette and the lighter would not catch. She rapped on the window. She appeared agitated and distracted. He rolled the window down and turned to her. She did not say anything. The little twenty five automatic she pulled from her purse was in his face and he tried to duck but she shot him between the eyes and he slumped forward over the steering wheel. She put the muzzle of the twenty five on his left temple and fired again. The motor was still running and there was music coming from the radio. She recognized Randy Travis singing but she could not place the song.

The pretty red head turned and walked briskly to the corner of the pool room, turned the corner and got into a brown 1998 Toyota Camry. Al put the car in drive and they went down an alley behind the pool hall and turned back onto the highway and headed towards Alpine.

The girl took off the red wig. Her hair was short and black and she had big brown eyes. She would be twenty five in the spring.

Al said, "Look in the glove box. Take the white envelope out and count it. Should be fifty five one hundred dollar bills."

She took the money out of the white envelope and fanned it and put it back in the envelope and put it in her purse. She unloaded the twenty five and put it back in her purse and lit a joint and took a deep hit.

In a few minutes, Al said, "Rene, you're good but always count the money. Always."

They made it back to Alpine a few minutes after dark and Al went in his office after telling the bartender to order him a pizza from Domino's. And he wanted a cold pitcher of Bud when the pizza came.

Rene drove her little blue Tacoma back to El Paso. She went to sleep that night while studying for her Civil War History exam on Monday. Grant at Vicksburg. She was a junior at UTEP and wanted to get her doctorate in History and teach somewhere. Somewhere with a beach and an ocean and a big yellow moon.

Francine and Claudia never could figure out why anyone would kill Danny Boy. It just made no sense to kill such a handsome boy who worked hard and was a good husband and father. No sense at all. The Sheriff's department never developed a suspect. Danny Boy was buried on the next Wednesday. Right next to Jack Fant. Francine and Claudia would be able to visit both graves at the same time and it just seemed right to Francine that they would spend eternity together. Side by side with the soft noises from the gently rippling waters of the Concho River to comfort them.

Chapter Ten

Lim Gets Up and About

Lim Couch was moved out of the Intensive care unit in less than a week. He began the slow journey to recovery. After a few more weeks, Lim was moved to the home of Karen Saunders. Karen was an occupational therapist. She was a retired registered nurse. She had moved to Tucson in the late nineties when she turned fifty five and could retire from the Trauma Unit of the hospital in St. Paul, Minnesota she had worked in for years.

She and her husband retired to Tucson and bought a three bedroom adobe home on Presidio Street, just a few blocks south of Fort Lowell. She lived three blocks east of Country Club. Her husband died in 2000 and she wanted to supplement her income and be useful. She used the second bedroom of her home as a patient room.

Her usual duties were to care for someone in their home in the last stages of life or to care for someone injured in an accident. Karen had worked cases before for Randy Price and she took Lim Couch into her home and cared for him as best she could.

The main problem Lim had was boredom. He didn't like to read much, he only watched a few ball games on TV, and he was a loner. He spent a lot of time in the back yard sitting in a wheel chair and doing nothing. One of the things Karen watched for was signs of depression. She told Lim about cases she had handled during her years as a registered nurse and Lim began to understand his problems were not so bad. But he still got bored.

Soon Karen worked a routine out for him. But it was three months after the accident before Lim could start rehabilitation. He would swim and do pool exercises at the LA Fitness on lst Avenue on Monday, Wednesday, and Friday, and do some limited stretching and weight work on Tuesday, Thursday, and Saturday. On Saturday afternoon, Karen would carry him home to the Circle S. Lacey would bring him back to Tucson on Sunday night or Monday morning.

Sometimes during the week, Lacey would stop by and carry him out to dinner. He could talk to her easier than anyone else. Even Iris. He only wanted Iris to see the good side of him. He did not want her to know his fears and anxieties.

He told Lacey that he still had dreams about being trapped in his truck. Being confined scared him more than anything. He did not like small rooms and he longed to be back at the Circle S on horseback, riding in the long flat pastures and rolling hills. He liked to go to Guero Canelo on Oracle and eat two Sonoran hot dogs with Lacey.

It was spring before the cast on his ankle was removed. Karen intensified his pool workouts. She began to swim with him. She was almost sixty now but she had an attractive figure, blond hair, and a ready smile. Lim and Karen would leave the gym every morning and go to The Egg Connection on Fort Lowell near Country Club. They would eat breakfast. Lim felt he could relax there. He would eat eggs over medium, grits, bacon and whole grain toast most mornings. Karen had orange juice, poached eggs and toast. They both drank a lot of coffee. It was a family owned business and had been in the neighborhood for over thirty years. Most days a nice young girl named Libby waited on them. She was the daughter of the owner. A big guy named Frank who had come west from New York City.

The atmosphere in The Egg Connection was intimate and friendly with the pictures of John Wayne, the Rat Pack, and Marilyn Monroe on the walls. The Egg Connection had a Workman's Special for $1.99. Frank, the owner, was a Mets fan and would stop by Lim and Karen's table some times and Lim would ask him baseball questions. Frank usually knew the answers.

When he got home after breakfast, Lim would usually sit in the den and read the Arizona Daily Star. Sometimes he would fall asleep in his chair and not wake up until the middle of the afternoon. After a month of swimming, he could swim half a mile. He felt like he was getting back in shape and was ready to get back on his horse.

It was July before the doctors released him from Karen's care and let him go back to the Circle S. Lacey drove him home one Thursday night. Iris and Sherman came over. Iris brought a chocolate cake. Dewey made spaghetti. Vern brought Fat Tire and dominoes. Charley Webster was back. He and Raul came down from the bunk house and stayed a few minutes. They did not eat. They said they ate before they came down. Raul said he was riding Little Molly and Dewey was riding Louie. Sherman said Lim timed his return just right. The second cutting of hay was next week. Lim asked about Louie. Dewey said with a little training he could be an automatic. Just like Davey and Little Molly. He was maybe a year away but he was getting close. Dewey said Lim could have Louie now. Dewey said he would ride his old bay gelding from now on

Iris said she wanted Lim to ride with her the next morning. Sherman said he could lollygag for a day but he could take up some of the fencing duties the day after he went riding with Iris. After dinner, Vern and Lim played dominoes on the front porch. Vern was drinking a Fat Tire from a frosty mug. Lim looked at the clear night sky and saw a lot of stars off in the distance. He could see the faint grey outline of the Whetstone Mountains in the East. A big, powerful, yellow moon shed a calming and soothing light on the Circle S.

The next morning when Iris came into the horse barn, Lim already had Pepper and Louie saddled. They rode out into the soft morning light. Soon, the temperatures had climbed into the nineties. They rode first to the hill overlooking the Cienega Creek where Davey was buried. There was a headstone. It read "Davey - A Good Horse".

Lim got down and went to the headstone and knelt on one knee for a few minutes. Iris hung back for a while then walked up to Lim and put her left hand on his right shoulder and gently squeezed. She did not say anything. Lim said, "I got to remember to thank Sherman for this."

When they were riding down the hill towards the Creek, Lim said, "And I might start by thanking you. I know you had something to do with it."

Iris said, "It was Sherman's idea. He pays attention to the horses on the Ranch. He can tell you stories about every one of them."

They rode east until noon. They checked pastures, herds, and fences. Iris knew when a pasture was grazed down and the cattle needed moving. She kept records of the cows and knew which ones had calved and which ones had not. Iris told Lim she had packed a lunch. Nothing fancy, she said. They sat under a mesquite tree and ate turkey sandwiches. Iris wanted Lim to take college courses over the Internet when he had his feet on the ground and was settled down in a routine again.

Iris said Pepper was stiffening up in his back end. His trot was just a little rougher. Lim said he could have a stifle joint problem. Iris said he was over twenty years old now but he was still the prettiest horse in the Tucson Rodeo Parade and Grand Entry. They rode for most of the day and then headed back into the fading, late afternoon light. Lim trailed behind Pepper. He was moving a little stiffly in his hind quarters, but he was not fidgeting or throwing his head. Lim did not think he was having any pain. Just getting older.

On Saturday, Tommy came down from Tucson. He waited for Lim until he came back to the horse barn at the end of the day. They went down to the house and sat on the porch and Tommy slowly drank a beer. Lacey was in the house. She was cooking supper. Dewey was slicing mushrooms for the salad. Lim could smell chicken frying.

Tommy had unsaddled Louie in the horse barn and fed and watered him for Lim. Lim had sat on a hay bale and drank a cold Dr. Pepper.

Tommy had not said much at the barn. He spent a lot of time just looking at his horse. When they were sitting on the porch, Tommy said, "Well, Lim, things are not progressing very positively in my divorce proceedings. When you got hurt, Sherman called and said he was not going to even charge me board because you were not here to ride Louie. Well, Dewey has been riding him and he looks great. My wife wants the divorce but she won't compromise on any of her demands, so it looks like it may take another year. I got almost seven thousand in Louie. You make me a decent offer, pay me what you can down, and the rest as you get it and Louie is yours. Best for him. Best for me."

Lim said, "Randy Price has settled with our insurance company for the truck, trailer, and Davey. I can offer you eight now."

"Eight is a fair price. Even as good a horse as he is. He is still a gelding and you do not plan to show him. Eight is a deal."

Lim went into his room and looked in his desk and found his checkbook, wrote the check for eight thousand, and handed it to Tommy on the porch.

"I will miss him. I had dreams of my daughter and me going on a nice trail ride up near the Yellowstone. Her on Louie. Me taking pictures and riding some mule the outfitters would assign me. Never happen now. Never. That's the bad thing about divorce. You lose your money and your dreams. Rough."

Lim did not know what to say. Lacey came on the porch a few minutes after the sun set and invited Tommy for dinner. He said he had better get back to Tucson and walked back up to the horse barn and turned the lights on. He went to Louie's stall and talked to him a few minutes. Louie was eating hay and did not pay attention to him.

Tommy turned the lights in the horse barn off and walked back to his car. He passed by Dewey Couch's home. All three were at the table eating. Tommy remembered the smell of the chicken frying and turned his black BMW toward Tucson.

When it came time for the hay to be gathered, Sherman told Lim his job would be to drive the tractor that pulled the flatbed trailer they stacked the hay on. When the hay was stacked in the barn, Sherman broke out a cold six pack of Coors. Charley Webster said he and Raul should get two each and Sherman and Dewey should have one. Lim told Charley that would be fine with him. He could drink a cold Dr. Pepper and be happy.

When Charley was through with his first beer, he handed his second beer to Lim. Charley said, "I need to watch my drinking. I think I will have me a Dr. Pepper."

Sherman said, "Friday and Saturday nights are your downfall, Charley. You get lonely and go somewhere and drink the time and your troubles away. We have all done it."

Lim sat and listened to the easy banter between the men. It relaxed him. He was glad to be back at the ranch. He liked being outside working. But Lim soon saw that he was not needed. Charley Webster and Raul worked hard and they were all the help Sherman and his father needed.

Lim was glad to see Randy Price drive up late one Friday afternoon a few weeks later. He and Lim sat on hay bales in the horse barn and talked. Lim had received a few medical bills since he had returned to the ranch. Randy said for him not to bother opening any of them. Randy told Lim to buy some big envelopes at Walgreens in Nogales and some stamps and mail him any medical bills that came to the ranch.

Settlement talks had not even started. The insurance carrier for Fant Trucking had contacted Randy but nothing would be done until all the medical bills and reports were all submitted. And then the haggling would begin.

Randy told Lim to drop by the Worth Ranch near Tubac on Saturday and talk to Lamar Tisdale. Lamar was a Quarter Horse trainer. He needed an assistant. Randy said that Tisdale was not only a trainer but he was a respected Quarter Horse judge. He usually had his pick of shows he could judge. Randy said Amy Worth was the owner of the ranch. She was high strung, rich, abrasive, and attractive. She had retired at age fifty after a successful career as a plastic surgeon in Beverly Hills.

Randy said the Worth Ranch was not really a working cattle ranch. There were around sixty head of Angus. There were three bulls and the rest were cows. No one paid a lot of attention to the cows or the fences or the pastures. There was no hay equipment so hay had to be trucked in. The main focus of Amy Worth was showing quarter horses. She had grown up around horses. Her father was a butcher in a grocery store in Williams in Northern Arizona. She had ridden with some of her school friends on their ranches. On their horses. Never enough money in her parent's household to buy a child a horse.

Now things were different. She owned a ranch. Her son was in Portland running a restaurant and bar. She had dumped her husband years ago. She had leased Socks from the Circle S and shown him to an AQHA Championship. The Sniders had sold him for over eight hundred thousand dollars. Lim had started Socks out at halter when he was a colt.

Lim went over to the Worth Ranch on Saturday afternoon. He found Lamar Tisdale in his office in the horse barn. Lamar was almost as tall as Lim. He moved around the office slowly. He told Lim he would be doing a lot of grunt work around the barn and taking care of sixty head of cattle. He planned on hiring someone else to help as soon as he could but it would be tough for a while.

Lamar rocked back in his chair and said, "Now, I will give you some background. I was in Viet Nam during the Tet Offensive. Marine. I saw combat. I didn't get hurt. Nothing. Lucky as I could be. A little later I was redeployed to Saigon. I drove a jeep for a Colonel. The Colonel played some golf, went to a lot of meetings, and stayed out of the combat zones."

"Every Wednesday afternoon, he had a standing appointment with this lady. Vietnamese and French blood. I got him there right at two o'clock. One Wednesday, I was at a bar down the street from his girl's house. I was sitting outside at a table. Drinking beer with this whore who had just shown up. All of a sudden, this motorbike drives by. Two young guys tooling down the street. Nothing unusual. When they got even with the bar, the passenger threw a satchel bomb through the door of the bar. Next thing I knew, there was a big explosion. Dead and wounded soldiers and civilians everywhere. I was on the ground and when I got my wits about me I looked around and there was my lower left leg. Severed at the knee. Still in my boot. Laying under a bunch of debris. "

"I was fitted for a prosthetic in California and learned to walk almost like a normal person. Reason I am telling you this is because if I am a little slow getting around, know it is not because I am lazy. I just get tired easily."

He pulled his left pants leg up. The prosthetic fit in his boot nicely. He told Lim that when he was discharged from the Marines, he went home to his parents' ranch just south of Hereford in the Texas Panhandle. Lamar would not talk to anyone about his three tours in Vietnam. So people in the county supplied the details. His friends and neighbors made him into a war hero and Lamar stood mute.

The Hereford Brand was published five days a week. The daily circulation was less than five thousand but the newspaper had plenty of advertising and most families in the area read it. They wrote an article describing Lamar as a combat veteran who had completed three tours of duty.

Lamar showed and trained quarter horses through the 1970"s and in 1984, he was certified as an AQHA judge. He had learned who to drink with, who to stay away from, and which wives would kiss and tell. Everyone liked a tall, quiet, war hero.

He told Lim he was scaling back now and only trained a few horses. Amy Worth had three horses. A gray colt who was not halter broken, a four year old, sixteen hand, bay mare she showed in English Pleasure, and a six year old sorrel gelding she showed in Western Pleasure. Lamar's plan was for Lim to bring the gray along like he had done with Socks years ago.

Lamar walked Lim down to a small two bedroom adobe house that sat underneath a large Arizona sycamore. Lamar offered Lim two hundred dollars a month more than he was getting at the Circle S and told him he could train two horses on his own as long as it did not interfere with his duties at the ranch. And he could bring Louie to the ranch to help with the cattle.

Lim took the job and moved to the Worth Ranch. It was exciting. He had to do for himself. No more coming home at night to a cold Fat Tire and a frosty mug waiting for him. He had to fix his own meals. At first he ate a lot of food out of cans, but he learned gradually to cook for himself. If he was tired at night, he could always boil some pasta and warm up some meat sauce he kept in meal size packages in the freezer of his noisy old white Kenmore refrigerator.

The first two months were frantic. Amy Worth did not make matters easier. She barely spoke to him when she came around and if she had a question, she always asked Lamar. Lamar hired another hand before Christmas. His name was Jamie and his wife, Rosa, cooked and cleaned for Amy Worth.

Jamie was Irish. Rosa was Hispanic. Jamie was in his late forties and Rosa was still in her late twenties. After they came to the ranch, Lim had less grunt work and more horse and cattle work. And he had someone else he could talk to. Jamie was like Lim. He liked to be out on the ranch working. Jamie noticed that the calving barns were in pitiful shape.

He and Lim cleaned them up and repaired structural damage that had been neglected. When calving time came around, Amy did not show any interest in how many calves were born or how many cows did not have calves. Jamie and Lim took the three bulls and kept them in a separate pasture until it was time for breeding. Amy never knew. It was just something she was not interested in.

Lim told her there were some cows that had not calved in a couple of years and she said to keep them around. She had more grazing land than she needed to keep up her herd. Lamar helped with the branding. Lim talked him into buying a calving table.

Lim's first spring at the Worth Ranch was in 2005. He would turn twenty in the summer. Either he or Jamie drove the truck and horse trailer to the horse shows. There was usually one a couple of weekends every month. Lim and Lamar would hang out at the shows. Lim would usually be grooming the three horses at five in the morning.

cl 255

He saddled all the horses and warmed them up for Amy. She would ride her horse an hour or less before she showed him. Sometimes she would be in two consecutive classes and Lim would hand one horse off to her and then unsaddle the other one. Things were hectic at the shows but when there was time, Lim watched the classes and Lamar would tell him his top five horses and give his reasons for his choices. Lamar's picks were usually the same as the judges or mighty close to their picks.

After the show ended, Lamar and Lim would usually go eat at some steakhouse or bar that the trainers and exhibitors frequented. It was not long before Lim had two horses to train. One was a colt and the other one was a two year old. The money was good and Lim was even saving some money every month.

Lim still had time to ride Louie at the ranch. Comparing Louie to the young horses Lim watched at the shows, Lim felt he could be a good show horse. Western Pleasure, Trail, and Reining were all classes he felt Louie could do well in. Lamar told him to try his hand at showing. Amy said it was a good idea as long as Lim had her horses ready for her to show.

Lim showed Louie in the summer and fall of 2005 and got three Western Pleasure points on him in six shows. He showed him in trail and got one point. This got horse and rider noticed by other trainers, exhibitors, and horse owners. Lim did not have time to take on any new horses but he got his name out there to the right people. He turned down chances to train horses because of his work on the ranch. He turned down twenty seven thousand for Louie. He knew a horse like him only came around a few times in a person's life time. Louie, Little Molly, Socks, and Davey.

He got a call around Christmas of 2005 from Jody Race in Safford who wanted to buy Louie. Jody was in her sixties. She was a retired CPA. Lim did not let himself hear what kind of money she was talking about. He remembered Davey and how he felt lying in the hospital wishing Davey was alive. Now Davey was buried on a lonely hill. You found a horse like that and you just did not sell. He remembered his Dad getting that faraway look in his eyes when he talked about his good roping horse Tommy that he sold before he moved to Benson to sell tires and raise a family.

Jody Race asked Lim to find her a nice horse if he could. She wanted one like Louie with some chrome and with a calm, easy disposition. Jody had an easy way about her. She drank with the guys after the shows. She had bought Lim several beers one night after a show in Sedona. Lim had told her about Davey and the wreck and she had said he had to count himself lucky to have owned a horse of that caliber. Many people had never even owned one outstanding horse. She said she was looking for her first one.

A few weeks later, Vern told Lim about a colt he had seen on a ranch near Bernardino. Lim went to see the colt on the next Sunday. He had already looked at over a dozen colts and had not been impressed enough with any of them to recommend them to Jody Race.

Vern rode with him over to the ranch. The ranch was a few miles from the Pedregosa Mountains. It was owned by James Ray Smith and had passed through five generations as the Smith Ranch. James had a generous Forest Service grazing allotment that had been in his family for over sixty years. He raised Angus cattle. He had two sisters who did not live on the ranch but shared in the profits from the ranch.

Vern was Smith's long time farrier and drinking buddy and when they were through trading friendly insults, they took Lim to the horse barn and showed them the colt. He was a nice bay. He had no chrome. Lim put a halter on him and walked him down a pasture fence. He saw alertness and good confirmation. The price was five thousand dollars with no room for negotiations.

When he got home that night, Lim called Jody Race and told her he had found a colt he liked. He told her he did not have any chrome at all but he wanted her to look at him. The next Sunday they drove to the Smith Ranch in Jody's pickup. She had picked him up at five that morning. She said she wanted to avoid any chance of meeting Amy Worth. She said Amy was a double dog bitch if there ever was one. Lim kept silent.

Lim and Jody walked the colt down a pasture fence and talked for a little while. Lim said he liked the price of the colt, his solid Three Bars and Poco Lena breeding, his alertness, and his calm and friendly nature. He did not tell her that the colt was a better prospect than Amy Worth's gray. Nor did he tell her that Amy had paid almost twenty thousand for her colt.

Lim did not crowd her. He told her if she was not confident the colt had potential, she should not buy him. Jody bought the colt. On the way home, Jody told him that she had never spoken two words to Amy Worth. She said the reason she disliked her was her cold and impersonal attitude toward her horses. She had watched Amy get on one of her horses, show him, then hand him off to Lamar after the class and walk away just like she was leaving her car to go shopping in a mall. Once again, Lim was silent. But he knew she was right. He saw the same thing every day. She never groomed her horses. She never showed any affection towards them. They were a means to win a competition. And that was all.

By the end of 2006, Lim had settled the injury case, invested his money, and grown tired of the travelling he had to do as part of the show circuit. He called Randy Price and met him down at Amado Steak House. They sat in the bar, drank beer, and ate Porterhouse steaks and baked potatoes. Lim told Randy he was ready to move on. Things were fine with him and Lamar but he knew he did not like to travel and show horses.

Randy had moved his law office to Tubac. His little spread was only a few miles south of his office. He had renovated an old building next to the Big Horn Gallery. His office was in an old adobe house with a large front porch and kiva fireplaces in the waiting room and Randy's office. He had a large window in his office and had a good view east of the foothills and the Santa Ritas. There were old, shady mesquite trees on either side of the front porch.

Randy had tired of the grind. Living in Tucson and commuting to his small ranch was time consuming and draining. Most of his clients were ranchers, cowboys, or just plain good, hardworking people. He also had some lowlifes mixed in with the good clients. Randy had made a lot of money practicing law and he had saved a lot and plowed a goodly portion of his earnings back into his ranch. He had no debts.

One of the low lifes was his only hand at the ranch. Randy always told people it would be hard to explain why he even let Harvey Mote on his ranch, much less take care of it. Randy had represented Harvey when he was seventeen. He had stolen a Mercedes out of a parking lot in Nogales, Arizona and was taking it to Tucson to sell when he was picked up on the old Nogales Highway near Sahuarita. He did some juvenile time and Randy forgot about him until he got a call from Harvey a few years later.

Harvey was in jail again. This time in Benson. He had killed a man over a woman. The victim had a butcher knife and Harvey had a thirty eight. Harvey was caught coming out of a motel room with the victim's two hundred and fifty pound wife. Harvey shot the husband three times before he fell dead in the parking lot by Harvey's old blue Dodge pickup.

Harvey got ten years for that one. Randy got paid seven hundred dollars of a five thousand dollar fee plus the title to Harvey's pickup. Randy sold the truck for twelve hundred dollars and thought he had seen the last of Harvey. Harvey went to Florence and did most of the ten years.

One Friday night in 1998, Randy drove down to the ranch for a peaceful weekend of horseback riding, reading, and drinking. When he pulled up in front of his house, Harvey was sitting on the front steps. He was wearing an old blue t-shirt, blue jeans and a broken down pair of brown boots.

Harvey said, "Heard you was short a hand. I could use the work."

Randy said, "You flatten your time or are you on parole?"

"Flattened it out. Worked in the kitchen and stayed off to myself and out of trouble."

Randy let him in the house, fed him, and drank some whiskey out on the porch with him. He told himself he knew better than to do this. But he said to himself that he would give him one chance and if he messed up, he would have to throw him off the ranch. He would probably have to get the Sheriff or one of his deputies to help him do that. It never came to that. Harvey worked hard and stayed off to himself most of the time.

Now Randy lived in the ranch house and saw Harvey every day. Besides Randy, Harvey's only company was an erratic procession of loud, overweight women who liked the five foot eight, one hundred and thirty five pound Harvey Mote.

Randy told Lim about the murder case. He said that what confounded him was the story that would never be told. Randy often wondered during slack times in his life how the two hundred and fifty pound woman and the hundred and thirty five pound Harvey had managed the sexual coupling.

Lim laughed and said he was a novice in all of that. After the steaks came, Randy said Lim was too hard on Amy Worth. He said that during the time, twenty something years ago, when Amy Worth broke into the highly competitive Beverly Hills medical community, there were few women in the hunt.

She had to be tough. Randy said there were lots of tough women in business and Lim had better get used to dealing with them. Iris Snider was an exception. She had a good business head on her shoulders and she was super good with figures. But she had a gentle side to her. Randy said Iris had a tough side to her and when business was on the table, she was tougher than Sherman. Lim was like a son to Iris but he could not expect that but one time in his life. Lim agreed. He knew Randy was right but he told Randy the thing that stuck in his craw was the way Amy Worth treated her horses. So cold and impersonal.

Randy said it was a business to her. The horses were performance athletes. She expected results. But her checks did not bounce and she paid Lim's wages on time and did not interfere with what he did. Lim said the cattle part of the operation was just for tax purposes and he knew that was true because she had told Lamar and him that one night over dinner in Chandler after a show. She had said spend what you have to spend, and no more, and do not bother me with the details.

Randy was drinking a cold mug of draft beer. He tilted the mug and took a healthy swig.

"Give me a week and I might have a good deal for you. Just might have something you would like," Randy said.

Friday of the next week, Randy was waiting in the bar at the Amado Steak House for Lim after work. They ordered beer and food. Tonight Randy went for the barbequed chicken and potato salad and Lim stuck with the big Porterhouse and baked potato.

Randy said, "I was raised on the High Meadow Ranch in Williamson Valley. Twenty miles north of Prescott. About a hundred and twenty miles north west of Phoenix. I have a twin brother. Name is Jim."

"Jim is the oldest. By fourteen minutes. He went to Arizona State and moved back to Prescott after getting his Dentistry degree. I went to U of A and finished law school and practiced all this time down here in Tucson and southern Arizona. Our parents are dead and we have no other siblings. My dad died about ten years ago and Jim sold his dental practice and moved out to the ranch. He runs it. Mother died three years ago. Jim's wife, Sonia, died a few years back. He has a son in the Marines. He served two tours in Iraq and one in Afghanistan and now he is in Washington. When he retires, he is probably going to come back and take over the actual running of the ranch. Talked to Jim and told him about you and he said for you to come up and see if you like the spread and maybe you two can work a deal out. He said you could train horses and help around the ranch. I told him you were a good hand as long as he did not depend on you for a lot of roping."

Lim told him he could take off a few days next week and drive up to the ranch and see if he liked the set up.

On Sunday Morning, Randy and Lim rode up to Prescott. Randy showed him the Rodeo Grounds, the Plaza and Courthouse, and then Randy drove up a steep hill to the Hassayampa Inn. Lim liked the old hotel. They ate breakfast in the dining room and then drove north on 89 some twenty miles and turned left on Ash Fork Road. They drove another three miles and turned right onto a winding gravel road. They topped a hill in another half mile and Randy stopped his car.

"No offense, Lim, because I know you think the Circle S is the prettiest place in the world, but just look around you."

The land was mostly flat and green. Angus grazed peacefully in fenced pastures. There were a few rolling hills but for the most part the land was flat. Lim saw the big ranch house and a few other buildings. Barns painted white with green roofs. It was impressive.

Jim Price was in his office in the horse barn. He looked ten years older than Randy. You had to look hard to see they were twins. Jim's hair was gray. Randy still had dark brown hair with a few random streaks of gray mixed in. Jim moved slower than Randy and he had a very slight limp. He had been thrown from a horse a few years ago. His left hip had been replaced and he did not ride anymore.

Jim and Randy showed Lim around the ranch. It was bigger than the Circle S by a few thousand acres and there were no brushy slot canyons. Everything was open. There were a few trees, but not many. Wide open spaces with mountains way off to the east and Granite Mountain to the south west. You could see for as far as your eyes would let you.

When they were back at the horse barn, they sat in the office and drank cold iced tea Jim had made earlier. Jim said, "Now Lim, this ranch is like most others from a cowboy's point of view. Long hours and low pay. No benefits and no retirement. Course, you might be riding out one morning to check fences and see a pasture full of Pronghorns. And Deer. They come down and eat with the cows. Not much use in trying to chase them off. They just go off another mile and go on back to eating. But they roam. Our place today, someone else's place tomorrow. But they come and go every year. And I let you off early when the Rodeo comes to town. Mighty fine Rodeo we got here in Prescott. Some say it is the oldest Rodeo in the country. Others dispute that. Nobody disputes the fact that is a damn good Rodeo. Held over Fourth of July Weekend every year."

"Randy says you are not scared of hard work but you are sort of stuck in a dilemma. You want to halter train colts and start young horses under saddle. And help some of your old Quarter Horse friends find horses. Well, I can use you. We get shorthanded sometimes. When I need you, you help us. Paco will be your boss. Paco grew up on this ranch. Now he is the foreman. Man works hard and is easy to work with."

They left the horse barn and walked across the hill to a small white stone house with a green roof. The house had two bed rooms, a kitchen and a small den. There was a large stone fireplace in the den and a smaller stone fireplace in the larger bedroom. A small mudroom with a washer and dryer, was at the back of the house. There was a wide, but shallow front porch.

Jim said, "This will be your house. You can hook up to my DirecTV if you want to. They will just charge me a little more. I buy enough wood every year to last us all."

They left the small house and went to a larger house and found Paco. He was slim, close to fifty, with coal black hair and a full black mustache. They all went back to the office and sat back down.

Jim said, "Paco, I am going to hire this boy. He will be our horse wrangler, help when you need him around the ranch and in his spare time train some horses."

Paco said, "That is good. The first thing I would like you to do is look at our stock. We have too many horses. And some need selling. I want you to thin our herd out. We got seventeen horses. We have three cowboys on the spread counting me. No need for all these horses. Will you be bringing a horse with you?"

Lim said, "Yes."

Paco said, "What can he do?"

Lim said, "Anything we need him to do."

Paco said, "I would like to see this horse."

That night, Jim took Paco, Randy and Lim to the Palace Bar on the Plaza in Prescott. They ate in the restaurant and then went to the long, oak bar. The bar had a brass foot rail.

Jim said, "There is a history to this place. Back in the 1800"s, this whole area on Montezuma Street was called Whiskey Row. Whiskey, gambling, and whores. All you could pay for, you could get it on Whiskey Row. The Palace Bar was a gambling hall and bar. The dining area was full of slot machines, faro, blackjack, and poker tables. Everyone said the bar at the Palace was the best. Hands down. Well, that all changed in 1900. Whiskey Row burned down. But patrons came in and salvaged the bar before the place burned down. I been coming here as long as I can remember. Our dad and mom would bring me and Randy to town when we were just kids. Not even old enough to go to school. We would eat big old cheeseburgers with fries and when we would leave, Randy would always run out ahead of us and crawl up on one of those bar stools. Dad would jump his ass and tell him, "Goddamn son, you got plenty of time for that later on. Give me a break and be a kid for a little while."

They stopped in the bar and had a drink. Jim had scotch. Randy had a shot of Jim Beam. Paco and Lim drank shots of Herradura Reposado tequila. Paco ordered the tequila for Lim and said it was the best. Even better than Patron. Jim said, "One more task you got, Lim. And it is to be taken seriously. Now, Paco and I come in here most every Thursday night. Eat a good meal. Have a shot or so of good whiskey and talk about business. What we need you to do is come in with us, leave us alone while we are talking business, cut your drinking off at one drink, and drive us home. We buy your meal and one drink at the bar."

Lim said he could handle that and Jim asked would he start tonight because he wanted another drink. Jim and Randy had a couple more drinks. Paco stopped at two. They stood at the bar and talked. Randy told Lim some scenes from Junior Bonner had been filmed in the Palace Bar. Lim nursed his tequila and when it was done, he drank a cup of black coffee. Jim told Paco there were two old brood mares he did not want sold. He would just let them die on the High Meadow. Randy said there was an old gray gelding he was partial to. When they left the long, dark bar, Lim got Jim's truck keys and drove them back to the ranch. The sky was clear. Stars and a big yellow moon drenched the country side with soothing light. Granite Mountain loomed large and sinister in the west.

When Lim got back to Tubac and the Worth Ranch, he told Lamar he was leaving and gave him thirty days' notice. The day before he left for the High Meadow, Lamar called him into his office. He gave him a framed picture of Zan Parr Bar. It was painted by Orren Mixer.

Lamar said, "Lim, when I first started training and showing horses at the AQHA shows, I was in Abilene one spring day. I think it was seventy six. Might have been seventy five. Carol Rose came into the arena leading Zan Parr Bar. He looked just about like he does in that picture. I bought that picture first thing after I got to be a judge. Reason was that he had the best confirmation of any horse I had ever seen. That day in Abilene, I stood at the rail and tried to remember everything I could about him. When the class was over, I trailed Carol Rose to where she had him stalled. Her husband was one hell of a horseman. Name of Matlock Rose. I introduced myself and we stood around and talked for a while. "

"You look at that picture. Zan Parr Bar was a chestnut with a star. That's all. No white socks or stockings. But what he had was that classic Three Bars confirmation, only better. Three Bars was a race horse but he had that high, strong hip and highly muscled shoulder and front end we look for. And he had a long graceful, but well-muscled neck and a nice head with a small nose. And alert, but not skittish eyes. Zan Parr Bar had all that and more. He was foaled in 1974 and he died of colitis in 1987. During his brief life, he was an AQHA Champion, AQHA Register of Merit Performance Horse, AQHA Superior Halter Horse, AQHA Superior Steer Roping Horse. He was the World Champion Three Year Old Stallion and the World Champion Aged Stallion in both 1979 and 1980. He was a grandson of Three Bars. As a sire, he was just hitting his prime when he died. He still has a legacy of champions he sired."

Lamar picked the picture up and looked at it and smiled. "Now Lim, this is the gold standard. Right here. Put this up on a wall somewhere in your office or your house and look at it when you are buying a horse for someone."

Lamar said his second favorite all time horse was Zippo Pine Bar. "Zippo Pine Bar was bred to be a halter horse. He was a grandson of Three Bars. His mother was a daughter of Poco Pine. Her sire was Poco Bueno who was a son of King. Anyway, the halter dreams never panned out but I judged him at the All American Congress and the World Show in Western Pleasure and he had the most natural ability of any pleasure horse I have seen. Your Louie is nice. He has the same traits, but he has more chrome. Zippo Pine Bar was a sorrel with a blaze and right back stocking. He lived to be twenty nine years old. Because of his longevity, he surpassed Zan Parr Bar as a sire."

Lamar and Lim spent most of that last day looking through old Quarter Horse Journals Lamar had kept over the years. Lamar showed him pictures of horses he had judged and results of big shows he had helped judge.

When Lim left the Worth Ranch the next morning, Louie was in the trailer eating hay. Lim stopped at the ranch house. He wanted to say thank you to Amy Worth for letting him work at the ranch. He walked up on the porch and rang the doorbell. Rosa answered and Lim asked to speak to Amy. In a few minutes, Rosa came back and said Ms. Worth was on the phone and would be tied up for a while and it would be best if Lim came back in the afternoon.

Lim went back to his truck. He had bought a nice gas grill last summer and he checked to be sure it was tied down snug. He walked back to the trailer and checked the hitch and looked in on Louie. The sorrel was eating hay. Lim got back into the truck and left Worth Ranch and headed north and west to Williamson Valley and the High Meadow Ranch.

Chapter Eleven

The High Meadow Ranch

Lim Couch

I got to the High Meadow just before calving started in 2007. The ranch had good clean calving barns and things went fairly smoothly. Only difference was there were a lot more calves to deal with than at the Circle S. I did not even try to start taking outside horses. I got all of the High Meadow horses ridden and rated in my mind the first few months. Paco liked Louie and I told him he would be doing me a favor if he would ride him while I was riding the ranch stock.

One of the old brood mares Jim Price had wanted to keep was a decent ranch horse. Her papers said she was twenty three but she reminded me of Little Molly. A nice slow trot and good cow sense. She was a big, gangly bay with no markings but I rode her a lot and grew to depend on her. The other old mare was not much use to anyone. She was twenty one and I thought she had a stifle problem. I never even rode her. I put a halter on her and lunged her some and put her back in the pasture.

Paco had two horses of his own and the two other hands on the ranch had a horse each. I found six horses I thought we could sell and Paco and Jim agreed. We kept the old gray gelding Randy rode when he came up to the ranch.

In the spring of the year, we branded and Randy came up to help his brother. Randy rode the old gray gelding when we were gathering and sorting the cows and calves. Jim and Randy had cousins that lived in the Prescott area. They had children and grandchildren and it was a tradition for the children in their families to come out and help during branding. They mainly got in the way, but that was fine. With the calving tables, branding was so much easier. The older kids could help with tagging the calves ears and giving them shots.

Later that spring, Randy came up on a Friday and he told me he needed to talk to me when the work was done that day. It was almost dark when we quit for the day. Randy came down to my house. I only had the picture of Zan Parr Bar on the wall of my den. My only decoration except for a few pictures of Davey and Louie and the folks at the Circle S I kept on a coffee table in the den. I had put my nice picture of Carrie Ann in a drawer underneath my tee shirts and underwear.

I gave Randy a cold bottle of Fat Tire and opened one for myself. He said, "Lim, I do not know exactly how to tell you this but the gist of what I want to say is that Jimmy Dale Scruggs is in a lot of trouble and I am afraid he is going to prison for a long, long time. And Lita is back at the ranch by herself. But she won't be by herself long. She is about four months along. I can't get him out of this. All I can hope for is an early parole date."

I asked what he had done and Randy said to let him tell the whole thing, so I sat back and listened.

"A few months ago, the Sheriff back in Davey Waddell's and Jimmy Dale's county got a call from a police office in LA. Jimmy Dale's mother, Nancy, had been found dead in a motel room with a spike stuck in her arm. Bindles of heroin were found in her purse. Jimmy Dale and Davey went out and buried her there in LA. From then on, Jimmy Dale started drinking something awful. Lita left and went back to Sierra Vista and one weekend a month or so ago, Jimmy Dale drove down to Douglas and went in this pool hall and was eating and drinking a beer when two of those Ragsdale boys came in. There was bad blood between the Ragsdale brothers and Ray Scruggs, Jimmy Dale's dad, for a long time. Anyway, one of them came up to Jimmy Dale and asked if he was Ray Scrugg's boy. Jimmy Dale didn't say anything and the guy said he would be quiet too. Nobody could be proud to be Ray Scrugg's son."

Randy drained his beer and I got up to get him another one. He shook his head. He said he would wait 'til suppertime. I put some logs in the fireplace, started some kindling and sat back down to watch the fire catch and build.

Randy said, "Well, the Ragsdale boy that started it all was bigger. A lot bigger than Jimmy Dale, but Jimmy Dale busted a beer bottle on the bar rail and stuck it in his right eye and then took a pool stick to the other one who was running out the door. When the second boy was down, Jimmy Dale went back to the first one and almost killed him. Might have been an easier law suit to defend if he had. What will get Jimmy Dale the big penitentiary time is the damage he did after the fight was over. In the eyes of the law, it could be the worst thing. When the police came, Jimmy Dale was going berserk with that cue stick and he struck an officer with the stick and broke the officer's hand. Of course, then Jimmy Dale got a good whooping, but nothing like what the first Ragsdale got. Head injuries. Broken jaw. A bunch of teeth knocked out. All with a pool cue. So add it all up and you have aggravated assault, assault with a deadly weapon. The deadly weapon being the cue stick. Two counts each and assault on a police officer. So he is facing some serious time."

"I am trying to get him ten years. His age, he could probably parole out in four. Davey will keep the ranch going. I know that. But Jimmy Dale might not see that child of his until he or she is in high school. I just do not know. He won't see anyone now except Davey and me. He saw Lita once and told her to go make a life for herself and she told him she was pregnant and would stay on the ranch and live her life the best she could. But Lita is an attractive woman. Still got a lot of color in her cheeks. Big brown eyes, long black hair. A woman like her might not be around long and who could blame her. She is smart, too. Real smart. Looks like she will have to put her plans to go to college away for a few years."

Turned out, Randy got Jimmy Dale an eight year sentence for assaulting the police officer and the other charges were dropped. I wanted to go see him in Florence but Randy said he would not come out of his cell to see anyone but Randy.

That first year I did not take any new horses until June. June of 2007. By then we were through with branding and had sold or traded our excess horses. By Rodeo time in July, I had three two year olds under saddle. I spent a lot of time riding them in the pastures with Paco and Louie. Paco called Louie his Cadillac. Paco told me Louie was a horse of a lifetime. Paco started working him with cows a lot. He had more patience with cows and horses than I did. I was getting paid to train other people's horses and I was getting my own horse finished off for free.

The Rodeo was the Fourth of July weekend and the Sniders and Lacey and my Dad came up and stayed at the Hassayampa Inn and went to the Rodeo. After the Rodeo, we would all go to the Palace Bar and pull a couple of tables together in the dining room and eat. We finished the night off in the bar. Sherman got me a room near theirs so I would not have to drive home. When we left the Palace, we had a long walk up the hill to the Inn. My dad was just like he always had been except he was happier. He laughed more. Lacey and he looked comfortable. Iris told me she missed me and worried about me even though she knew there was no cause for her to worry.

The week after the Rodeo, we moved a lot of cattle from pasture to pasture. Jim Price rotated his cattle a lot. He was constantly riding a little red ATV through the pastures checking the grass. We wanted to get the cattle settled for a while because we had the second cutting of hay coming up next week. We wanted to get the hay in before the monsoons came tearing through the valley. Monsoon season is the name given to the big summer rains that come in late July through parts of September in Arizona. They usually come late in the afternoon and last anywhere from ten minutes to four hours. A good rain is one that starts in the morning and lasts 'til sunset. Those are few and far between.

The Thursday of that week after the Rodeo, I figured we would not bother going into Prescott on Thursday night. I was in charge of the remuda and we were all riding two horses a day. When I got through feeding and was turning the lights off in the barn, Paco and Jim Price showed up and said they had already cleaned up and were hungry for a steak. I would have to go like I was. Dirty and tired.

We ate steaks and baked potatoes and apple pie with ice cream. No one talked much. Jim said it looked like we would finish moving the cattle by the middle of the day on Saturday and we could start cutting hay on Monday. There was no forecast of rain in the near future. Usually the monsoons started for real in August.

We moved up to the bar after we settled our checks. I was nursing a shot of Wild Turkey 101 and listening to Paco and Jim talking about buying three or four good young horses. Two year olds or coming two year olds. One stud and three mares. The idea being to upgrade our horses. Ride the mares for a few years and then breed them to the stud. Paco said we could use a remuda of fifteen good horses and right now, counting Louie, we had eight. Paco said the O RO and the Babbitt ranches all bred their own stock.

Some of our horses were showing signs of getting worn out this week. I was there to drive, listen, learn, and keep silent unless spoken to. I thought Paco had a good handle on what we needed to do and he did not need me to help him make his point with Jim. Jim said he would see if he got a good price on the cattle he sold this fall and if the year showed a decent profit, he would buy a stud and three mares this winter and I could start them under saddle in the spring. He said if we did this for two years, we would have two good studs and up to six brood mares.

Jim was drinking scotch and Paco was sipping his Herradura Reposado. Donna, our waitress, was a tall, rangy blonde in her middle forties. She had a tough, raspy voice. I figured she would be a lot of fun in the sack. She told me there were some girls looking at me and giggling. They were sitting at a table next to the far wall. I turned around and looked at them. There were six of them. Most about my age and a couple a few years older. I turned back to the bar and forgot about them for a while. I listened to Paco and Jim talking about the best place to buy some good ranch bred horses. Jim said he liked the idea of buying horses to bolster the remuda but he hated the actual act of buying horses since he had been burned several times before. Talked into paying premium prices for mediocre handling horses. He said he would take me with him so he could have someone to blame if we picked a dud. But he was joking with me. The scotch and the tequila and the bourbon and the good food were all kicking in to make our long, hard day on the range easier.

One of the girls walked up to the bar and stood by me. She was just a little shorter than me and had pretty, long black hair and blue eyes and a pretty face. She wore heavy, black rimmed glasses. She had mischief in her eyes and she looked me straight in the eye and before she said a word, I said oh shit to myself. I had the same feeling I had when I was first around Carrie Ann way back in high school.

She said, "I am Sheila Ann Hancock. My girlfriends are curious about you. We want to know if you are a real cowboy or if you just got off your shift at Walmart or Lowes or Ace Hardware or Home Depot and went home and changed into your duds."

Jim Price said, "Miss Sheila Hancock, I am Jim Price and my little brother and I own the High Meadow Ranch in Williamson Valley. Now, to answer your question, let me say this. There are stages to being a cowboy. Things you have to learn. This young gentleman is Lim Sanders Couch and he is in the earliest stage. It is the stall cleaning stage. He is doing quite well and we may let him on a horse around Christmas."

Paco said, "I am Paco and I am the foreman of the High Meadow Ranch. Lim is in charge of our remuda and he trains horses, also. This week, we are trailing cattle from one pasture to another. We did not give him time to shower and clean up before we came to town. He can only have one shot of whiskey or one beer because he has to drive us home."

Sheila said she would be back in a minute. She went back to her table and talked to the other girls for a minute and then picked up a half full mug of beer and came back to the bar and stood by me. She told me one of the girls at the table had finalized her divorce today and everyone was celebrating with her.

Sheila stayed at the bar and talked to me until Jim and Paco were ready to go. We had a hard day and a half or longer ahead of us. Sheila told me she lived over an art gallery on the south side of the Plaza. She said her office and living quarters were in one open area. Sheila made her living as an actuary. She had graduated from MIT and then moved west. She had visited Prescott as a child. She had ridden horses with cousins during the summers in the Chino Valley. She knew exactly where Ashfork Road was. She was three years older than me.

She gave me a card with her phone number on it and then wrote another number on the back. She said this was her private cell phone. She took business and routine calls on one cell phone and had another one for private calls.

I walked her over to her apartment and asked her to come out to the High Meadow someday soon. I told her I was going to be working long hours for the next few weeks moving cattle and stacking hay but I wanted to see her again.

She walked upstairs to her apartment door. When I saw she was safely inside, I left and went back to the truck. Jim Price said it looked like I had hooked up with a winner and if I needed any pointers to come see him. Paco laughed. I drove on home and when I was through cleaning myself up, it was after midnight. I went out on my little porch and sat down and drank two shots of Jim Beam and thought about Sheila Hancock.

When I finished up Friday at the horse barn, it was after dark again and I knew it would be hard for us to push the last bunch of cattle into their new pasture before dark tomorrow. Way it worked out, we finished around five on Saturday. When we got back to the horse barn, I saw Jim Price and Sheila standing at the horse pasture fence rail.

The sun was going down. There were red and gold streaks all across the western horizon. Granite Mountain was drenched in red and gold. Paco was riding his good gray gelding, Pat, and I was riding Louie. They had their heads down and were both hitting a good, comfortable lick. A nice slow trot that they were extending into a longer gait as we got closer to the barn.

Paco said, "Careful, Lim. Take it slow and easy. Do not do something stupid and run her off. A woman like that will not come back once you piss her off. This is my belief."

I did not say anything. Sheila came into the horse barn and helped me feed and water the horses. They would all get a break for a week while we got the hay cut, baled, and stacked. Jim sat on a plastic bucket and drank a Miller High Life. Paco went on home to his family.

When we had the horses fed and watered, Sheila said, "Hope you do not mind. I brought some groceries. I thought I might make our dinner. And Jim's. He told me Thursday night you were not much of a cook. You eat a lot of tamales and chili and beans out of a can."

We all three went back to my house and Sheila started supper while I got cleaned up. I put on a clean pair of 501s and a blue shirt and my black Paul Bond boots my father had bought for me when I graduated from high school.

There was a bottle of wine on the table. I picked it up and looked at the label. It was La Velona Brunello. There were wine glasses on the table and Jim was laying out silverware and plates and napkins. We had Italian spinach, Chicken Parmesan, and pasta with a marinara sauce. The wine was full bodied and rich. I had some vanilla ice cream in the refrigerator freezer and I spooned that out for dessert. The wine was gone by the time we ate the ice cream. I can not remember what we talked about at dinner but I remember how everything tasted. And Sheila was wearing tight blue jeans and a gold blouse and a gold necklace.

After Jim left, Sheila and I cleaned the kitchen up and I poured us each a shot of the good stuff. Basil Hayden 12 year old Kentucky Bourbon. Smooth as a good whiskey can be. We drank it sitting on my old brown leather couch I had bought second hand a few years ago. It came with a nice old brown leather chair.

Sheila said, "I would like to spend the night. I can sleep on the couch. I think I have had too much to drink. But don't you get any ideas. For some reason I trust you. You are bashful but a girl never knows."

I told her she could sleep in my bed. I changed the sheets and pillowcases and put the old ones in the washer and closed the door. She called me back into the bed room and told me I should at least kiss her and I did and I did not want to let go of her but I remembered what Paco said and I closed the bedroom door. My other bedroom was empty. I had nothing in it and no need to put anything in it. I went back on the porch for a few minutes and then made myself a pallet on the den floor and went to sleep.

In the middle of the night, Sheila woke me up and asked me to come to bed with her. She said she was not ready for sex with me yet but she wanted me close to her. So I went to bed and pulled her close to me and we slept till morning.

One Saturday night a few weeks later, I stayed at her place and we made love on her big king sized bed. As the summer began to fade away, we spent most nights together. In October, she moved a computer desk, some bookshelves and books, and a small couch into my second bedroom. We spent a lot of time in front of the fireplace. I would read the paper and she would read magazines or trade journals. A lot of days, she spent working in the office in my spare bedroom. She loved to cook.

One Sunday night in November, we were in Prescott in her apartment. A nice fire was going strong in the fireplace. We had been sitting on a bench on the Plaza talking for most of the afternoon. The town was quiet. A few tourists looked in gallery windows or ducked into some of the few businesses that were open. But the traffic was quiet and we felt like we had the Plaza to ourselves.

I had to get up early the next morning to get back to the ranch and get the horses fed and watered. We had moved the cattle up to the winter graze on Forest Service land. It was an eight mile cattle drive from the High Meadow to the Forest Service graze. We had gathered the cattle and driven them up the road and gotten them all settled in last week. Paco and I were going to trailer our horses up to the Forest Service land and check on the cattle on Monday.

That Sunday night, Sheila fixed lasagna and after we had eaten and cleared things away, she said she wanted to talk to me for a few minutes. We moved over close to the fireplace and I put some more logs on the fire. Sheila told me about growing up just south of the Tennessee line in North Alabama. Her father was a prosperous farmer and her mother was a contented housewife. Her dad was alone now on the farm. Sheila's mother had died a few years before Sheila went off to college.

Sheila said her mother was always the most optimistic and cheerful person she had ever been around. She described her childhood as ideal. No family drama other than her older brother teasing her all the time. Her mother had a circle of friends she had known since school days. The family attended a Methodist Church not far from their farm and her father had plenty of friends in the church and in the small farming community they lived in near Cedar Grove.

After her mother's death, Sheila's father had kept the farm prosperous. The fencing was all attended to, the tractors were kept in good running order, and the crops were never neglected. But slowly, the social life in the community died away. The Church grew smaller as the younger people moved to Chattanooga, Atlanta, Huntsville, and Birmingham. People went where the jobs were.

When she was growing up, she had ridden horses and helped around the farm. Her main interest was cooking. Her mother was a traditional southern cook. Fried chicken, fruit cobblers, big pies with meringue, vegetables cooked with bacon, and banana pudding were all dishes her mother excelled in preparing. After her mother died, her father ate very little. He hunched over his plate and showed no interest in his food.

When she was growing up, she remembered going down to Hawthorn's with her father. Hawthorn's was at a busy country cross roads a few miles north of Cedar Grove and five miles from Sheila's home. It was a hardware and feed store with a store room in the back. The store room had a pool table and some card tables in it and a small bar and grill. Sheila's dad would stop in and get a ham and biscuit in the mornings after Sheila's mother died. And drink coffee with the other farmers. On Thursday night there was a dollar limit, dealer's choice, poker game for the regular customers. No outsiders could play.

This was her father's social life after her mother's death. Last year, Hawthorn sold out and retired and moved to Panama City. Now, the store was up for sale again. The poker game and the ham and biscuits were gone. The only activity her father had now outside the farm centered on the church. His duty was to keep the grounds clean. The grounds included the cemetery his wife was buried in.

He would go up to the church on Saturday and cut the grass, trim the hedges, and care for the flowers. When Sheila was there in April, the azaleas around the house were in full bloom. But her dad moved slower now. Her brother lived in Chattanooga and worked as an engineer for the Southern Pacific. He saw his father when he could and he helped around the farm some.

Sheila said her father was going to die alone and she did not want that to happen to her if possible. She told me she wanted me to tell her where I wanted our relationship to go.

I told her I had only fantasized about having a wife and family. My family had been Dad, Vern, Sherman, and Iris. Only Dad lived under the same roof as me. Now Lacey was in the picture and my Dad was happy, but I was on my own and I had not thought about the future. I told her I would like to see how we were getting along in a year or so and if we were happy, I thought we should settle down together.

She asked if that meant marriage and I said yes. But we should wait at least a year or so. She said she wanted to have children. She wanted a girl and a boy. I said that would be fine with me. But she had to realize that I only made so much money as a cowboy and she said she understood that and the money questions would work themselves out.

We did not wait a whole year. In 2008, Vern and Dad and Lacey and Sherman and Iris all came up for the Rodeo and stayed at the Hassayampa and Sheila and I bought rings and Jim and Paco and some of Sheila's friends all crowded into a small chapel along with everyone from back at the Circle S. The chapel was at the Hassayampa. We were married in a short ceremony.

After the wedding, Iris fussed at me because she had not brought a dress with her and she had been caught by surprise and I told her we made up our minds to do it the same day they all got into town. We all went into the big lobby of the hotel and Sherman ordered champagne from the bar and we all stayed in the hotel drinking champagne and eating oysters on the half shell and shrimp cocktails. We missed the Rodeo that night.

In the winter months of 2007, Jim, Paco, and I did some traveling around the State looking for three mares and a stud. We found two mare colts we liked at Davey Waddell's ranch. I knew the sire and dams of the two colts and the price was right. Both were dark bays with high hips, wide, clear eyes, straight legs, and strong shoulders. I knew the sire was a good cow horse and the dams had sired some decent cow horses.

I finally found the third mare at a ranch near Wickenburg, just north and west of Phoenix. She had Poco Pine, Poco Bueno and Doc Bar breeding. She was a coming two year old. She was a sorrel with a nice star in her forehead and no other chrome. The stud we chose we bought in March from a rancher in the Peeples Valley, about midway between Prescott and Wickenburg. He had Doc Bar breeding on the top side and Poco Bueno breeding on the Dam's side. Doc Bar was a legendary cutting horse. This stud was almost two and Jim paid a nice sum for him.

The summer of 2008, I told Jim and Paco I was not going to take any new horses to train. I concentrated on the young horses we had. Jim said we should just buy three more broodmares. I agreed. That would give us six colts on the Ranch each year. That would keep me busy.

We bought another mare colt from Davey Waddell in the fall of 2008 and a two year old mare from the same rancher who had sold us the stud down in the Peeples Valley. Just after the first of year in 2009 Paco, Jim, and I were at the Palace Bar one Thursday night and Jim told us we had five mares and he wanted to hold off on buying anymore. That was fine with us. We were tired of spending Saturday and Sunday on the road.

I took two young horses in the spring of 2009 to train. They were both two year olds. Sheila and I were happy. She spent her days in Prescott during the week, but she had set a computer up in our den and some days she would stay home and work. In the spring of 2009, Sheila asked Jim if she could have a horse if she paid for its board. Jim said he would take the board out in chicken parmesan, banana pudding, and lasagna, and an occasional meat loaf with mashed potatoes and gravy. She found a five year old Appaloosa gelding she liked and she rode him a lot. I let her handle her own horse. His name was Jack and he was black and had a white blanket and a pretty black mane and tail. He had a small blaze but no chrome on his legs and feet.

Jack was a quick footed and nimble horse. I rode him a couple of times and he had a nice, easy handle on him. Sheila would ride him early in the morning or late in the afternoon. I was so busy we did not get to ride together very much. A lot of afternoons, Paco and I would come into the horse barn and Sheila would be unsaddling, grooming, or feeding and watering Jack.

Louie was as good a horse as I could ask for. He was settling down nicely. He had a good head for cows and he had a good long trot that I called on him to do when we were trailing cattle or coming back to the ranch late in the afternoon.

Sheila and I went back to Alabama after we had the cattle settled on the Forest Service winter graze in 2009. We landed in Chattanooga the Tuesday before Thanksgiving, rented a car, and drove to the family farm near Cedar Grove. The farm was well taken care of but Sheila's father was not doing well. He had diabetes and his blood pressure was high. He was on a restricted diet and did not have much to say about anything. It was obvious he loved Sheila but once the thrill of seeing each other again began to wear off, it was up to Sheila to get a conversation going. Mainly, her father sat in his old green recliner and stared at the fireplace or television. The only real sign of life he showed after the first day we were there was when he showed me around the farm. He had about fifty nice Herefords. He raised corn, soybeans, and millet. All his crops were in and each day I would go with him and we would throw out hay for the cattle.

We left on Friday after Thanksgiving. Sheila cried on the way to the airport and once we were on the plane, she put her head on my shoulder and cried some and slept some. When we touched down at the Phoenix airport Friday night, we were bone tired. We had had a three hour layover in Dallas. I drove on back to the High Meadow and when I got the last of the bags in, Sheila was starting a fire. We drank some good zinfandel and made a pallet in front of the fire and fell asleep watching the red and orange flames.

In May of 2010, Jim came over one Friday night for supper. Sheila said she was running late because she had been to the doctor in the afternoon. When we sat down to a dinner of meatloaf, potatoes, gravy, asparagus, sour dough rolls, and chocolate pie, Sheila opened a nice bottle of Beringer's Knight's Valley Cabernet. She told Jim and me this was a special occasion because it was the last night she could drink wine or any alcohol for a long time. Jim smiled and asked if that meant she was pregnant and she said, "Yes, it does."

I did not know what to say. I knew my Dad would be proud. And I was going to try to be as good a father as he was. By making my children learn to make do with what was in front of them. What fate and circumstances dictated. And to live their lives with dignity and pride. And I wanted them doing chores at an early age. I did not want them to grow up strangers to hard work.

So now, here it is, May of 2010, and I will soon be a proud father. Sheila had the test done and she found out our first child will be a boy. We still have not decided on a name but we have a few months. We know we are going to name him Dewey but we are looking for another name to put with it.

The new mares are all bred to our stud and we should have foals in the late summer. I have never taken care of a new foal. But Paco and Jim have and I will learn from them. Sheila is tall and rangy and you can't tell she is pregnant yet. Jim goes down to the house every day and checks on her.

Sheila asked me to ride Jack for her until the baby is born and the doctor gives her the green light to ride again.

Paco is riding Louie a lot now and Jack is catching on to being a ranch horse. Our son will be born in the late fall. Probably after we move the cattle to the winter graze and before Thanksgiving. Nowadays, when I come home late in the afternoon with the sun setting over Granite Mountain, Sheila will be in the house fixing supper or working at her computer. She is letting her hair grow longer. Sometimes I wake up in the middle of the night and look at her and I get a feeling of total completeness. I think about our son. I hope he is interested in horses and cattle and western sunsets and saddles and cowboy boots and big Stetson hats. For that is all I know. I will tell him about the nights Dad and I ate tamales and chili with beans. All out of cans. And talked about good horses he had known and ridden over the years.

I can tell him about my good horse Davey and the Tucson Rodeo and the fight with Jimmy Dale and Henry, the big old bull on the hill, and Pepper and Iris and Sherman Snider and Vern. Dad's legacy to me will be my legacy to my son. All you can do is hope that it is enough.

Chapter Twelve

Cowboys

Jim Price

I have seen sixty years of cowboys. Growing up on the High Meadow, I saw some shiftless reprobates on the run from the law. Cowboys who would load up their belongings in the back of their old, rusty pickups and leave a few days before the Sheriff came by with a warrant for child support, car theft, assault and battery, or manslaughter.

But for the most part, they have simply been wanderers. People who did not want to stay in one place for a long time. Honest, hardworking, and hard drinking men. Some would knock on our door and ask to see my father and ask for their check. The reasons usually had something to do with a desire to see another part of the country or a desire to go back home and patch things up with a wife or girlfriend or their parents.

So over the years, I have learned not to expect a long term commitment from my hands. Some are different. Paco was born on this ranch. He is content to stay here, work hard, raise a family, and not worry about the future. He knows every hill, every pasture, every irrigation pipe, every bull, every horse, every piece of machinery and every vehicle on the ranch. He is my foreman and he can hire and fire on the spot. We have three cowboys besides Lim and Paco.

Two are young guys that grew up around Prescott. One wants to get on the Rodeo Circuit and he is saving up enough money to give it a try. Another is content to earn his keep and maintain his old red Silverado pickup. He doesn't seem to have a worry in the world. The third cowboy is named Wiley Black and Wiley has a drinking problem. His driver's license just got reinstated and he has paid a lot of his salary out to the court system in fines and costs and lawyer fees.

Wiley is short and dumpy and came here from Florida. Most people do not realize it, but Florida has a big cattle industry. Wiley grew up on a ranch and is closing in on forty now. He has never been married and is a good hand. Not only can he ride and take care of cattle, he can fix most any vehicle on the place. Tractor, hay baler, or truck. Even my little red ATV. He has been here for three years. The younger cowboys have only been here a little over a year.

Wiley is a good example of how the life of a cowboy has changed. Wiley is fine on a horse. He is a natural even though he is short and dumpy. But nowadays, cowboys, or more accurately, ranch hands have to be able to handle mechanized equipment. The calving table has made branding easier. Irrigation equipment has to be set up and dismantled and moved and set up again. I have tried to get Paco off his horses and onto an ATV but he says he wants to ride as long as he can.

I can help gather cattle on my ATV. I can get to a pasture faster on an ATV than the ranch hands on horses. Most cowboys resent the time they spend away from their horses. They do not want to become farm hands. They want to gather cattle, check fences, and stay in the saddle. But that is not the way it is now and it is sure not the way of the future.

The best cowboy I ever had was Juan. Paco's father. Juan's wife was killed in a traffic accident in Phoenix one Christmas Eve when Paco was ten years old. Juan started working here when he was seventeen and raised Paco and a daughter here on the ranch. After Juan's wife died, my parents pitched in and did what they could to raise the two kids. Juan's daughter married and moved off to some little town on the Deschutes River up in Oregon.

Juan was our foreman for many years. He taught Randy and me how to ride and he never ratted us out when we spooked cows or forgot to close a gate. He followed behind us and was a gentle and good natured teacher. He would fire a cowboy if he thought he was mistreating a horse or one of the cattle. Fire him on the spot. I saw him do it to a cowboy who got mad at his horse and jerked on the bit until there was blood dripping off the shank of the bit.

I always thought Juan would stay on the High Meadow until he died, but as Paco became older and more skilled, Juan saw that Paco should be a foreman somewhere, so he up and got a job at the O RO and left the foreman job at the High Meadow to Paco. The O RO is one of the largest and best run ranches in the west. It is north and west of Prescott. Probably forty to fifty miles away. One hundred and fifty thousand acres of the ranch are traceable all the way back to a Spanish land grant. The segment of the original land grant that is now in the O RO was called the Baca Float for many years.

Another one hundred thousand acres has been added over the years. It now sprawls over two hundred and fifty thousand acres. The altitude ranges from four to seven thousand feet. The ranch covers over four hundred square miles and is divided into five camps. Each camp has an old World War Two 6x6 Army truck that has been converted to a chuck wagon. The cowboys at the O RO still do things the old fashioned way. They are out gathering cattle for months at a time. The job of gathering cattle is made harder by the hilly and mountainous terrain.

Juan was the head wrangler at the Mahon Camp. It is the most remote camp on the ranch. He came on back to the High Meadow after about a year and said it was hard work but he liked it because all he had to do was break new horses and take care of the large remuda. Each cowboy would have six or eight horses assigned to him.

Because of the treacherous terrain, the O RO bred and trained their own horses. Their horses were all agile and sure footed. After Juan had been there for six years, he was out riding a green two year old and the horse spooked, lost his footing, and rolled over on Juan. The young horse went back to base camp and a search was launched for Juan. He was found dead the next morning lying under a small manzanita bush.

I was back at the High Meadow then. It has only been ten or so years ago when he died. I got the call about Juan and I had to go and get Paco out of a pasture where he and the rest of the cowboys were moving cattle to another pasture. I did not feel like telling him there in front of the other cowboys. This was before I busted my hip. We rode on back to the horse barn and I told Paco we had to go somewhere and we unsaddled the horses and grained and watered them. I told him right there in the horse barn. The worst moment of my life. He sat down on a hay bale and looked out the door of the barn for a few minutes and then he stood up and said, "I am ready to go get my father now."

I drove on up to the O RO. They warned us not to look at the body. Juan's face had been smashed and a closed casket funeral was held at a Catholic Church in Prescott. Since that day, Paco talks less than he ever has. And he never talked that much before his father died. Paco's wife is named Elena and Elena cooks for me and keeps the two houses up. The house I live in and the original ranch house I grew up living in.

My mother passed on a few years after my father and one Sunday afternoon before she died, she asked me to keep the big ranch house in order and to find a way to keep the High Meadow in the family forever. Now, I stay in a nice house under some big cedar trees and I keep up Mother's rose bushes and cut the grass and keep the bushes trimmed around the big house that we grew up in.

The only people that stay in the house are Randy and some of our cousins and their families. Randy will come and stay and help with calving and branding and the fall gather when we separate the cattle ready for sale from the mother cows and bulls. And he comes up for the November drive up to the Forest Service winter graze. I will call him when we are cutting hay, just out of meanness. He hates loading hay on the trailers and stacking it in the barns.

No one who visits stays in Mother and Dad's bedroom. I keep it closed. Elena is the only one who goes into it. She keeps it clean and neat. Just like it was when Mother and Dad were alive. I just did not feel right about living in the big house once Mother was gone. I left everything like it was. Kachinas Dad and Mom bought on the Hopi Reservation are still on the same shelves where my Dad put them. Pots from Acoma, Zia, Zuni, and Santa Clara Pueblo are everywhere Mom and Dad could find to put them. A big red and white Ganado storm pattern rug hangs on the wall in the entry way. A large elk head from one of Dad's early Colorado hunts presides over the large stone fire place in the den. Bronzes by Fred and Diane Fellows are on the mantel over the fire place. A large pencil drawing Mother bought for Dad at the Phippen Museum Art Auction hangs on one wall in the dining room. It is a drawing of three cowboys trailing cattle down a dusty trail. It was done by Robert Shufelt. On another wall in the dining room is an early Howard Terpning painting depicting Apache warriors preparing for battle.

Randy will come and stay a week or ten days and sleep in his old bed in our room. When we grew up, we shared a large bed room. It was big enough for each of us to have a closet and a dresser and a desk to study on.

Randy will ride out with Paco and help when he comes. He is still a fair hand but he gets tired like me at the end of a long day.

I had this cowboy that worked for me right after I took over the ranch. Bob Tracey. He was a typical cowboy. Dropped out of high school after football season was over in his senior year. Said he knew he could not make the grade in college as a student or a one hundred and sixty pound running back. Too slow and too little. He worked for us for a few years. He did his share of work and was turning into a decent cowboy until one day he came up to the house and stood on the bottom step of the back porch and told me he had taken a job driving a propane gas truck. He would be delivering propane all over the county. He said he was marrying one of the Upton girls.

Now almost twenty years later, he still comes around. You can tell he misses the cowboy life. He will drive up late in the afternoon when he has made his deliveries and we will sit out in the horse barn and drink a cold beer or fire up the ATV and ride out on the range and look at the cows and horses and deer and the Pronghorns. His kids are just about grown now and he and his wife and kids live on two sections of land they bought on Puntenney Road. Their property is right next to the large railroad right of way that cuts through the valley. Bob and his kid still ride and Bob has a few head of cows he takes care of. He is the only cowboy that has left that comes back to see me.

I think Bob got attached to this land. A piece of ground can do that to you. Just like a woman that you can not do without. A piece of land can get under your skin. The High Meadow is like that for me. I never get tired of watching a western sunrise or sunset. And where our house and barns are located is high ground and when I look out over a seemingly endless horizon as the sun sets with all its multi colored streaks that never repeat themselves, I get a sense of peace. My time may come soon. I am in my early sixties. I can square my shoulders and handle whatever comes down the pike.

Now this Lim Couch is cut from a different cloth than most cowboys. I tell him he is a tweener. What I told him is that he does not want to be a regular horse trainer with a training facility and a bunch of clients. He does not want to travel to horse shows a lot. But he wants to train horses. Young horses that are just getting started under saddle. He does not want to specialize in cutting or reining or trail or Western Pleasure or Halter horses. He wants to stay on a ranch and do ranch work and train horses, too.

He is our wrangler. He has told me he eventually wants to go back to the Circle S down near Sonoita. Lot of cowboys have told me the same thing. They want to ramble some. Work on different ranches in different settings in different states and then go on back home to where they grew up and find a job. Some do, most don't. Lim is lucky. He has Sheila and she can pick up and move anytime without losing business. She told me the computer and Internet makes everyone your potential next door neighbor. I like to go down there to their home and eat supper and talk to them. Sheila knows a lot. Lim says she can read a book faster than anyone he has ever known and she retains what she reads. They seem happy. They will have a child this fall. Sometime before Christmas.

Lim is training our first two year olds from our stud and mares. He stopped taking outside horses to train since we will have new two year olds every year. We agreed to wait on some of them to get them started until they were closer to three years old. Lim has this knack for knowing when the time is right. I bumped his pay up some since he is not taking in new horses of his own.

Like I said, I don't expect too much from cowboys. They are born misfits and wanderers. They come and go. But I remember how Randy and I both felt when Juan left. I just imagine I will have some of those same feelings if Lim and Sheila and that boy they are going to have in the fall ever leave the High Meadow.

Chapter Thirteen

Going Home

Lim Couch, June, 2010

I asked Randy Price to call and tell me when Jimmy Dale was to be released. I figured it would be in three or four years from now. We had just made the first cut of hay for the year and I was settled in to riding our first crop of two year olds when Randy called. It was a surprise to me. I thought Jimmy Dale still had several years to go before he could get parole. I was reading late one night when Randy Price called.

I got the date of his release and went up to Jim's house and told him I needed to take off a few days starting on Thursday of this week. It was Monday night and I told him what it was all about and he said he understood and he thought it might do those two year olds some good to stay out in the horse pasture and graze for a few days. I told him I would drive back on Monday and he said that was fine. Paco said it was alright for me to go as long as I did not forget the way back and I told him I would be home late Monday afternoon.

I told Sheila this was something I needed to do on my own. I knew Jimmy Dale had done wrong. No excuses for him from me. But I still remembered the good I had seen in him. Sheila said to just hope that Florence Prison had not taken all of the good away and put some more badness in its place. She said she would fly down on Friday afternoon.

She had not been to the Circle S. We called Dad and told him what we wanted to do and Lacey was there with him and she said she would bring Sheila to the Circle S from the Tucson Airport on Friday afternoon. I asked Dad not to tell Iris I was coming.

Randy Price had told me the prisoners to be released were usually out of the prison after eight and I should get there before eight. I got up early on Thursday and left the High Meadow before the sun came up. I was on Interstate 10 going south towards Tucson when the sun finally came up. I cut off the Interstate and turned east on Highway 387 and turned at the junction with Highway 87 and followed it on south and east into Florence.

I checked in at the prison and I was directed to a small drab building. I told the guard who I was and who I was waiting on. He never looked up from his clipboard. He told me to sit down and Scruggs would be out in a few minutes. A few minutes turned into an hour. There were several other people in the release room waiting for freed prisoners. There was some crying and some laughing and I felt nervous and I could not help but look at each prisoner and ask myself if I thought he would be back soon.

Finally, a little after nine, a frail, unsmiling, Jimmy Dale Scruggs came through the door. His head was shaved and he had a scar on the right side of his forehead that ended in his eyebrow.

I said, "Jimmy Dale."

He gave me a hard stare and said, "What you doing here?"

"I came to carry you home."

"I could'a took the shuttle into Tucson and hitchhiked on down to the ranch."

I asked him if Lita knew he was coming home and he said,"No. Randy Price got this all worked out. Happened out of the blue. Big surprise to me."

We got in my truck. There was a hat box in the right front seat. Jimmy Dale said, "What is this?"

I told him it was a new hat for him to wear when he saw his son for the first time. He did not say anything and he kept the hat box in his lap. I asked him if he was hungry and he laughed and said, "Of course, I'm hungry. I been hungry since I got here. Never anything worth eating. You stay hungry."

I stopped at a Circle K before we got out of Florence and bought us both a hot dog and coke. We drove down Highway 79 past the Tom Mix Memorial. Jimmy Dale said word was Tom Mix was going to try to make a comeback and had a lot of cash in his car when he crashed and died. And that was about all he said until we were in Tucson going south on Oracle. Jimmy Dale was wearing flip flops, baggy blue jeans, and a white tee shirt that had some holes in it.

I stopped at the Boot Barn on the west side of Oracle near Prince. We went inside and I bought him two new pairs of boot cut 501s, a pair of black Tony Lama calfskin boots, a black belt with a good silver buckle, some socks, and two Wrangler shirts. One was solid blue and one was white. They each had nice pearl snap buttons. He wore a pair of the new 501s and the blue shirt and the boots and belt out of the store. He left his old clothes there and told the pretty sales clerk to put them in the dumpster.

He asked me where we were going now and I told him the Silver Saddle for some lunch. We sat in a comfortable booth near the salad bar. The lunch crowd was thinning out. Jimmy Dale had his new black hat pulled low on his head and he said when he grew some hair the hat would fit perfectly. It was a Stetson Rancher. I had a black one and a brown one. The Silver Saddle had Dos Equis Amber on draft. We each had one with our New York Strips and baked potatoes.

Jimmy Dale looked around and said, "It ain't changed. I remember one day. A Sunday. When that girl Rhonda rode your good horse

Davey in the Grand Entry at the Tucson Rodeo. We came here afterwards. Me, You, Dave Waddell, the Sniders, your dad, and Vern. We sat at a big table in the bar and ate the same damn fine meal we just had. One of the good times."

Before we left, I asked Jimmy Dale about the fight we had in front of my Dad, Vern, the Sniders, and Davey Waddell. I asked him if he had done a tank job. I told him I had thought about that day a lot and I was just not convinced that he had put his all into it. I told him I thought he did not want to whip me in front of all those people I lived around. And my dad. It would have crushed me and probably changed my whole life. I did not tell Jimmy Dale that last part.

He smiled and said, "You will never know. Now let's go home. I want to see Lita and my boy. I have never seen him. No way a son of mine is coming to Florence Prison to see his dad."

It was not long before we were out of the Tucson traffic headed east on l-10. Jimmy Dale said he was one lucky bastard because Davey had kept the ranch going and even showed a profit while he was gone. He had two hands working the ranch. Jimmy Dale said he felt like he could stop drinking now.

He said there was a little short, fat girl about his age who was a counselor in the prison. Her name was Gail and she had helped him a lot without preaching to him or talking down to him.

When we drove onto the gravel road that led to Jimmy Dale's home, I thought he might be tearing up so I looked straight ahead. When I pulled up in front of the house, Lita was in the yard playing with their son. He was digging in the flowerbed with a plastic shovel. It had a red blade and a yellow handle. Lita ran to the truck and she had tears coming down her cheeks. Jimmy Dale said, "I'm obliged, Lim," and opened the truck door and took his sack from Boot Barn and his hat box with him. Lita helped him carry the sack and the box to the porch and then they went to the boy. He was looking up at Jimmy

Dale. He was thin and his head was shaped like Jimmy Dale's but his eyes were big and brown. Jimmy Dale and Lita knelt down and talked to the boy.

I drove slowly out of the driveway and in less than an hour I was at the Circle S. I pulled my truck in front of Dad's house. It was almost dark and he was still up at the horse barn. Vern was puttering around in his Airstream. I could hear Webb Pierce on Vern's radio.

I walked up to the ranch house and knocked on the door. Iris came to the door and hugged me for a long time. Then she said, "Why, Lim Couch, you could have called. We are eating left overs tonight and I just have a small piece of chocolate cake and I cannot give you that. You know how Sherman is about his chocolate cake."

We sat on the porch and I told her I had brought Jimmy Dale home and I was going to stay 'til Monday with my Dad and Sheila was coming tomorrow night. I told her I was her yard man tomorrow. I wanted to help her do whatever needed to be done. She asked about Jimmy Dale and I told her he had a hard edge to him but he only drank one beer at the Silver Saddle and had told me he was going to quit drinking. One beer with a steak after you been in prison for a while does not qualify as drinking, I said, and Iris agreed.

When it got dark I went on up to the barn and talked to my Dad and Sherman. Sherman said he had some things to show me. The first was a black two year old he had bought. His name was Mark. He had two white stockings and a blaze. He was long and rangy. He had that Three Bars look. He needed to fill out some but he had the high hip, straight back, teacup nose, strong shoulders, straight legs, and alert eyes you look for in a Quarter Horse. I walked into his stall. He looked at me and came over to me when I called his name. I rubbed his head and ran my hand up between his ears and rubbed. He dropped his head.

Sherman said, "I called Jim Price up this morning and asked if I could send Mark back with you to train. I had to wait until Iris went to the grocery store in Nogales. I knew you wanted to surprise her. I want you to take your time with Mark.

"Lamar Tisdale called a few months ago. He up and left Amy Worth a few months after you left her. He moved back to his wife and their ranch. She is about ten years younger than him and she is a pistol. Feisty as hell. He said he had a nice colt he wanted me to look at. We drove all the way up there to Hereford in a long day and stayed with them at their ranch. His wife's name is Betty. We was eating supper and she told us it was hard for her to change her bossy ways but she and Lamar were going to make it if she had to snatch a knot in his neck and kick his ass all the way to Hereford.

"Lamar is judging just enough good shows to keep him traveling a little. He says Betty even goes with him some now. They got a nice spread with a bunch of Angus and some real good brood mare Betty has bought over the years. Lamar said he just got to missing Betty and went on home to her and they both knew it was time for them to start getting along.

"Keep Mark until he is a finished horse. My mule is getting old and I am going to turn him out to pasture when Mark is ready to work on the ranch. No hurry. I worked a deal with Jim. Some money for you every month and some for him. He said you were in a little strain right now with these new two year olds you are riding but if I was not in a hurry, he thought you could do it."

I said, "I will do it, but I did not bring a trailer."

Sherman said, "I got a little two horse trailer you can carry him up there in and I will come and get it when the baby is born. You know Iris is going to wart the hell out of me to come see that baby. We got no need for it. We got stock trailers."

I took Mark out of the stall and put him in crossties and brushed and curried him. He was going to have a nice full mane and tail when he got his growth. He needed work and a lot of grain and good hay before he would fill out. Probably take a year or so.

Sherman said, "Mark is out of Playgun. A great cutting horse champion trained and shown by Dick Pieper. Lamar and Betty bred one of their good mares to Playgun and when I saw him in the stall, I knew he was coming home with us. Now Playgun is strong on his top line with him being a son of Freckles Playboy. He was a great cutting horse, also. And a better sire. Playgun is a nice grey stallion. He is starting to sire some good colts. Mark's dam was a grey and here Mark is, black as he can be."

Dad went to a stall in the back of the barn and brought out another horse. He looked familiar. I looked at him a long time before I was sure. It was Socks.

Sherman said, "You moved off, Jimmy Dale went to prison and Little Molly died. The colic. And we never have much to do with our son or our grandchild. It all hit Iris at once this spring and she took some of her own money out of her account and went up to Santa Fe and bought Socks from a so called rancher out near Chimayo which is northeast of Santa Fe. She left in a big huff. I tried to talk to her about spending the money and asked her to think about it and she said it was her money and there she went."

Dad handed each of us a Fat Tire and put Socks in crossties facing Mark. Sherman took a healthy swig of beer and said, "I wasn't against buying him back if the price was fair, but she took what I said the wrong way. She said I was acting like I did not trust her to make an intelligent business decision. I told her it was her money that she had saved and invested from her share of the family ranch earnings. Her brother runs the ranch and they split the income. Anyway, I had not seen her like this ever before. I give her a good head start and I went on to Santa Fe the next day.

"I went to La Fonda when I got there. We always stay there when we go up that way. She had a suite for us on the third floor and there was a message for me to wait for her in the bar. She would be back as soon as she finished her business. I put my suitcase up and went and ate a late lunch in the restaurant there. The La Plazuela. A long slow lunch and when I was through she had still not showed up.

"Finally, I went on to the bar. One of my favorite places in the whole world. The bar in the La Fonda Hotel. We were there once years ago and Don Meredith told Iris she was the finest woman in the bar and then bought a bottle of French champagne and drank it with us. Long time ago. Just past sundown, here she comes marching into the bar like her hair was on fire. She saw me and said, "Those sons of bitches have let Socks get almost gaunt. A pair of real squirrels at that ranch. He is a fat shit that never gets out of the house and she is an animal hoarder. Goats, cats, dogs, all just running all over the place. Course that means no birds with all those cats running wild.

"She said Socks was standing in a dirty stall. All gaunt looking. She offered them a sum of money less than a hundred thousand dollars and told them to sign the goddamn bill of sale and give her the AQHA Registration papers or she was going to the SPCA and every radio and TV station in Santa Fe and Albuquerque and show them how they treated their animals. Iris has got one of them new type phones that can take pictures and she took a bunch at that ranch. All showing the sad condition of the animals. Come to find out that crash on Wall Street a year or so back had just about wiped them out. They had made a lot of money in California real estate and it all went bust in 2009. The woman got all mad and the man looked at the check and signed the bill of sale and filled out the transfer papers so we could register him with AQHA under our name. This was Socks' third owner since we sold him.

"She wasn't mad anymore and she said it was just frustration. We went to La Casa Sena and sat outside and ate a nice meal and drank a good bottle of Bordeaux and brought Socks home the next day. A long day in a pickup. We had Doc Siegfried check him out and he was low on iron and we have been riding him a little and feeding him a lot and he is coming around. As soon as he is back to normal, we are offering him at stud. Might be next year before he gets all fat and slick."

Dad and I put the horses back in the stall after we all finished our beer. It was good to have Socks back on the Circle S. I remember walking him down the pasture fence line when he was young.

Dad, Vern, and I ate grilled hamburgers that night. Vern brought some more beer down with him but I stopped after one more. Dad went on in and went to bed and Vern and I played dominoes. Vern said for me to never ask Jimmy Dale why he got out of prison early. Vern said he had talked to a recently released inmate a few months back in a bar in Benson and he told him Jimmy Dale had been assaulted by some guys in Prison and when his counselor called Randy Price, Randy threw a fit, then drew up a lawsuit against the Governor, the Warden, everyone he could think of including the convicts who did it and took it up to Phoenix and showed it to the head lawyer for the Department of Corrections.

Vern said the word in Florence was that they settled the case without a suit being filed by cutting Jimmy Dale's sentence and giving him a decent chunk of money. Vern said he had not talked to Randy Price about it because he knew Randy would not tell him anything. Vern told me not to tell anyone and I did not. Vern said he believed if Florence Prison had not ruined Jimmy Dale, he still held out hope that he could make it now that he had a son and Lita. Lita named the boy Roger Dale Scruggs.

On Friday, I got up early and went and fed the horses and let Dad sit at the kitchen table and drink coffee a little longer. When Dad and

Sherman came up to the horse barn, I went on down to the ranch house and sat on the front steps and waited on Iris Snider. She came out of the house wearing another one of those big straw hats with a big yellow band. We put out mulch, weeded flower beds, went into Nogales and bought some more plants, and came back and planted them. We planted blue lantana, orange marigolds, red geraniums, and a pink rose bush I bought at the nursery for Iris. I told her when I saw it, it reminded me of her. Soft pink petals on strong, healthy green stalks. Iris said that was the nicest thing anyone had said to her in a long time. We ate at Las Vigas and came on back to the Circle S. At the end of the day, my back and neck were sore from stooping down so much.

We quit a little after four so Iris could fix supper for all of us. Lacey and Sheila came around sundown. I took Sheila up to the barn and showed her Socks and Mark. Then we walked down to the bull pasture and Henry was on his hill looking west toward the setting sun.

We had a loud and happy meal at the ranch house. Pot roast, mashed potatoes, gravy, baby lima beans, sourdough rolls, and a blackberry cobbler. All my favorites. Iris told Sheila I was well trained to plant flowers and take care of plants. Sheila was just beginning to show and I thought she had a special glow in her cheeks that night. I had planted red geraniums on both sides of our front porch steps.

Saturday, Sherman, Dad, Vern and I moved cattle from one pasture to another and we got through around four. We all crowded into Dad's house Saturday night. Sheila cooked Chicken Parmesan, Italian spinach, and angel hair pasta with a marinara sauce. We had Breyer's strawberry ice cream for dessert. We drank a couple of bottles of Monsanto Chianti Classico with our meal. We sat outside and talked for a long time that night.

We were leaving on Sunday morning. I had planned on staying until Monday but now that I had a new horse to ride, I thought I might get on back on Sunday. I got up before dawn and hitched the trailer to my pickup and pulled up to the horse barn. I left the barn and walked east past Henry on the hill. He saw me when I was coming up the hill and he raised his head up and I called out to him and he dropped his head and went on back to sleep. I cut through the pastures and at first light I could see the hill I was looking for off in the distance.

I walked on up to the hill and when I was at the top, I could see small red and gold streaks on the eastern horizon. The sun was fixing to come up over the Whetstones. The Whetstones would soon turn gold for a few hours in the early morning sun light. I found the headstone and knelt by it and took my hat off and closed my eyes and thought about Davey. The day I bought him from Davey Waddell. Riding him up and down the long hill that leads to the front gate of the Circle S. He was my first good horse. I thought of his arched neck, his flowing mane and tail, and his black, slick and muscular body as he carried the Flag down the west rail of the Tucson Rodeo arena.

When I looked up, I saw a family of quail walking toward the silvery Cienega Creek. The sun was up. Doves were flying away from their roosts in the sycamores and cottonwoods by the creek. Hereford cows and calves were grazing in the long, broad meadow between the hill and the creek. Red penstemon flowers were on the hill side and a small stand of orange and yellow globe mallow was swaying gently a few yards from where I knelt.

I knelt there in the early morning light with my hat in my right hand and I tried to remember it all. The light. The flowers. The grama grass in the meadow. The red and white Herefords grazing in the meadow with their calves nearby. I looked for a red tailed hawk but I did not see one. The Whetstones were shiny and gold in the early morning light. Sherman had picked a good spot for my good horse Davey.

I heard Sheila call my name. She was at the bottom of the hill. I did not know how long she had been there. Her hair was down her back in loose curls. She did not come up the hill. She stood at the bottom. That was the way Sheila was. I stood up and asked her to come up. She walked up, pulled me to her, kissed me, knelt by the grave, bowed her head and looked at the headstone. She stood up and put her arm around me and hugged me. We walked down to the creek and looked at the golden slopes of the Whetstones in the early light before we turned around and slowly followed the pasture fence up to the old stone horse barn.

ABOUT THE AUTHOR

Jerry Harris was adopted as an infant and grew up on a farm in Yazoo County, Mississippi. He rode horses, fished, hunted, and after moving to the Mississippi Delta developed an intense interest in Hemingway, Faulkner, Eudora Welty, and John Dos Passos. After high school, he attended Millsaps College and received a degree in English. Eudora Welty was the Writer in Residence at Millsaps and Jerry took Creative Writing classes from her his last two years at Millsaps. While at Millsaps, Jerry achieved recognition from the Southern Literary Festival for his short stories. Jerry has published another novel, A Broken Circle, a detective story, set in Memphis and the Mississippi Delta and Yazoo County, Mississippi.

After Millsaps came law school at Ole Miss. After graduating from Law School, Jerry relocated to Memphis, Tennessee in 1969. He became a trial attorney with the Shelby County District Attorney's Office in Memphis in 1974. His specialty was Homicide cases. He was head of the Major Violators Unit, Chief Homicide Prosecutor and Legal Advisor to the Homicide Squad of the Memphis Police Department. As advisor to the Homicide Squad for 30 years, Jerry worked with detectives and other policemen on an almost daily basis. Many of Jerry's trials were broadcast on Court TV.

After retirement in 2004, Jerry and his wife, Audrey decided to move to Tucson in 2007. Audrey is an ophthalmologist who still does surgery and maintains her medical career for three days a week. Jerry has two grown children. Paige, his oldest daughter, lives in

Sharpsburg, Georgia and teaches school and is a riding instructor and horse trainer. She uses many lessons Jerry taught her when she showed horses in her youth that Jerry trained for her. His youngest daughter, Alexis is a Phi Beta Kappa Scholar who received her Doctorate in Psychology from Penn State University and is on the faculty of the University of Virginia. She lives in Louisville, Kentucky where she is in charge of a research project for the University of Virginia.

Jerry can be contacted at phillipgharris@yahoo.com.

18818301R00176

Made in the USA
San Bernardino, CA
30 January 2015